TAKING LADY GIBRALTAR

★ ★ ★

GRANT'S CONVOLUTED *TOUR DE FORCE* IN THE WEST

DICK SCHWIRIAN

SUNBURY PRESS

Mechanicsburg, PA USA

Published by Sunbury Press, Inc.
105 South Market Street
Mechanicsburg, Pennsylvania 17055

www.sunburypress.com

NOTE: This is a work of fiction. Names, characters, places and incidents are the product of the author's imagination or are used fictitiously, and any resemblance to actual persons, living or dead, business establishments, events or locales is entirely coincidental.

ISBN: 978-1-62006-650-8 (Trade Paperback)
ISBN: 978-1-62006-651-5 (Mobipocket)

Library of Congress Control Number: 2016944955

FIRST SUNBURY PRESS EDITION: July 2016

Product of the United States of America
0 1 1 2 3 5 8 13 21 34 55

Set in Bookman Old Style
Designed by Crystal Devine
Cover by Amber Rendon
Edited by Christin Aswad

Continue the Enlightenment!

To my wife, Jo

★ HISTORICAL NOTE ★

As history would have it, the Battle of Gettysburg and the Siege of Vicksburg were concluded on the same day—July 4, 1863, Independence Day. Both were major Union victories. Except in these respects, the two events bear little resemblance to one another.

To start with, the battles of Gettysburg and Vicksburg were initiated under completely different circumstances: the Battle of Gettysburg was the result of a chance meeting in a small Pennsylvania town between two hostile armies, yet the Union campaign against Vicksburg was anything but an accident. Vicksburg was a strategic Union target. Save for its proximity to major northern cities, Gettysburg had no strategic significance.

At Gettysburg, the Union forces quickly seized the high ground and played defense. At Vicksburg, the Confederacy had the high ground from day one and used it to advantage. Gettysburg was resolved in three days, but the campaign to seize Vicksburg took Ulysses S. Grant more than a year of planning and execution. When failure reared its ugly head, he simply started over again.

When the fight was over, the Confederates under Robert E. Lee fled the Gettysburg battlefield and lived to fight another day. The troops under John Pemberton, the Vicksburg commander, were captured. To be sure, John Pemberton was no Robert E. Lee. On the other hand, Grant actually had two Confederate armies to contend with—Pemberton's in Vicksburg, and Joseph Johnston's in Jackson. Had those forces been able to link up, the outcome of the Vicksburg conflict might have been different.

In short, Vicksburg was much more of a victory for Ulysses S. Grant than Gettysburg was for George Gordon Meade, the Union commander at Gettysburg. Why, then, does history generally regard the battle of Gettysburg more compelling in the annals of Civil War conflicts than the battle(s) of Vicksburg? There is no straightforward answer to this question. The fact that Gettysburg took place in the North, where it could be widely appreciated by a panicked citizenry, undoubtedly has something to do with it. To Northerners, the Gettysburg victory removed the fear that Robert E. Lee would take Washington, or Philadelphia, or some other major city, and leave them to the tender mercies of a ruthless foe.

Southerners were burdened by the same fears, but their fears became reality, and they did indeed suffer for it. The victory at Gettysburg was a morale boost for the North. The Union victory at
Vicksburg was merely substantive, splitting the Confederacy in
two, denying its trade access to the Mississippi and thus guaran-
teeing its eventual demise. Nothing exciting, no melodrama, no
fanciful headlines.

A final note, at least one Union citizen understood the importance of Vicksburg—President Abraham Lincoln. His reply to critics of Grant is telling: "I can't spare this man. He fights."

In less than a year after Vicksburg and Gettysburg, Lincoln elevated Grant to the rank of lieutenant general and gave him command of all Union armies, including Meade's Army of the
Potomac. The rest is, obviously, history.

★ CAST OF CHARACTERS ★

Union Military (listed alphabetically)

Charles Dana—A journalist by training and experience, he has been sent by Secretary of War Edwin Stanton to spy on Grant's drinking habits. In spite of this chronic sore spot, a friendship develops between Grant and Dana.

Admiral David Farragut—Naval Commander at Vicksburg early in the campaign. He makes a run past the Vicksburg batteries and concludes they cannot be overcome by naval bombardment alone.

Aaron Ferguson—An infantryman left behind on the Raymond battlefield and partner of infantryman Salvadore Zemprelli.

Frederic Dent Grant—Grant's twelve-year-old son, an unofficial member of the Army of the Tennessee, sporting a sword and sash designed by his father.

Major General Ulysses S. Grant—Commander, Army of the Tennessee. A complete failure in civilian life (he has tried clerking in his father's leather goods business, farming, and real estate), Grant seeks a position as an officer in the regular army that is being expanded to confront the secessionist states of the South. At first rebuffed, he is eventually appointed commander of the 21st Illinois on June 17, 1861. Grant has found his *niche*. After his victories at Fort Donelson, Fort Henry, and Shiloh Church, he sets his sights on Vicksburg, the "Confederate Gibraltar."

Colonel Benjamin Grierson—Leader of Grant's cavalry, charged with executing diversionary cavalry raids against Confederate rail links. Despite his fear of horses (he was kicked in the face by one at an early age) Grierson successfully achieves his objective.

General-in-Chief Henry Wager Halleck—Grant's boss, sometimes mentor and occasional nemesis. He is a capable administrator but has no talent for field command. Lincoln describes him as "little more than a first-rate clerk."

Charlie Johnson—An infantryman and "sapper."

Major General John A. McClernand—Commander, Thirteenth Corps, Army of the Tennessee. A close friend of Abraham Lincoln, Illinois politician John McClernand proposes and is granted the responsibility of raising an army to invade Vicksburg. Grant and the professional soldiers on his staff must grudgingly accept McClernand as one of their own. They do, but continue to despise him as a "political general."

Darren McGlover—An infantryman, "sapper" and sidekick of Charlie Johnson.

Major General James Birdeye McPherson—Commander, Seventeenth Corps, Army of the Tennessee. Entering service with Grant's army as Chief Engineer, McPherson, is given command of the Seventeenth Corps. His engineering skills are put to good use when he is appointed the leader of the Lake Providence expedition, a scheme to make use of the myriad of bayous near the Mississippi River to bypass Vicksburg and land troops south of the city.

Rear Admiral David Porter—David Farragut's foster brother and successor at Vicksburg. He, too, makes a run later in the campaign to move Grant's army below Vicksburg onto the eastern shore of the Mississippi.

Lieutenant-Colonels John A. Rawlins and James Wilson—Members of Grant's staff who, sensitized by the appearance of Charles Dana, assume roles as Grant's protectors.

Major General William Tecumseh Sherman—Commander, Fifteenth Corps, Army of the Tennessee. With the help of politically influential relatives, Sherman is appointed a colonel in one of the newly-authorized units being formed in Washington, D. C. Unnerved by the Union defeat at the first Battle of Manassas, he demands to be demoted to a position no higher than second in command. After suffering something akin to a nervous breakdown, Sherman is sent west, where he eventually becomes Grant's most trusted lieutenant.

Salvadore Zemprelli—An infantryman left behind on the Raymond battlefield and partner of infantryman Aaron Ferguson.

Confederate Military (listed alphabetically)

General Pierre Gustave Toutant Beauregard—Known as the "Creole" general, Beauregard assumes command of the Army of the Mississippi after General Albert Sidney Johnston is killed on the first day of the Shiloh blood-bath. Unaware that the army of Don Carlos Buell has joined Grant's army overnight, Beauregard's forces are overwhelmed on the second day of the battle and beat an orderly retreat to Corinth, Mississippi.

Jasper Bennett—An infantryman left behind on the Raymond battlefield who is confronted by Union infantrymen Ferguson and Zemprelli.

Brigadier General John S. Bowen—Commander, Bowen's Division. Before the war, he was a neighbor of Grant in Missouri.

Brigadier General Nathan Bedford Forrest—Legendary Confederate cavalry leader.

General Joseph E. Johnston—Commander, Department of the West, He is nominally Pemberton's boss, although there is a critical uncertainty as to who actually owns that position—Pemberton or Confederate President Jefferson Davis.

Jim Jones—A Confederate soldier who asks Charlie Johnson to find his brother Tom, a Union soldier.

Brigadier General Stephen D. Lee—Commander, Second Brigade, Stevenson's Division. Lee has been in the war since its inception, at Second Manassas, Sharpsburg, and now Chickasaw Bluffs, preventing the Yankees from entering Vicksburg via a northern access.

Major Samuel H. Lockett—Chief engineer for the Department of Mississippi and East Louisiana. To save the Confederates fleeing from the carnage at Champion Hill, he must burn the bridges over the Big Black River that he designed and built.

Major General William W. Loring—Commander, Loring's Division. He is one of several Confederate officers who despise Pemberton for his northern roots. His hatred is particularly intense.

Lieutenant-General John C. Pemberton—Commander, Department of Mississippi and East Louisiana. A northerner by birth, he has joined the Southern cause through the influences of his Virginia-born wife Martha, Jefferson Davis, and his military experience in the South. He achieves the rank of lieutenant-general and takes command of the forces defending Vicksburg.

Civilians (listed alphabetically)

Benjamin Boudreau Carter—The other member of Bobby Thomas's team.

Julia Grant—Grant's wife, the former Julia Boggs Dent. She is the cousin of Confederate General James Longstreet, who served as best man at the Grants' wedding. Ironically, Longstreet is engaged in another epic...at Gettysburg.

Sally June McGowan—A freed slave and loyal citizen of the Confederacy. She is the first to spot the Union flotilla headed for Chickasaw Bluffs.

Emil Meyer—Confederate telegraph officer and partner of John Shank.

Martha Pemberton—Pemberton's wife, the former Martha Thompson of Norfolk, Virginia.

John Shank—Confederate telegraph officer and partner of Emil Meyer.

Bobby Thomas—Younger member of a two-man team smuggling much-needed percussion caps to the Vicksburg defenders.

Tub—A plantation slave who agrees to carry messages between Sherman and Porter during the Black Bayou expedition.

★ PROLOGUE ★

April 6, 1862, Pittsburg Landing, Tennessee

Despite being named after a heroic Shawnee chieftain, William Tecumseh Sherman did not feel courageous. He was tired. He'd had three horses shot from under him during the battle, one of which was his own prize sorrel race mare. The Confederates, under General Albert Sidney Johnston and then, when he was killed, commanded by the Creole General Pierre Gustave Toutant Beauregard, had overrun Sherman's encampment near Shiloh Church. It rankled Sherman that Beauregard was now sleeping in his tent.

But his rancor was no match for the state of exhaustion in which he found himself. As he searched for Ulysses S. Grant at the foot of the seventy-foot bluff overlooking Pittsburg Landing and the Tennessee River, he could feel the rain pelting his brow and hear the myriad clatter and chatter of Buell's army arriving from Nashville. None of it registered. He wanted to find Grant to assure himself that the Union commander felt as he did: that the battered Union Army should be removed to the other side of the river and allowed to regenerate itself, to recuperate. It *would* be a retreat, but a small one.

It was not hard to find Grant. It was never hard to find Grant, only to convince oneself that this simple man, with his perpetual deadpan expression and half-mast beard, was indeed the commander of all the Union armies in the Western Theater. Grant's expression could easily be mistaken for disinterest. It was merely a diversion of biological energy to where it was needed most—the brain. Sherman found Grant standing beneath a tree, a crutch under one arm to support the leg his horse had fallen on and a cigar between his teeth. The only homage paid to the inclement weather was an upturned coat collar and a "slouch" hat, from the brim of which a steady stream of water flowed.

"Evening," Sherman offered awkwardly. They were not well acquainted. The battle at Shiloh Church was the first opportunity either man had had to observe the other in action. Both were impressed.

"Any casualty figures yet?" Sherman asked.

"Eight thousand dead, wounded, or missing...thereabouts."

The number was both shocking and depressing. Angered, Sherman prayed the Confederate losses were comparable, then hastily downgraded the prayer to a fervent wish. His gaze drifted to the Union soldiers huddled by the riverbank, shivering, most of them runaways ashamed of their actions. They would get a chance to redeem themselves.

"Well, Grant, we've had the devil's own day of it, haven't we?" Sherman said, unsure how to broach the subject of beating a retreat across the river.

Pushing himself away from the tree, Grant engaged the crutch and started toward his headquarters.

"Yes," he said, removing the cigar from his mouth. "Yes, we have."

Briefly halting in front of his colleague, he added thoughtfully, "Lick 'em tomorrow, though," and immediately shoved the cigar home again.

The first day of the Battle of Shiloh was coming to an end.

Inspired by Charles Bracelen Flood's account of this event in his book "Grant and Sherman, The Friendship That Won The Civil War," Farrar, Straus. and Giroux, New York, 2005.

*   *   *

★ ONE ★

April 7, 1862 - The Shiloh Battlefield

On the second day of battle, Union skirmishers began forming their lines at 3:00 AM and were ordered to find the enemy. They did. The evening before, P.G.T. Beauregard had entertained great hopes for taking the day for the Confederacy but was unaware of the Union reinforcements under Don Carlos Buell, who were then arriving from Nashville under cover of darkness. Beauregard had lost half his men on the first day of battle; Grant had gained twenty thousand more. The fighting on the second day was intense but brief. By 4:00 PM, Beauregard ordered a general withdrawal to Corinth, Mississippi in the middle of a cold, relentless hailstorm, some of the hailstones as big as eggs and as hard as musket balls.

Had he wanted to, Grant could have pursued and destroyed Beauregard's exhausted army. Pursuit of a defeated foe was, after all, a maxim of military tactical manuals. However, pursuit was an undertaking that his own bone-weary, mud-caked army might not be able to sustain. They were tired too.

April 8, 1862 - The Road to Corinth

Sherman rode his sorrel to the crest of the highest hill he could find and gazed southward. The army Albert Sidney Johnston had put together and Gustave Beauregard now commanded was strung out on the Corinth Road like a snake chopped into several pieces, each wriggling with mindless life. The hailstones had melted, and the accumulated water in the mud holes had created miniature swamps into which man, beast, wagon and artillery piece first plunged, then emerged like chocolate phoenixes.

"Where are we?" Sherman barked, his expression betraying confusion, then concern as Lieutenant James Fulton, his aide, rode up behind him.

Fulton shook his head. Tentatively, he pointed at the tattered column heading south and said, "That's the Reb army, sir."

Sherman tossed his head back, annoyed by the response, and ran a hand through his mottled, reddish-brown hair.

"I can see that, Lieutenant! But where is the damnable skirmish line that's supposed to be ahead of us?"

It was a damnably good question, Fulton thought but did not say. If the infantrymen were not nearby, he and the general were clearly exposed.

Suddenly, both men heard a loud, commanding "Charge!" emanate from the rear of the retreating Confederate column. Their eyes snapped toward the source of the battle cry and spotted a Rebel officer galloping toward them with murder in his fiery eyes.

"Jesus, we better get out of here," Fulton gasped.

Preparing to do just that, Sherman asked, "Is that who I think it is?"

"Yes, sir," Fulton replied, the fear in his expression obvious. "That's Nathan Bedford Forrest."

If Sherman was afraid, Fulton couldn't see it. What he did see was Sherman's furrowed brow and the intense glare he shot at the approaching Rebel general and his entourage, before turning to flee toward a copse of trees from which the remainder of his staff was just emerging. Frantically, he waved them back and, when several did not respond, yelled, "Back to the trees, it's Bedford Forrest!"

It was enough to get their attention. Fortunately, the skirmish line Sherman and Fulton were looking for had been found by Sherman's staff. The skirmishers were kneeling in line for battle at the tree line.

The general passed through, turned, waited for his staff to follow and shouted his orders.

"Gentlemen, shoot that man!" Sherman bellowed, pointing at the charging figure of Nathan Bedford Forrest, his twin pistols blazing as he penetrated the skirmish line twenty yards from Lieutenant Fulton.

Suddenly realizing where he was, Forrest leveled one pistol at Sherman, aimed, and fired. Nothing happened—the pistol was empty. Then, the unmistakable sound of a musket discharging echoed through the trees. Bedford Forrest jerked to attention. He had been shot but, rather than fall to the ground, he seized the nearest Union soldier, hoisted the man onto the back of his horse, and galloped to join the rest of his cavalry brigade, who were just arriving. Because of the captive Union soldier, not a single shot was fired at the retreating figure.

"That man is crazy!" Fulton groaned.

Sherman, who had drawn and raised his pistol to a firing position, gave his nervous aide a long, dubious look.

"It comes with the territory," he said.

He might even have smiled when he said it.

April 10, 1862 - Pittsburg Landing, Tennessee

Sherman tied his horse near the paddle wheeler *Tigress* that Grant was using as his headquarters. He expected the staff meeting to be a short one, dealing as it would with the fruits of victory rather than the leavings of defeat, and with how the army and navy would pursue its next objective, which would surely be Corinth, Mississippi. Grant's army was still encamped on the west side of the Tennessee River, but Sherman sensed a disquietude, an amplification of the background chatter among the troops. Particularly noisy were the utterances leaking from a large wall tent fifty yards from the wharf, situated between two tall beech trees.

He stared disapprovingly at the tent. Not only were argumentative voices coming from it, but the tent itself was being jostled about as if bodies inside were bumping its support posts. A fight? Momentarily, he wondered if he should intervene, but decided against it on the grounds that, whatever was going on, no cries of pain were yet in evidence. Sherman turned, then moved and re-seated his "slouch" hat so that the brim leaned forward and to the right. He continued toward the gangplank.

"Sir!" a voice called from his right.

Sherman's head turned to view a short, pudgy young man with a blond goatee and discrete knots of blond hair nestled close to a pink skull. He recognized the man, who was saluting him, as one of Grant's administrative staff.

Returning the salute, Sherman said, "Corporal . . ."

"Smith, sir," the youngster said, snapping the salute with a broad grin. "Corporal Aaron Smith."

"Yes, Corporal Smith," Sherman said, gesturing with his thumb towards the rowdy tent. "What's going on over there?"

Smith snorted. "Reporters, sir," he said with a frown. "Some of them are causing trouble. Some of the boys are causing *them* even more trouble."

Sherman could tell that Smith was pleased with the clever turn of phrase he had just uttered, but he offered no encouragement. He disliked reporters as much as the next soldier, more in fact, but was interested in finding out why trouble was brewing.

"We just won a major battle, Lieutenant. Why should reporters be causing trouble?"

"Some of them are saying the casualties are too high," Smith replied.

"What is the casualty count? Do you know?"

Blinking, Smith muttered, "Not quite sure, sir. Something like eleven thousand in all, eighteen hundred dead."

In a more casual conversation, Sherman might have whistled his incredulity. Instead, he cocked his gaze toward the tent and said, "What do they expect? A bloodless battle?"

"I heard some of them saying we were unprepared," Smith added.

Sherman glowered at the young man, unhappy with the implications of what he was saying. The "we" to whom he referred would probably include Sherman himself. Before the Confederate attack, he had rebuked Colonel Jesse Appler of the 53rd Ohio for reporting "a line of men in butternut clothes moving in the woods around Shiloh Church," and told the old man to take his "damned regiment back to Ohio." He had eaten those words when the Confederates launched their assault early in the morning of April 6. That scrap of bad judgment had cost the life of his orderly, Private Tom Holliday of the 2nd Illinois Cavalry, who took a musket ball while Sherman was surveying the terrain where Confederate infantrymen were reported to be. He still had Holliday's binoculars.

War is hell, Sherman thought to himself. Resting his hands on his hips, he paused to listen in on the clamorous conversation inside the tent. While he was struggling to decipher one of the more energetic entreaties, the tent flap was flung aside, and a civilian in a plain black suit, white shirt and black bow tie emerged. His thin lips were engaged in a rapid-fire monologue directed primarily at a clean-shaven, emaciated soldier who followed. The civilian's hairline receded to the rear of his skull, the ears of which supported thick-lens glasses. The fervor of the monologue was causing the glasses to vibrate, as well as the sparse tufts of hair just above the ears, and especially the long but formless beard jutting sharply from an underdeveloped chin.

Turning to Fulton, Sherman asked, "Who is that?"

"Benjamin Stanton," Fulton replied. When he saw the quizzical expression on Sherman's face, he added, "He's the Lieutenant-Governor of Ohio."

Sherman, as a resident of Ohio, recognized the name.

"He's no relation to Secretary Stanton," Fulton offered, referring to Edwin M. Stanton, the United States Secretary of War.

"I know," Sherman said, beginning a slow but purposeful stride toward the combatants. When he arrived, the clean-shaven soldier snapped to attention and saluted.

"Is there a problem?" Sherman asked in a tone indicating he knew there was.

Taken aback by the sudden appearance of an officer wearing a determined scowl, Stanton said, "General, I don't believe we've met. I'm Benjamin Stanton, Lieutenant-Governor of Ohio," and offered his hand.

Sherman took it, pumped once, and said, "William Tecumseh Sherman. Is there a problem?"

Stanton looked around, searching for allies, and seemed relieved to find several friendly members of the press corps interspersed among the troops. Some soldiers were only half-dressed and preparing for an evening of blessed inactivity.

"General Sherman, I am very happy to meet you," Stanton bubbled, then turned serious. "But I must tell you; I am not at all satisfied with the performance of your General Grant."

Stanton paused to assess Sherman's reaction. Sherman's return stare was ice cold and utterly free of nuance.

"Sir, I tell you, the blundering stupidity and negligence of Grant is criminal," Stanton scolded, wagging a finger in Sherman's face. "I have heard many disturbing reports this day, stories of Confederates killing Union soldiers while they slept, charges that General Grant was too drunk to prepare an adequate defense . . ."

"Mr. Stanton, you are completely wrong," Sherman stated with bristling resolve as he touched the brim of his hat and turned his head. "General Grant is the most competent officer I have ever met and quite possibly the only Union commander capable of winning this war. I will not listen to your slanderous accusations."

"General Sherman, we are both men of Ohio. I have brought five thousand dollars for the men of our state, and I wish you to assist me in its distribution . . ."

"I will not assist you in any of your nefarious activities, sir."

"Sir, I am the Lieutenant Governor of Ohio!" the insulted Stanton croaked. "And I *will* have your attention!"

Sherman turned so suddenly that Aaron Smith, who was nearby, nearly bumped heads with him. Sherman saw Smith's lips silently forming the un-word "Shh-h-h-h." His eyes locked on Stanton.

"And I am the brother of John Sherman," Sherman said, meting out the words like poker chips. "I assume you know who he is."

"Yes . . . of course," Stanton replied, puffing his chest.

"Then, sir, you know that my brother is a *full* senator in the United States Congress, whereas you are merely a *lieutenant* governor of Ohio. I would contend that his is the superior rank, would you not agree?"

Fulton tried but could not quite suppress a giggle.

Preparing to explode, Stanton once more resorted to finger wagging as he carped, "General, I have considerable resources at my command. If I were you, I would be wary of picking a fight."

"Ha!" Sherman bellowed, rocking on his heels. "Pick a fight indeed! The Rebels tried that yesterday, and you can see what it got them—a forced march to Corinth. As for your resources, can I assume you are referring to the *honorable* gentlemen of the press?"

The word "honorable" was spoken with anything but honorable intent.

Stanton's eyes fixed on several non-military men in dark suits who were generally accompanying each other among the onlookers. None appeared anxious to cross verbal swords with Sherman. After sizzling Stanton and his press sycophants with his most contemptuous glare, Sherman uttered a snort of disgust and headed for the *Tigress*'s gangplank and Grant's staff meeting. Fulton followed on his heels. Behind them, the rumble of opinionated men vehemently agreeing with one another filled the air.

"By God, I do hate newspapermen," Sherman complained. "They come into camp, pick up rumors, and print them as facts. They're no better than spies!"

Fulton was not quite ready to draw such a conclusion.

"Maybe you're right, sir, but I think it would be better for us if you tried not to aggravate them so much . . ."

"Aggravate them?" Sherman roared. "We should kill them, Lieutenant. That would be *my* preference."

Forcing his plump body to keep pace, Fulton watched Sherman's face, waiting for a sign that he was joking. None was forthcoming.

Instead, Sherman barked, "But if we did kill them, I'm sure we'd be getting reports from Hell before breakfast."

This *was* a joke. The twisted grin on Sherman's face confirmed it. Fulton flashed a meek smile.

"Lieutenant, why are you here?" Sherman asked. "I've never seen you at a staff meeting before."

"Oh . . . oh," Fulton stammered, happy to avoid further discussion of civilian homicide. He dug into the breast pocket of his coat and removed an envelope. "I have a message from the War Department for General Grant."

"From General Halleck?"

"Yes."

Halting on the *Tigress* side of the gangplank, Sherman swung an arm toward an open door and said, "You first, Lieutenant. Whatever news you're carrying trumps anything I could possibly have to say."

* * *

Seated in a wicker chair next to an oval table on the starboard side of the Tigress's deck, Grant studied Halleck's telegram. Sherman did his own visual study of the staff members present. James Birdseye McPherson, whose face was almost as pudgy as Fulton's, was seated away from the table in a chair like Grant's. He was a capable engineering officer who had been sent to Grant by Halleck. Also present were Generals John McClernand and Don Carlos Buell. McClernand was a political general from Illinois with no meaningful military experience who had been appointed by Lincoln, one of many such appointments made by the president. While regular army officers generally abhorred the practice, it gave Lincoln a way to reward those who managed to recruit entire divisions, brigades and regiments into the army. Both Grant and Sherman considered McClernand incompetent—his division had fled the field at Fort Donelson—but were not in a position to do anything about it. Although he was regular army, Buell was another thorn in Grant's side. He had outranked Grant until Grant's promotion to major general after the capture of Fort Donelson and remained resentful of his *de-facto* demotion. Having brought the reinforcements that made the difference at Shiloh, he was actively portraying himself as the battle's hero, at Grant's expense.

Grant dropped his hands to the table, releasing the telegram as he did so. Then he stood and, foregoing the crutch, limped to a position where he could be seen and heard by all. Straightening, he inhaled deeply and announced, "Halleck is coming."

There were no overt expressions of surprise, but there might have been. Major-General Henry Halleck, Commander of the Army of the Department of the Missouri, was Grant's and Sherman's commanding officer but had no significant field experience.

"Why?" Sherman finally asked.

Grant's expression, usually somewhere between pensive and stoic, seemed tainted by sorrow.

"He's taking command of field operations."

"Halleck is planning to command field operations?" Sherman echoed incredulously. He respected Halleck, in fact he owed the man a debt of gratitude for reinstating him in the western theater after a near nervous breakdown in Kentucky. But Halleck, known as "Old Brains" by his peers, was a military intellectual, not a combat veteran. He had written the well-regarded military text *Elements of Military Art and Science*, but, as far as Sherman knew, had never fired a shot in anger or personally directed other men to do so.

"When?" Sherman asked Grant.

"As soon as he can get here from St. Louis. His title will be 'Commander of the Western Armies.'"

"What does that make you?"

"*Assistant* Commander of the Western Armies," Grant said with a shrug. He limped across the deck to the railing and gazed across what had been the Shiloh battlefield and was fast becoming a scene of political conflict. Sherman wondered if the mild-mannered Grant could win such a contest. If he needed Sherman's help, it would certainly be made available.

Grant pulled a cigar from his vest pocket and lit it, then returned to the table, reseated himself, and unrolled a map of the area.

"As my first act as Assistant Commander of the Western Armies of the United States, I plan to boot Beauregard out of southern Tennessee and northern Mississippi. Has he made it to Corinth yet?"

"General Grant, may I ask a question?"

It was Don Carlos Buell. Grant held the map in place and looked at him.

"Of course."

Buell seemed to stiffen as he said, "Do the general's orders give any information on the command structure of this army?"

Grant paused, glanced around and found a sea of curious faces. Sherman empathized with him. Grant had just received a slap in the face and wanted to put the incident behind him. But the others were anxious to know how they would fit into Halleck's new organization.

"Yes, yes it does," Grant replied, retrieving the telegram and holding it before him. "General Buell, you will have the center, General Thomas the right, and General Pope, because of his present position in Hamburg, will take the left. That's all I can tell you right now."

Grant waited briefly for comments and questions, then said, "Gentlemen, please understand; I plan to recommend to General Halleck that we pursue Beauregard immediately before he has a chance to entrench himself in Corinth."

Heads nodded politely as Grant presented his plan. Sherman seated himself near Grant's end of the table and wondered if any of the others felt as he did, that "Old Brains" would never move quickly. It was not in his nature or his repertoire of military strategy.

★ TWO ★

April 15, 1862, Corinth, Mississippi

Damn the Yankees! was the dominant curse in the mind of Pierre Gustav Toutant Beauregard as he watched his army dig in at Corinth, Mississippi from his vantage point: the porch of the "Duck Pond" House. *Damn the Yankees!* There were too many of them; they had too much food and too many supplies. His own men, some virtually barefoot and all of them hungry, had magnificent *elan*, but that spirit was bound to cloy with time.

Damn the Yankees and damn Albert Sidney Johnston for getting himself killed! Johnston's was not a command Beauregard wanted, nor was he prepared for it. The first day at Shiloh had gone well until Johnston was shot. Then everything had shut down as night fell, with both sides exhausted and needful of the time to recover the wounded and dead. Beauregard had needed that time to assume the burdens of command. Time was everything, and he had inadvertently given it to the Federals to bring in Buell's reinforcements under cover of darkness. *Most of all, damn Ulysses S. Grant!* Why couldn't he be like the other Union commanders: slow, deliberate and unwilling to attack unless victory was guaranteed?

"Tea, General?" a saccharine vibrato voice to his left intoned. It was gray-haired Mrs. Ripley, widow of ten years and proprietor of the "Duck Pond" house he now occupied. She had arrived with her goodies, which she'd done at least five times a day since he'd been there.

"Why, yes, Mrs. Ripley, I believe I will," he said, gazing politely at her smiling, ancient face.

"I have ladyfingers, General. Would you like one or two?"

"No, thank you, Mrs. Ripley. The only ladyfingers I would care to possess are those attached to your lovely hands," he said, then took her hand and kissed it. As a Louisiana Creole, neither his accent nor his instinctive charm were up to southern standards, but he was learning.

Mrs. Ripley beamed, which is to say she turned nearly apoplectic. With skin the color of a ripe peach, she reddened easily.

"Why thank you, General Beau-re-gard!" she drawled as she poured tea into a new cup and retrieved the used one from a wicker table next to Beauregard. The general sipped slowly and nodded his favorable opinion.

When Mrs. Ripley vanished inside the house, Beauregard gulped his tea and wandered down to the street. *Washburne should be back soon*, he thought. Beauregard had sent him along with a cavalry patrol from Bedford Forrest's outfit to ride west and look for signs of Earl Van Dorn, who was bringing his divisions from Arkansas. God knows he needed all the reinforcements he could get. Corinth was located at a key juncture of the east-west Memphis and Charleston Railroad and the north-south Mobile and Ohio Railroad. Both provided communications and supply that were vital to the Confederate war effort. The loss of Corinth would be a devastating blow.

It was not until evening that Beauregard spotted a lone rider, framed by the orange ball of the setting sun on top and the track of the Mobile and Ohio Railroad on the bottom. By that time, he had returned to Mrs. Ripley's porch and was dining on ham, succotash and a port wine from the Gulf. The cavalryman was riding slowly but steadily towards him and was in no hurry. When he finally arrived and tied his sorrel to a post at street level, Beauregard noticed it was not Washburne, but a younger, clean-shaven man with a high forehead and a blunt nose, with whom he was not acquainted. The soldier climbed the stairs to the porch, removed the crumpled *kepi* from his head, and saluted.

"Corporal Dabney reporting, sir," he muttered nervously.

"Captain Washburne sent you?" Beauregard asked.

"Yes, sir," Dabney replied a little more vigorously than was necessary. "The captain wanted you to know that General Van Dorn will arrive within the hour."

"Good, good, I'm pleased to hear it," Beauregard said, restraining a sigh of relief.

"Oh, and sir, there have been Yankee troop movements," Dabney added.

Beauregard snapped upright in his chair, nearly dropping the wineglass poised at his lips.

"Is Halleck moving?"

Dabney laughed and said, "He's movin,' about a half mile a day. Then he digs in and waits maybe another day and then moves another half mile. He should get here by Christmas."

Beauregard was tempted to correct Dabney's math but realized he was only joking. Halleck was indeed moving very cautiously but, at half a mile a day, would cover the twenty miles from Pittsburg Landing in little more than a month. Nevertheless, he was reassured to be confronting the kind of fastidious Union commander who not only looked before he leaped but often found a way to avoid uncoupling his feet from the ground altogether. Despite Dabney's depiction, it sounded to Beauregard as if Halleck might only be conducting maneuvers at this point.

"What are his numbers?"

This time, Dabney's response was less sanguine.

"About a hundred thousand."

Had his heart not sunk into his bowels, Beauregard might have whistled. Even with Van Dorn's Corps, Confederate strength would be only fifty thousand. Slow as he apparently was, Halleck would be hard to stop. Leaving Dabney on the porch, Beauregard went inside the house and returned with pen and paper.

"Corporal, get yourself something to eat from Mrs. Ripley," he said, sitting down and removing his nearly consumed meal from the table. "I'm going to issue some orders, and I want you to transcribe them for distribution to all corps commanders."

Dabney did as he was told, happy to eat a general's meal. Mrs. Ripley, happy to oblige, put him in a corner chair next to an end table, and let him devour ravenously to his heart's content. After half an hour alternating between scribbling and introspection, Beauregard sat his writing implements down and said, "Corporal Dabney, when you have finished, please join me."

Which meant "now," Dabney quickly realized. Taking a final mouthful of ham and swallowing it prematurely, he rejoined his commander.

"Sir!" he said, snapping a precautionary salute.

Beauregard handed him the orders and five envelopes, each addressed to a corps commander, and said, "Please transcribe these orders and deliver them to my staff: Generals Hardee, Bragg, Polk, Breckenridge and Van Dorn. If any have questions or reservations, they may, of course, express them, but I want to emphasize the need for preparedness and expect you to convey that attitude. Do you understand, Corporal Dabney?"

The words were not harsh but had an edge to them Dabney had not expected.

"Yes, sir, of course," he responded curtly.

Beauregard rose, brushed the dinner debris off his butternut uniform and strolled as silently as his boots would permit to the porch steps, halting when he reached them. For a minute, he did nothing but clasp his hands together behind his back and gaze northward. Then he spoke.

"It is always this way, Corporal. They always have more than we do. Even in our own country, they have more. That is why we must be better than they are, why we must be more persistent, better prepared . . ."

Perhaps sounding more desperate than he intended, Beauregard brought his entreaty to an abrupt end and turned to face Dabney.

"But all that is contained in my orders," he said hastily. "Carry on, Corporal."

Once more, Dabney saluted and turned to go. When he was halfway to the street, Beauregard called, "Impress upon them the need for diligence, son. We must construct strong earthworks to stop the Yankee! We must bring every cannon in our arsenal to bear upon him and drive him back! We must build an impregnable fortress Corinth if we are to succeed!"

Dabney could only nod his acceptance of Beauregard's vehement exhortations. He boarded his horse and galloped away.

Beauregard watched him go, hoping his words of encouragement would somehow bear fruit. After all, the armies of the Confederacy had often succeeded before when none had expected them to. It could happen again.

On the other hand, it might not. Purging his mind of the fervent exhortations he had just expressed, Beauregard sat down and started planning how he would get his army out of town . . . just in case the Yankee assault was as overwhelming as he expected it to be.

May 29, 1862, The "Siege" of Corinth

When Henry Halleck reached Corinth after taking a month to travel twenty miles, Beauregard was waiting for him. He could hardly have done otherwise. Dutifully, the Creole general threw up extensive breastworks north and east of town, strengthened the "Beauregard Line," and created an inner ring of rifle pits. Although reinforcements had increased the size of both armies by twenty percent, their relative strengths remained the same: two Union soldiers for every Confederate. Halleck deployed his command with Thomas's Army of Tennessee covering the north, Buell's Army of the Ohio in the center, and Pope's army to the southeast. The Siege of Corinth, if it happened, would engage more troops than any previous military operation of its type on the North American continent.

But it was not to be. Pierre Gustav Toutant Beauregard, hero of Bull Run and co-designer of the Confederate Battle Flag, saw that he was outnumbered, had no siege guns, and would soon be unable to feed his troops. His decision to escape southward along the Mobile and Ohio Railroad to Tupelo would not be popular among the Confederate general staff, including Jeff Davis, and it was not truly popular among his men, but they breathed a sigh of relief nonetheless.

He did it with a degree of stealth that even purists might consider excessive. Just prior to Halleck's formidable encirclement of the town, Beauregard issued his men three days' rations and announced that he planned to attack. Given the dire circumstances, the normal efflux of deserters increased with the inevitable result that the Union forces learned of the "attack." Beauregard obliged by displaying a menacing array of dummy "Quaker" guns and staging a bombardment that froze the Federals in place. To encourage the deception, troops were ordered to cheer as if reinforcements had arrived, to maintain their campfires, and to play the drum and bugle music of a vast army on the march. When Union patrols probed the streets of Corinth the morning of May 30, the Rebels were gone.

It was a well-planned, well-executed retreat . . . but it *was* a retreat.

May 30, 1862, Corinth, Mississippi

Henry Halleck was not nearly the horseman Ulysses S. Grant was, a fact that was all too evident as the two men entered the battleground that might have been. Balding and bug-eyed, Halleck tended to bounce in his saddle, the epitome of a military administrator accustomed to stationary seating. Grant was an excellent horseman. During the Mexican War, he had once carried a message through enemy lines by riding on one side of his horse, shielding himself with the animal's body. Fortunately, the Mexicans had not thought to shoot the horse.

Halleck pulled at the reins and brought his white stallion to an awkward halt near a Confederate rifle pit. The loss of momentum nearly toppled him, but he seized the horse's mane and prevented a fall.

"They're gone," he said after regaining his balance.

"They are," Grant agreed without removing his cigar.

"I thought they would fight," Halleck said, bewildered.

Since his demotion to second-in-command, Grant was not favorably disposed toward his commander. He would have liked to point out that any Confederate commander with a grain of strategic insight—and Beauregard filled that bill nicely—would have known what Halleck had in mind for Corinth. With a month to observe the enemy's meticulous approach, Beauregard would also be keenly aware of how precarious his situation was.

Grant was not a man to deliberately provoke his superiors, so he said, "We would've whipped them good, and maybe even captured the whole Rebel army. Beauregard couldn't let that happen."

Halleck stared at Grant as if his second in command were mocking him. Grant's poker face revealed nothing.

"I'm sure you're right, general," Halleck conceded, clearing his throat.

He might have said more, but Sherman and McPherson seized the moment by riding in from the northwest, dismounting as they joined Grant and Halleck. Strolling to the abandoned rifle pit, Sherman gazed at it thoughtfully, then turned to his companions, a wicked grin somehow merging with his chronic scowl to produce a devilish expression.

"By God, they've lit out!" he shouted. "I wonder what fault the damn newspapers will find with this."

"They'll probably say it was too easy," Grant suggested. "Or that it was a Pyrrhic victory."

Sherman and McPherson laughed. Halleck did not.

"Pyrrhic victory! I think not," Halleck complained.

The three subordinate officers cast doleful glances at each other. Apparently, Henry Halleck was not attuned to battlefield humor.

"You're right, sir, there is nothing Pyrrhic about this victory and no newspaperman worthy of the name could see it that way," Grant said, and added, "But it would be a more satisfying victory if we were to go after Beauregard."

Whatever ground Grant had gained to that point was instantly lost. Even before Halleck spoke, Grant could sense the disapproval in his commander's protruding eyes. Once more he wondered if Halleck's shabby treatment of him was due to the differences in their philosophies of armed conflict, or was simply a personal dislike.

"That will not be necessary, general," Halleck grumbled. "The enemy will continue his retreat, which is all I desire."

Halleck looked at the three officers one by one, seeking approval, if not absolution. Neither was in evidence. Sherman's blank stare was free of emotion while Grant and McPherson merely averted their eyes.

"Besides, there is much to do. The President wants to liberate East Tennessee, and I must send General Buell to achieve that end. General Pope is needed in Virginia . . ."

"Sir, do you mean you are dismantling this army when we have the Rebels on the run?" McPherson asked, incredulous.

Halleck was dumbfounded. The remark might have been expected from Grant or even Sherman, but not McPherson. The young man was his protégé; an engineer like himself— logical, meticulous in action and thought. The shock of it gave Halleck's voice an uncharacteristic screech.

"Need I remind you that this is not the only front in the war, gentlemen? We cannot abandon our colleagues in the east, or anywhere the armed might of the Union is needed . . ."

Halleck declaimed mightily for another ten minutes, sounding more like a candidate for office than a commanding general. Dutifully and courteously, his officers listened. Grant could not help feeling it was an engineer's point of view Halleck was expressing: Make sure no branch of the army is overstressed or under-strength, and maintain all at an even, safe level. The trouble with that philosophy was that it was not likely to result in victory. Warfare was not like building a house brick by brick to achieve stability and balance. Warfare was like bringing a house down with a fatal blow to its key support. Grant understood this; so did Sherman and, somewhat unexpectedly, McPherson. Only the highest-ranking Union commanders like McClellan and Halleck seemed congenitally unable to abide the chaos of spontaneous battle.

"Sir, I believe we take your point," Grant said during a hiatus in Halleck's discourse. "But I would like to make a proposal on strategy. With or without the entire army, I think we should take Vicksburg."

Had he been asked about it later, Grant could not have said which of his colleagues was more astonished by the suggestion. Halleck was aghast, but he was always distressed by the possibility of precipitous conflict. Confusion reigned on McPherson's features while a tensing of his perpetual scowl highlighted Sherman's skepticism.

"Take Vicksburg? Take the Gibraltar of the Confederacy?" Halleck howled in disbelief. "I do not dispute the quality of your target, General Grant, but how do we assault a fortress bristling with armament and poised on a two-hundred-foot cliff overlooking the Mississippi? How could we even approach it?"

Grant brought his horse around to face his companions and leaned forward on his saddlehorn.

"I think it can be done. As we all know, Commodore David Farragut recently captured New Orleans. The navy can now steam all the way from that city to Vicksburg unimpeded."

"That's more than a hundred miles!"

"It doesn't matter," Grant argued passionately. "Farragut has an overwhelming force of gunboats, some of them ironclads. The Rebels can't stop him."

"But the Rebs in Vicksburg can blow anything out of the water that tries to get past those damn cliffs," McPherson asserted. "They have the high ground, and I mean the *really* high ground! Farragut would have to elevate his cannons like mortars just to land shells inside the city."

Grant drew in a breath and stared with melancholy eyes at two of his critics. The third, Sherman, chose that moment to seat himself on the ground and pick at the clovers growing among the blades of grass. His slouch hat concealed his face.

"I haven't worked it all out yet," Grant said patiently. "But look at the situation. The U.S. Navy controls the Mississippi from New Orleans to Vicksburg. To boot, General Pope and Commander Walke have given us Island Number 10, seven thousand Confederate soldiers, and a hundred sixty guns. The only impediment between Cairo, Illinois and Vicksburg is Memphis, Tennessee, and we'll soon have that."

Sherman's head lifted and Grant spotted a fledgling grin on his face. He wondered what was going on in his new friend's perceptive, but not always steady mind.

"We do not have Memphis yet, general!" Halleck chided, emitting something like a moan of horror. "That will require much preparation and effort . . ."

And, of course, time, Grant thought. Memphis was not twenty miles distant but sixty miles to the west. At Halleck's tortoise-like pace, the army would not reach the city before late summer.

Grant decided he had said enough for the moment. He had not expected Halleck to look favorably upon any plan as radical as an assault on Vicksburg, but he felt the subject needed broaching, and Halleck needed someone to build a fire under him. As second in command, he mused, perhaps that was a role he could properly assume.

A patrol of cavalry arrived to escort "Old Brains" back to his temporary headquarters near the intersection of the two railroads. Grant, Sherman, and McPherson decided to familiarize themselves with Corinth and tour the various Union commands to determine if the Rebels had left any spoilers behind. They headed east on Child's Street from the Mobile and Ohio track.

"Grant, how in God's name did you come up with Vicksburg? I thought Old Brains would keel over," Sherman said in his typically direct manner.

Riding between the other two officers, Grant said, "Strategically, it's the ideal target. Think of it. If the Union controls the Mississippi, it splits the Confederacy in two. The southeastern Confederate states become an island, with the Atlantic Ocean to the east, the Gulf of Mexico to the south, the Ohio River to the north, and the Mississippi River to the west. We already control three of those four waterways; the Mississippi would be the fourth, and the key to the Mississippi is Vicksburg. The Rebs wouldn't be able to carry on trade with anyone, least of all the Confederate states and their sympathizers in the west."

"It's no wonder you and Old Brains don't get along. He wants to waddle along at a mile a day while you propose to attack one of the most heavily fortified, unapproachable strongholds in the Confederacy," Sherman gibed. "You've frightened the poor man to death."

With a sly smile, McPherson said, "Perhaps that's what you had in mind, General?"

"Oh, no," Grant retorted. "I wish nothing but the best for General Halleck. It could be worse. We could be moving backwards . . ."

"McClellan's favorite direction," Sherman intoned sarcastically, soliciting belly laughs from his companions.

Grant reined his horse toward a line of tents to the south, and what looked like coffee brewing over an open fire. Sherman and McPherson followed.

"Seriously," Grant began. "I'm in a very uncomfortable position. "Being second in command of an army is like being the vice president. You are thoroughly conspicuous but have no real authority. If I don't occasionally startle Old Brains with my rashness, he may forget I exist."

"Sir, I believe you are exaggerating," McPherson said. "Everyone knows what you accomplished by capturing Forts Donelson and Henry. And, in terms of casualties, Shiloh is no worse than Antietam . . ."

"You do recall," a wide-eyed Grant exclaimed, "that the president fired General McClellan for that victory, don't you?"

"Not for the victory," the younger man argued. "But for failing to act upon it."

"Gentlemen, let's cease the chatter and take some refreshment," Sherman said, sliding down from his horse to shake the hand of a burly, red-faced sergeant who was saluting with one hand while thrusting a mug of coffee at him with the other.

Grant and McPherson were quickly out of their saddles and enjoying the steaming brew. As it happened, they had set down in one of George Thomas's divisions. Thomas, a Virginian, who had remained with the Union, was widely respected and apparently well liked by his men. To Grant's question about whether the Rebels had left anything useful behind, the burly sergeant replied, "Just them damn Quaker guns; they're only good for firewood."

Grant, Sherman and McPherson finished their coffees and departed under a hailstorm of snapping salutes and sharp cries of, "Sir!" The western sky, expansive above the flat Mississippi landscape, was turning a burnt orange as the sun dipped below the horizon. McPherson bade his colleagues a good night and rode off toward the west as if chasing the retreating sun. Grant suggested that he and Sherman relax beneath the umbrella of an ancient and twisted magnolia tree in their path. When they had seated themselves with their backs against its massive trunk, Grant removed a pint of whisky from his breast pocket and downed a swig. Then he offered the bottle to Sherman, who looked disapprovingly at it and then at Grant.

"Yes, Sherman, I drink whisky. Sometimes I even get drunk," Grant said. "You must know that by now."

"I do," Sherman replied stiffly, clearly uncertain how to react. Hesitantly, he took the bottle, downed a hurried gulp, and handed it back.

"If we are going to work together, you'd better understand this," Grant said, stuffing the bottle back into his pocket. "I am a very good drunk, by the way. I am never obnoxious but am occasionally entertaining, and my drunkenness never persists into the next day, much to the displeasure of my critics."

"Why do you do it then, if you know you'll be criticized?"

"Because it clears my mind. I do some of my best thinking when I'm drunk."

After he said it, Grant flashed Sherman a quizzical look with a hint of a smile beneath the close-cropped beard.

"You're joking," Sherman ventured.

"I am and I'm not," Grant said, pulling two cigars from another pocket and offering one to Sherman. "I don't get drunk very often, but when I do, I often conceive brilliant strategies in the process. However, I always re-examine them in the light of sobriety."

"Thank God!" Sherman exclaimed, accepting the cigar. "So, you drink for inspiration?"

"Not always. Sometimes I'm just unhappy, like all of us."

Both men were silent while Grant lit the cigars. With neither man being quite aware of it, the allusion to unhappiness had created a melancholy void in the conversation. As he puffed his cigar to life, Grant's melancholy seemed to deepen.

Eventually, he turned and said, "It really doesn't take inspiration, though."

"What doesn't?"

"Winning battles. It doesn't take inspiration, or creativity, or brilliance, or any of the other grand virtues. Are you a smart man?"

"I was sixth in my class at West Point."

"If you count from the bottom instead of the top, that's about where I was," Grant said with a mellow guffaw. "Best thing I ever did at the Point was jump a horse named York over a high bar. Even set a record doing it. Are you impressed?"

"I am," Sherman quickly responded. "But what are you implying, that horsemanship is more important to a military man than academic performance?"

"No, 'course not," Grant rejoined. "An officer has to learn strategy, tactics, and all the rest. Can't do without them. But war is not an academic exercise; it's a physical struggle. One thing I learned in the Mexican War is that, above all else, a commander must act. He can't afford to wait for the perfect strategy to reveal *it*self or the enemy will reveal *him*self in the most unpleasant way imaginable."

"Jump the horse before you have too much time to think about it. Is that your philosophy?"

"Something like that. Just don't act like an A-student."

Sherman was silent, but the scowl on his face was telling. He had no idea what Grant was talking about.

"Henry Halleck is an A-student. George McClellan is an A-student. What are we taught at the Point? Don't attack unless you have superior numbers and tactics. Who learns these lessons the best? A-students! That's why Halleck and McClellan are so God-awfully slow. What they should do is the unexpected. It's better to be quick than clever. It's even better to be unpredictable. Lee and Jackson are masters at this."

Sherman leaned forward, wrapping his knees in his arms. His head, cigar smoke encircling it like clouds surrounding Mount Olympus, nodded in uncertain affirmation.

"Robert E. Lee was an A-student. How do you fit him into your theory?"

The cigar gripped tightly between his teeth, Grant eyed his colleague mischievously.

"Never take a drunk too seriously," he warned sarcastically. "But my *besotted musings* do have an answer. As an A-student, Lee has also learned the obverse lesson just as well: *Don't wait for superior numbers if you know you can't get them.* He can't beat us that way and he knows it."

Sherman's head was nodding with renewed energy.

"So that's your secret? Attack with superior numbers if you can, but if you can't, then find another way that does not require superior numbers."

"Yes."

"What's the other way?"

"That's my *other* secret," Grant joked.

The two men laughed until inhaled cigar smoke choked them. Then they laughed at their discomfort. Sherman could not help wondering about his friend. Was Grant right about the lassitude of Halleck and McClellan, about the importance of doing the un-expected? Alexander of Macedonia had been a master of surprise and he had conquered the known world. Not the least of the shocks he had inflicted upon the nervous systems of his Persian enemies was cutting off his army from its home base and living off the land. Sherman shook his head. As quixotically appealing as it sounded, no modern commander—least of all a Union commander —would dare make such a bold move. The risk was far too great and, Sherman reflected, the menu of modern commanders offered no latter-day Alexanders.

"Sherman, I'm going to apply for thirty days' leave."

Grant's announcement was so matter-of-fact that Sherman was not sure he'd heard it correctly. He glanced at Grant, whose eyes met his, awash in something akin to despair, then turned sharply away.

"But why? We're winning. We just took Corinth. We'll take Memphis soon, like you said."

Grant hesitated, his jaw quivering with tension. It was as close to anger as Sherman had ever seen the man.

"You know why. You know I'm in the way here. I've stood it as long as I can. I won't endure it any longer."

As quickly as he'd lost it, Grant regained his self-control. His teeth clamped down on the cigar, nearly cutting it in two. After several frantic puffs, the muscles of his face relaxed, signaling a resumption of stability, if not normality. With forearms raised and fingers splayed, he stared with evangelical intensity at his companion.

"I'm not much more than an observer here. I send orders out to the right wing and they're ignored. Advances are made without any notification to me. I tell Halleck I think he should have Pope move his army at night for a daylight advance and he silences me as if he thinks I'm out of my mind. It's . . . it's . . . frustrating!"

Sherman was at a loss for words. Grant's was a predicament he had never experienced. Second in command was about as high as Sherman's aspirations had ever soared. On the one occasion when he'd been in command of the Department of the Cumberland, he had come damnably close to a nervous breakdown. But Ulysses S. Grant was different. Not only did Grant want command, he knew absolutely that he should have it. It was a quiet, understated, but implacable confidence that could easily be, and often was, mistaken for a cool detachment. It was also an objective recognition that he was the best man for the job, perhaps the only man. Not many men could harbor such knowledge without descending into arrogance and narcissism.

"When do you plan to go?"

"Soon, but I'm not sure how soon."

"Before you do, come talk with me first."

"So you can persuade me to stay?" Grant said, leaning forward to mimic Sherman's pose.

"So I can *convince* you to stay," Sherman corrected. "I have the wherewithal. Don't forget, I *was* an A-student. I'm a master of polemical procrastination."

This brought a rare grin to Grant's face.

"Seriously, something good might happen. A happy accident . . ."

"Hah!" Grant bellowed. "You want me to wish for Halleck to keel over? That's hardly . . ."

"No, no, of course not. I simply meant that something could occur that would restore you to your proper place. Lincoln is running out of generals to command the Army of the Potomac. Maybe he'll give you a shot at it."

"You're joking, of course."

"I'm joking, of course."

They traded jokes, laughter and stories like old friends, which they ultimately would become. It was as if they sensed that their lives were bound together, at least for the duration of the war. Perhaps it was simply a recognition of a common goal, coupled with an appreciation of each others' talents and weaknesses. The source of this intuitive conviction was a mystery, but mystery or not, its presence was palpable.

With daylight waning rapidly, Grant rose, stretched and said, "I think I'll get some sleep."

"Me too. We'll need it if Old Brains decides to make a forced march to Memphis," Sherman gibed.

Picking up on the sarcasm, Grant said, "That's eighty miles. What do you think we'll do, maybe a mile a day?"

"Maybe *two* miles a day! By God, if there are any Rebs in Memphis, they'll think we're the Golden Horde. We'll scare the bejesus out of them with our lickety-splittin' speed."

The two men strolled to their horses, mounted them, and headed west toward their respective camps. The Halleck jokes soon dried up, leaving a hollow space in the conversation that neither man was anxious to fill. Sherman was concerned that his commander would suggest another swig of whisky and was relieved when he refrained. The sun finally sank beneath the western horizon, leaving a smear of orange, red and gold framed in black to mark the spot of its descent to the underworld.

"Do you really think Vicksburg can be taken?" Sherman asked, directing his words to the lighted cigar ahead of him.

It was a moment before Grant responded, "We have the numbers—men, guns, ships, just about everything. If we can't, maybe we should look for another line of work."

"What about the two-hundred foot bluffs, and the artillery?"

"We'll figure it out," Grant replied. "The artillery is the navy's problem, not ours. What we have to do is figure out a way to get up there without getting everyone killed. That won't be easy."

No, it won't be, Sherman thought. *Not with those two-hundred-foot cliffs in the west, swamps to the south, thick woodlands to the north, and Jackson, the Mississippi Capitol, to the east. Maybe we can fly in, like a flock of geese.*

"But then, maybe we won't have to do anything but occupy the place," Grant said in a droll tone. "The navy's had a string of victories lately. We need to see what they can do."

It was another ten minutes before Sherman saw Grant's fingers extract the cigar from between his teeth and heard the soft-spoken pronouncement:

"All right. I guess I can stay a while."

★ THREE ★

June 28, 1862, The Mississippi River below Vicksburg

The red lanterns had been hung to signal the attack. At 2:00 AM there wasn't much to see except the mild glow of random firelight that inevitably betrayed the presence of a city as large as Vicksburg. Commodore David Glasgow Farragut hoped the Confederate soldiers manning the numerous hilltop batteries guarding the city were having similar visual difficulties. He was not anxious to stir his cannons—the 32-pounders, 42-pounders, and 10-inch Columbiads—into explosive life.

"Where are we?" he whispered to the pilot of the *USS Hartford*, one of the ironclads leading the charge past the city.

The pilot paused before pointing to the northwest and answering, "I think the first batteries are over there."

Doesn't know any more than I do, Farragut thought.

"I can't see a damned thing."

Farragut waited for a reply but heard nothing except the dull throb of the engines and the rush of water against the bow as the *Hartford* fought the unpredictable Mississippi current.

"Is there a good reason why we're doin' this, sir?" the pilot's quavering voice murmured.

"We have to meet Flag Officer Davis."

"Why do we have to do that, sir?"

Farragut could think of no good reason why he should risk destruction to meet with Charles Davis at the upstream end of the city three miles away. As far as he knew, no military actions were being planned. It was either an experiment to see if Union naval ships could successfully run the three-mile gauntlet past Vicksburg or some idiot's idea of a show of force.

"Orders are orders, sailor," he said lamely. "We have to let them know what we're made of."

The pilot's expression looked as if he might like to say, "I don't know what you're made of, sir, but I'm made of skin and bone."

The bombardment began with a muzzle flash off the starboard bow. A moment later the sound of a shell whistling through the dank air reached the collective ears of those manning the ships of Farragut's flotilla. A shell exploded in the water between the column of ships led by the *Hartford* and a second column of gunboats to the west. Farragut had intentionally placed the *Hartford* at the head of the first column to shield the smaller boats. The fact that a shell had landed on the *Hartford's* port side did not bode well for that strategy.

"Captain MacAdams, do you have a target?" Farragut barked.

A lanky officer with angular features and extravagant mutton-chops stepped forward into the light of a bonfire the Vicksburg defenders had just ignited.

"Yes, sir."

"Then fire at will."

MacAdams saluted so quickly that he nearly knocked off his Captain's hat. Soon the cannon fire from the Vicksburg batteries and the Union flotilla was so deafening that Farragut wished he could plug his ears with cotton. Instead, he ventured outside the wheelhouse amidst the brilliance of bursting shells and the cacophony of their detonations and tried to observe what was happening. He did not consider himself more exposed by doing so. The *Hartford* was a large vessel, a steam-powered "screw sloop" with masts and sails for service on the high seas. Even if she were struck with a direct blow, it would not likely be fatal. The ships most likely to suffer crippling damage were the gunboats. Even the "Pook Turtles," the ironclads designed by Samuel Pook, were vulnerable. Though covered by two and a half-inch iron plate, the Pooks moved through the water with the sluggishness of their reptilian namesakes. While it might not be able to penetrate their armor, a well-placed Confederate shell could wreak havoc on the exposed deck of a Pook, or incapacitate some piece of equipment vital to its seaworthiness - which, in the best of circumstances, was not much better than that of an overloaded dinghy.

A tall, broad-shouldered man with lieutenant's bars on his navy blue coat emerged from the stairwell and approached. The mandatory salutes were quickly exchanged, after which Lieutenant Asa Lindstrom said, "Commodore Porter signaled that the mortar flotilla has found the range, sir. He wants an all-out attack on the lead batteries."

Farragut was well acquainted with David Porter, whose father was Farragut's former commander.

"All-out attack? Nothing more specific?"

Lindstrom was nonplused by Farragut's reaction. His lips fluttered anxiously before any sound emerged.

"Poor choice of words on my part, sir. Commodore Porter wants to lay down maximum fire here because it will be more effective. The Rebel guns of those batteries are only fifty feet above the water."

Leaning over the starboard side railing, Farragut looked for cannon flashes coming from the downriver batteries Lindstrom had referred to. He spotted several, as well as some flashes coming from the mortar flotilla. He couldn't see whether the mortar rounds were reaching their targets, but each flash was followed by an explosion within or near the Rebel batteries a second or two later. Circumstantial evidence was good enough.

"Signal Porter to keep at it, but to save a few rounds for later. I want to see how far up those cliffs we can shoot."

"Yes, sir," Lindstrom said, then retreated down the stairwell to the lower deck.

While he watched the deadly fireworks display surrounding him with fascination, Farragut could not help thinking about his life and how he had come to be where he was at this moment. Not only had he *not* been born to a seafaring family, but the land-locked home in which he had spent his formative years was in Tennessee. *Tennessee!* A border state to be sure, but one with strong Confederate ties. However, those ties had been effectively broken when, at nine years of age, Farragut entered the navy. *Fifty-four years in the United States Navy was certainly enough time to alter one's loyalties*, he thought. But that wasn't an accurate appraisal; his loyalties had never strayed. They had always been with the Union.

"Sir, coming up on Fort Hill. You'd better come inside," came the pilot's voice from the wheelhouse.

"Fort Hill," said Farragut, turning. "That means we're almost there."

"Yes, sir," the pilot said, peering through the doorway. "But it also means there'll be hell to pay."

Farragut chuckled, took a final glance at the violent festivities and strolled back to the wheelhouse, stationing himself beside the pilot.

"How old are you, son?"

It was a moment before the pilot, his glassy eyes reflecting the conflagration outside, said, "Twenty-four, sir."

"You may be surprised to know that I'm sixty-three. Almost old enough to be a revolutionary."

"You and Bobby Lee, sir."

"That's right," Farragut laughed appreciatively. "But neither of us is *quite* that old. I was in the War of 1812, though, with Commodore Porter's father. I was nine years old. Saw a lot of hell there, let me tell you."

"Did you ever have guns trained on you from a ship's deck two hundred feet above the waterline?"

The pilot was obviously alluding to the formidable black monolith taking shape ahead of them: the two-hundred-foot cliffs at the northern end of Vicksburg where the infamous guns of the Fort Hill battery could rain terror down on any Union vessel foolish enough to venture into their crosshairs. Adding to the venture's handicap was the nearly one hundred eighty degree bend in the river that extended the time during which they would be exposed to artillery fire. It was, in a word, a *duck shoot*.

"No," Farragut replied, conceding the point. "Can't say that I have."

For a breathtaking instant, the atmosphere behind them became suddenly luminous with white fire and bellowed with the agony of a wounded beast. Farragut and the pilot turned to see the afterbirth of an explosion engulfing one of the ironclads trailing behind. The explosion probably wouldn't sink the boat, but men would die. Farragut shifted his eyes to the front, increasingly mesmerized by the grand and terrible sight emerging before him: the tall canyon wall on his right and the narrow finger of land called De Soto Point on his left. It was like a theater, a maritime Coliseum with the ships of his flotilla as the Christians and the raging cannon of the Fort Hill battery playing the bestial counterpoint.

"Sir, do you want me to get Lieutenant Lindstrom?" the pilot asked.

"What?" Farragut stuttered.

"Lieutenant Lindstrom. You told him you wanted to try the mortars here."

Farragut took a critical look at the high bluffs and shook his head.

"No, that won't be necessary," he said, trying to conceal the dejection in his voice.

Farragut ordered the guns of the three lead vessels—*Hartford, Richmond,* and *Monongahela*— into coordinated action, but little was accomplished by the effort. Even the heavy nine-inch Dahlgrens on the *Hartford* could not compete with Confederate guns that had only to lob their shells onto targets below instead of first battling the force of gravity to reach their prey.

More bonfires appeared on the west bank of the Mississippi as the flotilla pushed upstream amidst the rockets and incendiaries blasting overhead.

"Sir, permission to turn to starboard," the pilot blurted.

"What?"

The pilot waited for Farragut to regain his equanimity and repeated, "Permission to turn to starboard. We don't want to run into those mudflats."

For a moment, Farragut wondered what "those mudflats" were. He couldn't see a thing except the glare of the bursting shells and the red-hot glow of the bonfires. Then he realized the pilot could not see them either, but being a pilot, knew instinctively where they would be.

"Yes, of course, turn to starboard," Farragut murmured. "Maybe those damn guns will overshoot us if we hug the Vicksburg side of the river."

And maybe a divine curtain will fall on this foolish melodrama and permit us to exit stage right, he pondered.

"The artillery of heaven is playing on earth," he murmured.

Before Farragut had a chance to reflect on his descent into cynicism, a shell smashed into the mainmast, sending shards of debris to the decks below. It was followed by another shell that blew up the captain's cabin on the upper deck.

"Try hugging the shore a little more tightly," he suggested.

The pilot obeyed.

As the *Hartford* swung around the sharp bend in the Mississippi and was suddenly headed south, the intensity of the cannonade gradually diminished. *Maybe we've passed the last battery,* Farragut dared to hope. Within five minutes Lieutenant Lindstrom returned. He wasn't smiling, but Farragut could sense the relief on his Nordic features.

"That's the last one, sir," Lindstrom confirmed.

"Good. Have you contacted the other ships for a damage report?"

"With your permission, sir," the lieutenant said, his features tightening again.

"Go to it."

Which the lieutenant promptly did. While he was gone, Farragut moved to the port side of the Hartford and focused his gaze rearward. The Rebel defenders, unable to find sufficient targets, had cut back on their rate of fire. This and the steadily increasing distance between the shell bursts and the Union flotilla made the cannonade no more frightening than a fireworks display. For Farragut, the flames and thick smoke he could see engulfing several of the gunboats were more disturbing. The big ships, he was happy to note, were barely visible in the moonless night.

Lindstrom returned, breathless.

"Fifteen killed, thirty wounded, sir," he barked.

Farragut nodded, then asked, "The flotilla?"

This time, Lindstrom smiled as he announced, "No ships sunk, sir. A few boilers damaged, but only three vessels had to go back. I don't think the Rebs knew exactly where we were."

Nor did I, Farragut thought.

Passing beyond De Soto Point, Farragut sent orders to the flotilla to reduce speed to five knots. The Vicksburg guns could no longer reach them and there was no sense testing the already compromised integrity of damaged boilers. It was an hour before they reached the next bend in the river, a slow turn to the north-west that would eventually lead to another jog to the southwest called Milliken's Bend. As they entered the turn, the three men heard the distinctive churning of paddlewheels.

"Gunboat off the starboard bow," whispered Lindstrom.

"Ours or theirs?" Farragut demanded.

Lindstrom hurried to the rail and leaned his head into the night, as if moving ten feet closer would actually improve his vision.

"I can't tell. It's too dark."

"What is it, ours or theirs?" echoed the high-pitched voice of a man rushing up the stairs. It was Captain MacAdams.

"MacAdams, give them a call sign and have them signal us back. Blow them out of the water if they don't."

"Yes, sir."

MacAdams rushed back down the stairs as quickly as he'd as-cended. From the wheelhouse, Farragut could now see the gun-boat cutting its speed while the *Hartford* followed suit and flashed a challenge to the newcomer. The gunboat continued cutting its speed and flashed a response. Then a pause ensued, which Far-ragut took to be a good sign.

On his return, MacAdams announced: "It's the *Tyler,* sir, with a message from Commodore Davis."

A collective sigh of relief was breathed, followed by a spate of nervous chatter. They were not going to die tonight! The *Tyler,* which was not an ironclad and therefore resembled a steamboat instead of a gargantuan turtle, tied up alongside the *Hartford.* Its enclosed side paddlewheels slowly spun to a halt. Within two min-utes, a rope ladder was affixed to the *Hartford's* starboard bow and lowered to the deck of the smaller vessel. An officer with the double-barred shoulder boards of a lieutenant made his way up and onto the deck of the *Hartford,* where Farragut was waiting. When the man saluted, Farragut noticed he had a pleasant smile, complete with straight white teeth and a trim brown mustache be-neath a striking aquiline nose.

"Lieutenant Eggleston, sir," said the officer, shaking Farragut's hand. "Commodore Davis sent me to receive you. It's a pleasure to meet you, sir. We've all heard about your capture of New Orleans."

"Where is the Commodore?"

"At Milliken's Bend, a few miles upstream," Eggleston said, then gave the *Hartford* a long, appraising look.

"We're fine. Lost a mainmast, the captain's cabin, and fifteen men. Thirty more are wounded."

Eggleston nodded solemnly, then asked the inevitable questions about damage to the flotilla. Farragut repeated what MacAdams had told him.

"Losing men is always unfortunate, but in all, it's better than I would have expected," Eggleston opined.

"The trouble with being in the Navy is that you never get to choose the high ground."

Eggleston gave an ambiguous chortle and said, "We—I mean Commodore Davis's fleet—captured Memphis on June 6th. General Sherman has been appointed as military governor and should soon have matters pretty much under control."

Farragut's eyebrow lifted as he said, "I knew about Memphis. I didn't know about Sherman. Is Halleck still in charge of the army?"

"Yes."

"Has Commodore Davis been in contact with him?"

At this, Farragut detected a note of consternation in Eggleston's reaction.

"Yes, we've been in touch with General Halleck. The general is content to sit in Corinth and send his army in all directions, Pope to chase Beauregard into Mississippi, Buell to go after Kirby Smith in Tennessee, and the rest of the army to repair railroads."

"Halleck is using 120,000 men to repair railroads?"

Eggleston glanced away and said with a deep sigh, "It's a necessary activity and . . . the general *is* an engineer."

Rather than risk acknowledging Eggleston's sarcasm with a cynical chuckle, Farragut turned away as if something on the Mississippi shore had caught his attention. He was a Navy man, not an army man, but he could not help thinking it was gross folly not to pursue an enemy on the run. And from what he had heard, Beauregard was definitely on the run. If his army were captured, it could mean the end of the Confederacy as a viable military power.

Turning his attention back to Eggleston, Farragut snapped, "What does Commodore Davis want with me?"

Eggleston took in a breath and said, "He wants to discuss naval strategy."

"What navel strategy? Davis owns the Mississippi from Vicksburg to St. Louis and I own it from Vicksburg to New Orleans. What we don't own is Vicksburg itself!"

"That would be the point, sir: naval strategy to take Vicksburg."

This ignited the frustration Farragut had been feeling all day.

"Naval strategy to take that damned fortress? I can run a fleet past those cliffs every day of the week and suffer no more damage than I did tonight, but I can't attack. My guns are useless against those heights. What does Davis expect me to do, keep running the gauntlet until the enemy runs out of artillery shells?"

Eggleston dropped his gaze, looking uncomfortable. For an instant, Farragut felt sorry for the man and regretted allowing his anger to erupt. It seemed incompatible with the calm of the night and the rhythmic undulations of the two vessels in the unsteady Mississippi current.

Repressing his humiliation, Eggleston looked up and said, "There must be a way, sir."

"A way to do what?"

"To use the Navy. What good does it do to hold a river if you can't take the land bordering it?"

Since arriving at Vicksburg, Farragut had asked himself the same question many times. He didn't have an answer but had developed a germ of an idea.

"Only infantry can take Vicksburg. We can support them with our guns, but it's not enough. The army has to dismantle the Confederate defenses."

Farragut leaned on the port side railing and stared down at the *Tyler*. God, he loved being a sailor. But the Vicksburg stalemate was beginning to drain his confidence in the effectiveness of naval arms. Something had to be done if that faith was to survive.

"I don't understand, sir. How can the Navy assist the army except with its big guns?" Eggleston queried, obviously confused.

Grinning, Farragut eyed his younger colleague and said, "We can take them wherever they want to go. Tonight's mission did serve one purpose. It proved that we can get past the Vicksburg batteries without being annihilated in the process. We can land troops wherever we want."

Eggleston paused to reflect on this and then said, "The eastern shore?"

"Of course. That's where Vicksburg is."

"But where on the eastern shore? The army can't climb those cliffs."

Farragut sighed and stretched his body erect.

"And therein, lieutenant, lies the rub. There is no good place to land, which is why I intend to leave that decision up to the commandant of the Army of the Mississippi."

"General Halleck?" Eggleston laughed derisively. "He won't move his army on land. Can you imagine trying to persuade him to move his troops onto Navy transports and sail them past Vicksburg?"

Farragut could not, but he would not say so. He certainly owed Henry Halleck no debt of gratitude, but the general was his military equal and deserved his respect. He sent Lieutenant Eggleston packing with instructions to inform Commodore Davis of his pending arrival at Milliken's Bend within the next day or two. Then wistfully, he made a silent prayer that God preserve Henry Halleck but kindly move him to some other field of operation. He was *not* so naïve as to believe God would grant such an obviously self-serving wish.

★ FOUR ★

July 11, 1862, Union Army Headquarters, Memphis, Tennessee

Galahad Gilmore was not a spy, but he was the next best thing—a Union sympathizer. Unfortunately, he knew nothing of Confederate troop dispositions, Confederate railroad schedules, or anything of military value, for that matter. Seventy-three years old, with a face overlaid with liver spots, Galahad claimed to have met Davy Crockett just before his fateful journey to the Alamo. Ulysses S. Grant liked the old man, who, like Grant, appreciated a good cigar and an occasional snort of whisky. At the moment, as Grant sat behind his desk with his feet propped up and Galahad slumped cross-legged in an ancient maple chair opposite, only the cigars were in evidence. With both of them puffing steadily away, there was no danger of any intruder overstaying his welcome.

"I'll tell you, general, the only way to come at Vicksburg is from the east. Them cliffs is too steep and the ground north and south ain't much better," said Galahad, making smoke rings in the air as he gestured with his cigar.

"Jackson's over there. That's where Johnston will attack from. What do I do about him?" Grant asked, as if he were in a position to do anything.

"Hell, I don't know, general. I ain't no army man. I just know that comin' from any other direction but east is suicide," Galahad lamented.

Grant sat up, thinking. The old man served less as a source of information than as a catalyst for the various schemes Grant had been concocting to attack Vicksburg. As Halleck's *second-in-command,* he had plenty of time for such intellectual diversions.

"What if we go overland to Grenada, catch the Yalobusha and Yazoo Rivers all the way to Haynes' Bluff?"

"Haynes' Bluff is just north of Vicksburg and they don't call it Haynes' *Bluff* for nothin'. How you gonna get up there from the Yazoo? Oh, and by the way, the Yazoo and the Yalobusha ain't the Mississippi. They're just a little bit better than bayous. How you gonna keep your boats from bein' blasted to smithereens by the rebs on shore? You ain't gonna be able to move any faster'n a snail on a window pane and you'll be just as easy to pick off."

Galahad was probably right, Grant concluded. He looked down at the map of western Mississippi laid out on the desk before him and cursed its limitations. You couldn't really get a feel for terrain from a map and you couldn't tell if a river was actually a river or just an oversized creek. In the Mississippi Delta, there was water everywhere—in rivers, creeks, bayous, swamps, canals and an unbelievable number of lakes and ponds that were little more than large puddles. Except for the Mississippi, most were navigable only a fraction of the time. Droughts dried them up and storms flooded them to overflowing. Neither was good for navigation, especially by the ironclads, which ran lower in the water than other gunboats.

"Look here, Galahad," Grant said, pointing to the network of rivers and bayous north of Vicksburg. "Now I know some of these streams are too shallow and overgrown to move troops on, but there must be some I can use. Which ones are they?"

Gilmore moved to the desk, studied the map, sighed, and said, "I'm from Tennessee, general. I don't know much about rivers in Mississippi except they is generally shallow and swampy. Now, if you'd asked me about Tennessee rivers, they is deep and wide . . ."

"I know about Tennessee rivers, Galahad. I fought three or four battles on them. Can't you . . ."

He suddenly realized he was pressing too hard. The old man was looking away and pursing his lips as if trying to subdue an emotional outburst. While Grant paused to assess how to handle their tenuous relationship, Galahad pulled a handkerchief from his pocket, blew his nose, and surreptitiously wiped the moisture from his eyes.

"It's difficult, isn't it?" Grant said.

"What's that, general . . . what do you mean? Gilmore stammered.

"Helping us. Helping me. It must be hard."

Galahad rose, tried to straighten his back and found it would not fully cooperate. Bent slightly forward, he placed one booted foot tentatively in front of the other and walked stiffly to a window looking out on Memphis.

"It is, general. It surely is," he murmured.

"Why do you do it?"

Galahad looked over his left shoulder at Grant and brushed a hand through unkempt steel gray hair. A hesitant smile on his clean-shaven but corrugated face revealed at least one gold tooth.

"I was born in another century. The war against the British was all I ever heard about as a boy. General George Washington was my president. Ain't been nobody like him since."

Grant turned in his chair, sucked mightily on his cigar, and said, "You're right, but I wonder what he'd do if he was alive today."

Galahad grunted a distinct *harumph* and added, "You mean, would he be a Union man or a secesh?"

Surprised to hear the slang word *secesh*, a contraction of *secessionist*, used by a man of the South, Grant said, "Yes. He was a Virginian, after all."

"No."

Galahad Gilmore's jaw went rigid and his sea green eyes stared coldly at Ulysses Grant.

"No. No! To George Washington and the rest of them from that time, the Union was a holy cause. They would no more secede from the Union than secede their fingers from their hands or their hands from their arms."

Despite Gilmore's tortured metaphor, Grant felt his respect for his "turncoat" colleague growing. There was no doubt Galahad would be considered a traitor by many of his fellow Tennesseeans. Of course, there were Tennessee units fighting for the Union, but that was usually construed as an honest difference of principle. To be a spy, or even an informant, was something else. It was either an act of abject cowardice or supreme bravery; Grant thought the latter in Galahad's case. He wondered what he would do if faced with a similar situation.

"I hear Sam Houston refused to join the Confederacy."

"Yup, and they booted him right out of the Texas governorship."

"I guess it doesn't matter who you were before the war, does it?"

Galahad did not reply immediately. Grant saw his arm lift as if positioning fingers to rub his temple. Then Gilmore turned his head and looked at the general, a sparkle in his eyes.

"No, it don't. It certainly don't matter who I was before the war," he said, smiling as he spoke. "Don't worry about me, sir. I'm fine."

The door opened and Grant's aide, Lieutenant-Colonel James Wilson, entered. As he walked past, the colonel's gaze alighted briefly on Galahad Gilmore, but his eager gait quickly carried him beyond casual visual range. He strode directly for Grant's desk and extended his hand toward the general. In it was a sheet of paper.

"Telegram sir," Wilson announced.

Grant sat up in his chair, his lips slightly parted and his brow furrowed. He hated telegrams. They usually contained bad news or unexpected orders, neither of which he liked very much.

"Who's it from?" he demanded.

"General Halleck, sir."

"Halleck?" Grant mumbled, anticipating the worst. "What's he want?"

"Read it, sir," Wilson implored, a fledgling grin appearing on his face. "Please."

Grant leaned back in his chair and read the telegram. His curiosity aroused, Galahad Gilmore made his way back to the desk and hovered.

"Well, I'll be damned. I've been ordered to Corinth to take command of the Armies of the Mississippi and Tennessee. I'll be . . ."

Cutting his self-damnation short, Grant glanced sharply up at his aide and said, "You knew."

Embarrassed, Wilson allowed a grin to creep onto his face and said, "News like that is hard to keep quiet. I don't know the details, though."

The hint was not lost on Grant, who permitted himself a relaxed smile.

"Halleck is taking over supreme command of all Union armies. I guess the president is uncomfortable being his own commander-in-chief."

The President's tendency to take direct command of the army was a bit of an embarrassment for any West-Pointer, which both Grant and Wilson were. In frustration at West-Pointer George McClellan's reluctance to act against the Confederacy, Lincoln had taken personal command of all Union forces. For this action he had been bombarded with unceasing criticism, not only for assuming a position for which he was completely unqualified, but also for dismissing a popular military officer. McClellan enjoyed wide support among his men and the members of the northern press. Except for Antietam, "Little Mac" had achieved few victories for the simple reason that he seldom attacked; the enemy always seemed to *outnumber* him. When he did attack it was with graceless hesitation, a tactic distinctly unsuited for combat with Robert E. Lee.

Those who knew McClellan—like Grant and Wilson—agreed with Lincoln that, while Little Mac was good at whipping an army into shape, he suffered from a bad case of the "slows" when it came to field command.

"Washington is a good posting for General Halleck," Wilson commented. "Moving armies around on paper is better suited to his temperament."

After an appreciative giggle, Grant suddenly dropped his feet to the floor and laid the telegram on his desk.

"Colonel, get off your feet. Galahad, bring over a couple of chairs and sit with me and the colonel."

Gilmore obeyed, retrieved two chairs by the door, shoved one behind Wilson and seated himself in the other. Grant leaned forward.

"Gentlemen, I think a small celebration is in order," he said, gazing conspiratorially at the Southerner. "Galahad, I know you've got a swallow or two of good Tennessee sour mash in your breast pocket. Wouldn't you like to share it with us?"

"Why, general, whatever gave you the idea I got whisky . . ." Galahad protested.

"You've got whisky, Galahad, and I would dearly like to have some," Grant said.

Gilmore gazed into the general's gentle, persuasive but steadfast eyes. It was not an order and he was not a Union soldier, but he sensed he could not refuse. Mumbling a string of incomprehensible expletives, he searched for the bottle, found it, and extracted it. As its owner, he gave himself first dibs, then handed the bottle to Grant. Wilson looked on stone-faced and clearly unhappy.

After tossing a gulp of the stinging liquid down his throat, Grant looked at his aide and offered him the bottle.

"No . . . thank you, sir," Wilson stuttered.

"Colonel, I know you and the others of my staff disapprove of my drinking and, I admit, I do enjoy the occasional down-and-outer with the devil's concoction. But I only drink when it is not essential that I be able to think at the same time. You must admit, thinking is not a necessary requirement of my present—excuse me, former—position as General Halleck's second-in-command."

The logic was so impeccably tortured that Wilson had to laugh. His cohorts in vigilance— Charles Dana and Grant's Adjutant-General John Rawlins—would definitely not approve. Dana had been sent by Lincoln specifically to keep an eye on Grant. Before Dana's arrival, Rawlins had been doing just that and vigorously expressing his displeasure with the commanding general's drinking in terms that often bordered on insubordination. With Wilson as their infantry, the three defended Grant against temptation and tempters disguised as Union soldiers.

But today Wilson was in a conciliatory mood.

"I suppose I could reason that the more I drink, the less will remain for you," Wilson said. "Galahad, you don't have another bottle hidden away somewhere, do you?"

Panic-stricken, Gilmore sputtered and stuttered and looked decidedly sheepish.

"I mean . . . on your person," Wilson clarified.

Relieved, Gilmore quickly regained the power of speech.

"Oh, no, no. That's the only one," he said, pointing to the bottle caressed in Grant's hand. "Got no more on me."

With some hesitation, Wilson took the bottle, downed one swallow, and waited for the fire of its presence to abate. It was actually quite good.

"That's a decent brew," he announced, returning the bottle to Galahad.

Galahad immediately transferred the bottle back to Grant's hand and said," Best liquor there is, Tennessee whisky . . ."

"Almost as good a Kentucky bourbon," Grant joked, but only after taking a final swallow of the bottle's diminished contents.

"Kentuck . . . bourbon . . ." Gilmore stammered indignantly, but to no avail. Grinning, Grant returned the bottle and its few remaining drops of whisky to the Southerner. Shaking the bottle and sensing from its hollow feel that only fumes remained, Galahad frowned, tossed his head back, and dumped the minimal remnants onto his frog-like tongue, where they were instantly absorbed.

"What happens now, sir?" Wilson asked. Although he was seated, his stiff back made it seem that he was at attention.

"First thing is for you to relax. Slouch a little."

Wilson tried to slouch but achieved only a self-conscious droop, which invoked a belly laugh from Gilmore.

"My intention is to bring the several pieces of our army back from the four winds to which Old Brains scattered them."

"That won't be easy, sir . . ." Wilson said, casting a sidelong glance at Gilmore.

Grant caught the gesture and said, "Galahad, Colonel Wilson is hinting that he wants to speak to me alone. Would you go and get some cigars from my private stash?"

He lifted the lid of the cigar box on his desk to reveal its emptiness.

"I ain't no spy," Galahad complained.

"I know you're not, but it's just not smart for officers to discuss army matters when civilians are within earshot. You *are* a civilian."

Gilmore considered that, a wrinkled scowl transforming his face into a leathery prune. It was a short-lived display.

"I s'pose I am," he conceded reluctantly, then departed with a sigh to pursue the errand Grant had given him.

When he was out of sight, Wilson leaned forward and laid his gloved hands on the desk.

"As I was saying, sir, bringing the army back together won't be easy. Buell is going to have his hands full with Bragg in Eastern Tennessee . . ."

". . . And Lincoln considers the 'liberation' of East Tennessee one of his highest priorities even though it's of no strategic significance. Yes, I know all that, Colonel. I suspect we may even have to send General Buell some reinforcements."

"Then how?"

"I don't know how," Grant said, punctuating the statement with a groan. He looked up at Wilson with a gentle expression that caught Wilson off guard. Grant's soft, empathetic eyes were unusual in a military man, but they were one of his most engaging assets.

"I don't know how . . . yet," Grant said, in a voice more subtly earnest than his expression. "But I will."

★ FIVE ★

Late Summer and Fall of 1862, Northern Mississippi

Now commander of the Union Armies of the Mississippi and the Tennessee, Ulysses S. Grant might well have wished he'd remained Henry Halleck's second in command. Buell's Army of the Cumberland was not likely to return anytime soon from Eastern Tennessee; he was too busy trying to wrest Chattanooga, a critical railroad junction, from Confederate hands. In July, Halleck ordered Grant to reinforce Buell with G.H. Thomas's division of six thousand men. In August, two more divisions were sent, and September saw the loss of a fourth division to the struggling commander of the Army of the Cumberland.

Buell now had a larger army than Grant: fifty thousand to forty-six thousand. For Grant, offensive operations were out of the question. Though a valuable railhead in itself, Corinth was deep in southern territory, vulnerable to attack, so he moved his headquarters back to Jackson, Tennessee. Meanwhile, Buell's approach to Chattanooga was proceeding slowly, allowing Confederate General Braxton Bragg a golden opportunity to invade Kentucky, hoping to detach that state from the Union by capturing its capitol, Frankfort. When his left flank was enveloped by Kirby Smith, Buell was forced to retreat to Louisville, where he was effectively immobilized.

Despite shifting his headquarters to Tennessee, Grant's armies faced imminent danger. Confederate Generals Sterling Price and Earl Van Dorn, each with sixteen thousand men, were fifty miles south of Corinth and a hundred miles south of Grant's headquarters. With Grant in Tennessee were Stephen Hurlbut's nine thousand and McClernand's six thousand. Sherman, with seven thousand, was guarding Memphis and the Mississippi River, while Edward Ord's eight thousand and William Rosecrans's nine thousand constituted the left wing. Numerically, the Union and Confederate armies were comparable, but Grant's only mobile troops were those of Ord and Rosecrans. Sherman could not leave Memphis and the troops with Grant had lines of communication to protect. For Grant, it was almost like being under siege.

To take advantage of Buell's isolation and prevent Grant from sending further reinforcements to him, Bragg decided to attack Corinth. On September 1, Sterling Price and fourteen thousand men attacked the village of Iuka, Mississippi, thirty miles south of Corinth on the Memphis and Charleston Railroad. The small Union garrison fled without offering resistance. Realizing he must act before Bragg could send Van Dorn to reinforce Price, Grant sent Rosecrans and Ord to crush Price with a pincer movement. On September 19, Ord attacked from the northwest and Rosecrans from the west to block the Confederates' line of retreat.

The Union attack failed because of miscommunication and bad timing. One division of Rosecrans's corps prematurely engaged the Confederates and was driven back. Ord's divisions, waiting for the sound of gunfire that could not penetrate a strong northeast wind, never entered the fray. It was a clear, if not necessarily decisive, victory for the Confederates. But Bragg thought the capture of Iuka so inconsequential that he ordered Price to join Van Dorn at Ripley, thirty miles southwest of Corinth. Rosecrans and Ord repossessed Iuka on September 20 but had not achieved Grant's objective: Price was still in the field.

With Price's troops joining him at Ripley on September 28, Van Dorn now had twenty-two thousand men and was in an excellent position to strike a blow for the Confederacy. The question was: Where? Sherman and the Union navy held Memphis, and were a little too formidable. Bolivar, forty miles northwest of Corinth, was also rejected as a target because Grant had wisely rushed Hurlbut's division to occupy that city. Van Dorn chose Corinth and attacked on October 3.

The attack came from the northwest. Union troops manning the trenches dug by Beauregard in April were driven back two miles to the trenches dug by Rosecrans in September. But that was as far as the Confederates could penetrate, despite the savagery of the fighting along a two-mile front. Exhausted, both sides settled in for the night.

When he learned of the Rebel assault that evening, Grant ordered McPherson to march his reserves to Corinth and Hurlbut to cut off Van Dorn's retreat. On October 4, Van Dorn and Price resumed the attack and had moderate success on the Confederate left wing. Rosecrans counterattacked and won the day, a very hot, sultry one. Van Dorn withdrew just in time to avoid encirclement by Rosecrans, Hurlbut, and McPherson, the latter arriving at Corinth a tick of the clock too late. Grant ordered Rosecrans to pursue the enemy, but he did not, excusing his inaction with ". . . the darkness of the night and the roughness of the country made

movement impracticable by night and slow and difficult by day."
With Hurlbut blocking his retreat, Van Dorn turned back toward
Ripley, from whence Price and he had come, and eventually farther south to Holly Springs, Mississippi. Fearing his forces might
become too dispersed, Grant ordered a halt to further pursuit. He
had his victory, had rid himself of a pesky enemy, and had a clear
road south.

The time had come to move against the Gibraltar of the Confederacy—Vicksburg.

November, 1862, Corinth, Mississippi

But how could Vicksburg be attacked? Farragut and Porter had
made a valiant attempt but had failed to achieve much except
make it through the Vicksburg gauntlet relatively unscathed.
There were too many choices and too few good ones. It was a
question that had resonated inside Grant's head ever since taking
command of the army from Halleck.

"Ulys, have you finished?" Julia Grant inquired, gazing down
at her husband with quizzical eyes.

His reverie interrupted, Grant stared into his wife's critical
eyes and said, "Of course not. I'll finish it up and then have some
clams and a pickle."

"You're going to have clams after you finish ham and cabbage?
Isn't it bad enough that you eat ham and cabbage for breakfast?"

"Certainly, I'm going to have clams. I have an iron stomach.
You know that. It all goes to the same place."

Julia, a pretty if plump mother of four, shook her head and
made for the stove and the clams.

"Well, if you don't throw up, I will!"

"But I've gained weight since you've been here. Your cooking
has added fifteen pounds to me."

"It's all sitting at the bottom of your stomach like refuse in a
garbage dump. Your bowels refuse to let it pass."

Grant smiled and drank some coffee. His thoughts had not
completely disengaged from the Vicksburg problem, but he shoved
them into a corner of his mind for later inspection.

"Can't we visit the Shermans soon? I haven't seen Ellen in the
longest time," Julia inquired.

"I need Sherman in Memphis. He has a real talent as a military governor. I think he learned it when he was a banker before
the war."

Julia noticed the void in her husband's coffee cup and filled it.

"Don't you two ever call yourselves by your first names? All I ever hear is 'Sherman did this' and "Grant, how *do* you *do?*' What's wrong with 'Bill' and 'Ulys?'"

Grant's eyes widened in speculation. It was something he had not pondered before.

"It wouldn't sound right. Besides, 'Ulys' is your name for me. No one else would ever use it."

"Don't you like it?"

He was being baited, and he knew it. He decided to tread carefully.

"Of course I like it, but I'm used to it. Most of the time, people have to think twice when they hear you call me 'Ulys." It's like being named after a Polish general."

Julia *harrumphed* and returned the coffeepot to the stove to eat her own meal. After swallowing two mouthfuls of ham and cabbage, she said, "Why do you say Bill Sherman has a real talent as a military governor?"

"Because he does. Sherman is one of the most organized men I've ever known."

She didn't miss the emphasis on "Sherman" and blessed her husband with another *harumph.*

"I think he just scowls and growls at people to get his way. He's got one of the most penetrating scowls I've ever seen. I think it's permanently attached to his face."

"It is," Grant joked. He has to really exert himself to look cheerful."

Julia's laughter was cut short as Fred, Jesse, Nellie, and Ulysses, Jr. thundered downstairs to eat breakfast. Finished with his, Grant put on his coat, ventured outside, and braced himself against a porch column. He lit up a cigar and gazed southwest over the rolling Mississippi countryside. Though winter was in the air and overcast filled the sky, the weather was mild. Good weather for a battle, he thought, if there was a climate that favored the killing of men on a grand scale. It was not long before his mind returned to Vicksburg and how to overcome her natural and man-made defenses.

When she finished feeding her famished children, Julia donned a white cardigan and joined her husband. It did not take long for her to recognize the glazed, faraway look in his eyes.

"Vicksburg again?"

"Always."

"I'm jealous."

"Why?"

"Vicksburg is like another woman. She consumes you."

He placed his arm around her shoulders and said, "I don't think you'd be jealous if you knew what I have I mind for her."

December, 1862, Corinth, Mississippi

"McClernand did what?" Grant demanded.

James Wilson sighed and lifted Halleck's letter as if to re-interpret it.

"General McClernand has convinced President Lincoln and Secretary of War Stanton to let him recruit a corps of volunteers to attack Vicksburg. Halleck says McClernand has already raised at least two regiments . . ."

"McClernand, leading an army of raw recruits into battle against the fortifications at Vicksburg? That's insane! The man is totally . . ." Grant fumed, grasping his forehead to ease the pain behind his eyes.

"Incompetent," came a voice from across Grant's office. It was James McPherson, sitting in a chair beneath a portrait of Washington. "We all know it. McClernand is incompetent. Why not say it?"

Grant looked at his young friend, whose well-groomed face normally displayed a sanguine temperament. Now it was lined with frustration.

Grant shoved a fist into his pocket and paced back and forth between his two subordinates.

"Why would Lincoln approve such a thing? His judgment is usually good, or at least well-reasoned. This makes no sense at all."

Grant told himself to settle down; it would do no good to react in anger. He had a keen sense for politics. One could not survive in the officer corps of the Union Army without one. And yet he had happily granted McClernand extended leave, which the former lawyer had used to betray him. It was galling and yet Grant could not help wondering if part of his rage was self-serving, a fear that his own plans for the Gibraltar of the Confederacy might not be fulfilled. The thought sobered him enough to decelerate the pace of his deliberations.

"McClernand is a lawyer," Wilson explained. "An Illinois lawyer and a Democrat. Lincoln and he know each other. They've both been members of the Illinois legislature, and Lincoln needs support from all the Democrats he can get, even if they are . . ."

"Incompetent!" McPherson finished ruefully.

Suppressing a grin, Grant cocked an ear and spoke to Wilson. "What else does Halleck say? Is he with us or McClernand?"

Wilson rubbed his chin thoughtfully and replied, "I don't know whose side he's on but he wants you to set up headquarters in Memphis."

"Why?"

"I don't know why. He doesn't say," Wilson said with a shrug.

Annoyed with his aide's fixation on what Halleck's letter did *not* say, Grant started to express his displeasure. Then he thought better of it.

"I'm supposed to move my headquarters to Memphis?" he queried.

"Yes."

"With General Sherman?"

Wilson and McPherson looked at each other, neither wanting to reply with the obvious answer. Sherman was the military governor of Memphis, appointed by Grant. *Ergo*, Grant and he would be together if Grant moved his headquarters there.

But Grant did not expect an answer. Instead, he stood straight, smiled, and said, "I need to send a telegram. I'll talk to you two later."

He saluted and left for the telegraph station.

*   *   *

Wilson and McPherson were too curious to let well enough alone. Half an hour later, they found Grant sitting in the telegraph room next to old Pete O'Rourke, a hairless skeleton of a man who was the current operator on duty. The general had a telegram in his hand and appeared to be perusing it with what was, for Grant, a modicum of glee. Spotting Wilson and McPherson, he turned.

"I sent him a telegram," he said.

"Who?" McPherson asked, more curious than ever.

"General Halleck. I asked him where he was planning to send McClernand's new regiments."

"Is that the telegram you sent?" Wilson asked, pointing to the paper in Grant's hand.

"No, it's Halleck's reply," Grant said, then picked his slouch hat off the table behind him and flattened it on his head. "He said they'll report to me in Memphis."

The smile on Grant's face actually grew a little at the edges, although it remained a shallow conveyance of his delight. To his subordinates, it was like watching their commanding officer swoon in ecstasy.

"I'll read it to you," Grant said, abashed by the stunned expressions on their faces. Pete O'Rourke gazed silently at all three officers, wondering what the fuss was about.

"All the troops sent into your department will be under your control," Grant read, affixing his eyes to the telegram. "Fight the enemy your own way. I consider it advisable to move on the enemy as soon as you leave Memphis."

"I'll be damned!" McPherson gasped in awe. "Old Brains has finally done something sensible."

Wilson remained skeptical.

"Are you sure he means 'all the troops sent into your department?' Maybe he means 'all the troops but McClernand's new regiments.'"

Grant moved the slouch hat back on his head and resumed reading. His smile had reached its apogee and retreated, but his disposition remained buoyant.

"You are hereby authorized to relieve General McClernand from command of the expedition against Vicksburg, giving it the next officer in rank or taking it yourself."

When he finished, Grant looked up, his face calm and free of expression. For Wilson and McPherson, the momentousness of the occasion was starting to sink in.

Wilson stated the obvious: "McClernand won't like this."

"No, he won't," Grant agreed as he rose to his feet, "but he has to obey orders."

"Not if he can help it. Lincoln may still be in his corner," McPherson said.

Grant gave a snort of displeasure and rested his hands on his hips. Then he looked straight at McPherson and said, "That's entirely possible, but I'll have to deal with that when and if it happens. Right now, we have to get the Army of the Tennessee to Memphis, and the sooner, the better."

He patted Pete O'Rourke on the back, thanked him, and saluted his subordinates as he headed for the door. Except in the saddle, Ulysses S. Grant had never moved so fast in his life.

★ SIX ★

December 20, 1862, Holly Springs, Mississippi

General Earl Van Dorn was a man of action if not always good judgment. The Federals had pushed his army south from Corinth to Grenada and now held Holly Springs. He had no stomach for further retreat, but he did have thirty-five hundred cavalry, which, if God would just play it even-handedly, should permit him to do something worthwhile. It had taken four days of hard riding in miserable weather to reach Ripley, thirty miles east of Holly Springs. On one wet night, a campfire had set fire to a tree on which gun belts had been hung, and the explosions had temporarily caused a major rout, until it became clear what had happened. But Van Dorn was not discouraged; his attack plan was sound, and his men were in place.

"Sir, may I speak with you, sir?"

Van Dorn jumped at the sound of a voice immediately to his left. His black horse felt the movement and tossed its head. Van Dorn settled the horse and lowered the binoculars he had been using to observe the Mississippi Central railroad depot through which the Federals were pouring supplies and weapons. Something was afoot. He turned toward the voice.

"Dammit, son, you shouldn't sneak up on people like that," he scolded.

The corporal, a stocky, moon-faced farm boy with uncombed blond curls flowing over his shoulders, took the criticism in stride. Saluting, he said, "Sir, all three columns are in place. What are your orders?"

Van Dorn looked at the rising sun, which had popped up in the east only an hour ago. Then he raised the binoculars to his eyes and gazed at the railroad depot again. Something, indeed, was going on; he had never seen so many railroad cars before. They stretched to the northern horizon and beyond.

"Attack, of course. Hell, we have all day."

The corporal rode off to do his duty, which was to pass on the attack order to the three units, each of which was to subdue one of the three Yankee detachments garrisoning the city. The Tennessee unit in Van Dorn's army attacked from the northwest and caught the pickets of the Sixty Second Illinois in their tents and preparing for breakfast. With the Union infantrymen in their underwear and the Confederates on horseback, it was an unequal fight. In fact, it wasn't a fight at all; the soldiers from Illinois were too embarrassed to resist in their half-naked state.

There was Union cavalry at the fairgrounds, but they too were asleep. When they were frantically mustered to roll call, there was some clashing of swords and firing of guns, but the Federals soon realized they were outnumbered by at least two to one. Within two hours of the start of the attack, all had fled or surrendered.

At the town square, the Union garrison was least prepared for the Confederate assault. The post commander, Colonel Robert Murphy, was drunk, as he had been all night along with a majority of his officers. Murphy should have been aware of an impending attack; he had received a telegram from headquarters warning him that hostile cavalry was in the vicinity. But Colonel Murphy did not have a sufficient stock of awareness to expend much of it on this particular topic. He was promptly taken prisoner at the railroad depot, to which Van Dorn proceeded once the outcome of the battle was obvious. The surly blond corporal, whose name was Jacob Metzger and who had proudly returned with the word that the Federals had been completely routed, rode by his side.

"My God, look at all that!" Van Dorn exclaimed in awe as he watched his men wrench massive quantities of sugar, crackers, cheese, sardines and coffee from the bellies of the Union boxcars. "They must be planning a big one."

"A big one, sir?" Metzger asked. He was, Van Dorn remembered, a farm boy from Arkansas.

As he observed a soldier walking off with a crate of pistols, a pair of boots, two blankets, and a bottle of Kentucky whisky, Van Dorn said, "A battle, son. This is too much for the federal garrison at Holly Springs. It must have been passin' through, on its way to somewhere else."

"Where?"

Van Dorn considered the question, shrugged, and said, "South."

Although the battle was over, the soldiers made liberal use of the Rebel yell to express their joy with the manna from heaven with which they had been blessed. It just went to show that God was not pleased that so many earthly goods had fallen into the hands of the wicked northerners. To further proclaim their Christian virtues to the Almighty, Van Dorn's men gave many of the captured supplies to the townspeople and destroyed the rest. Notably absent from general distribution or destruction were two items: whisky and cigars.

The excess Union supplies were not the only thing to suffer devastation—much of the town was ravaged by the battle. The railroad roundhouse and auxiliary buildings were turned to rubble. The Magnolia Hotel on North Center Street, because it had housed Union officers, was blown up. Dynamite lifted the building where Union munitions were stored ten feet into the air before internal explosions shattered it to pieces. East of town, the three huge armory buildings were blown up, leaving nothing but chimneys and brick flooring.

When Earl Van Dorn and his cavalrymen left Holly Springs, they were well fed, well clothed, and well armed.

For the citizens of Holly Springs, it was proof that victory was sometimes not much better than defeat.

December 21, 1862, Union Encampment outside Oxford, Mississippi

"Son-of-a . . ." Ulysses S. Grant muttered as he read the telegram.

"Son-of-a-BITCH!" William Tecumseh Sherman finished. "It's a good word. I use it all the time. Good for what ails you."

"It's not a word; it's an expletive."

Sherman paused, then said, "Whatever it is, it's still good for what ails you."

Grant peered out from under the brim of his slouch hat. Sherman noted the dazed look in his eyes.

"May I see the telegram?" he asked, stretching a hand toward his friend and commanding officer.

Grant leaned one hand against the support pole of his headquarters tent and jabbed the hand holding the telegram toward Sherman, who took it and started reading.

After a moment, he uttered a peremptory "Humph!" After another, he looked at the disgruntled Grant and said, "It appears our pending invasion may come up a little short on supplies."

"A little short? Van Dorn got the whole damned trainload!" Grant groaned in frustration.

Sherman grinned and patted Grant's shoulder.

"You used 'damned' in a sentence. I'm proud of you, Grant. I fully expect a 'sonofabitch' or two in the next five minutes while you're in the proper mood."

"You'll get more than that," Grant growled, pulling another telegram from his breast pocket and thrusting it at Sherman.

"That sonofabitch Bedford Forrest is tearing up the railroad all the way to Jackson. Even if we had supplies, we couldn't take them south!"

Sherman unfolded the telegram, but since he already knew what was in it, refolded it.

"Which solves the supply problem. If we don't have supplies, we don't need a railroad to transport them," he said, trying to lighten the air.

"Sherman, this is a godawful debacle. We both know it, and if we don't do something about it, Halleck might put that sonofabitch McClernand in charge of the Vicksburg campaign just to make Lincoln happy. How would you like that?"

Still trying to temper his friend's anger, Sherman shrugged, rolled his eyes and said, "Of course I wouldn't."

Puzzled by the mild reaction, Grant stared skeptically at his companion and barked, "What's the matter with you? You're never in a good mood. How can you be cheerful now?"

"I'm not in a good mood. It's just a better mood than you're in," Sherman teased. "I have to be careful with my moods because some people think I'm crazy. I have to show some sanguinity now and then, or they'll be convinced of it."

"Sanguinity?" Grand echoed sardonically. Had he not been overwrought by the Holly Springs debacle, he might have laughed.

"It's a word . . . I think," Sherman replied and pointed to the black, eerie clouds gathering over the Mississippi. "Right now I suggest we move inside or risk being rained on."

Grant concurred, entered the tent, and struck a match to an oil lamp. A comfortable luminescence filled the limited space, revealing a map of Vicksburg and its environs laid out on a table at the tent's far end. Sherman headed directly for it.

"I see you've been thinking," Sherman commented as he gazed down at the map. He pointed at two proximate north-south lines sketched in pencil. One paralleled the Mississippi Central Railroad to Jackson. The other followed the general direction of the Mississippi from Memphis to Vicksburg.

"Which one?" Sherman asked.

"Both."

"Both? What did you have in mind, a pincers?"

"Yes. I'll come down the railroad and approach Vicksburg from the east. You'll come down the Mississippi and attack from the north."

"Where?" Sherman asked, searching for a logical entry point on the eastern shore of the Mississippi.

"There," Grant said, pointing to the land between the Mississippi and its tributary, the Yazoo River.

"*Yazoo!*" Sherman exclaimed, rolling his eyes upward. "What kind of a name is that? It sounds like some obscene Rebel taunt. 'Take this river and shove it up your old *ya-zoo*.'"

"Which they might do if you don't get there before the Rebels arrive," Grant said.

Sherman gave his friend a suspicious look, wondering if Grant's haste might have something to do with the possibility of McClernand making a grab for his recruits before Grant could mold them into his own troops.

Pressing a finger to the corner of land Grant had indicated, he said, "Does this place have a name?"

"Haynes' Bluff."

"Bluff? I'm not fond of attacking bluffs."

"They're not as high as the Vicksburg Bluffs."

Grant is in a hurry, Sherman realized, sensing a ghost of foreboding pass by.

"What kind of land is it?" Sherman queried.

Grant sighed and crossed his arms.

"It's next to the Mississippi River. What else would it be but trees and swamps?"

"Trees, swamps, *and* bluffs," Sherman corrected. "How soupy is the swamp and how dense is the forest?"

Shrugging, Grant said, "I don't know. All we have are reports from local sympathizers and not many of them. They seem to think there's nothing exceptional about the place."

"They live here. They probably think slogging through swampland and underbrush is normal human activity."

Suddenly, a thunderbolt cracked and rain fell from the sky like grapeshot from a Columbiad. The suddenness of the heavenly assault momentarily silenced both men. Each took the opportunity to compose a silent prayer.

"When?" Sherman asked plaintively.

"Tomorrow," Grant replied, his anxiety showing. "My half of the army is already beyond Holly Springs. We'll just keep going."

Given Van Dorn's destructive incursion into Holly Springs, Sherman was not sure he shared Grant's optimism, but there was no point in arguing.

"Are there enough boats?"

At this question, Grant seemed to gain confidence.

"You've met David Porter?"

"The commander of the mortar boat squadron in Farragut's run past Vicksburg last summer?"

"Yes. He'll be taking you and your half of the army downriver."

"Thirty-five thousand men? All in boats?" Sherman remarked, somewhat startled.

"You'll have seven gunboats and about sixty transports," Grant retorted, then struggled with a quick calculation. "That's six-hundred per transport."

The figure did not inspire Sherman. Shaking his head, he said, "Six-hundred men in one boat, probably not much more than a barge, sitting in the middle of the Mississippi River waiting to be sunk by the first Rebel battery it passes? Not my idea of sound tactics."

"It's not tactics, it's just transportation," Grant argued, seating himself in a chair next to the map table. He lit up a cigar and offered one to Sherman, who accepted and plunked himself down on a tall wooden stool next to a half-emptied duffle bag.

"It's something we have to learn how to do," Grant continued. "Use the navy, I mean. In this country, there are only two ways to move an army swiftly, by train and by boat. We know how to move men by train, but Rebels like Van Dorn are making a great sport out of tearing up railroad track. We have to use boats, but getting troops off a boat onto ground that might be swampy, forested, hilly, or any combination thereof is a skill we have yet to master. There's no choice; it has to be done."

Sherman lit his cigar, drew the smoke into his mouth, and released it before speaking.

"And you want me to learn that lesson for you?"

"For the army," Grant corrected. Then he leaned one elbow on the map and bent his wrist so that a forefinger landed on the stretch of railroad between Holly Springs and Jackson. "Meanwhile, I'll be learning another lesson—how to keep Earl Van Dorn and Nathan Bedford Forrest from robbing us blind."

"And if you don't?"

Grant pursed his lips in concentration. He looked stoically at Sherman and said, "If I don't, we'll just have to learn how to live off the land."

★ SEVEN ★

December 24, 1862, Point Lookout, Louisiana

It was Christmas Eve and the two Confederate telegraph officers John Shank and Emil Meyer were not happy to be on duty. Shank was the younger and more restless of the two and was busily pacifying his disquietude with a bottle of Tennessee whisky. Meyer, middle-aged, gray-bearded and wearing a tattered Rebel kepi on his egg-shaped bald pate, kept an ear out for the telegraph but was otherwise content to sit at the table, which, with the exception of the chairs on which the two men sat, was the lone piece of furniture in the room. The light from a coal oil lamp filled the room with a ghostly illumination.

"Emil, why don't you just relax and have a drink?" Shank said. "Ain't nothin' gonna come through on the telegraph. It's Christmas Eve."

Meyer turned his grizzled face toward his younger companion. "We're on duty," he chided.

"It's Christmas Eve. We need a little cheer. We deserve it."

Shank knew he was a little drunk, and would have let a giggle or two escape if he hadn't been afraid of incurring his partner's displeasure. Emil Meyer could be quite stiff-necked when he put his mind to it.

To Shank's surprise, Meyer said, "Maybe later, maybe midnight," and resumed his vigilance.

Shank stood and was about to begin his ninth orbit of the room when the sound of footsteps rose above the background noise of dogged rainfall, followed by a knock on the door. Shank sat the bottle on the table and opened it. To his amazement, a pretty young black woman in a soaked white cotton frock, with tight pigtails on both sides of her head, stood before him. Her hands were wringing nervously.

"Suh," she said, looking meekly up at him from deep brown eyes. "I has somethin' important to tell y'all."

Shank motioned her inside and offered his chair. She shook her head and said, "Nah, I got to help my mama fix supper. It's Christmas Eve, y'know. But I got somethin' important to say. 'Less you already know."

Shank and Meyer looked at each other, then back at the woman. Shank shrugged.

"What is it?"

She pointed out the front window toward the river and said, "They is boats out there. Lots and lots of 'em."

Boats, Shank repeated in his mind.

"What kind of boats?" he asked.

"*Big* boats," the woman exclaimed, her outstretched arms expanding as if forced apart by a swelling balloon. She looked anxiously at Shank, then at Meyer, thinking they might not believe her. "I seen 'em myself."

As she spoke, Shank saw her gaze fall on the bottle and then him. He felt a quick surge of anger course through him. He had always prided himself on his tolerance of Negroes, but this woman was staring sullenly at him in silent criticism.

"Miss," a calmer voice interjected from across the table. Meyer rose from his chair, walked toward the woman and placed a gentle arm around her shoulder. "Please sit and tell us your story."

Meyer walked her to the chair. She cast another glance at Shank, but this one held more wariness than animosity. Shank's anger had not completely abated, but he averted his eyes and said nothing as he sat down.

Her name was Sally June McGowan and she had been returning home from the Price's farm upriver with two plucked chickens, which were still in her carpetbag outside.

"I heard 'em before I seen 'em," she said with some enthusiasm. "It was already dark an' I heard noises comin' from up the river. Like, like engines an' steam an' water rushin' by. You know, like riverboats does."

Once again, Meyer and Shank exchanged puzzled glances. Meyer studied the resolute gaze of Sally June McGowan and said, "Can you show us?"

Sally June smiled, revealing white but imperfectly aligned teeth with a slight overbite.

"Yes, I can," she said fervently and got quickly to her feet. "But we gonna have to do some walkin' and it's dark outside."

She marched back to the door, opened it and stepped into the rain. Rather than shrink from it, she untied a kerchief from around her neck and laid it on her head, finishing the relocation by tying two of its corners under her chin.

"Come on, come on. We got to go," she said impatiently.

Meyer obeyed and followed, happy to have the kepi's protection against the steady downpour. Shank hesitated, grabbed his bottle, and sauntered toward the door. When Sally June saw the whisky, her expression turned hostile. For reasons he could not identify, Shank yielded before her gaze and returned the bottle to the table. Sally June turned and headed upriver, waving the two men forward.

"I seen 'em about a mile up this way. Them boats should be comin' down soon."

"Can we see them from here?" Meyer asked, cocking his head toward the intervening forest.

"No, but they's a path goes down to the riverbank a half mile up. We'll take it."

Shank thought he knew the path she was referring to but kept his mouth shut. He was both ashamed of himself and embarrassed that he'd allowed a black woman to instill such shame in him. He was also angry, but that emotion took a poor third.

It was ten minutes before they reached the cutoff, which was a narrow path through rain-drenched grasslands. The traverse was flat for a quarter mile but started sloping at a shallow angle after another quarter mile. They reached a sand, deadwood, and rock-strewn fragment of shoreline at the outside of a bend in the Mississippi's course. Had it been daytime, they would have been looking directly upstream.

"Can you hear?" Sally June asked. Shank could see her cupping a hand around one ear in the fog-filtered moonlight.

Shank and Meyer each cupped a hand around one ear and listened. It was faint but they could hear the medley of sounds Sally June had described: engines, steam and rushing water. The intensity was growing.

"Get down," Shank said, then hastily obeyed his own command. Sally June and Meyer followed suit, but with a lesser degree of urgency.

"What do you think, Emil?" Shank asked, peering over a mound of sand and dead grass toward the river.

"Nothin' to think about yet," Meyer replied.

"I got to go," Sally June said, quietly but insistently.

"You can't go yet. They might see you. They might shoot you," Shank said, flashing a glance at a hazy moon overhead.

Sally June snickered and responded, "So what they see me? I jus' a black woman strollin' along the river."

"But they might be Yankees."

"Maybe. But Yankees s'posed to be on my side. They s'posed to be savin' Negras, not shootin' them," Sally June said, the whites of her eyes glowing like ivory marbles in the moonlight.

The dissonant river symphony was loud enough that individual instruments could be discerned: the intermittent hiss of steam from pistons, the chugging of smokestacks, the lapping of bow waves on multiple hulls. John Shank saw the outline of the lead boat take shape in the mist and a Union flag flying from a bow pole. These were the war wagons of the Yankee navy. He glanced at Meyer to gauge his reaction but his partner seemed to be enjoying himself; so fixated was his wide-eyed stare.

"You gonna turn us in?" Shank demanded of Sally June.

She cast a cold, deadly stare at him.

"No, 'course not. I ain't in this war."

"They could set you free, like you said."

The young Negress smiled and said, "I don't need settin' free. I already free."

"You're a freeman?"

"I a free *woman*," she said, with a smile but no further explanation. "Free as a bird."

Shank was shocked. He had never met a free black man before, let alone a free black woman. In fact, the whole idea of a free black woman was alien to his established mindset. What did it mean?

"Don't fret, John. It's all right," said Emil Meyer in a subdued voice.

Shank glanced at his companion and saw something like compassion in his face. Sally June turned her attention to the river as if she hadn't heard.

"I'm not frettin'," Shank insisted. "I'm not frettin'."

There were now two boats to be seen, one a gunboat and the other whose bulk identified it as a transport. Soon more boats came into view, far more of them transports than gunboats. The Yankees were moving troops downstream, probably to Vicksburg. The shore along which the two Confederates and the woman lay was subjected to a violent pummeling by the whitecaps generated by the huge armada. As each boat passed, the spectators could see men on deck and dim oil lamps illuminating their movements.

Meyer whistled and said, "How many you count, John?"

"Five big ones, one little one . . . so far."

"You mean five transports, one gunboat. We need to be accurate when we telegraph De Soto Point."

De Soto Point was the peninsula opposite Vicksburg, formed by a tight, nearly one-eighty degree bend in the Mississippi. Its position gave it a unique vantage point for both upstream and downstream river activity.

"But they're still comin', Hell, there might be a hunderd of 'em for all we know," Shank said, awestruck.

"Then we gotta wait 'til they all pass, get an accurate count, like I said," Meyer's steadier voice intoned.

Suddenly, Sally June McGowan rose, brushed herself off, and began a return journey along the path they'd come by.

"Miss . . . Miss McGowan!" Shank croaked, trying to accomplish a shout and a whisper at the same time. He was confused about how to address a Negro girl, so, in the moment's anxiety, had settled on 'Miss.'

"Miss, you have to get down. They'll see you."

She turned and waved the argument away.

"Them boats is in the middle of the river and they movin' too fast. Ain't gonna stop for you, me, or Robert E. Lee. I gotta pick up the chickens I left at your buildin' and get home."

Although it was too dark to see anything but the outline of a moving figure, Shank sensed that Sally June was beating a hasty retreat. For reasons he could not explain, he felt a wave of panic pass through him. He was terribly exposed and all he had as a companion was a cranky old man.

As if to confirm that opinion, Emil Meyer said, "We can't go, John. We gotta stay right here 'til this thing passes."

Propped up on the sand by his elbows, Shank shook his head fretfully and said, "I know, I know, I know, I know . . ."

"Don't worry, boy; we'll be all right. We just have to stay a while . . ."

". . . And get an accurate count. I know. I know."

Meyer proposed, and Shank agreed to an independent count by each man, again for the sake of accuracy. The procession of floating Yankee might was so long that they lost track of time. When, finally, the last boat passed and the night air was once again still, Emil Meyer stood and turned to his partner.

'Fifty-nine transports."

"Fifty-nine."

"Seven gunboats."

"Yup, seven."

It was a good night's work but neither man was happy. There was too much to do. Meyer raised himself to a standing position, brushed himself off, and shot a challenging stare at his companion.

"Come on, John, let's go," he said, stepping briskly down the path.

Hurrying to catch up, Shank said, "Are we goin' after the . . . woman?"

"No, why should we do that?"

"She might tell the Yankees we know about their fleet."

Meyer gazed at his partner with something just short of contempt.

"Now, why should *she* do that? She already told you she wouldn't. Besides, how's she gonna do it—swim after those damn boats and hope they'll spot her black head in the dark?"

Shank ignored Meyer's impeccable logic and said, "She's a Negra. We can't trust what a Negra says, Emil."

"We took her on her word about the boats, and she was right," Meyer barked, his contempt no longer concealed. He shook his head and accelerated ahead of Shank.

They were nearly back to the telegraph station before Shank caught up again and muttered, "Emil!"

"What?"

"Maybe you're right. Maybe she won't tell, but . . ."

Meyer halted, waiting for a complete sentence to emerge from his colleague's lips. Finding none forthcoming, he said, "But what?"

Shank steeled himself and said, "Why wouldn't she? She's a Negra!"

Meyer snorted his displeasure and turned his deep-set black eyes and rock solid jaw back to face Shank.

"She's a free woman, and she lives here. She don't want them damn Yankees trampin' over her and hers any more'n we do."

With that and a despairing shake of his bald head, Emil Meyer re-entered the telegraph shack and began preparations for transmitting a message to De Soto Point. He left a dumbfounded John Shank standing outside in a cool Christmas Eve breeze. It would take several hours of mental muscle-flexing for Shank to comprehend what Meyer had just told him: that a black woman could be as loyal to the Confederacy as he was.

* * *

December 24, 1862, De Soto Point, Mississippi

"Jesus!" Colonel Philip Fall murmured under his breath as he gripped the deciphered message.

"What was that, sir?" asked Lieutenant Rankin Boucher, the operator at the De Soto Point telegraph station from his comfortable chair facing the fireplace.

"The Yankees are coming," said Fall, foregoing further blasphemy.

Boucher lifted his massive form from the chair and waddled across the room. Fall handed him the message.

"Jesus!" Boucher said, glancing up in horror. "Sixty-six. That's the devil's number!"

Fall ignored the comment. It was well known that Lieutenant Boucher's family came from a clan of Louisiana swamp dwellers whose belief system could have served as the billboard outside a freak show. They also danced with snakes.

"I believe six-six-six is the devil's number," Fall said. "We have to get this message to General Smith."

"What do we have?" Boucher inquired.

"Just the skiff."

Exhaling through flared nostrils, Boucher rested his hands on his considerable girth and said, "You better go alone, sir. I might sink the boat."

Fall shoved the message in the pocket of his gray uniform and thanked Boucher's bizarre God for blessing the man with a rare crumb of common sense.

"I'll be back in an hour or two," Fall said, heading for the eastern door.

"I wouldn't count on it, sir," Boucher said, settling back into his chair. "The general's goin' to ask a lot of questions."

"I have one answer: sixty-six."

Fall exited the station, ran to the skiff, thrust it into the turbulent Mississippi, and hopped aboard. Before starting to row, he got a visual fix on the Balfour House, where most of the Vicksburg garrison were attending a Christmas Ball. Alive with lamplight, it was easy to spot. Fall judged the speed of the current at approximately five knots and aimed the skiff for a spot about a hundred yards upstream of the Balfour House, estimating that the current would take him downstream by the same amount. He didn't like boating in the Mississippi, particularly at night and particularly in the skiff. It was not a swift river, but it was wide and had so many bends and sandbars that you could never predict where the next whirlpool would reach out and grab you by the tail.

After fifteen minutes of hard rowing, he landed and pulled the skiff onto the eastern shore. He was almost directly below the Balfour House, with the Vicksburg Bluffs between him and his objective. Setting off at a trot, he began to climb, weaving his way through the hilly streets of the town until he reached the intersection of Cherry and Crawford Streets, where the Balfour House shone brighter than the full moon. He could hear faint music—a waltz, he thought—and saw men and women in their formal finery standing beneath the front portico. He paid them no heed as they watched him scurry through the front door, wondering at his haste on such a blissful occasion.

Two Confederate soldiers stood guard just inside the entrance. Fall recognized one of them.

"Corporal Cahill," he said, gasping. "Where is General Smith? I must see him."

Cahill, a square-faced descendant of Scotch-Irish parents from the eastern part of the state, stood on his tiptoes and gazed over the heads of the dancers. When he found what he was looking for, he pointed and said, "Right there, sir. He's dancing with his wife."

Fall mimicked Cahill's example and stood on his toes, stretching his neck to give his eyes a clear line of sight. He quickly spotted his commanding officer hovering in front of the small orchestra, enjoying the vibrant interplay of violins, piano and wind instruments. Thanking Cahill, he hastily crossed the dance floor, drawing curious eyes along his path as if he were a magnet.

"General, sir," he said, halting to salute. Reaching into his pocket, he withdrew the message and added, "An urgent communication from the Point Lookout station."

Nodding to his wife, the general ran fingers through his long and chronically unruly hair. Mrs. Smith drifted off to invisibility while her husband took the telegram and unfolded it. Apprehension lay heavily on him until he realized it could not be bad news about Grant's current offensive through Holly Springs. If it were, the news would have come from the northeast, not Point Lookout farther west. But as he read the message, the apprehension returned.

"My God, fifty-nine transports and seven gunboats! Where are they going?" he demanded.

Fall shook his head and said, "This is all we know, sir. But I seriously doubt they would attack Vicksburg directly from the river. They've tried that before without success. Upstream somewhere, maybe the Yazoo River."

General Smith nodded in agreement, his head seeming to precess like a top on its spinal column.

"Yes, yes, you're right. The bluffs, Chickasaw Bluffs," he said, suddenly stiffening his posture and forcing his head erect. He turned to an aide and added, "Lieutenant Emery, find General Stephen Lee and have him send some of his boys north to the Yazoo to look for Yankees. They'll be coming ashore from fifty-nine transports. Tell General Lee to stop them if he can, but if he can't, to slow them down until we can get more people up there."

Lieutenant Emery's bulging fish eyes nearly popped out of their sockets at Smith's words. He saluted, planted a kepi on his pointed head, and uttered a hoarse, "Yes, sir," before departing.

Smith's attention returned to Philip Fall.

"Colonel, I need you to send a message to General Pemberton right away."

Having just arrived in haste, Fall did not want to withdraw in the same frantic state. But he was a soldier.

"Yes, sir," he said.

"Tell him about the Yankee flotilla. Tell him he needs to get back to Vicksburg and take command of her defenses. You choose the words. Tell him I'm sending patrols out."

"Yes, sir."

"Now, please!"

"Yes, sir," Fall snapped and made his exit. Now the revelers *were* staring at him, some with concern on their faces, others with hostility. He had spoiled the party, after all. Before he reached the door, Fall heard General Smith's *basso profundo* booming behind him.

"Ladies and gentlemen, may I please have your undivided attention!"

Fall turned in his tracks to see the general poised before the orchestra beneath an enormous crystal chandelier laden with burning Christmas bows and candles. His raised arms and the shadowy light gave him the aspect of an evangelist preacher. The strength and commanding richness of his voice brought an immediate hush to the ballroom.

"I am sorry to tell you that this ball is at an end. The enemy is coming down the river, and all non-combatants must leave the city."

Without waiting for questions or even for the conversational buzz to resume, Smith strode purposefully from the room, his gaze fixed on the back of the aide who was running interference for him. When he was gone, the room burst into a cacophony of shocked, bewildered and angry utterances.

Colonel Fall fought to deflect the sea of humanity rushing past him toward General Smith. Except for those who bounced off him, no one paid any attention to the messenger. Few citizens of Vicksburg were prepared to leave the city, some out of fear, others from an in-bred recalcitrance in the face of the enemy. But most wanted to make their arguments loud and clear to the general who, anticipating their concerns, successfully made his exit.

As did Colonel Philip Fall. Being downhill most of the way, the journey back was quicker than the climb up to Cherry and Crawford Streets had been. When he arrived at the beached skiff, Fall found a gray-clad soldier with long red locks down to his shoulders standing guard, a musket braced between his hand and the ground. Apparently, he was standing guard.

"Sir, Corporal Dan Seeger to row you back, sir," he said, saluting. The loose locks quivered with the disturbance.

"Who sent you, Corporal?" Fall asked, pushing the skiff toward the river. "And why do I need you to row me back?"

Seeger took hold of the skiff's bow and added his energy to the launch.

"You don't, sir, I'm sure. And no one sent me," said Seeger. "I just wanted to ask you . . ."

The skiff made an audible rippling sound as it entered the water.

"Ask me what?"

"Ask you . . ." Seeger stammered. "Ask you what you think of our chances, sir."

Fall thought about that, now that he had the opportunity. As both men stepped aboard and Seeger started to row, he replied, "I think we have a good chance. There are a lot of Yankees coming downriver, but they won't attack here. Farther north, maybe the Yazoo."

Seeger belched a sigh of relief.

"That's good, isn't it? I mean, we can handle them up there, can't we?"

We could handle them here better. Maybe sink the whole damn fleet.

"I think so," he said noncommittally, adding, "If everyone does his part."

Once they reached deeper waters, Seeger deepened his stroke, propelling the boat forward.

"You'll have to aim the bow upriver, toward the Point. The current's pretty strong."

Fall saw Seeger's face nod in the shadowy moonlight. Then the skiff made a low right turn upriver so that its direction vector was at a forty-five-degree angle to the opposite shoreline. The balance of swift current and Seeger's propulsive efforts made it seem as if the skiff were standing still. But Fall could sense an agonizingly slow movement to the west.

"Good night for a battle," Seeger said conversationally.

Rather than respond—as no night was a good night for a battle—Fall said, "There won't be a battle tonight. The Yankees aren't ready, and we're not ready. General Lee will let us know what they're up to."

"Who do you think is the Yankee commander?" Seeger inquired.

Fall shrugged and heaved a weary sigh.

"I'm not sure. We know Grant has his hands full at Holly Springs with Van Dorn and Bedford Forrest. Couldn't be him. I guess I'd expect either Sherman or McPherson, probably Sherman."

Seeger nodded. His strokes fell into an efficient rhythm and Fall could feel the skiff accelerate with each thrust. Still the western shore seemed far away. He shifted his gaze upstream and, as expected, saw nothing but candlelight shining through the windows of homesteads in the Walnut Hills opposite De Soto Point, and a blazing bonfire at the Fort Hill Battery in northern Vicksburg. *Another Christmas celebration*, he thought, wondering if the celebrants had received the news of the Yankee invasion.

"Corporal, could you row a little faster?" he said.

Seeger immediately accelerated the pace of his strokes.

"I need to send a dispatch to General Pemberton," Fall explained.

"It must be urgent," Seeger remarked.

Fall fell silent, took another quick glance upstream and unexpectedly snickered.

"It is, Corporal," he said. "But I must also admit to an ulterior motive."

Hesitantly, Seeger inquired, "And what would that be, sir?"

Fall sucked in a breath and said, "I truly do not believe the Yankees will come this far downriver to attack Vicksburg. I've already said that . . ."

Silence once again reigned as Philip Fall struggled to express himself.

"Yes, sir, you don't think the Yankees will come this far . . ."

"But if they do," Fall cut in, finding his voice. "If they do, Corporal, I don't want to be stuck in the middle of the Mississippi River with nothing but a skiff between me and a watery grave while a sixty-six boat Yankee armada bears down on my position."

Seeger was tempted to laugh but managed only a cheerful grunt. Mimicking Fall, he cast a surreptitious glance upstream, then shifted his rowing rhythm into a higher gear.

"Neither do I, sir. Neither do I."

★ EIGHT ★

December 29, 1862, Chickasaw Bayou, Mississippi

Standing beside Navy Commander David Porter, Sherman watched while the transport on whose deck he stood approached the shore. A small company of Union soldiers and sailors had already been sent ashore to secure the beachhead against any of the enemy who might be prowling around. It had been nearly two days since they had come up the Yazoo River from its mouth at the Mississippi, but had been forced to halt at a small tributary called Chickasaw Bayou before reaching Haynes' Bluff. No Confederates, army or navy, had yet been encountered.

"How in God's name are you going to land fifty-nine transports and seven gunboats on that shoreline?" Sherman asked Porter. "There's no beach!"

Porter sucked air into his lungs and stretched himself to his full height, causing the two rows of brass buttons on his double-breasted navy blue coat to snap to attention. Like many of the officers on both sides, and distinctly unlike his barefaced foster brother, Rear Admiral David Farragut, Porter sported a long, thick beard.

"On the other hand, there is no shortage of trees. We can use them to tie up," Porter said in an ascetic voice.

Which was what the flotilla did. Adjustments were made as some captains found their boats approaching a segment of shoreline blocked by cypress trees, vines and other varieties of dense Mississippi vegetation. But the mouth of the Yazoo provided plenty of shoreline, and each transport eventually found a vacant piece of it to cling to while unloading its human cargo.

When Sherman stepped ashore, his boots sunk ankle deep in the Yazoo mud. He pulled a disgusted face and looked at Porter, who had no reason or inclination to leave the deck of the boat.

"My God, how are we supposed to move artillery through this?" Sherman bellowed in frustration.

If Porter was amused, he steadfastly refused to show it. Pointing a finger to the southeast, he said, "I'll help you out if I can, General, but I think the bluffs are too far away for our guns."

Sherman gazed in the direction of Porter's pointing finger and spotted the upsurge of the forest roof at the extreme range of his vision. It appeared to be several miles distant and was as heavily wooded as the swampland below. He looked at the sky and then at the shoreline several yards from where he stood. The sky was gray with rain clouds and the Yazoo current was on the verge of overflowing onto the land, if a substance consisting of fifty percent water, thirty percent earth, and twenty percent grass could be called "land." Extracting his boots from the mud, he stepped back onto the deck of the transport, kicking the boat's hull to remove the surface filth.

"This is not my idea of a battleground, but that's not always something we get to choose," he said to Porter, enunciating the words as he might a curse on his worst enemy. "We'll lose five thousand men before we take Vicksburg, and we may as well lose them here as anywhere else."

It was a rancorous remark, born of consternation, and Sherman thought he might ultimately regret having said it. But Porter ignored it, and Sherman saw no compelling need to indulge in self-criticism before he had even met the enemy. Porter excused himself to supervise the unloading of equipment and supplies. Sherman spotted one of his aides, James Fulton, and motioned him over to the transport.

"Lieutenant, find the brigade commanders and tell them to meet me here on deck. Promptly."

With much suction pulling his feet, Fulton plodded away to do his duty.

When the officers arrived, Sherman moved them to a spot that had just been vacated and explained what he had in mind.

"Gentlemen, welcome to Chickasaw Bayou," he said, indicating the lazy stream behind them. "As you probably know, we can't get to the original objective, Haynes' Bluff, because the Yazoo is mined just north of here."

A murmur of voices ensued. Sherman couldn't tell whether its tone indicated satisfaction or dissatisfaction, so he continued.

"We'll approach Vicksburg by way of the Walnut Hills, otherwise known as Chickasaw Bluffs, which are that way," he said, pointing southeast. "It's actually a shorter trip to Vicksburg from there than it is from Haynes' Bluff."

The sight lines of all projected beyond the line of Sherman's raised arm as far as their eyes could see, which was not far because of the forest.

"We'll be marching along that little stream to the hills, which I estimate to be about three miles distant. Brigadiers Blair, Steele, and Thayer will take the left. Brigadier A. Smith, Colonels G. Smith and T. Smith will take the right. Which leaves Brigadier Morgan and Colonel De Courcy in the center. Are there any questions?"

There were questions; Sherman could see it in their faces. But they were not questions about tactics, or line of battle, or any of the myriad questions that always faced soldiers at the onset of a deadly struggle. They were questioning the wisdom of pursuing a battle, so the unasked questions remained unanswered.

Sherman dismissed his staff to initiate the approach to Chickasaw Bluffs. Skirmishers were sent ahead to engage the Rebels and gauge their strengths and weaknesses. Within the hour, troops, horses, artillery and loaded wagons were moved off the noisy, steaming transports and onto the spongy earth. While the attack force got sluggishly underway, David Porter showed up and offered his hand.

"I wish you good luck, General," he said.

Sherman cocked his slouch hat slightly forward and shook the proffered hand. Then he stared into Porter's eyes.

"Good luck?" he said solemnly. "I think we've had all the luck we're going to get, and none of it is good."

Withdrawing his hand from Porter's grasp, Sherman straightened and turned his horse into the swamp, steadying it as a twelve-pounder Napoleon artillery piece splashed its way ashore. The horse hesitated as its front hooves engaged and then sank into the soft soil. A lightning bolt flashed from the direction of Chickasaw Bluffs, followed by a thunderclap that nearly made the horse rear up. Then a quiet, persistent mist began to fall.

Positioning the flat of his hand to catch the rainfall, Sherman turned toward Porter one last time and said, "Even God doesn't want this battle."

★ NINE ★

December 29, 1862, Chickasaw Bluffs, Mississippi

"Fire!" ordered Brigadier General Stephen D. Lee.

The Confederate artillery responded with deafening and deadly effect. Under normal circumstances, Union artillery would dominate artillery duels, but this was home ground, and the Yankees were bogged down in the swampy bayou at the base of Chickasaw Bluffs. The Rebels had the high ground.

While the cannoneers reloaded, the Yankee artillery took its turn, lobbing several exploding shells among the reserve troops of the 17th and 26th Louisiana infantry farther back from the bluffs. The duel had been initiated by the Yankees two hours before as the prelude to an attack. That attack had failed, partly because of the inhospitable terrain of Chickasaw Bayou, and partly because Lee had sent his infantry to check it. Despite being outnumbered by at least five to one, the Confederate counterattack had succeeded in its objective of delaying the Union advance. The Rebel cannons were still spreading havoc and carnage among the Union troops trying to ascend the steep bluffs.

Lee stiffened his posture and raised an arm above the redoubt walls from which he was directing the cannon fire. He needed to be heard and, if not heard, seen.

"Fire!" he shouted, dropping his arm like the blade of a sword.

Once more the Confederate artillery roared to life, sending swarms of grapeshot, canister, and mini-balls to decimate the fragile Union line. When the smoke cleared, Lee saw blue-uniformed men moving toward him, with gray-clad, armed men behind them. One of the gray-clad men, a lieutenant, approached Lee.

"Sir, Lieutenant Jasper McKee, sir!" he said, snapping the requisite salute.

Lee returned the salute and said, "You have prisoners, Lieutenant McKee. What is their unit?"

"4th Iowa, sir."

Lee gave the artillery barrage to his second in command and looked over the band of Union prisoners. Like all prisoners he had ever encountered, there was a blend of despondency and relief on their features—despondency at being captured, and relief that they were not dead.

"Is there an officer among them?"

"Yes, sir, a captain."

"Bring him to me."

Lee moved to a gnarled cypress tree and leaned an elbow against it. He thought of himself as a simple man. Some had likened his placid, vacant expression to that of a farmer, or at least to someone unaccustomed to social intercourse. But the blank face was a facade. Stephen D. Lee had been in the war since its inception, at Second Manassas, Sharpsburg, and earlier. His reticence was not a sign of mental indolence.

A captive was marched before him, a man with a dark complexion, thickset, with chocolate hair, and dark, deep-set eyes that could barely be seen under prominent brow ridges.

"Sir, this is Captain James Hargraves of the 4th Iowa. Captain, this is General Lee," McKee said.

Hargraves's jaw dropped an inch or two while he tried to formulate a response.

"Sir, are you . . ." he managed to sputter.

"No, I'm not *that* Lee," the Confederate general snapped, weary of what had become, for him, a standing joke. "I'm half the age of Robert E. and all my relatives are from the Carolinas. Besides, he's a Johnny-come-lately. I'm the Lee who started this war."

Which was literally true, but failed to convince Hargraves. A gnarled brow reflected his puzzlement.

"Sir?" he said.

Lee paused for effect. Then he folded his arms and said, "I'm from Charleston, South Carolina. I'm the man who delivered General Beauregard's ultimatum to Major Robert Anderson, demanding the surrender of Fort Sumter. I'd say that constitutes the official start of the war, wouldn't you, Captain?"

Hargraves hesitated, wondering if Lee could actually be boasting of what was, for a Union officer, a monstrous act. He half expected a punch line but, when none came, said, "I . . . suppose that argument could be made."

"Brigadier General Stephen D. Lee," the southerner declared, offering his hand.

Hargraves dutifully shook it.

"You're a member of the 4th Iowa, Captain?"

"Yes."

"And your commanding officer is . . .?" Lee quickly interjected, hoping for a reflexive reply. It didn't happen.

Walking away from the cypress, Lee turned his back to the prisoner and tried again.

"Never mind, I already know. General Sherman, correct? What I really want to know is how many men he's got."

Hargraves remained silent.

The Confederate turned, gave his captive a bland smile, and rubbed his hands together.

"Ah, but we know that too. Thirty-thousand or so, I expect."

"But how . . ."

"Don't worry, Captain. None of your fellow prisoners gave us the information. We simply counted the boats and made an educated guess at the human cargo in each. Though your opinion of us may differ, we are not complete bumpkins."

If the captain had ever thought of Rebels as bumpkins, the notion was quickly dispelled. To Hargraves's embarrassment, Lee now had confirmation that thirty thousand Union troops were attacking Chickasaw Bluffs.

"You seem to know more about our plan of attack than I do," Hargraves said.

To his surprise, Lee snickered, an action that instantly painted an emotional context on the Rebel general's face. It was a brief but telling glimpse of the man inside. As if aware he had bared his soul, Lee hastily clamped his jaws shut, erasing the grin he'd let slip by his defenses. Hands resting on his hips, he strolled to the edge of the bluffs and looked down.

"I don't know more about your attack plan than you do, but I don't have to," he said, pointing down the slope at the bayou below. "That bayou down there is a natural barrier, and there's only one corduroy bridge over it. To get up here, your army must cross over that bayou. They . . . you have already tried and failed."

Hargraves knew it was true. John DeCourcy's and Frank Blair's brigades had crossed over and assaulted Confederate positions.

"We captured your advance positions."

"Not for long. Most were driven back. Of the rest, half are dead, the other half prisoners."

"Why are you telling me this?"

Lee straightened and returned to Hargraves.

"I want you to understand, sir," he said icily. "I want you to understand that you cannot win this battle. This is Vicksburg and Vicksburg is a natural fortress. It is our Rock of Gibraltar. There is no approach to Vicksburg that cannot be successfully defended by a handful of men. Here, for instance. We have one-third your number, and yet your army is the one in retreat."

"I still don't know why you are saying this to me. I'm a captain, not a general."

Lee snorted, wiped a broad hand across his chin and beard, and glanced away. After a thoughtful interlude, his gaze shifted back to the prisoner.

"Not counting yourself and the men with you, we have taken approximately three-hundred Union prisoners. We will take more before this battle is over. When it is, I expect there will be a prisoner exchange. If you are included in that exchange, I would request that you relay this message to the highest Union officer who will listen. You may think you can win the war, but it will not be done here. It is a fool's errand. Vicksburg is excellent ground, and we have done everything to reinforce her natural defenses. Go back to Memphis. Go back to Corinth. The only thing you will accomplish in Vicksburg is the slaughter of countless Union soldiers and a lesser number of their Confederate counterparts. Will you do this?"

Hargraves reflected a moment, judged Lee to be sincere, and answered, "I will, but I do not expect your warnings to be heeded."

"They are not warnings. They are statements of fact."

"Nevertheless, I do not believe they will be interpreted as such."

"That is unfortunate," Lee said sharply. Satisfied he had done his best to avoid further bloodshed, he turned away and signaled his lieutenant to take charge of the prisoner.

"Sir, do you know General Grant?" he heard Hargraves ask.

Lee pivoted around and said, "General Grant is not here, Captain. He is either in Holly Springs or retreating from it."

"That is not my point, General, sir. I asked if you knew him."

Lee wondered at the purpose of the Yankee's insistence. It was a challenge of some sort; its hard edge bespoke of anger, hostility, determination . . . but the reason for it eluded him. He could only assume that Hargraves was inquiring about a possible acquaintance between Grant and himself in the Mexican War. During that war, many friendships had sprung up between officers above and below the Mason-Dixon Line, when the country was still united. But Lee could not have been in that war; he was too young. So was Hargraves.

"I regret I have not had the pleasure, sir," Lee replied.

"And you will not," Hargraves said boldly, the darkness in his cavernous eyes suddenly luminous. "General Grant is not known for pleasing his enemies."

As McKee led Hargraves away, the Confederate guns continued their crushing cannonade. Unperturbed by the prisoner's assertion,

Stephen D. Lee resumed his command, content in the knowledge that the day belonged to the Confederacy.

* * *

December 30, 1862, Chickasaw Bluffs, Mississippi

The smell and taste of cordite permeated the air well after the Union and Confederate guns fell silent. Stephen D. Lee stood with his commanding officer, staring down from Chickasaw Bluffs to the bayou below. There was not much to see now. The dead, mostly Union soldiers, were being removed from the slopes, and the invasion force led by William T. Sherman was gone. Lee sniffed the air again, not to test its odor but to feel its texture. It was wet; a fog would be settling in soon.

"Congratulations, sir, you've won a great victory," Lee said exuberantly. Unlike some of his southern comrades, he did not resent the fact that his commanding officer, General John C. Pemberton, had been born and raised in Philadelphia, Pennsylvania.

Pemberton was not a melancholy man, but he mistrusted the act of celebration. He considered it a precursor to letting one's guard down and he certainly did not wish that upon himself. Vicksburg was his first real field command, and he did not want to disappoint President Davis, the man who had appointed him to that post. As a former northerner, he felt this dread more keenly than other members of the Confederate officer corps.

"It was a victory, yes," he concurred, twisting the tips of his well-trimmed mustache between a thumb and forefinger. "I suppose we could even call it a glorious victory. What are the numbers?"

Lee had them memorized.

"Eighteen hundred enemy casualties and only a hundred eighty-seven of our own, sir. Do you want me to break it down into killed, wounded and missing?"

"No, not now. I would like to inspect the battlefield if you don't mind."

Lee did not reply. It was not his place to mind or not mind. Motioning for Pemberton to follow his lead, he led the way down the slope the Yankees had charged.

"I understand Grant has retreated to Memphis," Lee said conversationally.

Struggling to secure his footing on the steep incline, Pemberton said, "He has indeed. General Van Dorn did not treat him very hospitably at Holly Springs—destroyed all his supplies. And General Forrest was successful in persuading General Grant not to move south by removing the rail lines with which he could do so. A retreat to Memphis was the general's only option."

By "removing all the rail lines," Lee knew that Pemberton was referring to Bedford Forrest's practice of detaching railroad tracks, heating them until they warped and, if the warping was sufficient, tying them in neat bows. Railroad track treated by this process could never be used again.

When Lee and Pemberton reached the flatland at the base of the bluffs, Pemberton halted and cast a critical gaze across the heavily forested ground. The intensity of his commander's stare surprised Lee. He was not well acquainted with Pemberton but had been led to believe that the former Philadelphian had little talent for field command. Yet the General had directed this battle —albeit from a position well in the rear—and here he was inspecting the battlefield. Maybe the rumors were just another example of southern chauvinism.

"Show me how it happened," Pemberton said with a quick glance at his compatriot.

Hastily organizing his thoughts, Lee breathed deeply and began his exposition by pointing west.

"The Yankees landed on the east shore of the Yazoo a few miles that way, on Christmas Eve. About thirty thousand men. They weren't all ashore until December twenty-seventh and even then they weren't ready to fight for another day or two. You were back from Granada by then.

Pemberton nodded but gave no indication that Lee should cease his discourse, so he continued.

"Union artillery bombarded us the morning of December twenty-nine but didn't do much damage. We were dug in pretty well. We fired back with our artillery, and I suspect inspired a lot more fear in them than they did in us . . ."

Lee paused while a pair of Negro stretcher-bearers carrying the bloodied body of a Union soldier passed by. It was not obvious whether the man was dead or alive.

"Then the Yankees came at us, mostly regiments from the west —Iowa, Missouri, Illinois, places like that. Good soldiers but on bad ground. They didn't want to come, but they did. Charged up at us and even captured a few rifle pits, but we drove them back."

"Who stood against us, besides Sherman?" Pemberton asked while picking at a food particle lodged between two of his upper teeth.

Lee meditated briefly, then answered, "The officers I'm aware of are George Morgan, John DeCourcy, Frank Blair, Giles Smith, John Thayer, James Williamson . . . Do you know any of them?"

Pemberton removed the finger from between his teeth and flicked its prize toward the bayou.

"I don't think so. I may have met some in Mexico. A few names are familiar, but I don't recall where the familiarity comes from— Mexico or West Point."

Standing with his feet apart and his hands clasped behind him, Lee fell silent. There was really very little he could say. His age and Pemberton's were too far apart to share any West Point acquaintances, and Lee was too young to have been in the Mexican War. Though few expressed the sentiment openly, younger officers envied their older colleagues' experiences in the Mexican War of 1846-1848. While it was considered by some Americans to have been an unjust war, entered into by a bellicose and power hungry James K. Polk, it had, nonetheless, been won by the United States. To a career soldier, combat experience was as valuable as minted gold, and experience in the Mexican War carried with it the added benefit of social intimacy with the new enemy—the Yankee.

Pemberton suddenly shifted to a position directly in front of Lee, a fledgling grin underscoring an otherwise impassive expression.

"General Lee, I must express my deep satisfaction with the way you've handled our defenses. You have put to rout an enemy force of thirty-thousand with a mere three thousand of our own troops . . ."

"It was more like six thousand toward the end, sir, with the reinforcements from General Bragg and yourself . . ." Lee said.

The Pennsylvanian looked puzzled, but his ebullience would not easily be dislodged by details.

"Nevertheless, General," he said, cutting a swath through the air with one arm, "you have done well. I am proud to communicate your success on the battlefield to President Davis."

Although he was not sure this meant the president of the Confederacy had been or would be informed, Lee thanked his commander for the compliment. Jefferson Davis was a distant man, widely respected but rarely beloved. A good word in the proper ear, however, could do wonders for a military career.

"Tell me, General Lee, what do you think of this battle?" Pemberton queried.

Lee bowed his head, then looked up and replied, "I think the Yankees were foolish to attack us here, sir. They must have known we could seize the high ground. Then there's the additional problem of transporting men, wagons, and equipment over unfavorable terrain."

"Swamp and woodland, you mean?" Pemberton said, sweeping his eyes in a hundred-eighty-degree arc.

"Yes, sir. And the bluffs. It's very difficult to attack up a steep hill when grapeshot is being thrown at you. We could defend these hills against twice as many."

Pemberton nodded lazily and raised one eyebrow. The latter action seemed contrived, as if the general were putting on a mask of sagacity to demonstrate his comprehension. *What was he getting at?*

"Still, they will learn from their mistakes, don't you think?" he posited.

"Yes, sir, but . . ."

"And . . . having become aware of the obstacles, they will be better prepared next time."

Next time?

"I think we've beaten them soundly, sir," Lee said, distressed by the unexpected meekness in his voice.

"Yes, yes, we've beaten them soundly," Pemberton said impatiently. "But if they do return—and I believe they will—it will be here they return to."

"Here?"

"Here . . . north of Vicksburg. We have vulnerabilities . . . here."

"Vulnerabilities?" Lee asked querulously. Vicksburg would be difficult to attack from any direction. "Sir, we've just shown the Yankees we can beat them here. They aren't likely to try an attack by gunboat; *they* would be the vulnerable ones then. They won't attack from the east for fear of getting caught between General Johnston's army in Jackson and ours in Vicksburg. And the terrain south of the city is as bad as what we are standing on right now."

Reluctant to alienate his commanding officer by expanding his appraisal of the battle, Lee added, "Does this mean you intend to strengthen the northern defenses?"

"I do."

At the expense of the other fortifications? Lee would like to have asked, but didn't. Pemberton must have detected a hint of skepticism in his voice, his lowered head, or his stance because the commander's mood turned sullen.

"Thank you, General Lee," Pemberton said, his words clipped as short as a pig's tail. "I'll leave you to your duties."

Brandishing a crisp salute, Pemberton returned to the bluffs along the terrace road. A bewildered Stephen D. Lee returned the salute. When Pemberton had gone, he strolled across the battlefield, studying the detritus of the failed Union attack and subsequent re-treat. Bodies, pieces of bodies, dead horses, blankets, muskets, can-teens, overcoats, spent and unspent cartridges, everything an invading army could leave had been left behind. For a Confederate soldier, it was at once a pathetic and an inspiring sight.

Shaking his head, Lee looked around once more and started back. He could not agree with Pemberton. If he were a Yankee commander, he would *never* come back to this place.

★ TEN ★

December 30, 1862, Grant's Headquarters in Memphis, Tennessee

"Sir, where is my army?" John McClernand demanded. He was a small man with the kind of overgrown, unkempt beard that seemed to typify Civil War generals. His arrogance was part earned—he was a lawyer and had been a member of the Kentucky legislature—and part megalomania. To Ulysses S. Grant, he was a damned nuisance.

"Your army?" Grant said, glaring up at McClernand across the table separating the two men. Grant was seated, McClernand standing at attention while a persistent rainfall chattered on the roof of Grant's tent.

Oblivious of Grant's disquiet, McClernand proclaimed, "Yes, my army. The army I raised in Iowa, Illinois, and Indiana, by order of President Lincoln."

Grant leaned back in his chair and crossed his arms. Gazing between the tent flaps at the inclement weather outside, he wondered what he should do about the rogue general, or rather what he *could* do. To be fair, the man had handled himself well at Shiloh, but he had absolutely no military training. That, and the fact that Lincoln—through Secretary of War Edwin Stanton—had granted McClernand the right to raise and command a virtually independent army to attack Vicksburg were the issues that concerned Grant. Two armies with the same objective was bad enough. Two independent commanders was impossible.

Turning his attention back to McClernand, Grant said, "Your men arrived before you did, General, so they were given to General Sherman."

"I was getting married!"

"I understand, but we could not delay the attack. General Sherman had to depart Memphis December 22 . . ."

"But the attack failed!"

"Yes, it failed," Grant reluctantly acknowledged. "But we had no way of knowing it would fail. The fault was as much mine as General Sherman's. It was to be a two-pronged invasion: General Sherman from the west and me from the north. Unfortunately, the

Rebels destroyed the rail lines, and I could not progress any further south than Granada."

What he could not admit was that the mission had been hurried along so that the Iowa, Illinois, and Indiana recruits arriving in Memphis could be assigned to Sherman without interference from McClernand. Grant was not proud of this pretense, but the Shiloh campaign had taught him that success in the Union Army depended at least as much on politics as it did on military achievement. In fact, he was getting good at it.

He suddenly realized he had unfolded his arms and was pressing his hands against the surface of the table as if preparing to assume a standing position. Willfully, he allowed his arms to relax and clasped his hands firmly together.

"May I join my army, sir?" McClernand finally asked in a polite but contentious tone of voice.

"Certainly, General. You will join General Sherman at Milliken's Bend at your earliest convenience," Grant said.

Caught unawares by Grant's apparent acceptance, McClernand stammered and said, "What are your orders, sir?"

"Those *are* my orders," Grant said, then rose and strolled past McClernand to the tent's entranceway. Folding the flap over the tent's exterior, he added, "Just get there and take command. You don't need to do anything else."

"Will we be attacking Vicksburg again, sir?"

"Of course."

Fidgeting, McClernand looked decidedly uncomfortable, Grant thought. He suspected he knew why.

"I know you want to lead the attack on Vicksburg, General McClernand. And I know you persuaded President Lincoln to permit you to raise an army to do just that," Grant said, working his jaw muscles around the distasteful words. "But things have changed. My orders are that you may command *your* army, but I will retain command of any assault on Vicksburg. Do you understand what I'm telling you, General?"

If he knew Grant was reading the riot act to him, John McClernand didn't show it.

"Yes, of course, General Grant. May I ask if any thought has been given to a new plan of attack?"

"It's too early. We're still recovering from the last one."

McClernand smiled, but not enough to indicate enjoyment, only sympathy.

"I would appreciate being consulted, sir. I have a few ideas on how it might be done."

This did not surprise Grant. It had, after all, been McClernand's intention to attack Vicksburg with *his* army. Shuddering at the thought of such a debacle actually coming to pass, he diverted his gaze outside and saw John Rawlins, his chief of staff, heading in his direction.

"My officers are free to share their ideas with me at any time, General. That includes you."

From the front of Rawlins' slouch hat gushed a waterfall of grandiose proportions. The colonel was indeed hurrying this way.

"I'm going to call it the Army of the Mississippi," McClernand said.

The intensity of McClernand's voice startled Grant. He turned to find his subordinate's thickly bearded face no more than a foot from his own.

"Whatever you like, General," he said.

Evidently satisfied with the outcome of the meeting, McClernand grabbed his slouch hat—an excellent umbrella—and saluted Grant as he exited. Grant returned the salute as Rawlins passed McClernand in the entranceway. The two men grunted greetings at each other. Rawlins removed his hat, shook it, and laid it on the table.

"Damned rain," he said, offering a half-hearted salute. "It's cold out there. We'd be more comfortable with snow."

"Not likely in southwestern Tennessee," Grant remarked, cheered by the younger man's presence. Rawlins was an intensely decent man with an odd penchant for profanity. He was fiercely loyal to Grant and obsessively protective of him.

"What did that sonofabitch want?" Rawlins asked, wiping a rivulet of rainwater from his brow.

"He wants his army," Grant replied. "And I wish you would not refer to members of my staff as sons-of-bitches."

"He is a sonofabitch," Rawlins said, chuckling. "You know it, and I know it."

"Don't call him a sonofabitch."

"All right. *Bastard*, then."

Grant could not help laughing at Rawlins' audacity.

"What are you here for, John? Did Charlie Dana suggest I might be depressed by our failure to get anywhere near Vicksburg, and that I might need a swig or two of demon rum to lift my spirits?"

"Dana didn't send me."

"So, you're checking me out on your own initiative?"

"I'm not checking anything. I'm here for moral support and to find out what happens next. Just like everybody else."

Everybody else was Grant's staff, which included Generals McPherson, McClernand, Sherman and Thomas, Admiral Porter, staff officers Rawlins and Wilson and, semi-officially, Charles Dana. The two staff officers considered it their duty to defend Grant against all criticism, deserved or not, and had been initially fearful of Dana's interference when the Harvard-educated New Englander first arrived. They had been pleasantly surprised when, contrary to expectations, Grant and Dana appeared to genuinely like one another. Although Charles Dana would always, by the nature of his job, be a War Department "spy," he interpreted that duty as a mandate to head off trouble.

"I just told John McClernand I don't know exactly what will happen next," Grant said.

"Well, that sonofabitch is gone now. You're free to tell me what you have in mind."

"I have a whole list of things we *could* do," Grant said, making his way to a pot of coffee sitting on the ground beneath the table. "But we need to conduct a few experiments."

"Experiments?" Rawlins mumbled skeptically.

"Experiments," Grant confirmed, offering to pour a cup of coffee for Rawlins. The staff officer nodded, and Grant continued: "As I see it, we need to land our forces either above or below Vicksburg since we clearly cannot make a direct assault from the river. We just tried the *above* option, but the fact that we failed doesn't mean it's impossible; we may need to look into it further."

Grant paused to pour coffee for Rawlins and himself.

"And landing men and materiel *below* Vicksburg. How would we accomplish that?" Rawlins inquired.

"That's why we need experiments: to answer such questions. We have to either move south on the west side of the Mississippi or run our ships past Vicksburg. I'd rather move south through Louisiana if we can."

Rawlins nodded his agreement. Given the massive artillery bombardment that slow-moving military transports would be exposed to, a run past Vicksburg did not seem like a good idea.

"But the Louisiana side is mostly swamp. How can we get through that?"

Grant held up a finger and smiled as he reached under the table for a rolled-up map of Vicksburg and her nearby environs. He unrolled it and placed his fingertip on the Louisiana side of the river.

"Look at all those lakes and bayous," he said.

Puzzled, Rawlins swallowed a third of his coffee, then seated himself next to Grant and said, "That's the problem, isn't it? Swamps and mud?"

"And flood . . . maybe. But we have a whole army of men who have nothing to do until spring. What's to stop us from making some of these lakes and bayous wider and deeper? The draft of a riverboat is small; it doesn't need a lot of water to float in."

"You want to dig a canal!" the incredulous Rawlins exclaimed. "It might have to be ten miles long!"

"Or it might be as short as the width of De Soto Point."

Rawlins could appreciate the appeal of Grant's argument. The width of De Soto Point varied from zero at its extreme northern tip to about two miles at its southern base, over relatively flat land. Digging a canal from the northeasterly flowing Mississippi on the Point's western shore to the southwesterly flowing Mississippi on its eastern shore appeared to be feasible.

"Any boats coming through that canal will still be exposed to cannon fire," Rawlins said.

"But will avoid fire from the major batteries in Vicksburg proper, like Fort Hill."

With his finger, Rawlins traced an imaginary line across De Soto Point.

"It could work. How certain are you that it can be done?"

"Not at all. I called it an experiment, and that's what I meant."

"Do we have time for such . . . distractions?"

"We have the rest of winter and spring. What else are the men going to do except eat, sleep and drill? It's best to keep them busy. And . . . who knows . . . some 'experimenting' might actually succeed."

Experiments! It was a hell of a way to run a military campaign, Rawlins mused. Still, it might actually be a good thing to be able to recognize a flawed plan before it was too late to abandon it. Commanding officers were often ego-bound to pursue an attack plan of their own creation, even if its flaws became evident. A general who "experimented" before committing himself was something new under the sun.

"All right," Rawlins blurted, raising his hands in mock surrender. "I give up. I'll be damned if I'm going to fight against 'experiments.' What's the first going to be? The canal across De Soto Point?"

Grant finished his coffee and became thoughtful, resting his chin on one hand while striking a match and lighting a cigar he had promptly placed between his teeth.

"I don't know. I'll have to mull it over a little more. Talk to the staff. But I don't want to do that with Sherman and Porter absent."

"Where is Porter?"

"He's going with McClernand to join Sherman at Milliken's Bend."

"I thought you wanted the sonofabitch to sit on his ass. If Porter's with him, McClernand is bound to get him into some kind of trouble."

Leaning back in his chair, Grant cast a quick, circumspect glance at his subordinate. Then he said, "I can't very well refuse him access to the Navy or he'll complain to Stanton. He's got the only troops within striking range of Vicksburg."

"But you told him not to do that."

"And if he does, I'll court-martial him!" Grant grumbled, the fervor in his voice intensifying. "But I can't expect him to do nothing. I can strongly suggest it, but I can't force him to—as you put it—*sit on his ass.*"

Recognizing the limitations of rational discourse when it came to discussing the politically well-connected John McClernand, both men fell silent for a minute. Then Rawlins spoke.

"He won't, you know."

"Won't what?"

"Sit on his ass."

Grant snorted stoically, "I know."

"Not when he's got both Sherman and Porter to give orders to," Rawlins added.

"He's the senior officer," Grant said, a note of melancholy creeping into his tone.

Grant's demeanor became increasingly sullen, and Rawlins let him have the moment. Silence and meditation frequently energized the man, even though it looked like he was only drinking coffee and belching smoke like a Mississippi Central locomotive. Rawlins thanked his lucky stars that it was coffee, not whisky that his commander was drinking. But even if it had been, Grant would be lost to the army for only one night. He was not a binge drinker.

"Let's take a look at the map," Grant said, rising to his feet. Bending over the map, he examined the juncture of De Soto Point and the "mainland." Eager to deflect Grant's thoughts away from the McClernand problem, Rawlins followed his lead.

"You know, General Williams started digging a canal here last summer," Grant said, dragging a finger across the base of De Soto Point.

"And his men rapidly developed sun stroke and malaria," Rawlins merrily pointed out.

"You're a pessimist, John," Grant said, smiling.

"I'm a realist."

"Not much difference. Come on, help me figure this out. Where should we put it, the same place as Williams' canal?"

"Why not?"

"How wide, do you think, a hundred feet?"

Rawlins stared into space for a moment, then shook his head and muttered, "Too much."

"Fifty?"

"Not enough. Say, sixty-five or seventy."

"Fifteen feet deep?"

"Too much. Five to ten should be enough."

"How do we keep the water out while we dig it?"

"How the hell would I know? Ask the engineers . . ."

★ ELEVEN ★

January 28, 1863, Milliken's Bend on the Mississippi River

"General, McClernand, you have not followed your orders," said Ulysses S. Grant, more peevishly than he intended.

John McClernand stood stiffly before him, apparently willing to accept the dressing down with stoicism. Despite the disarray intrinsic to his hair and beard, the man exuded a certain willfulness.

"I did not disobey your orders, sir," he argued. "You ordered the Army of the Mississippi to Milliken's Bend . . ."

"Where I told you to stay put," Grant interjected.

Vigorously shaking his head and all the shagginess that accompanied it, McClernand said, "No, you said I didn't *need* to do anything else. You didn't say I *couldn't*."

Upon arriving at Milliken's Bend on January 4, McClernand had quickly organized an expedition up the Arkansas River, using Porter's gunboats and the "Army of the Mississippi" to attack Arkansas Post, a small settlement sixty miles upstream. Protecting the village and Confederate gunboats employed to disrupt Union operations on the Mississippi River was Fort Hindman. McClernand had taken both the village and the fort with minimal casualties, and would have continued farther into the Arkansas interior had he not been recalled by Grant.

Despite his legendary patience, Grant nearly choked on the bile rising in his throat. Here he was, a month after ordering McClernand to Milliken's Bend, once more chastising the man for insubordination. Despite the stupidity of the expedition, McClernand had succeeded, and had five thousand Confederate prisoners to show for it!

"General McClernand, Arkansas Post is not our proper theater of operations. You have taken your army on a wild goose chase!" he barked.

"I did no such thing, sir," McClernand said with equal, if measured vitriol. "I saw an opportunity to defeat the enemy, and I took it. You cannot argue with the outcome."

In fact, Grant could not argue with the outcome. Five thousand fewer Confederates and one less Confederate fort to deal with were nothing to sneeze at. But he was not about to concede the point. In his mind, McClernand had blatantly pursued a course of action independent of his own command, and that was simply unacceptable. He glanced across the intervening space of his headquarters tent at the three other officers present—Sherman, Porter, and McPherson—the first two of whom had accompanied McClernand on his reckless adventure.

"General Sherman, Admiral Porter, what do you have to say?"

Sherman turned his face away, an unexpectedly sheepish reaction. It was not like him. By contrast, Porter heaved a sigh, braced his hands on the table in front of him, and gazed cryptically at Grant.

"General McClernand was the senior officer. We followed his instructions," he said.

It was a non-answer, and Grant wondered why Porter was choosing circumspection over candor. Like most other officers on Grant's staff, Porter disliked McClernand and considered him incompetent. Even now he could see that Porter was choking down this antipathy, but he could not understand why.

"General Sherman, I'd like to listen to your perspective," Grant said, leaving his friend little wiggle room.

Sherman looked at Grant, then at McPherson, and finally at McClernand. With a pained expression on his face, he rose from his chair and stood directly in front of Grant, his arms crossed in front of his chest. Compared to Grant he was a physically imposing man, but it would not help him in the present circumstances.

"The idea to attack Arkansas Post was mine," he said flatly.

"Sir, that is not accurate," McClernand objected, his eyes widening. "Of course, we discussed the matter . . ."

"Admiral Porter, who proposed the expedition?" Sherman asked, directing his gaze at the Navy man.

But Porter was not anxious to be drawn into what was rapidly degenerating into a rancorous argument. His mouth opened, but no sound emerged.

"Sir!" Sherman insisted.

Porter's sigh of resignation was like a release of repressed flatulence. Without looking Grant directly in the eye, he turned his head and said, "Yes, you thought of it."

"General Grant, I obje . . ." McClernand started to say but was cut off by Sherman.

"I believed it to be a sound military operation," he said, but only to Grant.

Taken aback by the revelation that McClernand had only executed, but not conceived the expedition, Grant was uncertain how to respond. He threw his hands up in desperation.

"What could you have been thinking, Sherman?"

"We took a village, a fort, five thousand prisoners and removed a threat to our flank, when and if we ever attack Vicksburg."

Grant fumed, not only because of the adventure up the Arkansas River but because it had turned out to be, at least partially, Sherman's blunder. It was not nearly as satisfying to fault Sherman, a friend and an officer of demonstrated competence, as it was to blame McClernand. Had the expedition really been a mistake or had he found it so because he'd thought it to be exclusively McClernand's brainchild? It was not a pleasing experience to recognize vanity and prejudice in oneself.

A melancholy silence fell over the room. Only the steady beating of raindrops on the canvas roof and walls could be heard. Grant and Sherman stared at one another, each looking for a way to call a draw.

"General Grant, you called us here to discuss Vicksburg strategy. Perhaps it would be advisable for us to focus on that."

The speaker was James McPherson, and his words were more a plea for reconciliation than a request that they get down to business.

"Yes, that would indeed be advisable," Grant said, making a grand sweep of his arm toward the chairs around the table. "Be seated gentlemen, and I'll get the maps."

*   *   *

The huge map rolled out on the table showed the path of the Mississippi River, with all its treacherous twists, turns, and dead ends, from a point south of Memphis to Port Gibson below Vicksburg. In all, the north-south span of the map was three to four hundred miles. On both the east and west sides of the Mississippi River lay complex, tortuous networks of rivers, creeks, lakes and bayous, all of them, one way or another, tributaries of the Father of Waters. In this extensive marshland, gravity seemed to have lost its influence and water could apparently flow just about anywhere.

Standing with John Rawlins at one end of the table, Grant waited for the others to react to the "plan" he had just presented. At the other end of the table stood Sherman, a puzzled expression on his face and a hand stroking the beard under his chin. McPherson, McClernand, and Porter sat stiffly in their chairs, apparently waiting for someone else to comment, most probably Sherman.

As if to oblige, Sherman stopped stroking his beard and looked up at Grant, his expression shifting from perplexed to doleful.

"Let me try to summarize what you have in mind. You want to dig a canal across De Soto Point in the hope that the river will take a new course south of Vicksburg," he said, pointing to the finger of land opposite Vicksburg on the map. "And you also want to dig a canal from Duckport to an as yet unspecified location on the west bank of the Mississippi below Vicksburg?"

As he spoke, Sherman moved his finger upstream to Duckport and traced an overland path to the vicinity of New Carthage. Though his face had become impassive, a clear note of skepticism crept into his voice.

"While some of us are engaged in these endeavors, others will be excavating a channel from Lake Providence to the Red River, some three hundred fifty miles one way. The return trip, just as long, will mean sailing down the Red to the Mississippi and then north to a landing below Vicksburg."

As he listened to the sardonic timbre of Sherman's voice, Grant was tempted to burst into laughter. His experiments did sound absurd when described by a former academic and intellectual like Sherman. Of course, Grant did not think they were absurd; or rather, he did not think they were *all* absurd. He had absolute confidence that something would work. He just didn't know what it would be.

Strolling to the entranceway, he pulled back the tent flap and gazed searchingly outside.

"Sherman, we have to give the men something to do. We can't just let them sit in their waterlogged tents waiting for the river to rise and flood them out. This rainfall is ridiculous. Do you remember what the New York Times said?"

It was McPherson who responded with, "I believe their words were: 'Grant remains stuck in the mud of Northern Mississippi, his army of no use to him or anybody else.'"

"We could return to Memphis and plan another campaign for the fall," McClernand asserted.

"No, General, we will not do that!" Grant exclaimed, striding forcefully back and placing himself directly in front of McClernand. "That would be interpreted as a defeat, and I will not have it."

It was another dressing down, albeit a mild one. McClernand looked for support from the officers in the room; any officer would do. But none was forthcoming, and he had to turn his face away, the bitterness of his disposition evident in the lines of his face. His favorite expletive, "Damned West Pointers," cycled through his mind.

"Then there's the *Yazoo Pass*," Sherman announced, still reviewing the experiments Grant had conceived for his troops. His voice was loud enough to break the ice of the Grant/McClernand confrontation. "I must admit I do not fully understand this one. You want to connect the Mississippi and Yazoo Rivers somewhere north of here?"

"No, no, I want to reconnect the rivers. All we have to do is blow up an old levee, and it will happen by itself," Grant said, moving his pointing finger to a spot well upstream of Vicksburg. "This is the Yazoo Pass, or was so-called before the levee was built. If we remove the levee, the Mississippi will flow into the Coldwater, the Coldwater into the Tallahatchie, and the Tallahatchie into the Yazoo. We can send troops downstream and land them north of Vicksburg."

Sherman, who had come over for a better view of the Yazoo Pass logistics, said flatly, "That's over three hundred miles through bugs, swamps, and in all probability, Rebel soldiers. Besides, I've been to the Yazoo once, and I didn't like it."

"Then you can dig the canal across De Soto Point. Admiral Porter, would *you* like to try out the Yazoo Pass route with some of your boats?"

As much as it sounded like a request, it was, in fact, an order. But Grant preferred to soften his command presence when dealing with members of the sister service.

"Yes, of course," Porter replied, standing so that he could get a birds-eye view of the map. He did not sound as if he relished the prospect of inserting a fleet of gunboats into a maze of waterways that may or may not be deep enough and wide enough to accommodate them. He looked up and added, "But we'll have to be very selective. Only boats with shallow drafts. I don't want to get stuck while Rebel cannons tear us to pieces."

Grant nodded while Sherman suppressed a snicker. McClernand turned his head for fear of revealing the contempt on his face, and McPherson braced his elbows on the table, resting his inscrutable face between his palms.

"General McPherson, that leaves you and your corps the responsibility of digging out the channel between Lake Providence and the Red River," Grant said, with something approaching nonchalance.

If McPherson's expression could have defined itself in sound, it would have been a deep, persistent groan. He looked up at Grant, his head popping up from his hands, his gaze a plea for mercy.

"Yes, sir," he replied, his natural stoicism reasserting itself.

"General Grant, what task do you have for me?" McClernand suddenly demanded.

Sherman, Porter, McPherson, and Rawlins were shocked nearly into disbelief. McClernand was actually asking to be involved in one of Grant's bizarre schemes. The man was truly a god-awful fool. Surreptitiously, they glanced at one another, suppressing the urge to grin like Cheshire cats.

"Sir, there will be plenty for you and . . . the Army of the Mississippi . . . to do," Grant said in a more ingratiating tone than he normally used with McClernand. He motioned for McClernand to follow him outside and added, "Come with me to the commissary where we can have a bite to eat . . ."

"But it's raining cats and dogs," McClernand said, tentatively rising to his feet.

"Yes, it is, and that's one of our major problems. We're going to need your men to build some levees on De Soto Point so that General Sherman's men can dig the canal without being flooded out . . ."

Talking all the while, Grant directed his only enthusiastic volunteer for the De Soto Point canal experiment into the pouring rain. The four remaining officers congregated around Sherman, who presumably understood their commander better than they did. Both humor and perplexity filled their faces. It was McPherson, the most perplexed, who spoke first.

"I really don't understand. Why can't we return to Memphis and come back in the fall, like McClernand says? God knows I despise the man, but he may be right this time. It doesn't have to be painted as a defeat."

Sherman's eyebrows lifted at his young friend's naïveté.

"It may or may not be perceived as a defeat, but that doesn't matter," he said.

Sherman pulled out a cigar and, placing one foot on a chair so he could rest an elbow on one knee, fired it up. McPherson lost his patience.

"What *does* matter then, if victory doesn't?"

Scowling as if in pain, Sherman blew a smoke ring and glanced at his other two companions. He was satisfied they knew his mind.

Turning his attention back to McPherson, he said, "Think about it, Jim. What happens if we go back to Memphis?"

"We get a well-deserved rest."

"No, no, no," Sherman moaned, then gazed directly into McPherson's eyes. "What happens is that we are once more in direct telegraphic communication with Washington."

"What's wrong with that?"

For a moment, Sherman could only stare at his colleague, his teeth digging into the fuming cigar.

"Do you remember when Old Brains was in charge?"

"Yes."

"And do you remember how long it took him to march us the twenty miles from Pittsburg Landing to Corinth?"

McPherson meditated, then said, "A month . . . or thereabouts."

"Right. Not exactly an invincible army on the move, I think you'd agree. Now, can you tell me who gave our good friend General McClernand the sanction to raise his own army and attack Vicksburg?"

"President Lincoln."

Sherman shook his head and said, "Who persuaded Lincoln?"

"Stanton?"

"Yes, of course," Sherman sighed, confident he was finally getting through. "Now here's my final question. Once we are in direct communication with Washington and, naturally, once again in touch with Old Brains and Secretary Stanton, what do you think they are going to present us with?"

McPherson finally caught on and grinned ear to ear, his precisely trimmed beard rippling like a wave across his face.

"Orders!"

"Exactly," Sherman confirmed, giving his young colleague a hefty slap on the back. "And we don't need those, do we?"

"No," said Porter.

"No," McPherson agreed, his fleeting encounter with euphoria quickly vanishing.

Only Rawlins was uncertain. He lifted his hands in searching supplication, his face a study in confusion.

"But we have to follow orders from Washington, don't we?"

Sherman stepped toward Rawlins, sucked on his cigar, then turned his back and strolled a few paces toward the entranceway.

"We will not disobey orders from Washington, John," He said, tossing an over the shoulder glance at Rawlins. "But we will do everything in our power not to receive them."

"And if that means biding our time with every blasted experiment General Grant comes up with, so be it," Porter declared.

"Hear, hear," McPherson declared.

As low man on the totem pole—a mere adjutant general—Rawlins was not sure he wanted anything to do with something that had all the earmarks of a conspiracy, albeit a relatively benign one. He was only thirty-two years old but had been around long enough to know that the vast majority of officers, except for those who had received their commissions by political appointment, abhorred orders from Washington. The distances were too great and the turnaround times too long for the tactical situation in the field to be properly understood by anyone in Washington.

Straightening his posture and his demeanor, Rawlins said, "Admiral Porter, I think it's high time you honed your cursing skills."

"What's that?" the puzzled Navy man replied.

"I believe, sir, you meant to say 'biding our time with every *damned* experiment General Grant comes up with.'"

The final conspirator had been recruited.

★ TWELVE ★

February 2, 1863, Young's Point, Louisiana

Standing atop a levee protecting the worker's encampments from the rising Mississippi floodwaters, Sherman and McClernand inspected the canal that had been dug by Brigadier General Thomas Williams in the spring of 1862. Digging had ceased in July of that year because of the toll taken on the workers by the summer heat, and because the Mississippi had then been at a low ebb. That was not the situation now. The persistent rainfall was raising the water level in the canal at an alarming rate.

"So, this is Williams' ditch!" McClernand commented.

Sherman knew his colleague was making a casual comment, but he had discovered that his personal dislike for the man sometimes colored his reactions to him. Nevertheless, he managed to swallow his irritation.

"Yes, and a creditable job it is, don't you agree?"

Stiffly, McClernand replied, "Of course, of course."

It was a spectacular sight. The church spires and industrial haze of Vicksburg could be seen across the downstream end of the river that enveloped De Soto Point. Docked along the bank of the upstream end at Young's Point was the massive fleet of transports that had brought Sherman's XV Corps and McClernand's XIII Corps to De Soto Point. Thousands of men were traipsing through the Mississippi mud and searching for, but seldom finding, dry spots where they might catch a comfortable respite. Shielded by levees that surrounded the northeast bank of Williams' ditch, the camps were momentarily safe from rising floodwaters, but not from the rain. It was the primary ingredient in the foot deep soup that covered every acre of ground on the narrow sliver of land.

"My God, look at that!" McClernand cried.

Sherman turned to observe the object of McClernand's entreaty. As he did, the puddle of water accumulating in one corner of his slouch hat gushed over the brim and onto his nose.

"Sonofab . . ." he muttered, grabbing the hat and whacking it against his thigh. When he was satisfied the hat was dry—at least for the moment—he looked westward to where McClernand was pointing and saw it.

"I'll be damned!" he declared.

"What is it?" McClernand wanted to know.

"I've heard of them but never seen one," Sherman said. "It's a dipper dredge. Steam-powered. It'll dig as much dirt in a day as a hundred men."

The thing they were looking at was being maneuvered toward the canal entrance by port and starboard ropes held by two trains of men onshore. It looked like a two-story houseboat that had somehow grown a crab-like appendage on its front end. The "dipper" was essentially a large bucket. It was supported by a truss attached to the prow of the barge on which the "house" rested, and was controlled by a long arm that allowed the operators to manipulate the dipper remotely

"What will they think of next?" McClernand swooned.

"Probably a lot of strange devices, if this war lasts long enough," Sherman predicted.

As he spoke, the team of men on the starboard rope flung it over their shoulders and struggled to prevent the dipper dredge from drifting downstream with the current, while the port side team pulled it toward shore.

"Not exactly a seaworthy craft," McClernand said, then added with some dismay, "They're docking it in front of the canal entrance."

"Think about it, John," Sherman quipped with a grin. "That's where we will be digging first."

Before McClernand could reply, the sound of a cannon burst from Vicksburg reached their ears. Sherman and McClernand immediately turned their heads toward the sound and saw the remnants of a smoke ring lazily spinning away from one of the batteries south of the city. A fraction of a second later, the familiar drone of a cannonball in flight filled the air, to be followed by an impact and an explosion well to the northeast of the canal and the nearby workers' encampment. The blast sent mud and water skyward but did no damage to men or materiel.

"I suppose they'll be doing that all day," McClernand offered.

"Maybe, just to pester us. But the upstream end of the canal is out of their range. They'll do a lot more damage when we get close to the other end of the big bend."

"The dipper dredge?"

"That's what I'd shoot at," Sherman replied. "We've got a few more coming if that one gets put out of action."

McClernand nodded and took off his hat to whack it dry, as Sherman had done. The intensity of the downpour was increasing. Replacing the hat on his saturated scalp, he gave Sherman a skeptical glance and said, "As impressive as it is, that thing doesn't look big enough to dig a canal as deep and as wide as transports will need to make it through. Do you think it's really possible?"

Sherman watched the scene where the Mississippi and the two trains of men were engaged in a tug of war. Two teams of mules had also been enlisted to assist in the operation. It was touch and go.

"The theory is that all we have to do is get a trickle of water flowing through the canal and erosion will do the rest; scour it out, so to speak. Once that happens, it won't be long before we've got us a raging river. It might even drain the water from the big bend and leave Vicksburg high and dry."

"Whose theory is that?

"It's the joint inspiration of Admiral David Farragut and General Benjamin Butler."

"Are they here?"

"Not anymore. They left with General Williams."

Before McClernand could respond, a rider left the scene of the dipper dredge struggle and climbed to the top of the levee, steering his horse toward the two men.

"Who's that?" McClernand asked.

"One of Grant's aides. He's overseeing the digging operation."

It was less than a minute before Colonel George Pride brought his horse to a halt, dismounted, and marched for the two generals. He was a young man with a handlebar mustache and a flat, sloped forehead. His walk gave the illusion of a swagger but was really a consequence of hips that were disproportionately large and swayed with an effeminate rhythm. He removed his hat, saluted, shook the hat dry, and quickly returned it to his head. On a day like this, all officers wore slouch hats; they were quite effective as umbrellas.

Snapping to attention, Pride said, "Sir, Captain Prime plans to move the entrance two hundred yards upstream."

Captain Frederick E. Prime of the Army Corps of Engineers was in charge of the De Soto Point canal dig.

"Why?" Sherman inquired.

Pride made a half turn and answered, "There's an eddy causing all kinds of difficulties."

Sherman nodded. The Mississippi River was notorious for its "eddies;" suck-holes that disrupted river traffic and frequently sent swimmers and occupants of small crafts to early, watery graves.

"Is that the reason for the trouble over there?" McClernand asked, indicating the on-going tug-of-war with the dipper dredge.

"Yes, sir," Pride acknowledged.

"Is Grant aware of the change?" Sherman asked.

"Yes, sir."

"Then by all means get to it."

Pride hesitated, pulled in a breath and said, "Captain Prime also wants to dam up the two ends of the canal so it can be drained. It will be easier to dredge when it's dry."

The officers walked to the edge of the levee and gazed down into Williams' ditch. A large but nearly stagnant pool of water lay in it. The movement of the water was not enough to cause even a ripple.

"The water is not running fast enough to scour out the canal, but it's deep enough to keep men from digging it out with picks and shovels," Pride explained.

"Why not bring in the dipper dredge?" Sherman inquired.

Pride shrugged and said, "The dredge is on a barge. To get it in here, the water level in the canal has to be high enough to float it . . ."

Sherman groaned, appreciating the problem.

"So we have the perfect tool to dig a deep-water trench if only we had a deep-water trench to float it in with."

"That's about it," Pride said. "Besides, we need the dipper dredge to dig the new entrance."

"Can this really be called a *military* operation?" McClernand said, revealing the consternation he felt at having to participate in what he considered to be another of Grant's frivolous schemes. The Confederates chose this moment to launch another cannonball from the nearest Vicksburg battery. This one managed to make it into Williams' ditch several hundred yards to the east of where the three men stood. The explosion sent gobs of mud in all directions and left a soggy crater ten feet in diameter.

"I'd say the occasional cannonball makes it a military operation, wouldn't you, John?" Sherman noted.

McClernand acknowledged him with a terse "Harumph!"

Playing to Sherman's quip, Pride said, "Hey, if we could get the Rebs to move those guns a little closer, maybe they'd blast out the canal for us."

Sherman chuckled. McClernand discharged another "Harumph!" and drifted to the other side of the levee to watch for cannon smoke.

With a sly wink at his subordinate, Sherman said, "No sense of humor."

But Colonel Pride decided he had already stuck his neck out too far and was reluctant to trade witticisms with one superior officer at the expense of another.

"Sir, I should get back now," he announced.

Regretting the loss but understanding the Colonel's position, Sherman returned the salute and said, "Of course, Colonel. Good luck in all your endeavors, and give my best wishes to Captain Prime as well."

The combination of a smile topped by a handlebar mustache somehow gave Pride a porcine look, but it was pleasant enough. A moment later, he was well into his return jaunt.

Sherman gazed thoughtfully into the canal, wondering how much deeper and wider it would have to become for a decent current to establish itself. He imagined a dam at either end and could not help but dwell on the mental picture of the huge excavation that would transpire. It left him deeply apprehensive. This far south, the Mississippi was not a well-behaved stream; the adjacent land was not far enough above sea level. This, coupled with the drain-off from the Rockies to the west and the Appalachians to the east, could fill the river to overflowing in a geological instant. If that happened, Williams' ditch would fill up, and even the encampments would be threatened.

Sherman shifted his gaze to the segment of the turbulent Mississippi to the west of him. Removing his slouch hat, he rolled his eyes heavenward, let the rain wash over his face and, as if praying to God, muttered, "Grant, I hope you are a genius and not a damned fool."

February 10, 1863, Lake Providence, Louisiana

Despite the fact that the two junior officers were doing all the rowing, General James McPherson didn't feel comfortable on this reconnaissance. "Lake" Providence was not really a lake at all, but a residual puddle that had once been part of the Mississippi River. The fickle river had abandoned the bend that was now Lake Providence in favor of another track in which to romp southward to the Gulf of Mexico. McPherson needed the reconnaissance to assure himself that the parallel path proposed by General Grant was indeed open.

"Sir, there's the levee," the forward rower proclaimed, pointing to the tall mound of dirt and vegetation along the eastern shore.

"I see it."

McPherson was both the commander and the engineering officer of the Lake Providence experiment, the object of which was to find a water path parallel to the Mississippi that was deep enough to float transports. It was fitting that he should have the dual role since he had graduated in engineering from West Point in 1853 near the top of his class. Subsequent positions as West Point engineering instructor, various harbor projects, and serving as chief engineer on Grant's staff had assured his rapid promotion. With this project, however, his enthusiasm had faltered.

"Sir, I think that may be the entrance to Bayou Baxter over there," the aft rower said, pointing west.

With the continuing rainfall, McPherson could not make out what his junior officer was pointing to, but he trusted the man and waved the rowboat flotilla forward. In each of the crafts were men and equipment that would allow them to cut their way through whatever vegetation blocked their path. At least, that was the plan.

One of the rowboats was under the command of a bespectacled sergeant somewhere in his middle age by the name of Amos Gaston. Standing in the middle of his craft, between the standard pair of oarsmen, Gaston looked like a stunted crab tree whose limbs, by some perversion of nature, had been forced to project farther from his trunk than normal. This resulted in a bow-legged posture and elbows whose elevation was not much below his shoulders. Gaston managed to be the first to approach McPherson.

"Are we there, sir?" Gaston's gravelly voice rasped.

McPherson, who had been sitting, stood to get a better view.

"I think so," he ventured uncertainly.

"It's right there, sir," the aft oarsmen offered, pointing to the vague outline of a bay nestled between two clumps of cypress trees.

Shading his eyes from the midday sun, Gaston said, "It sure don't look like much."

"It may not look like much, and it may not be *enough*. That's what we're here to find out."

Gaston's lazily shaking head and skeptical squint betrayed his opinion.

"General Grant's idea, sir?"

"Yes, Sergeant. It's General Grant's idea and his ideas are usually pretty good, don't you think?" McPherson said a little testily.

Gaston was not about to express disagreement, though his sentiments were obvious.

"Yes, sir, they truly are . . . usually," he murmured. "Would you mind tellin' me again how this is supposed to work?"

McPherson directed his oarsmen to row into the apparent opening between the cypresses. Then, despite his irritation, he decided patience was the watchword and turned back to Gaston.

"I admit, the route is a complicated one, and long . . . nearly five hundred miles. It starts here at Lake Providence, enters Bayou Baxter, then Bayou Macon and the Tensas River. The Tensas flows into the Ouachita, which becomes the Black and, in turn, flows into the Red and finally to the Mississippi just above Port Hudson. Then we take the Mississippi back north to Vicksburg."

Gaston's whiskered visage fixed on McPherson. Finally, he said, "Yup, it is complicated. I got no idea where half those bayous and rivers are, but even I can see it's complicated. Circ . . . circ . . ."

McPherson's aft oarsman helped Gaston find the word he was searching for.

"*Circuitous*, Amos."

Offering a curt bow to the officer, Gaston said, "That's right. I thank you, sir. Cir-cu-it-ous! That's surely what it is."

Gaston eyed McPherson as if seeking approval.

"It is definitely that . . . circuitous," McPherson concurred. And by God it was! Two hundred fifty miles south, then two hundred fifty miles back, just to land troops below Vicksburg.

"But there's still one thing puzzles me," Gaston continued. Like the rest of the rowboat fleet, his had entered the small bay and stopped. His narrow green eyes remained fixed on McPherson, as the eyes of everyone else remained fixed on him.

"What's that, Sergeant?" McPherson inquired indulgently.

"How in the blazes are gunboats and transports gonna get in here? There ain't no water connection to the Mississippi."

McPherson pointed eastward to where the top of the levee they had passed was barely visible between infrequent breaks in the thriving vegetation.

"We'll cut through the levee."

"With what, shovels?"

"Mostly, but we'll probably use explosives too, and some digging machines we've brought," he said, thinking of the dipper dredges he'd heard about. "Any more questions?"

The last was proffered harshly. McPherson was getting tired of answering Gaston's questions.

"Oh . . . no, sir," the sergeant replied, clumsily seating himself.

McPherson took a long look at the assembled fleet of rowboats and then took another long look at the Bayou Baxter inlet. Although stumps, vegetation, and debris poked through or littered its surface, the bayou appeared to be marginally negotiable. Noting the sun's position—it was nearing midafternoon—he shifted his gaze to his makeshift navy. They did not look very soldierly in their heavy boots, leather gloves, thick outer garments, and red woolen underwear, which managed to show through in sundry places. They were dressed for hard labor.

"Lieutenant Sherbine, would you please make your way over here?" McPherson called to an officer three rowboat hulls distant.

The officer, Lieutenant Carl Sherbine, acknowledged the order and directed his men to row toward McPherson. A squat, hulking man of thirty-five, Sherbine was ill at ease standing in a rowboat, so he knelt instead. It was from this position that he saluted McPherson.

"Excuse me, sir, I'm a little unsteady in this thing," he said, gripping the cross-board on which he was kneeling.

"It's all right, Lieutenant. I want you to do something for me."

"What's that, sir?" Sherbine asked shakily, clearly wishing for orders that did not require nautical expertise.

"I want you to take five rowboats and penetrate into Bayou Baxter a mile or two. Take about a third of the saws and other cutting equipment with you. If the bayou doesn't get clear of all this . . . hard scrabble within a few miles, put the saws to it. I want to know if clearing a path is feasible. I don't want to be hacking away at vegetation all the way to Port Hudson."

Somewhat sheepishly, Sherbine picked his five rowboats, counted off the requisite number of saws and, from a seated position, led his squadron into Bayou Baxter. McPherson waited until they had disappeared around a bend in the bayou before addressing the remainder of his command.

"Gentlemen, you will need to get as many saws into action as are available. Those of you who do not have saws will assist by pulling and yanking and doing whatever is necessary to rid this damn stream of its damnable vegetation. Sergeant Gaston!"

Having resigned himself to obscurity, Gaston was surprised to hear his name. "Yes, sir," he chirped, struggling to elevate himself to attention.

"Sergeant, I want you and ten men to get yourselves into the water and do the same thing I told Lieutenant Sherbine to do— clear a path. Use the saws, use whatever axes and hatchets we've got, and your bare hands if need be."

"But, sir, it might be over our heads."

"That would be better. It would mean you don't have to clear as much away. You can swim, can't you? You're a soldier."

"Yes, sir, I can, but I never tried to swim with a saw in one hand."

McPherson snickered, trying to maintain a calm, relaxed atmosphere.

"You don't have to swim. If the water is deep, just hold your breath, submerge, and cut your way through anything that presents itself, rowboats excepted. When you need a breath, come up and get one, then start over again."

It did not sound as straightforward to Gaston as McPherson was describing it. He was not anxious to immerse himself in a stagnant pool of water with God-knew-what kinds of creatures, great and small. But . . . it was his duty. Along with ten others selected by McPherson on an undefined basis, Gaston stepped overboard into the water, expecting any moment to be swallowed by an alligator, bitten by a water moccasin, or at least attacked by a school of small, carnivorous fish. His pained expression and taut muscularity said it all; he was not happy to be there. At least half of the remaining ten appeared equally reticent. The rest were showing no signs of displeasure, but had stoically accepted their lot and simply wanted to get it over with. Silently, the amphibious members of the expedition lined up alongside the rowboats to receive their equipment. Saws, axes, and assorted dislodging devices were hastily, almost eagerly handed over by those left on board.

Wielding a saw, Gaston gazed pleadingly at McPherson and said, "Where to, sir? Any particular place?"

Seated but hardly comfortable, McPherson pointed to a copse of twisted branches breaking the surface of the water between the rowboat fleet and Bayou Baxter.

"Over there."

Looking as if he wanted to groan, Gaston directed his squadron of stump-sweepers toward the objective identified by their commander and spread out Indian fashion to attack the foe. The water was not over their heads but was up to the armpits of some and the necks of others. Sergeant Gaston and two other men tried the submerging tactic proposed by McPherson. After staying underwater for more than a minute, their heads popped sequentially to the surface, but the enemy remained steadfastly in place. After two more tries, a barrel-chested private named Nicolas Meyer emerged with a bouquet of naked branches in his raised hand. A raucous cheer burst from the amphibians, which was echoed by another from the rowboats when those aboard realized what had happened. McPherson, however, was not impressed.

"Mr. Meyer, how deep is your cut?" he asked.

Meyer's smile did not vanish but was adjusted to a less buoyant magnitude.

"About halfway, sir."

"That won't do," McPherson said, shaking his head. "We've got to have enough draft for the transports. Can you cut it closer to the bottom? That wood will make mincemeat of the boat hulls if we don't get it all."

Grudgingly, those in the water went back to work while McPherson sat and perused what he was coming to view as a predicament. He thought the Mississippi to be a sad excuse for a river and its tributaries to be even sadder. The river was too big and cumbersome. Like the proverbial bull in a china shop, you never knew what it was going to do. A period of heavy rainfall could overflow its banks and spread devastation for miles on either side. The Ohio River, with which McPherson had some familiarity, being a citizen of the state with the same name, did not do that. Its banks and the land adjacent to them were steep enough to contain most floodwaters, except for those who built their homes in the lowlands near tributary rivers and creeks. Even the Ohio's tributaries were to be preferred over the stagnant, turbid bayous branching off the Mississippi. The soft, marshy ground and the intermittent explosions of vegetation made the rare patches of bayou land both uninhabitable and impossible to navigate.

Which is what McPherson anticipated was fast becoming an accurate description of Bayou Baxter.

After an hour, the workers had detached enough scrub and snags from Old Lady River's womb to create what looked like a bonfire in preparation. Except for a fifteen-foot arc in front of the fleet, the inlet to Bayou Baxter was still the same morass it had been upon their arrival.

"Sergeant Gaston, Mr. Meyer, where are you?" McPherson called.

A soldier in a rowboat to McPherson's left pointed at the water surface, then reached beneath it and grabbed Gaston by the hair.

"Ow, what are you . . ." Gaston squealed as his head poked out of the water. The soldier whispered something and pointed to McPherson. Gaston stood as straight as the irregular bed of the bayou would permit and said, "Yes, sir!"

"Sergeant, gather your men in and come over here. Bring your . . . harvest with you."

Barking commands and disrupting the underwater forays of several men, Gaston eventually brought the ten into port clutching their prizes. McPherson stood and reached out to touch one of the scraggly wood offerings from the deep.

"I don't think that wood will burn well," he said, fingering its surface. "Too wet."

Gazing out over his command, McPherson heaved a sigh and said, "Well, gentlemen, what do you think?"

At first, no one said anything. Then a voice from the rear piped up and said, "Place is like a damn South American jungle!"

"How do you know what a South American jungle is like?" a skeptic scoffed. This was followed by snickers of laughter.

"I'll tell you what I think," McPherson said, then paused for effect and glanced sharply toward Bayou Baxter. "I think Lieutenant Sherbine is back."

All eyes quickly refocused on the returnees, who, with their backs to the soon-to-be-setting-sun, looked like expatriates from some netherworld. Sherbine looked no more comfortable than when he'd left, although he had managed to raise himself beyond his departing squat. Half the men appeared exhausted; the other half were soaked *and* exhausted. The oarsmen, made up of members of the drier contingent, rowed without enthusiasm. It took Sherbine's squadron ten minutes to reach their nautical brethren with his boat in the lead. Somehow, the lieutenant managed to lift himself to his full height and salute.

"Sir," Sherbine said wearily.

A full minute passed before either man spoke again.

"Sir, I don't think it's a good idea," Sherbine finally offered.

"You don't think *what* is a good idea?"

"Cutting our way through this damned swamp," the lieutenant said, accompanying the statement with a sweeping gesture toward Bayou Baxter.

"We've more or less come to the same conclusion," McPherson said flatly.

For this, Sherbine was unprepared, unaccustomed to the luxury of an agreeable superior officer. Before he could respond, McPherson asked, "What did you find out there?"

"Uh, well, as far as we could tell, Bayou Baxter is a long, long cypress brake with not much of a channel, if any. We tried clearing the stumps and trash out of the water, but there was so much of it . . ."

Sherbine went on to describe unpleasant experiences similar to those of the men who had stayed behind. McPherson nodded in a manner both grave and oddly cheerful. When Sherbine finished, McPherson called for silence and said, "Gentlemen, I believe we are finished here. I will inform General Grant that we have explored the proposed Lake Providence route and found it to be impossibly congested and unsuitable as a means for getting below Vicksburg . . ."

A cheer rose from the assembly. In the absence of fireworks, the various fragments of wooded harvest were lofted skyward, several clobbering unprotected heads on descent.

"However, I believe General Grant will probably want us to continue here for a while . . ."

Groans and murmurs. McPherson's lips curled up into a grin as he added, ". . . to make certain of our findings. We have at least a week to go on this expedition, and I am certainly not enthusiastic about chopping away at any more cypress roots than we have to."

Faces contorted in puzzlement. These were not the words of an officer bent on making their lives miserable. McPherson noted their perplexity and tried to keep his grin from widening.

"Can we go fishin'?" an unidentified voice asked.

The thought of such relaxation was absurd.

"I see no reason why not," McPherson said. "As long as we do what the general expects."

"What's the general expect?"

The query originated from one of the rear boats.

"Why, General Grant expects us to explore every possibility," McPherson answered, his tongue lodged firmly in his cheek.

"What if there ain't none?"

McPherson appeared to think about this, massaging his chin in thoughtful silence. Then he said, "I suppose we'll have to think of something. Any ideas?"

There was a salvo of crisp, sometimes profane exclamations.

"Sir, I seen a plantation house a ways back," spouted a sandy-haired youth with a fierce concentration of freckles on his nose. "By the lake, I mean. Can we go back there and see what's inside, like maybe whisky?"

McPherson gazed at the lad in shock. The boy didn't look old enough to have a craving for whisky. He wasn't sure he should encourage such behavior.

"Or maybe, just wine?" the boy stuttered, correctly reading his commander's concern.

"Certainly, why not?" McPherson said, happy to accept the compromise.

Their commander's apparently favorable disposition loosened the tongues and fired the imaginations of his men.

"Hey, can we take another ride on that steamboat that brought us?"

"How about we take a dip off the dock of that plantation house?"

McPherson could not understand why men who had spent an entire day muddying themselves in a bayou would want to spend any more time than necessary immersing themselves further. Maybe they just waned to get clean again.

As the levity became more intense and disorderly, McPherson decided to leave rather than risk putting a crimp in the party atmosphere. He sat down in the rowboat and said to his oarsmen, "Let's go back to the towboat. I have a few things to do."

The towboat had been "horsed" overland to Lake Providence and was serving as McPherson's base of operations. While the turbid waters of the lake passed by, he considered how the day's activities might be reported in a way that would indicate the improbability of success without completely closing off the possibility.

"Sir, could I ask you a question?" the rear oarsman asked. McPherson knew him only as Karl.

"Certainly, Karl.

"Did the general really expect us to find a way through all those rivers and creeks and bayous you talked about? Is he . . ."

Karl seemed unable to complete his query.

"Crazy?" McPherson finished sardonically. "No, he's not crazy, he's shrewd."

"How so?"

McPherson meditated briefly, then replied, "Well, for one thing, it might have worked. You never know about these things. Do you hunt turkey or grouse?"

"When I can."

"Shot or musket balls?"

"Shot, a' course. Can't hit a flyin' turkey with a musket ball. Can't shoot with that kind of accuracy. Shot puts a lot of deadlies around the turkey all at once. Don't need to be real accurate."

"That's what the general is doing: putting a lot of deadlies in the air all at once. Maybe one will nick the tail feathers of that lovely bird we call Vicksburg and bring her down. Then we can have her for supper."

Karl concentrated on rowing for a few strokes, then said, "That's a mighty high-flyin' chunk a' lead that finds its way two hundred and fifty miles to the Red River and back again."

McPherson laughed, pulled out three cigars from the breast pocket of his coat and handed two of them to his companions. The boat halted while all cigars were lit up. With renewed vigor, the oarsmen dug in and propelled the rowboat forward, a miniature steamboat with three smokestacks.

"You're right, Karl, Lake Providence to the Red River probably never was a likely candidate, but it'll keep us busy."

"Why do we need somethin' to keep us busy?"

Too late, McPherson realized he had spoken carelessly. "I don't mean to say we have to *find* a way to keep us busy. We *are* busy. But even if we weren't busy, we'd have to do something just to maintain discipline."

Karl looked skeptically at McPherson, but nodded his head and appeared to accept the argument.

"What's the rest of the army doin' to keep busy, sir?"

After blowing a smoke ring, McPherson said, "Oh, you'll be glad to hear we've got one of the easier missions. We just convinced ourselves the route we were assigned to look at won't work. That's a lot more than the other missions can say."

"Where are they, sir?"

"Well, there are a couple of canals being dug, one across De Soto Point, to land troops below Vicksburg."

Karl was silent, looking grim, and might have been wondering about how much work would be involved in digging a canal wide enough and deep enough to allow the passage of troop transports.

"That would be General Sherman. Then there's the Duckport Canal . . ."

"Duckport, where's that?" Karl inquired.

"Louisiana. Upstream of Vicksburg, on the other side of the big bend in the river."

"Where's the canal gonna go?"

"It'll connect with Walnut Bayou and then to New Carthage—also in Louisiana but below Vicksburg—before dumping into the Mississippi."

The towboat was in sight now, moored by towrope to a stake that had been driven into the alluvial mud. The horses were well back from the shore on long tethers, munching on the abundant grass. Karl and his aft cohort unconsciously picked up the pace. The rowboat surged forward. When they were within ten feet of their objective, Karl stepped into the lake and pulled its bow ashore. McPherson and the rear oarsman then disembarked.

"Where else, sir?"

"What?"

"Where else?" Karl asked, helping his fellow oarsman drag the rowboat farther onto the beach. "What other expeditions has the general got up his sleeve?"

"Karl, why are you asking all these questions? I swear, I'm tempted to believe you may be a Rebel spy."

Karl was suddenly embarrassed that he'd bothered his commanding officer with questions that shouldn't concern him. His fleshy white face turned a lively pink.

"I'm sorry, sir, I didn't . . ."

"He's just nosy, sir," the other oarsman cut in. McPherson remembered that his name was Vincent, and he was a sergeant. Vincent grinned through teeth so severely gapped they could have been used to comb hair. Then he patted Karl on the back, and added, "Nosiest sonofabitch I ever knowed."

McPherson smiled too, wondering whether he should be amused or annoyed by Karl's persistence.

"Well, there's one foray that's already started about three hundred miles upriver."

"Three hundred miles!" Karl and Vincent exclaimed simultaneously, glancing at each other in astonishment. Karl added, "That's further than ours is . . . was."

"It is," McPherson acknowledged, stepping aboard the towboat and heading for the box at the aft end of the towboat containing his papers and writing tools. "As I just said, it's already underway. The idea is to connect the Mississippi and the Yazoo at a point where the two rivers are only ten miles apart."

"By doing what, sir?" asked the sergeant, revealing his own curiosity. "Digging another canal?"

Pulling a nearby bench closer to a desk adjacent to the storage box, McPherson seated himself. Removing his hardly soiled gloves, he said, "No, by blowing up a hundred foot levee on the Mississippi."

"When's that gonna happen?" Karl asked.

"I believe the deed is already done."

"Will it work?" was Vincent's next question.

Anxious to get to work on his Lake Providence report, McPherson gazed at his two subordinates with tolerant impatience.

"I have no idea, but you boys should be glad you're here and not there. As I understand it, the place is swarming with Johnny Rebs."

Karl and Vincent got the message and nodded to indicate their silence would be coming soon. Karl did have a final question.

"Sir, one last thing. This expedition; does it have a name?"

"It's called the Yazoo Pass Expedition," McPherson replied, then turned his attention to the daunting paperwork before him.

★ THIRTEEN ★

February 24, 1863, Junction of the Tallahatchie and Yalobusha Rivers, Mississippi

The Yazoo Pass Expedition was starting to fray the nerves of Lieutenant Commander Watson Smith. He was a Navy man. When he gazed out over the decks of his gunboat, he wanted to see a calm ocean, or, at worst, an ocean with enemy ships scattered sparsely across its surface. Instead, he found himself surrounded by a jungle of cypress and willow trees, tangled vines, narrow straits, high banks, and Confederate soldiers trying to block the passage of his ten-boat flotilla by felling trees in its path.

"Gunnery-Sergeant, what is that ahead of us?" he asked Kyle MacAdam, who was a much more imposing physical specimen than Smith. "It looks like a boat."

MacAdam moved to the bow of the command gunboat and stretched his neck for a better view. Smith ordered a reduction in speed while MacAdam evaluated the obstacle. Except for the licking of waves against the gunboat's hull, all was silent.

"It's a sunken ship, sir," MacAdam reported. "We can't get past."

"How far are we from Fort Pemberton?"

Smith did not intend the question specifically for MacAdam, but the gunnery sergeant answered anyway.

"Fort Pemberton will be a few miles downstream on the starboard side. After we pass the mouth of the Yalobusha on the port side, Greenwood is the next village."

Smith was not sure what to do. On the open sea, he could have taken a wide swath around the two Confederate threats, but here the ocean was little more than a figment of his imagination. What he needed was an army.

"Is there no possibility of going around her?" he inquired desperately.

MacAdam offered a cursory grunt and shook his head, reflecting Smith's dour mood. Dutifully, his eyes scanned the river, searching for a channel. Then his posture became suddenly rigid.

"Sir, it's the *Star of the West!*" he exclaimed.

Smith and all hands aboard the gunboat were momentarily shocked into silence. The *Star of the West* was the first Union ship to attempt the relief of Fort Sumter at the war's genesis. She had failed in that mission and been eventually captured by the Rebels in the Gulf of Mexico. Smith did not know the full story but suspected the *Star of the West* had been chased up the Mississippi and then up the Yazoo by Admiral David Farragut along with a goodly number of other Confederate craft. Now here she was, battered and rotting in a southern swamp; a sad end for a noble vessel. Smith could not help wondering if he was destined to suffer a similar fate.

The crewmembers were emerging from their reverie when the scream of an artillery shell stunned them back into silence. The roar of the beast was evident only after it passed over the bow of the command boat and smashed into the *Chillicothe*, the ironclad leading the flotilla. A second shell followed and once more found the *Chillicothe*. The explosive one-two punch knocked out the ironclad's gun turrets and set it afire.

"Oh, Jesus! Oh, Jesus!" Smith babbled, reflexively ducking his head and fearing his boat would be next.

The *Chillicothe* remained afloat, despite the considerable damage done to her. Noting this, Smith ordered the flotilla to a halt and sent a message to the stricken ironclad, asking her captain if she was still capable of doing battle. While he waited for the answer, Smith retrieved a telescope from his cabin and pointed it southwest. With all the over and undergrowth in the way, there was not much to see, but the settling gunsmoke revealed the location of Fort Pemberton. Now that he had identified its location, Smith could see the fort's formidable palisades and parapets.

"Sir," MacAdam called from below.

When Smith looked, he saw MacAdam pointing in the direction the messenger had been sent. The messenger was nowhere in sight but the two Union gunboats—*Chillicothe* and *DeKalb*—were steaming past at considerable speed, clearly headed for Fort Pemberton.

"What . . . I didn't order that!" Smith complained.

On deck, MacAdam shrugged and turned to watch the two ironclads make their run. The *Chillicothe's* fire had been extinguished, but smoke still streamed from the mangled gun turrets. With cotton bales stacked on their decks to absorb incoming shells, the pair of attack boats looked like steamers taking their freshly picked product to market.

* * *

Lieutenant Joseph Pitty Couthouy glanced across the intervening space between his gunboat and the *Baron De Kalb*. He
wasn't looking for anything specific, just confirmation that he was
not alone. Though slightly behind the *Chillicothe*, the *De Kalb* was
indeed by his side. The gunboat's commander, Lieutenant L.
Paulding, was looking directly at him over a megaphone that was
pressed to his lips.

"Commander Couthouy, are you sure you can fire your guns?"
Paulding inquired.

The question annoyed Couthouy, as such questions often did.
He was a bit of a contrarian. On his first assignment—an expedi-
tion to Hawaii in 1840—he'd been a member of Andrew Jackson's
Scientific Corps, but had been sent home for disobeying orders.
His excuse was that his superior officer, Lieutenant Charles
Wilkes, "knew nothing of science, enjoyed a fat salary and was fit
only to unpack and take care of the specimens collected by the expedition." This disregard for military etiquette inevitably led to his
departure from the service. He eventually returned in 1862, the
Navy having become more receptive to Couthouy's talents and less
repelled by his rough edges in the face of a looming civil war.

Couthouy glanced at his two forward guns. Their support
structure was a smoking mess, but they could still be fired. What,
he wondered, was Paulding worried about? The *De Kalb* was a five
hundred and twelve-ton Cairo Class gunboat with casemate-pro-
tected guns around its periphery. By contrast, the *Chillicothe* was
three-hundred eighty-five tons and had only the two forward
guns.

Couthouy raised a megaphone to his lips and shouted, "They
will surely fire, Commander."

For an instant, he was tempted to add, "But I'm not sure they
can be aimed." He thought better of it and instead pointed his left
arm forward and said, "Let's go. Full speed ahead."

Which both boats proceeded to do, their twin smokestacks
belching sparks and smoke and their stern wheels churning the
calm shallows of the Tallahatchie River. The distance between the
two ironclads and Fort Pemberton diminished with astounding
speed.

*   *   *

Private Albert Belcher stuck his head up and over the riverside
parapet of Fort Pemberton to see what was happening. What he
saw were two Union gunboats rushing toward him, hell bent for
leather. Convinced that the sunken *Star of the West* provided ample

protection, he felt no fear. But he was a cautious man and, fearful or not, judged the circumstances to be worth reporting.

"Sir!" he called, turning and cupping his hands around his mouth. "Sir, we're under attack."

It was a moment before Major General William W. Loring responded with a skeptical, "Really?"

Belcher looked again. The boats were still coming.

General Loring, who preferred a black Stetson to the usual slouch hats favored by officers on both sides, waded through the mud to the wall of cotton bales, which, along with sandbags, served as the outermost parapets of the fort. The mud had been created by leakage between the cotton bales that had originally been placed well above the normal water level of the Tallahatchie. But the damn Yankees had blown up the Yazoo Pass levee, and now the Mississippi was feeding a goodly amount of its contents into the Tallahatchie. As a consequence, the cotton bale and sandbag emplacements of Fort Pemberton were partially underwater.

Poking his head above the top cotton bale, Loring took a good look and saw what Belcher had spotted.

"By God, they are attacking," he said in a voice that was almost cheerful. "Albert, go back and tell everyone you see to duck. Those Yankee gunboats are getting ready to fire."

Belcher glanced toward the gunboats and confirmed his commander's observation.

"Yes, sir," he blurted and started off.

"Oh, and, Private Belcher."

Belcher halted and said, "Yes, sir?"

Casting a knowing glance from beneath the brim of his Stetson, Loring said, "Tell the boys to fire every cannon we've got at those damn Yankees."

"We only have one cannon, sir, the six-incher."

"Yeah, I know," Loring said with a wink. "Tell them to fire it twice as often as the Yankees do."

"It's a rifle, sir, not a smooth bore."

The remark alluded to the fact that cannons with rifled barrels, while more accurate than smooth bore because of the stabilizing spin imparted to their projectiles, also required more time to load.

"I know that, too, Albert," Loring snapped. "And if we load it twice as fast, we'll hit them four times as often as they hit us."

Recognizing the irritation in Loring's voice, Belcher uttered a disconsolate, "Yes, sir," and continued on his mission.

Loring extracted a telescope from a case attached to his belt and leaned his elbows on the cotton bale to support it. The magnification of the telescope made the two ironclads look quite formidable, although their captains seemed a bit confused about how to attack with a sunken ship in their path. The more aggressive one had only two guns and had clearly suffered some damage from the last round his cannoneers had fired an hour ago. Because of that well-placed shell, Loring had expected the Union flotilla to turn tail and run, but here they were again, ready to trade blows.

Well, he would be happy to accommodate them.

This comforting thought had barely formed when it was shattered by the horrific scream of an eleven-inch projectile. The sound was immediately followed by two explosions—the delayed burst of the cannon that had launched the projectile and the blast of the shell hitting its target. Of the two, the latter concussion was by far the more intense.

"God-dammit!" Loring muttered, struggling to regain his balance after the earth stopped quaking. Hesitantly, he lifted his head to assess the situation. The men of the Mississippi and Texas regiments nearest him appeared to be in good order, although most were still lying face down in the mud with hands clasped behind their necks. His next sighting revealed the culprit. The lead Yankee gunboat, shrouded in gunsmoke, was facing him, its guns pointed directly at Fort Pemberton.

"Private, get your ass over to the fort and tell those sons of bitches to get that damn rifle into action. We can't take much more of this," Loring yelled at the nearest soldier.

Which might or might not be true, Loring reflected, but was usually an effective ploy.

Instinctively, the soldier knew Loring was addressing him and, rising to his feet, murmured "Yes, sir," and was on his way.

As his eyes followed the young private, Loring let his gaze scan the parapet that had been hit by the shell. He was relieved to see only light damage—a hole in the lower part of the structure where it met the ground, and the adjacent debris field.

Another eleven-incher screamed in, with the accompanying concussions and earthquakes. This was followed by two more, and there was still no return fire from the fort.

"Son-of-a-bitch!" Loring cried, dirt and vegetation falling on him like hailstones. "Sonofabitch! SON of a bitch!"

Several expletives later, it happened. The 6.4-inch rifled cannon was brought into action. The projectile made a distinctive, fading whine as it sped across the nine hundred yards separating the belligerents. The 6.4-inch shell struck the lead gunboat, the smaller of the two, setting off a huge explosion that sent a blazing fireball spinning skyward and scorching the limbs and leaves of the forest canopy enveloping the Tallahatchie.

"I'll be damned!" Loring whispered, shocked by the intensity of the explosion and the fact that his orders had finally been carried out. "I *will* be damned!" he repeated in awe as the two gunboats fell back, the larger one interposing itself between the smaller one and the gun of Fort Pemberton.

"Sir," said a voice behind him.

Loring turned to see Private Belcher standing at attention.

"Belcher, you did it!" Loring bellowed. "You did it, son!"

"Sir, your orders have been carried out," Belcher announced nervously.

"I can see that, Belcher," Loring said, pounding ham-fisted on Belcher's shoulders. "Did you see that fireball, son? That was a beauty. Don't you think?"

"Yes, sir."

Loring removed his Stetson and placed it on Belcher's head. The action revealed a continuation of Loring's forehead that penetrated all the way to the rear of his skull.

"Here you are, son. You did it. I hereby declare you a general for a full five minutes. How's that sound?"

Belcher did not look comfortable being a general, even for five minutes. His eyes bulged in horror at the sight of Loring's hair-free pate. The ring of dark hair between the ears and the Stetson had apparently fooled him.

"Oh, that," Loring said, letting his eyes roll upward. Then he grinned and added with mock seriousness, "I think the explosion may have singed my hair a bit."

The nearby soldiers, emboldened by the retreat of the *Chillicothe* and the *Baron De Kalb*, laughed heartily. Private Belcher chuckled more tentatively.

"All right, Belcher," Loring said, struggling to repress his annoyance. *The man simply has no sense of humor,* he realized. "You don't have to be a general. Just get back to the fort and offer those people my congratulations."

Loring patted his subordinate's back as he hastily departed once again. Then he turned around and leaned his elbows on the cotton bale, staring at the destruction wrought by the 6.4-inch cannon. The fireball had dissipated but the smoke, like an ethereal fog, lingered above the Tallahatchie. Some of the branches of the canopy directly above the spot where the *Chillicothe* had been hit were on fire.

Loring looked around and signaled to one of the soldiers in his vicinity. The soldier, a tall, crooked man with narrow features, promptly joined his commander at the cotton bale parapet.

"What's your name, soldier?"

"Wesley, sir. Matthew Wesley," said the soldier, flashing a smile with straight but discolored teeth.

"Matthew, I want to ask your opinion."

Wesley became instantly attentive.

"Surely, sir."

"Matthew, do you think our little old 6.4-inch rifle could make a boom as big as the one we just saw over there?" Loring asked, pointing at the hazy aftermath of destruction.

Wesley looked, squinting his already slit-like eyes in the direction of Loring's pointing finger.

"Surely looks like a big one," Wesley opined. "Maybe."

"Maybe? No 6.4-inch shell ever made that much fire and smoke."

"I'm sure you're right, sir."

There was a brief lull in the conversation as many of the Confederate soldiers who had been crouching close to the ground raised themselves and began jabbering in relief.

"You know what I think, Matthew?"

The reply was foreordained, but Wesley still seemed pained saying it.

"What's that, sir?"

Jabbing at the air, Loring said, "I think we got lucky. I think we hit some of their ammunition."

Wesley's face went blank for a minute, then he said. "I suppose that's possible, sir. Does it mean they won't be coming back?"

Loring sighed, leaning forward on the cotton bale, his chin resting on his hands. When he spoke, his spear-like goatee moved more vigorously than his lips.

"I don't know, Matthew. We'll see, but I think we can handle this one."

With the Yankee retreat in evidence, temporary though the respite might be, officers from inside and outside the fort made their way toward Loring. They would be asking for orders, he concluded. Loring spotted his adjutant, Lieutenant Harry Harrington, leading the pack.

"Lieutenant Harrington, I have an important task for you," he shouted.

Lightheaded from the sound of exploding eleven-inch shells and from the unexpected Yankee withdrawal, Harrington smiled and said, "You want me to break out the whisky for everyone, right, sir?"

Which was definitely not what Loring had in mind, but the enthusiastic roar from the Texas and Mississippi regiments persuaded him otherwise. He gave the bare-chinned, grinning Harrington a well-deserved sneer and said, "Exactly."

★ FOURTEEN ★

March 7, 1863, the De Soto Point Canal

The water level in the Mississippi was rising.

It worried Sherman. A rising water level was not in itself a problem—the canal needed to reach four or five feet in depth before it could pass transports and gunboats—but a prematurely flooded canal was worse than useless.

"Can't we do something about this?" Sherman asked Colonel George Pride.

Shrugging, Pride said, "Like what, sir? I do not have a direct line to the Almighty."

It was an impertinent answer, no doubt reflecting the stress Pride was feeling as the canal's chief engineer. Appreciating his subordinate's consternation, Sherman decided a rebuke would be ill advised.

"We need to do something, George. That levee doesn't look like it can take much more," Sherman said, pointing to the earthen mound that had been built to separate the canal dredging and digging operations from the upstream juncture with the Mississippi River.

The De Soto Point Canal was fast becoming a nightmare. The five hundred black laborers digging out the entrance had run into water four or five feet down. Disease was rampant among both the laborers and the thirty-five thousand soldiers encamped between the canal and Young's Point. In February, electric storms had flooded De Soto Point and the encampments and softened the ground to the consistency of hotcake batter. And, of course, the Rebel guns continued their relentless bombardment of the levees and the dipper dredges. It was a hell founded on water and mud instead of fire and brimstone.

"Suh!" yelled a frantic voice from below. "Suh, it's givin' way!"

The eyes of Sherman and Pride immediately shifted to the black man who had shouted the warning, and then to the levee to which he was pointing.

"Oh, my God," Sherman moaned.

The dam holding back the Mississippi was, indeed, giving way, but not with any flair for the dramatic. It was as if Old Man River were conducting a seminar on how easily it was for him to fling aside the flimsy toys of mankind and impose his watery will on the landscape. The first flaw to appear was a mere rivulet at the crest of the levee. Despite efforts by laborers and soldiers alike to toss sandbags and shovel dirt into the rivulet's path, it continued inexorably to expand and deepen. In five minutes it was a creek.

"Get those men out of there!" George Pride shouted to one of his officers supervising the digging operations. He pointed to the current shift of black workers directly below the levee and therefore below the water level in the Mississippi.

But the laborers needed no encouragement. They could see what was happening and, picks and shovels be damned, scurried for the nearest high ground. All made it to safety in plenty of time; the old man was in no hurry. While the water poured through, widening its path and flooding the bottom lands downstream of it —encampments, equipment and all—the dam slowly eroded until an equilibrium between the pressure of the Mississippi and the torrent rushing into the canal was reached. Men could only stand and watch as water filled the canal, threatening to top its levees and flood the encampments they protected. But it didn't happen. The flood's high water mark failed to overflow the canal levees by a foot or two. It was a blessing, if only a minor one.

With his hands on his hips and disgust filling his face, William Tecumseh Sherman said, "What a mess."

"It is that. It is that," Pride muttered, mesmerized by the wanton destruction.

Sherman strolled along the edge of the canal, staring down at it. One of the dipper dredges, which were mounted on floating platforms, had broken free and was being washed downstream by the burgeoning current.

"Corporal, get some ropes on that thing and bring it back," Pride yelled to one of the men watching the spectacle.

The corporal saluted and marched off to find rope and the men to handle it. Pride walked uncertainly toward Sherman, apprehensive about his commander's reaction. He was not fearful of being blamed for the debacle, but neither was he enthusiastic about dealing with Sherman's famous temper. The general had been known to vent his wrath on nearby subordinates for lesser disasters. When he arrived, Pride was pleasantly surprised by Sherman's deferential attitude.

"Can you fix it?" Sherman inquired, more desperate than angry.

"Given enough time, anything can be fixed."

"How much time?"

Pride reflected a moment and swung his gaze around in a hundred eighty degree arc that encompassed both ends of the canal. Then he pointed toward the levee separating the downstream end of the canal from the Mississippi.

"A week or two. First thing we have to do is blast that levee out to relieve the pressure on the canal levees," he said.

Sherman nodded that he understood.

Resuming his recitation, Pride brought his pointing finger around to the upstream dam and continued, "Then we have to fix that one. It won't be easy."

"Why not?" Sherman asked.

"Because there's a waterfall flowing across its face," Pride explained. "Unless we tear it down and start over, we have to plug that gap first."

Sherman looked like he wanted to groan again but restrained the urge.

"How would you plug it?" he asked, his words crisp and free of nuance.

"I don't know exactly," Pride admitted. "I need some time to think about it. Maybe we could . . ."

Pride's sudden hesitation made Sherman react with, "Maybe we could . . . what?"

Pride rubbed his chin thoughtfully while his mind wrapped itself around an idea.

"I was going to say maybe we could run one of the boats into the gap and plug it, but it doesn't have to be a boat. It could be a barge."

The thought was so encouraging that Sherman actually grinned through his five o' clock shadow.

"Once the dam is plugged, we'll shore it up with planks. It will probably mean tearing down some of the service buildings."

"They aren't much use if we don't have a working canal," Sherman said, then added, "Might as well widen the damn thing while you're at it."

The statement had the timbre of a question, so Pride answered, "That would be a good idea. Get rid of as many stumps as we can, too. Blast them out."

The conversation was interrupted by the boom of a Columbiad fired from one of the Rebel batteries at the south end of Vicksburg. Pride and Sherman turned to see the distant puff of smoke, then hear the shell roaring in. Most of the laborers and troops ducked for cover or flattened themselves on the sodden ground. Pride and Sherman didn't bother but tried to guess where the shell would land based on its audible signature.

It fell fifty feet short of the wayward dipper dredge, which by now had been captured by two ropes and six men who were struggling to pull the huge machine and its barge back to its original station. The blast of the cannon shell damaged neither the men nor the dipper dredge but did create a tidal wave that lifted the beast ten feet, nearly tossing it into the midst of its handlers. Fortunately, the six soldiers suffered only a good dunking and exposure to the rapid-fire cursing of their baptized brethren.

After juking at the blast, Pride looked back at the spot from which the shell had come.

"I wonder what those people think of us. Do you think they're afraid we might succeed?"

Sherman's response was deliberate. He wondered what the faculty and staff of the Louisiana State Seminary of Learning and Military Academy, where he'd been the first superintendent until 1859, would think. "Those people" had been his friends.

"I think *those* people must think the Yankees are out of their damn minds."

★ FIFTEEN ★

March 10, 1863, Young's Point, Louisiana

Ulysses S. Grant re-lit his cigar in the campfire roaring outside his headquarters tent. During one period of intense contemplation, while he was pacing like an expectant father, it had gone out. *Can't let that happen,* he thought. A good cigar, like an occasional drink, was essential to the proper functioning of the thought process. At least, it was to his thought processes.

He took a good puff, exhaled and turned to his companions: William T. Sherman, James B. McPherson, David Porter, and John Rawlins. His eyes fell on McPherson.

"So the Lake Providence passage is no good, is it?"

"It's not a passage. It's an obstacle course in a swamp," McPherson said.

"You're sure?"

"We've been there a month now. I'm sure."

"Hmm," Grant murmured, rubbing the bristles of his abbreviated beard. He turned to Porter.

"What about the Yazoo Pass?"

Porter stood and clasped his hands behind his back. Although he had been a member of Grant's staff for more than a year, he still felt a certain discomfort as the only Navy man in the general's circle of counselors.

"Lieutenant Commander Watson Smith made a decent attempt but the Rebels sunk the old *Star of the West* in the river channel. We couldn't get close enough to Fort Pemberton to do any significant damage, and we couldn't get past. They also had luck on their side."

"How's that?"

"Their first shot hit one of the eleven-inch projectiles we had stacked on the deck of the *Chillicothe*. The pair of explosions—their shell and ours—killed two and wounded eleven. We had to withdraw."

"Is Smith a good man?"

Porter took a deep breath before answering.

"He's a little high-strung, but I think so. Since I wasn't there, I can't be sure, but I have no reason to think he did not do his duty. He tried again on March 13 and 16, but with no greater success. There was no room to maneuver. The two gunboats are a mess."

It was an equivocal answer. Grant had anticipated that most of his assault schemes would probably fail, but he wanted to make sure they were given a good chance to succeed. Planning the conquest of the Confederacy's Gibraltar was not simply a matter of developing a grand strategy. The viability of any strategy for taking Vicksburg had to depend on an exploitation of weak points and Vicksburg had precious few of those visible to the naked eye. He had to search for less obvious vulnerabilities or create them himself.

David Porter raised his hand. "Sir, I have a suggestion."

Grant puffed heavily on his cigar, gazed critically at Porter, and asked, "What kind of suggestion? How to get past Fort Pemberton?"

"No, how to avoid the fort entirely and attack Haynes' Bluff."

"We tried that last Christmas."

Porter shook his head and stood.

"Not this way we didn't. We attacked from a position of inferiority below the bluffs. My proposal is to take the high ground upstream."

As the field officer in charge of the failed Chickasaw-Haynes' Bluff expedition, Sherman had something to say. Without rising, he cast Porter a frightful stare and said, "How would we get there? We can't get boats past Fort Pemberton in the north, and the Rebels have blocked the Yazoo on this end. Don't you remember . . .?"

"There's another way," Porter said, raising his hand even higher. "I've been looking at maps and charts and exploring the lower Yazoo for tributaries."

"Tributaries?" Sherman snarled.

Rather than reply immediately, Porter raised the other hand and thrust both hands forward in a patience-seeking gesture.

"Let's bring out a map. Colonel Rawlins and General McPherson, would you get General Grant's topographical map of Vicksburg and the Mississippi River? Thank you."

Rawlins scurried to the corner of the tent where most of the administrative paraphernalia of command was stored and brought back the requested map. Handing the exposed end to McPherson, he carefully unrolled it for viewing. When that task was done, Porter stepped forward and placed a finger on the point where the Yazoo met the Mississippi.

"We have control of the lower Yazoo. Five miles up the Yazoo—well within our sphere of operations—is a tributary called Steele's Bayou."

"If I remember correctly, it juts off to the west," Sherman objected. "We need to be on the eastern shore of the Yazoo."

"Bear with me, General," Porter pleaded. "There's more."

Sherman paused, shrugged, and waved a limp hand for Porter to proceed.

"Steele's Bayou is just the entrance," Porter began. "I'll try not to confuse you with particulars, but the entire route will involve not only Steele's Bayou but Black Bayou, Deer Creek, Rolling Fork, the Sunflower River, and back to the Yazoo."

With his last statement, Porter moved his finger to the mouth of the Sunflower River, which was about fifty miles above the Yazoo's mouth. Grant scrutinized the map through the cloud of cigar smoke enveloping his head.

"You *have* confused me. Can you show me the path you have in mind . . . quickly?"

Porter did so, tracing his finger clockwise from a seven o'clock position at the mouth of Steele's Bayou to a four o'clock ending position at the mouth of the Sunflower River.

"How far is that above Haynes' Bluff?" Grant inquired.

"About twenty miles."

"And how many miles does this route of yours traverse—as the fish swims?"

"About two hundred miles."

No one groaned, but everyone's expression suggested a repressed desire to do so.

"It's not as far out of the way as the Yazoo Pass or Lake Providence expeditions would have been," Porter argued.

"Well, there's that," Sherman offered sarcastically. "Travel two hundred miles for a net gain of twenty. It's hard to believe this is the shortest detour."

"Why haven't we considered this route before? Why are we just discovering it?" McPherson wondered.

"Normally the water level is too low, but when we blew up the levee to open the Yazoo Pass, the levels in all the connecting byways east of the Mississippi increased."

"The Yazoo Pass is four hundred miles upstream," Rawlins pointed out.

Grinning with the confidence of nautical insight, Porter replied, "It doesn't matter. Water flows downhill, and that's where Haynes' Bluff is."

"Is it deep enough now?" Grant asked. "For the whole two hundred miles?"

Porter stopped and bowed his head, facing Grant. It was a question he'd expected but had only an incomplete answer for.

"I think so. All the signs are favorable. Would you like to come aboard the *Black Hawk* with me? I can show you why we're optimistic."

Grant was still, only his eyes moved. They danced from one man to the next, assessing the probable opinion of each. Sherman's was obvious; his sour expression made it clear he disapproved. McPherson was his usual stoic self, although he looked weary. John Rawlins, on the other hand, appeared tense, but Grant put this down to his chronic concern for the general's state of sobriety. Grant knew that Rawlins had every right to be concerned, but he also knew that he had no plans in the near future that included whisky. However, if one of these damned schemes showed promise . . . well . . .

"Certainly. I can't think of anything I'd rather do than take a boat trip up a Mississippi bayou or two."

Except for a terse snicker from Sherman, the sarcasm was lost on his audience.

* * *

March 13, 1863, The Yazoo River, Mississippi

As he stood on the deck of the *Black Hawk* with David Porter, Grant could not help wondering what attracted men to Navy service. *It certainly couldn't be the opportunity to explore the inland waterways adjoining the Mississippi*, he thought. The air was too humid, the water too foul, the vegetation too thick, and any redneck with a gun could take a potshot at you without much fear of retaliation. Hell, Rebels with cannon could sink the damned *Black Hawk* without fear of retaliation. Floating like a giant duck in the middle of a narrow river surrounded by a tropical, enemy-concealing forest was not Grant's idea of an effective strategy.

The *Black Hawk* suddenly lurched to port.

"Whoa, what was that?" Grant demanded, ever mindful of being attacked.

"We're turning to port," Porter said, unconcerned.

For a moment, Grant had to scan his memory to find what "port" meant. After he decided it was a left turn, and the *Black Hawk's* motion confirmed that conclusion, he asked, "Why? Are we going ashore?"

"No," Porter answered. "You'll see."

Observing the boat's shoreward drift and the large cypress trees and thick brush residing there, Grant hoped it would not take too long for him to "see."

It didn't. Just as it seemed the boat would ram headlong into a tree, the leaves parted and the *Black Hawk* passed onto what appeared to be a placid lake. The leadsman at the bow pulled his lead line taut, looked at it, and called, "Fifteen feet!"

"Fifteen feet, is that enough?" Grant asked.

"Twice as much as we need for the ironclads," Porter replied.

Grant nodded. If a depth of fifteen feet was good enough for the heavy ironclads, it was good enough for the transports.

"Will it be that deep all the way?"

Porter pursed his lips and shrugged.

"There's no way to tell without traversing the entire route, but what we have seen so far looks good."

He left it at that because he had to; intelligence was necessarily limited.

"What about size? Width, I mean."

Placing his hands on his hips, porter inhaled and said, "Same answer. I think the connecting byways will be wide enough, but we won't know until we run into one that's not."

"That could present you with more difficulties than a shallow channel."

Porter smirked in acknowledgment. The Mississippi and its tributaries could flood or drain on a dime, and no one could predict exactly what land would and would not be underwater. Having his fledgling armada under attack by a Rebel army or even Rebel farmers with pitchforks and shotguns was a recurring nightmare he'd had to live with ever since Grant had begun conceiving his waterway experiments. The Federal Navy was designed to take on enemy navies, not enemy armies. It was a new concept in warfare, and it made him nervous.

"It could," Porter admitted. "And, of course, we'll have to keep the transports close at hand."

"Do you have any opinions on who should command the expedition from my side?"

By "my side" Porter knew Grant meant the army.

"If General Sherman weren't tied up with the De Soto Point canal . . ."

"He's not," Grant announced abruptly.

"He's not?" Porter echoed, uncomprehending. "I thought the canal was nearly finished . . ."

"We were flooded out," Grant said, disappointment showing in his expression. "I thought we were damn near done, but the water level came up and broke the dam at the upper end. We lost a lot of horses and equipment."

Another of the Mississippi's practical jokes, Porter mused. As if mourning the loss of horses and equipment, Grant became suddenly silent. Porter mimicked the silence, uncertain of the depth of Grant's distress. A minute later, after the Union commander had paced off his frustration and distracted himself by skipping flat shards of coal across the surface of Steele's Bayou, he turned to face Porter.

"At least you'll have the pleasure of Sherman's company," Grant said, grinning through his partially trimmed beard. "But I'm not sure 'pleasure' is the right word. He might be in a foul mood."

"General Sherman is always in a foul mood. It's just a matter of degree."

"At least he won't have to dig in the Mississippi mud anymore. That may improve his disposition."

Porter laughed out loud.

"That would be a sight to see," he gibed. "General Sherman with a happy face. A sight indeed."

March 20, 1863, Deer Creek, Mississippi

The Confederates had stacked cotton bales along both shores of Deer Creek and set them afire. Like the cotton, the smoke was a dirty white, but the flames flickered an ordinary orange and blue. If Deer Creek had been wider, the inferno might have been tolerable, but a mere two boat beams was so narrow that Porter could feel the heat from the flames licking his cheeks and neck. He had a new respect for roasted pig.

At the head of the gunboats, the *Black Hawk* was rendered temporarily immobile by a bridge. On the bridge facing Porter was the ugliest man he had ever seen, smoking a pipe and grinning down at him like a gargoyle on a balustrade.

"Who the hell are you?" Porter demanded.

The grin expanded, revealing fiercely sharp but surprisingly white teeth.

"I'm a Jeff Davis man; first, last and always."

Porter looked at the crowds gathering on both ends of the bridge. They were all Negroes, not a white man among them. Was this man a plantation owner?

"I hope you don't mind, but I'm going to steam into that bridge of yours and knock it down."

"You may knock it down and be damned," the man proclaimed, removing the pipe and spitting into the water. "It don't belong to me."

"You sound like a Yankee. Are you?"

The man's bizarre but amused expression turned dour.

"Yes, I am a Yankee by birth, but I gave up on the institution a goodly while ago."

With that, the man shoved the pipe back into his mouth, turned and headed for a cabin on the eastern shore. For a frozen moment, Porter was struck by the man's audacity. Then he turned to the *Black Hawk's* captain and said, "Go."

Making less than a half mile per hour, the *Black Hawk's* momentum was easily enough to crush the fragile bridge. When the deed had been done, Porter glanced back at the Yankee apostate. The man was sitting on the porch smoking his pipe, spindly legs propped up on a stick of firewood. He made no move to acknowledge the bridge's destruction or Porter's hostile stare.

"What a brute," Porter grumbled. "That man needs to be taught some manners.

The *Black Hawk's* skipper—a chubby, jovial man in his fifties—accepted the comment with a sheepish nod. He was not ready to volunteer to teach the man anything.

For the next four miles, the flotilla lazily proceeded along Deer Creek without incident, except for the burning cotton bales. But the creek had widened, and the flames and smoke were not as annoying as they had been at the bridge. Then ahead, he heard the thumping of heavy axes.

"God, I wish Sherman was here," Porter said, as much to himself as to his companion.

"Shall I send word that we need him?" the captain asked.

"Not yet. He's probably busy widening the creek so the transports can get through."

The captain nodded again, content with inaction. Porter, however, was not.

"Send the *Grope* ahead. Find out where that hacking is coming from and take care of it. The Rebels are probably felling trees in our path."

"It'll be dark soon, sir."

"I don't care. Give the order."

Again the captain nodded and did as he was told. Corralling an ensign, he gave the order for the mortar boat *Grope* to sail ahead and eliminate the source of Porter's irritation. The *Grope* was on its way in five minutes. Within half an hour, the mortar batteries opened up in a clamorous cannonade that endured for fifteen minutes. Fiftcen minutes after that, the *Grope* appeared in the mist, which was in fact partly smoke hovering around the stubby mortar barrels. To Porter's relief, the *Grope's* commander signaled the success of his mission. By this time, the sun had set, and Deer Creek was shrouded in darkness.

Putting a match to an oil lamp, the *Black Hawk's* captain held it up and gazed at Porter.

"I think it's time to settle in for the night," Porter said. "Pass the word to tie up."

"What about the general? How will he find us?"

With some incredulity, Porter replied, "There's only one road. He can't take a wrong turn."

★ SIXTEEN ★

March 21, 1863, Deer Creek, Mississippi

The morning was brisk and damp. After washing and trimming his beard, Porter strolled on deck to enjoy the morning. To his surprise, he spied a plantation house just beyond the east bank of Deer Creek that he had not seen in the gloom of the previous evening. It was a white, three-story structure with massive Doric columns dominating the portico. Between the house and the creek, farm animals—cattle, hogs, sheep, and chickens—marched by, some staring at him, others too busy filling their stomachs to be bothered. At first, he was appalled that the residents permitted their livestock to freely wander about the premises, but his hunger soon overwhelmed his concern for pastoral etiquette.

"Ensign!" he yelled to a sailor on the lower deck of the *Black Hawk*. "Get some men together and seize enough of those beasts over there to feed the officers and crew."

Following Porter's line of sight, the sailor quickly got the picture. He didn't have to be told twice.

It was a ham and eggs breakfast for all, officers and enlisted men receiving equal portions. The plantation owner, one Giles McDermitt, a haughty and be-whiskered southern gentleman, was properly outraged by the seizure of his property. Porter calmly explained the rules of war to him, emphasizing an army's right to take whatever it needed from the enemy. Neither McDermitt, nor his wife, nor his several offspring accepted the argument with grace. To himself, Porter justified his actions by issuing and enforcing no-looting orders and by condemning McDermitt as a tyrant. At least thirty slaves worked the plantation, and while none appeared to be starving, not a one possessed the aplomb of a free human spirit.

It occurred to Porter that the apostate Yankee was nowhere to be seen. Maybe he was exactly what he claimed to be; a Yankee whose loyalties had somehow shifted to the southern cause. Odd.

After breakfast, Porter called the gunboat commanders together to explain the plan of the day. It was simple: proceed up Deer Creek to Rolling Fork.

"What is Rolling Fork?" one asked.

"It's another stream," Porter explained. "But don't ask me if it's a river or a bayou because I don't know."

"Ain't a nickel's worth of difference, if you ask me," another burly captain opined. He was rewarded with a mild wave of laughter.

"The good thing about Rolling Fork is that it connects Deer Creek and the Sunflower River, and that river, gentlemen," Porter said with a smile. ". . . that river flows southeast to the Yazoo, twenty miles above Haynes' Bluff.

That was enough to inspire another wave of laughter, accompanied by a round of *huzzahs*.

The flotilla pushed off in late morning, just as the sun was finishing its daily task of burning off the heavy fog that had settled in overnight. The *Black Hawk* led the lazy parade, speed being imprudent in these shallow waters. None of the McDermitts attended the departure, but a good many of their slaves did. Some waved, a few even smiled. Porter was happy to wave back. The throng of Negroes never entirely vanished, the crowds of onlookers gradually giving way to gangs of black field hands working the land.

Surrounded by black smoke that could not readily penetrate the network of branches above her smokestacks, the *Black Hawk* traveled only several hundred yards before Porter spotted what looked like a green slime covering the water's surface.

"You, you there. What in God's name is that?" he shouted to one of the field hands closest to the shore.

The man, black as peat and endowed with a laborer's physique, stood up, leaned on his hoe, and answered, "Them is willers, sir, just willers."

"*Willers?*" Porter thought, then realized the man was referring to willow wands.

"Why are there so many?"

"We cuts them to make baskets. The women folk weaves them."

Porter looked skeptically at the undulating layer of green in his path.

"Ain't nothin' to worry over, sir. They jus' willers. Boats slide over them willers jus' like a eel," the black man said, shaking and moving his arm and hand to simulate an eel traversing a willow patch.

"Boats?" the still skeptical Porter asked. "What kinds of boats?"

"Canoes, skiffs, flat-bottoms, them kind," said the field hand. "Ain't got no battleships like yours."

The *Black Hawk* was, of course, not a battleship, but it was the closest approximation to one that this man would ever come across. He did not belabor the point.

"Go ahead," he said, with considerable reservation, to the captain. "Full steam."

The captain stared dubiously at the Admiral, then ordered full steam ahead. Black smoke bellowed like exhaled dragon's breath from the smokestacks, and the *Black Hawk* plunged forward. Porter surveyed his surroundings and found very little to be optimistic about. The banks of Deer Creek were well above the boat's guns, even at their steepest angle of inclination. After twenty yards, the hull seemed to groan, and the two side paddlewheels slowed, then made an unpleasant churning sound Porter had never heard before, and came to a near halt.

"What . . ." Porter demanded.

"What the . . ." the captain echoed.

The gaze of both men shifted to the starboard paddlewheel, which was barely rotating. The problem, it seemed, was that the willows were clogging the paddlewheel and its machinery. An inspection of the situation ahead of the *Black Hawk* revealed nothing less than a willow-jam obstructing the boat's forward motion. Far from moving over the sea of willows "like a eel," the *Black Hawk* was stuck. Designed for shallow water, her bow nevertheless needed two or three feet of clear water to proceed unhindered, and the willows were definitely not behaving like clear water.

"Goddamn!" Porter exclaimed.

The captain reacted with neither censure nor concurrence. He was merely frustrated.

"Get that godforsaken slime off my paddlewheels!" he shouted at the deck hands within earshot. "And clear it away from the bow. We can't stay here."

The captain's words were prophetic. Keenly aware that the flotilla could not "stay here" with high ground flanking them on both sides, Porter barked orders of his own to an *aide-de-camp*.

"Lieutenant, get some cannon on that hill over there, and some men to handle them. Take enough, but not too many, eight to ten I think. The rest will help cut us free from this . . . abominable stew we appear to be in."

Four howitzers were hastily transferred to the mound-like hill Porter had indicated, along with ammunition and powder. Ten men were assigned the duties of loading, firing and cleaning the stubby smoothbore barrels of the weapons. The rest of the crew, some wading in Deer Creek, others hanging from the *Black Hawk's* superstructure, hacked away at the willow wands, hoping to dislodge them or cut them into fine pieces. For a while, it appeared the boat would be freed from the spider web in which it had become entangled. The tension in his body dissipating, Porter's grip on the railing of the upper deck was just beginning to relax when he heard rifle shots. His fingers again tightened around the railing and his gaze moved immediately to the cannoneers he had sent ashore. One of them was down.

"Lieutenant, fire those damn cannons!" he screamed at an officer on the hill.

The officer cast a look of despair at his commander and mouthed the words "At what?" before resuming his duties.

Spotting a Negro slave, blithely observing the chaos from one of the plantations on shore, Porter hurried down the stairs and over to him. The Negro was young, strong, and, his thick lips parted in a frown, looked terrified.

"Sambo, would you like to make a dollar?" he asked.

"My name ain't Sambo, sir, it's Tub," the man replied.

"All right, Tub. Would you like to make a dollar?"

Tub grinned and said, "I surely would."

Porter took pen and paper from his breast pocket, composed a note, and handed it to the black man.

"Give this to General Sherman. Tell him to hurry.

Tub stared solemnly at Porter, only partially comprehending. He had never before seen a white man's face suffused with an emotion so close to despair. As much as he disliked being a slave, he found it unsettling that the heart of a white man could be gripped by such fear. Unsettling, but revealing.

"Yes, sir. I take it," he said, crushed the noted in his powerful hand, and scurried off.

*   *   *

Sherman was *not* in an agreeable mood. Black Bayou was like every other bayou, creek, or "lake" he had experienced in this campaign: dark, dank, narrow, and laden with creeping vegetation that hung like fishnets over unsuspecting prey below. This bayou had all of that, and it had bugs, lizards, mosquitoes, rats, cockroaches, snakes, coons, and the occasional wildcat, most of whom descended from the trees or, for the winged varieties, flew directly at their victims.

"Goddammit!" he snorted, swatting a mosquito on his cheek. He held the bloody corpse out for viewing. The smear on his hand was red with yellow frills of a thicker substance, no doubt mosquito meat. "I'll bet that blood is from a half dozen of us. Goddamn, miserable, little bastard . . ."

Lieutenant Copernicus Ledbetter turned off his hearing and interrupted with, "It's still on your cheek, sir."

"What?"

"It's on your cheek," Ledbetter repeated. "The mosquito, or parts of it anyway."

"Oh, I see," Sherman said, lifting his hand to the spot at which Ledbetter was pointing. "Well, it would be, wouldn't it?"

After wiping away the mosquito remains, Sherman said, "Lieutenant, if I have to deal with these damned insects, I'm going to do it with my gloves on."

The lieutenant understood he was being ordered to retrieve the general's gloves. He did. Sherman put them on and seemed to relax a bit. First, he looked up to see if any of the flying beasts were headed for him. Then he looked down at the *Silver Wave's* wake to see if any swamp creatures were slithering their way to the upper decks from below. There were none. Finally, he surveyed the *Silver Wave*, on whose upper deck he stood. The transport was an aging passenger steamer, with all the wedding cake architecture of that style.

"You know, Lieutenant, this is a fine ship, but it doesn't belong here," he said.

"It's a boat, sir."

"Yes, yes, I know, it's a boat. What I don't know is what makes it a boat and not a ship. Do you?"

Since Ledbetter did not understand the difference either, he fell momentarily silent. Then he said, "I don't think anything civilized belongs here, sir, man or machine, ship or boat."

Sherman gave a grudging smile and said, "Where do you think Admiral Porter is? How far ahead?"

"Hard to tell, sir," said the lieutenant, craning his neck over the railing as if doing so would give him a better sight-line through the dense foliage. "The gunboats are difficult to see, as low in the water as they are. Maybe a mile or two ahead."

"Where are we?"

"We're still in Black Bayou. Should be coming up on Deer Creek pretty soon, though."

Sherman contented himself with gripping the handrail and attempting to see far enough ahead to spot one of the lead boats making the left turn onto Deer Creek. He couldn't see much at first—the forest canopy filtered out too much sunlight. Finally, he saw the port side of some vessel—whether it was one of the five gunboats, a tug, or a mortar boat he couldn't tell. Just then a low-hanging branch struck the *Silver Wave's* smokestack, creating a tremendous, painful sound that nearly toppled the bonnet.

"Good God!" Sherman exclaimed, unconsciously ducking his head. "I thought Porter was knocking those things down with his heavy gunboats."

"We're higher above the water than he is, sir," Ledbetter explained.

"So we are, so we are," Sherman grumbled, watching the soldiers on the lower deck who had been sweeping vermin overboard, now engaged in clearing dislodged soot from floors, tables, chairs, and walls. Both Sherman and Ledbetter kept their eyes peeled for low-hanging branches that might be coming their way. Several did, but none was as destructive as the first. Within half an hour, the *Silver Wave* was swinging to port onto Deer Creek. It looked like Black Bayou with slightly more sunlight and smaller, more densely packed trees. When they were a half-mile into the waterway, Lieutenant Ledbetter thrust an arm forward.

"Look, sir."

Sherman looked. In the spaces between trees and vines, he saw a parade, or, more accurately, parades of boats passing by in several, often opposite directions.

"What the hell . . ." he muttered.

"Deer Creek must be very crooked, sir," said Ledbetter.

"Crooked is not the word for it," Sherman said, finally comprehending the strange phenomenon.

"Quite a sight, don't you think so, sir?"

Sherman could only nod; a verbal response seemed inadequate. He was becoming concerned.

"This damned swamp is like a shooting gallery in a maze. I don't like it one bit."

"We haven't been fired on. The gunboats are where they should be."

"The Rebs are out there somewhere. If they come at us in force, there'll be hell to pay. We'll never be able to maneuver in this . . ."

"Creek."

". . . Swamp," Sherman finished. No resident of the mid-west who had lived within spitting distance of the Ohio River would ever refer to this stagnant, waterlogged abomination of a waterway as a "creek."

Ledbetter's nose was suddenly in the air, sniffing. Sherman mimicked the gesture.

"Smoke," he said.

"Up there," said Ledbetter, pointing toward a white fuming mass near the lead gunboats.

"I hope . . ." Sherman began but was immediately distracted by a dark figure moving toward them with as much haste as the forest would allow. It was a Negro, his glistening eyes alternately focusing on the *Silver Wave* and the path before him. A slip of paper was clutched in his hand. Ledbetter looked forebodingly at Sherman, who returned the harsh expression.

"This can't be good news," he moaned.

Ledbetter caught the man's attention and signaled for him to come aboard. Tub was, at first, hesitant but soon found himself pleased with the idea. His first footsteps on deck were equally hesitant, not out of fear but from uncertain footing on the undulating surface.

"And who are you, sir?" Ledbetter asked.

Tub looked at the younger officer and said, "Got a message from Captain Porter."

"You mean *Admiral* Porter," Ledbetter corrected.

Embarrassed, the black man replied, "Yeah . . . Admr'l Porter. Got a message for General Sherman."

The announcement was accompanied by a flashing smile and an outstretched hand, revealing Porter's note. Instead of taking it, Ledbetter nodded toward Sherman and said, "You can give it to him yourself."

Which pleased Tub no end. He virtually sparkled with enthusiasm, despite the greasy perspiration on his brow, thick forearms and soaked into the armpits of his gray cotton shirt. After climbing to the upper deck, he presented himself in Sherman's front and executed a surprisingly good salute.

"Sir, got a message from Admr'l Porter," he declared.

Sherman took the proffered note and read it.

"He says you got to hurry," Tub added, remembering Porter's admonition.

"That's what the note says all right," Sherman acknowledged, showing concern. "What's your name? What's going on out there?"

"My name Tub, sir," the Negro said proudly, then added with careful articulation, "And they be under attack by the Con-fed-er-ates. Admr'l wants you to come help."

Sherman had figured that out for himself but the sun was setting, and it would not do to lead his men into an unfamiliar swamp in the middle of the night. Half of them would probably be lost before daybreak. He stared at the black man, wondering about his capabilities as a guide.

"Tub, can you take us back?"

Once more, Tub's enthusiastic grin emerged.

"I surely can, sir. I surely can," he said, executing another salute.

Placing a hand on the black man's shoulder, Sherman said, "We'll start early tomorrow. Why don't you go into the kitchen and get something to eat? Lieutenant Ledbetter will show you the way. After he does, tell him to report back to me."

Which broadened Tub's smile even more. Bounding down the stairs to the lower deck, he approached Ledbetter, spoke a few words, and was promptly directed to the kitchen. Ledbetter then climbed to the upper deck and presented himself to Sherman with a salute that was not nearly as buoyant as Tub's had been.

"Sir," he said crisply.

"Lieutenant, Admiral Porter is under attack, and we must go to his aid. Have the men prepare for departure an hour before dawn."

March 22, 1863, Black Bayou, Mississippi

Though it had been a while since he'd been to one, or to any religious service for that matter, the lighted candles, the quiet, and the reverent stillness reminded Sherman of a Catholic mass. It was a reminiscence that lasted only until the next man stepped on or tripped over some unseen obstacle and exploded with a wave of curses that would have embarrassed an Irish drill sergeant. Sherman halted the ethereal procession and grasped Tub's left shoulder. When Tub turned around, his face and languid smile were dappled by candlelight like a fall landscape at sunset.

"Tub, are you sure this is a shortcut?" Sherman asked.

"I sure."

"This doesn't look like a path anyone has ever traveled. It doesn't *feel* like a path anyone has ever traveled."

Tub gave him a reproachful look, as if to assert the primacy of his judgment on what did and did not constitute a proper "path" in this country.

"I sure," he repeated.

Sherman snorted, but ultimately decided he had no reasonable argument to make.

"Well, when will we get there?" he demanded irritably.

"Oh, jus' a little while," Tub said, looking up. "Sun be up, we be there."

Sherman gazed at the sky, assessing its brightness. It was still dark, but a faint luminescence was penetrating the blackness from the east. Maybe half an hour.

"All right, let's go. You first, Tub."

Tub was happy to lead, reveling in the opportunity. As a footpath, the trail left a lot to be desired. In most places, feet, even shins, were under water. As Sherman watched the pre-dawn parade, he saw exasperation and pique on many faces, but there was no despair. These were good soldiers, even the drummer's boys who balanced their drums on their heads to protect them when the water became waist deep.

One mile and a half-hour later, the blasts of mortar cannon and the sharp reports of random rifle fire reached their ears. Shortly thereafter, Lieutenant Ledbetter returned from the front of the ragged line.

"Sir, Admiral Porter's gunboats are ahead. They have a problem," Ledbetter said.

"I know that, Lieutenant. We wouldn't be here otherwise. What's his situation?"

Ledbetter scowled.

"He's stuck, sir, in . . . vegetation."

"Vegetation?"

"Leaves, or something like leaves. I didn't ask what it was, but he can't plow through it, and his paddlewheels are all clogged with the stuff."

"God . . ." Sherman began but restrained himself. "This is the most god-awful, the most infernal expedition I have ever participated in. Did you order the men into position?"

The last of Sherman's men passed by as Ledbetter replied, "Yes, sir, they're still in the woods. Rebs haven't spotted us yet."

But they will, Sherman reflected, *and when they do there will be hell to pay.*

"What is Porter doing to extract himself?" Sherman snapped.

"I'm not sure, sir. I sent a couple of scouts to reconnoiter but told them not to expose themselves until we bring up the whole regiment."

The Union forces did not constitute an entire regiment but were the only troops Sherman had on board the *Silver Wave.* He ignored the misstatement.

"Let's get them up then," he said.

The order was flavored with a resolve that Ledbetter could not fail to notice. The "regiment" was brought forward with little regard for stealth and much concern for speed. Soon, the Rebel muskets were turned on Sherman's men as well as Porter's. The

Confederate forces, however, turned out to consist primarily of snipers. When these relatively few pockets of resistance were eliminated, or ingeniously vanished into the *flora*, the Rebel attack ceased.

Sherman found Porter on the aft deck of the *Black Hawk*, steaming backwards down Deer Creek, led by the gunboats *Carondelet, Cincinnati, Linden, Louisville,* and *Pittsburg.* Sherman hopped aboard and joined the Navy man.

"What happened?" he asked. "I heard you got stuck."

Porter snorted unpleasantly and bent to pick up a willow wand, one of many cluttering the deck. He showed it to Sherman.

"We ran into a school of these. They clogged everything, the paddlewheels, the rudders, anything that sucked them in and tried to spit them out again. I'm glad you're here. We were like ducks . . . in a pond."

Porter smiled, his frustration giving way to a sense of relief. He pumped Sherman's hand and pounded him repeatedly on the back. Then he pointed to the boat's rudders stacked helplessly on the port side of the deck.

"We had to unship the rudders to get away from that place. Reverse was the only direction we could move in. You came just in time."

Despite his colleague's obvious elation at being rescued from a desperate situation, Sherman was worried. He observed the sluggish progression of the *Black Hawk* and the gunboats behind it and was not reassured. A narrow, crooked stream whose depth was as unpredictable as the rainfall did not seem a sensible place to float a massive flagship like the *Black Hawk.*

"I think we should get out of here," he said.

"I couldn't agree more."

"Do you need us to go after the Rebels?"

Porter looked around, gauging the danger and trying not to broadcast his embarrassment for proposing the Steele Bayou expedition in the first place. With the disappearance of the snipers, there did not appear to be much resistance left, although a residual crowd of Southerners lined both shores, taunting and jeering.

"Hey, Jack, how do you like playing in the mud?" cried one.

"By Jove, I do believe someone has stolen their rudders," another shouted through cupped hands.

Ignoring the gibes, Porter turned to Sherman and said, "No, I don't think that's necessary. Let's just leave."

Amen to that, Sherman found himself thinking.

The *Black Hawk* and her phalanx of gunboats finally reached a spot where Deer Creek was wide enough and deep enough to maneuver and restore some semblance of order to the inglorious retreat. Porter had the flagship's rudders re-installed and it was not long before the flotilla—with the transports and their human cargo now in the lead—was in full retreat. The mood on board the *Black Hawk*, especially for Sherman and Porter, was dismal. How many failures was it now? Sherman queried his memory. He thought six, but wasn't sure. The mind, he decided, does not register failure as well as it does success. More to the point, how many more failures would there be before Ulysses S. Grant took Vicksburg, or admitted that he couldn't?

"Genr'l Sherman, sir. Admr'l Porter, sir. Could I ask you somethin' impawtant?"

Startled to hear a voice in the midst of their spiritual gloom, Sherman and Porter reacted by jerking to attention. When they turned to face the source, they found Tub. The black man executed his now-practiced salute and waited for the two officers to come to grips with his presence.

"Genr'l, Admr'l, I wants to be a soldier," he announced, snapping his saluting arm to his side.

Sherman and Porter looked quizzically at one another, unsure whether to be amused or annoyed. Tub had been of considerable assistance to them but neither was ready to enlist a "contraband" into the armed forces of the United States. If that was indeed possible, it would have to be done at some higher level, by officers who understood the political ramifications of such an action. Sherman spoke first.

"Tub, you can't become a soldier just like that, or a sailor for that matter. You have to be trained. Can you shoot a gun?"

The question was disingenuous. Sherman knew that a slave owner who permitted his slaves to use firearms was likely to be a dead slave owner. Tub frowned, his eyelids falling over eyes that had danced with joy seconds before.

"No, can't say I know how," he said mournfully. But the doleful expression vanished as a new idea occurred to him. "But I learn quick, and I real good with a knife. Killed me many a hog. Ain't no white boy's throat goin' be harder to cut open than a mean old, jiggly-wiggly hog."

As he said it, Tub smiled gloriously and swiped the edge of a flat hand across his throat. Then he glanced from one officer to the next, seeking approval. What he saw, however, were two faces momentarily drained of blood.

"Oh, oh, no, I don' mean *northern* white boys," Tub reassured when he understood the reason for the officers' ghostly appearance.

"I talkin' about *southern* white boys. Thems is the only throats I goin' cut."

Tub's intentions were stated with such innocence that Sherman had a strong urge to laugh. He repressed the urge and said a silent prayer for whoever had been Tub's slave-master.

"You can stay with us, Tub," Sherman said sheepishly. "No need to cut anyone's throat just yet."

"O-o-o-o-we-e-e-e!" Tub cried, leaping into the air to a height that struck awe into the hearts of his beholders. When he came back to earth, his size fourteen feet landed square on the wet wooden deck with a magnificent thump. He danced away, singing, "I gon' be a soldier boy. I gon' be a soldier boy . . ."

"Do we need to watch him?" a concerned Porter asked.

"I don't think so. He's just enjoying his first experience as a free man."

Porter loosened his collar, stretched the tendons of his neck, and swallowed.

"I hope you're right. We don't need a band of Negro cutthroats killing off the white natives. Old Brains would have us drawn and quartered," he said.

Sherman gave his Navy colleague a curious look, wondering what Tub had done to inspire such a reaction.

"Tub is harmless," he said.

Porter's scowl was intense and immediate.

"Tub is *not* harmless," he insisted.

Each officer averted his gaze from the other, preferring instead to watch the euphoric black man dancing from one spot to another and introducing himself to the crew. Having had their home and transportation sunk less than twenty minutes earlier, few were prepared for such heedless vitality and frowned in disbelief. Several forced weak grins; one man shook Tub's hand.

"He's harmless right now," Sherman said. "And that's all that matters."

Porter nodded acquiescently and said, "Shall we head for home?"

Since the expedition had been Porter's idea in the first place, Sherman thought it appropriate that he be the one to abandon it.

"Certainly."

When the *Black Hawk* reached deeper water and was able to turn around, the flotilla began the return journey to Steele's Bayou. The mood aboard the flagship was, if not depressing, at least somber. Sherman strolled to the handrail, leaned on it, and tried to enjoy the lush scenery enveloping him. Inevitably, he found himself cursing the place as a theater of operations. Better a flat, dry desert than a swamp packed with cypress trees, swarming vegetation, and unfriendly creatures, especially the unfriendly creatures known as Rebel soldiers.

Porter joined Sherman at the railing but made no attempt to enjoy the scenery.

"Is it worth coming back and trying again?" he asked, his demeanor somewhere between uncertain and tentative.

Sherman opened his mouth to speak, but a large, airborne insect flew into it. He coughed once, twice, and brought it up the third time with a violent heave of his lungs. The semi-intact mosquito tried to fly away but was too severely wounded and drenched in saliva to do anything but drop to the water below. Sherman executed several retching spasms to clear his throat of possible bug debris and looked at Porter with disgust and malice suffusing his expression.

"I would rather lead an expedition to the North Pole," he said, then ejected a final "hocker" to punctuate the proclamation.

★ SEVENTEEN ★

March 29, 1863, Duckport, Louisiana

"Could you try to look interested?" asked the photographer, Emmanuel Skinner. He was a thin, hairless man with the best natural teeth Grant had ever seen in a human being. His employer was a newspaper in St. Louis.

"But I'm *not* interested."

"You have to be. You're a Union general, one of the most important. How would it look if you were not interested in defeating the Confederacy?" Skinner replied, his tone oddly ambiguous.

Grant removed his hand from the tree at which Skinner had formally posed him and leaned his shoulder against it.

"I mean I'm not interested in having my picture taken. I'm not photog . . ."

"Photogenic."

"Yes, I'm not photogen-ic," Grant said, forcing himself to conquer the unfamiliar word. "Never have been, never will be."

While he sighted through his camera, Skinner said, "It doesn't matter if you're photogenic, General, but you should try to *look* interested. You are the commanding general in the western theater of operations. If you don't, the public might think you are not concerned with the war's progress. You wouldn't want that, would you?"

Why in God's name should he care what the public thought? The "public" had no idea how to run a war and, through it surrogates in the press, usually made that job more difficult.

Grant tried to look interested.

"That doesn't work, General. You look like you're scowling. That's General Sherman's temperament, not yours. Can you try to look fierce?"

Grant threw up his hands and barked, "No one has ever accused me of looking fierce. I am not Attila the Hun, Mr. Skinner. I'm an American soldier of the nineteenth century. I don't get to stare down my counterparts in the Rebel army because I rarely see them. Even if I did, I would consider it a waste of time."

Skinner conceded the point and rubbed his bare chin.

"Can you look *commanding* then?"

Resisting the temptation to dismiss the man, Grant curbed his frustration and directed his gaze to the surroundings. If he were to try to look *commanding*, the environs certainly wouldn't support the illusion. The scraggly tree had no limbs below ten feet, the headquarters tent behind him resembled the side of an old barn, and the chair next to the tree, while comfortable, looked like something Julia would take to a church picnic. And the incessant groaning and hissing of the dipper dredges as they dug the trench for the Duckport Canal was definitely an unmilitary sound.

"Is this commanding enough?" Grant said, standing at attention beside the tree.

"No. Too stiff."

Grant switched to "at ease."

"Definitely not. You look like a toy soldier."

"Damnit, Skinner, just tell me what you want. I have better things to do," Grant barked. He briefly considered lighting a cigar and reached into his breast pocket for one, aborting the move when he realized Skinner would probably veto the cigar anyway. Finding his arms and hands unburdened, he put his right hand on the tree, adjusted his stance with his left hip cocked outward, and placed his left hand on it. He waited, impatience clouding his features, for Skinner to instruct him in the next pose.

"That's perfect," the photographer announced.

"What's perfect?"

"What you're doing right now."

Grant inspected himself: unbuttoned coat, slouch hat, muddy shoes, arms and legs askew. This was a *commanding* posture?

The commander of the Army of the Tennessee steadfastly held the pose, an expression of mild annoyance on his features, while the photographer fiddled, fussed, and generally toyed with the equipment. Although the snapshot would be of Grant, it was definitely Skinner who was strutting and fretting his hour upon the stage. Finally, Skinner ducked behind the camera and exposed the chemically coated glass plate to the light patterns emanating from the scene.

"All done, General," he announced.

Relaxing, Grant asked, "When will it be available?"

"Oh, about a day. I've got a few more to develop in my darkroom wagon."

Grant nodded, then stretched his legs. Skinner removed the photographic plate and stashed it away in a lightproof cloth wrapper along with several others.

"We should get you on a horse someday, General. You would look good on a horse."

"Everyone looks good on a horse. It is one of the functions of a horse to make his rider look good."

Skinner started to laugh but stopped when he detected no reciprocal laughter from Grant.

When a rumble of hoof beats met their ears, Grant and Skinner looked up to see three horsemen approaching. The profoundly bewhiskered John McClernand was arriving with two of his aides. McClernand descended from his horse and walked directly toward Grant, nodding a vacuous hello to Skinner as he passed. His aides remained in their saddles. Reaching his destination, McClernand snapped to attention and saluted Grant, who returned the gesture with somewhat less *panache*.

"Sir, the Duckport canal is complete," McClernand said.

Grant studied the man who dearly wanted to replace him. There was a strident edge to McClernand's voice that suggested, to Grant at least, that this was not necessarily good news.

"And what is its status?"

"The canal is in good order but the river has begun to fall. I fear the water level may not be sufficient for the passage of our ships.

Grant rubbed his beard, looked around and ordered an aide to saddle a horse for him. The aide quickly performed the task and brought a chestnut mare past the headquarters tent to Grant, who immediately mounted it. Patting the horse's flanks to steady her while McClernand re-mounted his horse, Grant turned to the photographer and said, "Skinner, we will have to be finished for now."

"Sir, I was right, you look magnificent on a horse," Skinner said hopefully. "Could you hold still a moment while I . . ."

"If I intended to hold still, I wouldn't be on a horse," Grant said bluntly and galloped the chestnut past McClernand's entourage before their leader had steadied himself in the saddle. When Grant was a quarter mile ahead, the trio spurred their horses to catch up.

Watching forlornly as Grant and then his followers disappeared into a copse of trees, Skinner weighed his options. He could pack up and go back to his wagon to develop the pictures he had already taken, or he could scour the camp for scenes that might accompany a human-interest story in his magazine. After making a hasty perusal of camp activities, he decided that nothing which hadn't been covered a hundred times in one publication or another was going on. He folded up his equipment and wheeled it back to the wagon, wondering on the way what it was like to be Ulysses S. Grant. He seemed like such an ordinary mortal in all things except warfare. Even in war, Grant's leadership was anything but exciting and, except in retrospect, rarely inspired admiration or awe. It was, simply put, businesslike.

With one exception, Emmanuel Skinner suddenly realized. Ulysses S. Grant could ride a horse like no one he had ever seen.

*   *   *

Colonel George G. Pride, the supervisor of the Duckport Canal Project, gazed querulously as the dipper dredge *Sampson* sank its huge teeth into the Mississippi slime, swallowed it, and then disgorged it on the west bank of the canal. Every time he saw one of the beasts in action, he could barely contain his awe. The steam-driven dipper dredges were marvels of technology. They were like metallic arms with shoulders, elbows and cavernous hands that could scratch tons of earth with gouging fingers and fling it aside with barely a grunt from its powerful engines. Floated on barges, the dredges could do the work of a hundred men, perhaps a thousand, and come back the next day without the plague of exhaustion and muscular fatigue.

"Sir, I thought you told General McClernand the canal was finished," said Lieutenant Joseph Parr. A younger man than Pride, Parr shaved as little hair from his face as possible to illustrate that he could, in fact, grow the stuff. As a result, his sideburns were like goose down stretching from his ears to just above his goose-like neck. By contrast, except for his handlebar mustache, Pride was clean-shaven.

"It is, but I want to see if it might be possible to keep pace with the Mississippi."

Skeptical, Parr said, "All thirty-seven miles from Duckport to New Carthage? That's a long way."

Pride raised a scolding finger and replied, "Lieutenant, the canal itself is only a half mile long at Walnut Bayou. We are not responsible for dredging Walnut Bayou the rest of the way."

"We may not be responsible, but there's nothing to stop Walnut Bayou from drying up too."

Pride reluctantly conceded the point with a wave of his hand. The level of the Mississippi River was notoriously fickle. Since it drained the entire midsection of the country, heavy rainfalls anywhere in that region or in the mountains bounding it on east and west could fill it to overflowing. A sustained drought could do just the opposite. Drought was the problem Pride had to face. Measurements of the Mississippi's plunging water level indicated that, when the separating levee was removed, the canal's depth would be only five or six feet. This was barely enough to pass transports, barges, and gunboats through.

Pride and Parr heard hoof beats from the northwest and looked to see Grant arrive and dismount in one fluid motion. By the time McClernand and his aides arrived, Grant was already at Pride's side, rubbing his beard and alternately gazing at the dipper dredge and the swath it had cut through the Mississippi landscape.

"Well, Pride, are you ready to bust the levee and let the old man come in?" Grant asked.

"No, sir," Pride responded, somewhat panicked by his commander's insistent tone. "We need to dig a little more. That's what we're doing now."

"General McClernand tells me the river is falling rapidly. Is that so?"

"Yes."

"Can you keep up with the drop? If you can't, we might as well bust the levee right now and bring our boats in. We need to get the army south of Vicksburg. I have no other way to do that safely."

Feeling the pressure, Pride squirmed and waited for McClernand to reach them before replying.

"I understand that, General Grant, and I can't predict how fast the Mississippi will drop. That's in God's hands."

This caused Grant's normally stoic face to screw up in irritation.

"I see no point in bringing God into this, Colonel. He has enough to do. What do you think, General?"

McClernand did not at first recognize he was the target of the question, but, realizing he was the only general present other than Grant, formulated a hasty response.

"There's no good way to predict how fast the river will fall," he said glumly, casting a sidelong glance at Pride. The Colonel's return glance was not contradictory, so he promptly added, ". . . or whether we can keep pace with the rate of drop."

Grant looked at McClernand with a blurred expression that tried to blend respect and surprise. He was not used to hearing intelligent, honest opinions from John McClernand.

"That's my opinion as well," he said, placing his hands on his hips and surveying Pride's work. Showing neither pleasure nor distress, he strolled along the edge of the canal and then returned, lifting his eyes to Pride's.

"And for that reason, I think it best to cut the levee and see what we've got. Do you agree, Colonel Pride?"

With a sigh, Pride replied, "Of course."

"General McClernand?"

Assuming his command presence, McClernand straightened and proclaimed, "Yes, I think it's an excellent idea."

"Good, we're agreed then," Grant said with little affectation, then turned to Parr. "Sergeant, go tell the men at the upper end to cut the levee."

Parr saluted, found his black gelding and rode off to perform his duty somewhat more enthusiastically than the occasion demanded. Like many soldiers Grant had observed, Parr tended to equate action and accomplishment, especially when it involved blowing something up.

It was ten minutes and less than thirty words of conversation before they heard the blast and saw the smoke. Grant listened hopefully for the sound of an approaching deluge but was disappointed. It was five minutes more before one of McClernand's men saw a muddy ripple casually making its way toward them, and another five before a steadily flowing stream was achieved.

Gazing in disappointment at the gurgling rivulet, Grant said to Pride, "How deep do you think it is, four feet?"

Pride shrugged, replying, "About that. Maybe it will eventually make five."

Snorts and harrumphs of opinions from the others suggested this was probably an optimistic estimate. A parade of workers from the levee end of the canal with a mounted Sergeant Parr at their head snaked toward Grant, McClernand, and Pride. They were anxious to observe the fruits of their labor. The dipper dredge *Sampson* was immobilized after its operators abandoned it to participate in the proceedings, such as they were.

"Colonel Pride, can we bring the boats in?" Grant asked. "Is it deep enough?"

"I think so. We'll have to measure. But . . ." Pride murmured hesitantly.

"But what?"

Pride pointed downstream, where a tangle of tree limbs and stumps littered the canal, blocking passage.

"We have to clear that first."

"And how long will that take?" Grant demanded, with as much frustration as any of them had ever heard in his voice.

Pride was loath to answer, but he managed to work up the courage.

"Four, five days."

"FIVE DAYS!"

"We'll probably have to clean out Walnut Bayou as well," Pride murmured meekly. "I'm sorry, sir, it's the damned Mississippi."

Though he tried not to show it, Grant was distressed.

"Colonel, we cannot afford to rely on this canal for transporting troops below Vicksburg. We'll have to find another way. But I would like to be able to float supply barges through here. Once we get the army and gunboats where we want them, they'll need as much coal, food, and weaponry as they can get. Can you get enough water flowing through here to do that?"

Like Grant, George Pride tried not to show his trepidation. He was being asked to ponder the imponderable: how the Mississippi River would behave in the next few weeks. No, it was more than that. He was being asked to assure his commander that the Mississippi would deliver enough water to the canal to enable it to pass barges through. He felt like pointing out to Grant that he could not assume the role of God but concluded that the general was probably not in the mood for sarcasm. He gazed at the still sputtering stream below and turned to Grant.

"We'll do our best," he said. "Even barges need a few feet of draught."

Grant frowned at the tepid response but accepted it.

"Good, good, that's all I can ask," he said, patting Pride's forearm. "Do you need more equipment?"

"Dipper Dredges, certainly."

"You'll get more," Grant promised.

"Thank you, sir," Pride replied.

"General Grant, we still have to get troops below Vicksburg before we can attack her. How do you propose to do that?"

It was McClernand. While Grant and he did not much care for each other, they were usually able to communicate in restrained utterances. But this remark was delivered with a barely concealed contempt that could easily be interpreted as insubordinate. Grant struggled to retain his equanimity.

"I propose to do that, General, by discussing the matter with my advisors," he said curtly.

"A council of war? Is that what you mean?" McClernand growled. "At the present time, we hardly have a war. The enemy's defenses are too formidable."

"That, sir, is the purpose of a war council," Grant said stiffly. "To determine how best to force the enemy into the open."

There was enough edge in Grant's voice to warn McClernand to temper his attitude. For a tense moment, the two men stared at each other with mutual if repressed hostility. Finally, Grant spoke.

"Besides, General McClernand, aren't you getting a little tired of dragging your feet in the Mississippi mud? I certainly am."

★ EIGHTEEN ★

April 16, 1863, the Mouth of the Yazoo River

In his relative isolation on the upper deck of the *Benton*, David Porter could easily have yielded to a black depression. The news about the De Soto Point and Duckport canals was discouraging. One had been flooded out and it looked like the other would never be finished. Even if one of them were to be successfully completed, the plunging water level of the Mississippi would prevent ferrying troops through it to the east bank. Only transports could accomplish this, and the only remaining way to get transports from Milliken's Bend to a bombardment-free position south of Vicksburg was to sail them past the Gibraltar of the Confederacy. While his Navy colleague and friend Admiral David Farragut had shown this to be possible, it was not an undertaking David Porter was looking forward to.

"Are the boats in good shape?" he asked his *aide-de-camp* Lieutenant Albert Day.

"As good as they'll ever be," Day sighed.

Porter understood Day's reservations. The gunboats and transports they would be exposing to bombardment from Vicksburg were the same ones that had been used in the Steele's Bayou expedition. They were, to put it mildly, banged up. God only knew which boilers and their associated plumbing would collapse when confronted by the explosive force of an artillery shell or two.

"We'll be moving fast. We're only going downstream," Porter explained. "*The Queen of the West* and the *Indianola* made it. There's no reason why other boats can't."

Except that the Confederates will have more targets to shoot at, Porter reflected. He gazed out into a foggy night crowned by a hazy full moon then back at his *aide-de-camp*. Not surprisingly, Lieutenant Day was unconvinced.

"Aren't we coming back, sir?"

"It's too risky. We can't fight the Mississippi current *and* the Rebel cannonade. It would be suicide."

"What if the Rebs attack north of Vicksburg?"

"That will have to be General Grant's problem, I'm afraid."

Both men fell silent. There was little more that could be said. Bringing Porter's fleet south of Vicksburg would expose the army north of the city to whatever Confederate military operations Pemberton and his staff chose to pursue, and Porter could do nothing about it. Grant's orders had explicitly recognized the problem when he had told Porter: "You must understand that when these gunboats go below, we give up all hope of getting them up again. If we do send vessels below, it will be the best vessels we have, and there will be nothing left to attack Haynes' Bluff."

It was vintage Grant: gambling the gains he had already made against the prospect of a much larger prize. He admired Grant's boldness but wondered if "reckless" might be a more apt description of the general's approach to battle. The other Union commanders, like Halleck and McClellan, insisted on having all their ducks in order before launching a campaign. But they weren't winning. Grant was.

Intruding on Porter's thoughts, the Lieutenant said, "We're not bringing the army with us?"

Porter replied, "No, just the gunboats and transports. That way, if any boats are damaged, it will minimize loss of life."

"How will the army get south of Vicksburg if we don't take them?"

It was probably a little more than he should reveal to a subordinate but Porter felt a need to allay Day's concerns.

"The canals haven't yet worked out and my guess is that they won't. Only one boat got through before the water level dropped too far. It's still dropping. As an alternative, General Grant has ordered General McClernand to dig a dry land route from Milliken's Bend to New Carthage."

Porter paused to let the information sink in. While such a route would certainly avoid the guns of fortress Vicksburg and place the Union forces in a strong position, it would have to pass through a piece of Louisiana in which "dry land" was an unfamiliar if not an unknown concept.

Porter looked at Lieutenant Day and, from the man's gloomy expression, knew what he was thinking: It was just another one of Grant's crazy schemes.

Though he could not have explained his logic, Porter said, "I have a feeling that this time General Grant is serious. Quite serious."

* * *

The *Benton*, Porter's flagship for this adventure, would arrive first. Before the thought had left his mind, Grant saw the lead boat, dark and silent, or at least as silent as a steaming paddle wheeler could be in the dead of night.

"Papa, look," said twelve-year-old Fred Grant, standing next to his father on the upper deck of the *Magnolia*, his finger pointing at the specter rounding the "Point" peninsula.

"I see, son, I see," Grant whispered, as if the Rebels in the Vicksburg batteries might hear him. He resisted the impulse to raise a finger to his lips to shush the boy to silence. Instead, he placed a steadying hand on his son's shoulder.

"It doesn't look like a river. It looks like a lake, it's so quiet," Julia Grant commented from the deck chair behind her husband.

"Let's hope it stays that way," Grant said, smiling at his wife. His gaze did not linger but did manage to take in the substantial contingent of onlookers who had come to witness the event. Lieutenant-Colonel James Wilson of Grant's staff was present, with ten-year-old "Buck" Grant on his lap. The ever-dutiful Charles Dana was also there. Stiff-necked Adjutant General Lorenzo Thomas, the newcomer from Washington, had come to keep an eye on both Dana and Grant, the colonel having become friendlier with the general than the War Department considered appropriate. Finally, a goodly number of Union officers and other significant personages had come in hopes of gaining a good view of the fireworks.

"The Mississippi is a river all right," Grant said. "If you'd ever had to sail a boat upstream, you'd know it."

Swinging his eyes back to the stage right entrance of Porter's armada, Grant listened, tensing at every creak and groan emanating from the river. Surely the Rebels would hear the flotilla's approach or spot some threatening apparition—like a smokestack—emerging through the fog. He wasn't sure that bringing a viewing audience along was a good idea but it was the politically expedient thing to do, assuming the run past Vicksburg achieved a modicum of success. There was no danger to his family or, for that matter, to anyone else on the *Magnolia*. The boat was anchored upstream of the Point, just outside the range of the most powerful of the Vicksburg guns.

Grant jerked involuntarily as the batteries opened fire at the northern end of Vicksburg, where the Union flotilla was negotiating the Point. It was like running a gauntlet in hell as explosions glistened around the gunboats and transports, rocking them with six-foot waves. The muzzle flashes of the Vicksburg cannons were like a swarm of fireflies gone mad, the delayed cacophony of their blasts a strange, disconnected counterpoint.

"O-o-o-oh!" Grant heard from Wilson's direction.

He turned to see Buck shrinking into Wilson's embrace as the reverberations of man-made thunder and lightning reached his ears. Grant smiled reassuringly at him, then took a position behind his wife's chair. After lighting a cigar, he placed his hands on her shoulders.

"It will be over soon," he said.

She grasped his hand but said nothing.

As time grudgingly passed, the Rebels sent fireboats after the flotilla. They were not especially effective, but the cannons were. Some boilers exploded, other boilers did not explode but hissed as the nautical structures around them collapsed from the unrelenting bombardment. The distance was too great to distinguish individual screams, but Grant thought he detected humanity in a shrill descant above the harsh, discordant symphony of destruction. An hour and a half later the Vicksburg batteries fell silent, but the Warrenton batteries downstream could be heard in the distance. At least some of the boats had made the passage successfully. Grant was anxious to know the extent of the damage.

He leaned over Julia, whispering in her ear, "I have to go."

Concerned and slightly indignant, Julia Grant looked up at her husband and said, "Why, Ulys, why do you have to go?"

"I have to see what's been damaged, and I have to check on General McClernand's progress. I have to know."

She seemed to accept that and said, "But why do you have to go *now*?"

"I just do," he sighed. "It's important."

He was tempted to add that he felt this was the critical moment, the one he'd been waiting for that would lead to the downfall of Vicksburg. But it was too soon for such optimism. There were too many looming obstacles in the way of success. Like most soldiers, he was superstitious enough to fear that a premature forecast of success would somehow "jinx" its outcome.

Julia cast her eyes downward in a gesture somewhere between anger and apprehension, but it was a brief lapse. She was an army wife. Her anxious but stolid gaze returned to her husband, her lips readying themselves to speak. But James Wilson beat her to it.

"Sir, I think I should accompany you," he said, lifting Buck Grant from his lap and cradling him in one arm.

"You don't even know where I'm going, Colonel."

Wilson hesitated, then caught Grant's eye and said, "I can make an educated guess, sir."

Knowing it would be partially concealed by his thick beard, Grant allowed a grin to form on his lips.

"No, Colonel, I need to do this myself," he said then cocked an eye toward his son. "Besides, you already have an assignment."

Wilson looked at Buck to discover that, in the absence of fireworks, the boy had fallen asleep.

Before further discussion was possible, Grant kissed his wife, bade her goodbye, and hastened down the steps to the lower deck and from there to the shore. On the way, several officers, Charles Dana among them, tried to engage him in conversation, but none was successful. Dana and Wilson, the latter with Buck Grant hoisted over one shoulder, ran into each other as they watched their commander depart.

"Where's he going in such a hurry?" Dana asked.

"To meet Admiral Porter. He's not good at waiting."

Dana gave Wilson a quizzical look, not quite comprehending the comment.

"He's not going to get drunk, is he?"

Before Dana had finished the question, Grant mounted his horse and headed south. It was the sound of galloping hooves that caught Dana's attention.

"My God, I've never seen a man ride like that before. What's gotten into him?"

"Whatever it is," Wilson opined, rocking the boy gently in his arms. "It's not whisky."

The Balfour House, Vicksburg, Mississippi

John Pemberton's wife, with whom the commander of the Vicksburg defenses was dancing, saw the flash before anyone in the ballroom heard the explosion. Her startled expression startled him. The subsequent blast, though moderate, startled both of them. Because it was a small shell and exploded high above the Walnut Hill batteries at the northern end of Vicksburg, Pemberton concluded it must have been fired as an alarm. That meant a Union attack—or at least Union activity—and that was very much his business.

"Excuse me, Martha," he said, trying to see past his wife's tall, beehive-like coiffure and make his way past the throng of dancers to the veranda facing the river. After several collisions with startled couples, he was out the door, accompanied by staff officers who had also heard or seen the alarm. The veranda was already agog with the Vicksburg aristocracy enjoying the fireworks while they sipped mint juleps and chattered. Pemberton hurried to the porch railing and tried to see through the fog to the Mississippi. He could make out little except the showers of sparks and billowing smoke from the smokestacks of riverboat engines operating at maximum power. He heard more than he could see: the unmistakable wash of paddlewheels churning, the subterranean growl of steam engines, and the exhausted hiss of spent steam discharging into the world. He spotted a lieutenant of his headquarters staff gawking at the sights and sounds, which included a buxom brunette at his side.

"Lieutenant, what's happening?" He demanded. "Are the Yankees attacking?"

As a former Yankee, Pemberton was uncomfortable using the term but decided this was no time to be observing the niceties.

"I don't know, sir," the Lieutenant stammered.

"Well, find out. If the Walnut Hills batteries haven't reported in, get someone over there. The same goes for the Warrenton batteries. We have to know what we are up against."

The lieutenant quickly downed his drink, saluted, and scurried off, leaving his lady friend to an uncertain fate with the commander of the Vicksburg defenses. Concluding there was not much fun to be had with the anxious Pemberton, she soon excused herself and left him with his thoughts. He stared down at the river, willing the fog to clear, and was rewarded with a blaze of orange light emanating from the north shore. He smiled, knowing exactly what it was. The soldiers in the northern emplacements had set fire to cotton bales and tar barrels to illuminate the Yankee flotilla, making better targets of them. It was part of the drill.

But the Union boats, some of which he could see were well downstream of Vicksburg, had not fired a shot. Not a single one! With their engines on full ahead, their sole objective seemed to be passing Vicksburg as rapidly as possible. Was it a challenge of some sort?

"Do you think they are getting ready to attack, sir? Why haven't our guns opened up on them?"

It was Corporal Robert Meyer, another of his aides, who had posed the question. Pemberton diverted his gaze to Meyer's face. The corporal was a head taller than he was and considerably more muscular. But the look on his face betrayed the uncomprehending anxiety of adolescence.

"I don't know why our guns are silent. Hopefully, they won't be for long."

As if reacting to Pemberton's command, the Fort Hill battery fired its heavy guns. The atmosphere was soon filled with flashes of light, thundering explosions, and a general fury that tormented all the senses. Smoke belched from cotton bales, tar barrels, smokestacks, and cannons, colluding with the already thick fog to shield the chaos from view.

"Thank you, sir," Meyer said.

"For what?"

"For reassuring me, sir," Meyer replied. Some of the anxiety had vanished from his face.

Pemberton shook his head. The only reassurance he had supplied was a supposition that the Vicksburg guns would not be silent for long. That supposition had proved true, but it could hardly be called reassurance. He wished he could eliminate apprehension from his own mind as easily as Meyer could, and found it a bit annoying that Corporal Meyer's attention was so easily diverted from reality.

"Corporal, this is a serious . . ."

At that moment, a shell from one of the Walnut Hills batteries struck home. The explosion had the intensity and rhythm of a descant of thunderclaps. Before his ears stopped ringing, Pemberton looked and saw one of the Yankee transports lying askew in the rippling water, fire and steam rushing skyward from where its boiler had been. At least a dozen men, half of them unconscious or dead, were floating in the river. The other half were struggling to put distance between them and the sinking vessel. Those that had not been blown into the Mississippi were abandoning ship to follow those that had. In the brilliance of the yellow-orange firelight, Pemberton saw the vessel's name painted on its side: *Henry Clay*.

Something about the scene wasn't right.

Pemberton noted that he was the only one on the veranda who was not screaming with delight at the *Henry Clay's* plight.

"Sir, this is a great victory!" Meyer squealed, then let out a series of howls that had come to be known as the "Rebel Yell." "Did you see that explosion? Did you see . . ."

Meyer was no longer talking to Pemberton but to a group of listeners who seemed enthralled by his every word. The commander drifted away, still irked by an inconsistency he couldn't quite put his finger on. The *Henry Clay* had been sunk, her crew killed or forced into the Mississippi. That was good, wasn't it?

Then he halted in his tracks. He knew what was wrong. There were no soldiers aboard the *Henry Clay*. If Grant had intended to attack Vicksburg tonight, the transports would be loaded with soldiers. That's why they'd moved so swiftly downstream. All they wanted to do was pass by the batteries and . . .

Get below Vicksburg!

Pemberton hurried back to Corporal Meyer and pounded him on the shoulder. Meyer, who had been participating in a spontaneous cheering session with several male and female attendees, turned to find his commander demanding his attention. Painfully, he suppressed his irritation.

"Yes . . . sir."

"Corporal, ten minutes ago I issued orders, the substance of which was intelligence gathering. I now find I need to modify those orders."

Meyer was instantly attentive, his demeanor evident in the rigidity of his posture and the set of his jaw. Pemberton gave him the name of the officer he had sent out and told him to intercept the man before he got too far.

"Tell the Lieutenant I want him to send a scouting party across the river."

"Across the river?" Meyer mumbled.

"Yes, *across* the river, somewhere upstream of New Carthage, where they won't be seen," Pemberton snapped. "I want them to look for troop movements, and I want to know which corps of Grant's army are involved and the number of troops in each."

The puzzled expression on Meyer's face gave way to a dawning enlightenment.

"Sir, do you think the Yankees are marching an army to New Carthage and the boats they sent past us tonight were sent to ferry them across?"

"I do."

It was enough for Meyer. After being dismissed by Pemberton, he ran from the veranda in search of a horse. For his part, Pemberton's first order of business was to find his wife. She was in the ballroom chatting with a clique of women friends and toying with a glass of champagne.

"Martha, I have to go," he announced.

She did not object but asked, "What's happening, John? Are the Yankees attacking?"

"No, but I'm afraid they will be soon."

"I don't understand."

The last thing Pemberton wanted to do was launch into a lengthy explanation of the tactics he expected Grant to use and why the Vicksburg defenses might not be able to deal with them. But he needed to say something.

"I'm convinced General Grant is sending an army to new Carthage. The boats that got by us tonight will transfer them across the Mississippi. It's very bad."

"What does that mean? Can't we just turn our guns on them, send an army after them? What about General Johnston? Can't he help?"

Anxious to depart so he could gather his staff and develop a military response, Pemberton strained to be patient.

"General Johnston is in Jackson and is in no position to assist us immediately. Of course we can send forces after the Yankees but we've lost one of our best defenses—the Mississippi River. Yesterday, they were on one side, and we were on the other. Now we'll both be on the east bank. If they get enough troops across, they can attack Vicksburg at will."

Wringing her small, alabaster hands, Martha Pemberton looked as if she might cry. Instead, she looked up at her husband and said, "You were with General Grant in the Mexican war, weren't you? Is he a good man?"

"He and I *were* in that war. We didn't know each other that well."

"What kind of a man is he?"

John Pemberton gently enfolded his wife in his arms. He understood the dread she was feeling. The conquest of Vicksburg was now a distinct possibility. Should it come to that, how would the victor treat the vanquished? Would he be cruel or would he behave in a civilized manner?

"Sam Grant is not Robert E. Lee. He did not distinguish himself in the Mexican War like Lee did. But, as far as I know, he is a good soldier and a gentleman."

"A gentleman," she echoed with a skeptical intonation. She gave Pemberton a final, apprehensive glance and, with a blank look and a curtsy, excused herself. Pemberton guessed she would find some place where she could cry without fear of being disturbed.

Without further delay, he departed the ball and the mansion, headed for the stables, and had a horse saddled. Launching himself into the saddle, he headed for the river, hoping, but not expecting, to find some Yankee prisoners to interrogate. He steered his horse close to the river's edge, parallel to the sinking Yankee transport. The *Henry Clay* was settling comfortably on the river bottom and, like an injured beast, groaned every once in a while to alleviate its pain. The boiler fires still burned, and black smoke was still issuing from the bowels of the vessel. He couldn't tell if there was anyone left on board.

"General, sir?" a hoarse voice said.

Startled, Pemberton looked to his right to find an aging, gray-bearded man wearing a kepi on his naked scalp and a grimy Confederate uniform on his crooked frame. The stripes on his sleeve identified him as a sergeant.

"Where is everyone? I was hoping to find some Yankee prisoners."

"Ain't no Yankees here, sir," the sergeant said, shaking his head and pointing at several bobbing heads. "They're bein' picked up by Yankee rowboats."

Pemberton squinted and eventually saw the rowboats picking their way from one bobbing head to the next.

"No bodies?"

"None that I seen."

Pemberton noticed the old soldier eyeing him curiously. In turn, he became curious.

"What's your name, Sergeant?"

"Crabtree, sir," the man said, executing a limp salute. "Sergeant Anselm Crabtree."

"Why are you here? Why are you the only one here?"

Crabtree hemmed and hawed, then replied, "There was a bunch of us down here, sir. Came down for the same reason you did, to find Yankees. Like I said, didn't find any."

Pemberton tried again.

"But you're still here, Sergeant Crabtree. Why is that?"

Initially puzzled by the query, the sergeant began to understand.

"Hold on, hold on, sir. If you're thinkin' I'm a spy, you got it all wrong. Ain't a spyin' bone in my body. I'm a Con-federate soldier all the way. Just wanted to see a Yankee up close. See if they really got them devil's horns and all. You know . . ."

Pemberton smiled, acknowledging the joke, but found he could not feign light-heartedness. He did make an attempt.

"I'm a Yankee myself, Sergeant. Do I have horns?"

Crabtree gazed uncertainly at his commander, unsure how to interpret his words.

"You mean you *was* a Yankee, sir. You ain't no more."

"That's right, Sergeant," Pemberton said, then added with forced good humor, "I *was* a Yankee from Philadelphia. That's about as Yankee as you can be."

Crabtree picked up a flat stone and hurled it toward the hapless Henry Clay. It skipped three times and sank into the river before covering half the distance to the Yankee transport. Retreating back to Pemberton, Crabtree seemed to have absorbed some of the general's melancholy.

"What do you think Grant is up to, sir?"

"He's going to attempt a crossing, probably at New Carthage."

"Got some army corps down there, did he?"

"I think so. We'll find out soon enough."

Pemberton promptly became engrossed in thought, provoked by Crabtree's question about Grant's intentions. He realized that, except for crossing the river and eventually attacking, he had no idea what Grant was up to. He wished he could expand his insight into Grant's thinking so he could not only answer such questions but predict what the Union commander would do next. What Pemberton knew about his opponent would not fill a page in a notebook. He did know that, as young men, both Grant and he had had no particular desire to join the military, but had been forced by dictatorial fathers to enter West Point. Neither had especially distinguished himself in the Mexican War, though both had fought bravely. After that war, both men had continued to serve in the military, but Grant had eventually resigned in favor of civilian pursuits, at which he had usually failed. Pemberton had remained in the United States military and been moderately successful in that career.

Was that the key difference? But how could it be? He, John Pemberton, was the more experienced army man, not Ulysses S. Grant. Shouldn't that count in his favor? And yet it did not. The quixotic Union commander not only had him bamboozled but, to a considerable degree, intimidated. Grant was crazy; he tried anything and everything, rendering predictions of his future behavior virtually impossible.

"Sir, may I be dismissed?" asked the sergeant.

"What? Oh . . . Sergeant Crabtree . . ." Pemberton stammered as he emerged from his reverie. "What is it?"

"I have to go. Get back to my unit. They'll be wonderin' where I am."

"Certainly, certainly, Sergeant. You are dismissed."

They exchanged salutes and Crabtree sallied off, in no great hurry. Only then did Pemberton realize Crabtree had not identified his unit. But he was headed in the general direction of the Walnut Hills batteries, so he must belong to one of them.

For no particular reason, he dismounted and took a stroll along the water's edge. The night had turned deceptively peaceful. Waves lapped steadily on the shore, and the Mississippi was still rushing past on its ceaseless journey to the Gulf of Mexico. Despite its groans of pain, even the *Henry Clay* seemed at peace, the raging conflagrations aboard her having mellowed to glowing red coals and smoke, the former reflected in the river like the eyes of river monsters.

The Vicksburg commander remounted his horse and led it up the steepening riverbank. Thoughts of his nemesis returned.

To ferry all his troops across the river, Grant would need more transports. He was sure of that. But when would the Union commander make another run past Vicksburg and how would he, Pemberton, stop him? There was also the possibility of other attack points. Were tonight's activities the main thrust or were they a diversion to cover something more threatening?

Pemberton did not know the answer to these mental queries and was uncertain of his ability to guess correctly. Nevertheless, he would have to make decisions, critical decisions.

No one could help him do that. He was quite alone.

Then, unexpectedly, he was not alone. The atmosphere around him was suddenly filled with blast waves and the sky with a rising mushroom of flames and smoke as the Henry Clay suffered the finale of her destruction.

"Jesus!" Pemberton muttered as he turned to behold the fresh conflagration. "Jesus God Almighty!"

★ NINETEEN ★

April 16, 1863, Vicksburg

The blast of the *Henry Clay's* final explosion still resonated in the ears of Christopher Spalding, even though he was underwater and struggling not to be. As a civilian member of the *Henry Clay's* crew, he was distressed that he seemed to have been singled out for abusive treatment by the Rebel cannoneers. Finally, he reached the surface and tried to rid his ears of the incessant ringing by popping them with quick palm strikes. It didn't work. *Damn, he'd lost his hat, too. What a nuisance!*

He took a hurried look around and discovered he was on the starboard side of the *Henry Clay*, which was in flames and facing downstream, riding low in the water. At least a half dozen heads other than his own were bobbing in the rough water and chattering with shock and cries for help. The pilot was still at the wheel, trying to steer the *Henry Clay* out of harm's way. Within a few minutes, a cannonball crashed into the boat's port side and sent a bouquet of flame and smoke spinning skyward. Spalding had no direct line of sight to view the damage, but he could tell by the boat's increased rate of submersion that the vessel was doomed. As if to punctuate that conclusion, the pilot finally abandoned ship. *About time*, Spalding decided.

Suddenly noticing that the current was transporting him downstream at a pretty good clip, he started thinking about what he should do next. The Mississippi current was not especially swift but it was turbulent, and he had heard about whirlpools that could suck a man under if he were not careful. He was closer to the Vicksburg side of the river but did not particularly want to spend the rest of the war in a Confederate jail. Could he make it to the west bank and, if he could, how far downstream would he drift before making landfall?

As he was considering which course to take, Spalding heard a gravelly voice saying, "Ahoy, sailor!"

Ahoy? Spalding mused. Thinking he was about to be captured by Confederates, he turned to see a rowboat headed for him, its bow plowing through the choppy water with all the grace of a swimming cow. Kneeling and extending a hand toward him was a Union officer with a stern visage and an equally harsh beard.

"Come on, sailor, grab my hand."

It was then that Spalding recognized his would-be savior. It was General William Tecumseh Sherman.

"Sir!" Spalding blurted. He would have said more but first tried to salute, which drastically reduced his ability to tread water. His head sunk below the waves and he came up coughing and spitting.

"Son, for God's sake, don't try that again. Just get onboard."

Resisting the impulse to salute again, Spalding said, "Yes, sir" and grasped the proffered hand. With the help of his two oarsmen, Sherman pulled Spalding aboard like a fisherman landing a prize marlin and left him squirming on the bottom of the rowboat. Next to him, Spalding discovered two previously rescued members of the *Henry Clay's* crew drying out.

"What's your name, sailor?" Sherman asked.

"Christopher Spalding, sir. But I'm not a sailor."

"You're not? Then what the hell are you *sir-ing* me for?"

"Force of habit, sir."

Sherman shot Spalding a wry look and said, "A civilian, eh? First time I've ever saved one of those lowly creatures. Sons-of-bitches mostly."

Spalding stared dumbfounded at the army man. He didn't want to argue but neither did he want to agree with Sherman's appraisal of civilians.

"Don't worry, son. You're helping us out so I can't honestly demote you to the rank of son-of-a-bitch."

Spalding's sigh of relief was audible.

"Not if you continue to help me. Are you up to it?"

Although he had no idea what kind of help Sherman was expecting, Spalding gave a nod of concurrence.

"Good, good," Sherman said, giving Spalding's shoulder a hefty slap and pointing to the nearby surf. "Now what we're going to do is pull the rest of these floating gentlemen aboard."

Spalding lifted himself and looked. At least a dozen heads were bobbing in the water.

"All of them?"

"No, there are three more rowboats out there."

Spalding extended the depth of his vision and found the other rowboats. One was relatively near; the other two were hugging the burning hull of the *Henry Clay* looking for waterborne sailors. All had picked up two or more crewmembers. He saw something else as well: the pilot strenuously swimming toward them.

"Swimmer off the port bow," he said instinctively.

"Where the hell is that?" Sherman growled.

Chastened, Spalding pointed at the pilot and said, "Over there."

The general growled again but with less zeal. Then he waved and yelled commands at the man in the water. The pilot, however, needed no encouragement and, on arrival, climbed over the gunwale with only minor assistance from Spalding and Sherman. Only then did he chance a look at the *Henry Clay*.

"She's smoking, Christopher," he said sadly.

Less sentimentally, Spalding said, "She is, sir, but I don't think she'll sink too deep."

The pilot offered a stoic shrug. Sinking the boats of the enemy was, of course, the paramount business of the Union and Confederate navies, but refloating the sunken prizes was almost as important an activity. Whether refurbishment was worth the time and effort depended on the boat and the kind of damage that had sunk her. Exploded boilers frequently made such a mess that a boat could not easily recover. But holes in the superstructure, or even the hull, could often be repaired. Nautical speeds on the Mississippi rarely exceeded five knots and were particularly low when moving upstream. To a shore battery, boats were, so to speak, like large ducks lazily swimming by—easy targets. Some boats had been sunk and refloated three or four times.

Before the fire and brimstone of the cannonades finally subsided, Sherman's rowboat picked up four more survivors. The other rowboats managed to procure similar amounts of human cargo. When it was clear that no more of the living remained in the water, Sherman turned the rowboat flotilla toward the west bank and then angled downstream.

"Where are we going?" Spalding asked the bow oarsman, a muscular man with no shirt.

Cupping his hands over his mouth, the oarsman replied, "He's taking us to the De Soto Point canal."

"Why are you whispering?"

The oarsman came closer, cupped one hand over his mouth again and gazed pleadingly at Spalding.

"The canal is an embarrassment."

"To who?"

Rapidly shifting his gaze toward Sherman and back, the oarsman said, "He hates the canal, but he hates the Mississippi for destroying it. In fact, he hates the whole Vicksburg campaign."

Spalding lifted himself and sat down on the seat opposite the oarsman. The big soldier was staring at him with a troubled expression.

"Why would General Sherman be embarrassed and why would he hate the Vicksburg campaign?"

"He's embarrassed because the canal came to nothing. He wanted to make it work for Grant's sake. Sherman and Grant are good friends; that's why he wants it to work. But his better judgment is telling him it won't. Most of the officers, Sherman included, don't think Vicksburg can be taken, with or without the canal, or with any of Grant's other ideas."

Which made it obvious where the oarsman's sentiments lay. As a deckhand, and a civilian one at that, Spalding's knowledge of Army politics was minimal, but he was curious.

"How does General Grant feel about this?" he asked.

The oarsman shrugged and began mumbling, then dropped his voice to a hush.

"No one really knows. He's a very private man, the general is. Some opinion has it that he's just trying to look busy so Halleck doesn't order him back to Memphis."

Judging the oarsman's words too cynical, Spalding remained momentarily silent. They were nearing the downstream end of the De Soto Point canal, or what would have been the downstream end if any significant amount of water had ever flowed through it. Sherman and the bow oarsman jumped out and beached the rowboat. Soldiers from Sherman's Corps rushed down to assist the members of the *Henry Clay's* crew. The bow oarsman laid down his oar and offered Spalding a hand, but the deckhand refused. He wasn't helpless.

As they walked up the beach, Spalding visually examined what he could see of the De Soto Point Canal. There were a few scattered puddles, but its bed was basically dry.

"What happened here? Why didn't it work? It looks like the canal is above the Mississippi."

"It is, but it wasn't always. The old man is fickle. It was just the opposite when we started digging. The water level was too high, so we had to build levees and dams to keep the water out. Had those things operating day and night."

The oarsman pointed to a pair of dipper dredges lying dormant in the canal.

Marveling at the technology that had produced such behemoths, Spalding asked, "Can't you just keep digging?"

The oarsman shook his head and, after removing a cotton undershirt from his pants pocket, slipped it over his head onto his massive frame. Since the shirt was saturated with sweat and river water, Spalding wondered why he bothered.

"I suppose we could, but it would take a while. General Grant's got another scheme now, and he's getting impatient to try it out."

"You mean the scheme he tried tonight? The one that got the *Henry Clay* sunk and me almost drowned?"

The oarsman chuckled with unrestrained glee at Spalding's raw cynicism.

"Yeah, that one," he said. "So far, so good, I'd say. You're alive, ain't you?"

"Well, there's that. I am alive—at least for now." After a lull in the conversation, he asked, "What do you think? Will it work?"

"Will what work?"

"This new scheme, the General's latest. The one that nearly got me killed."

The oarsman adjusted his undershirt to cover more of his potbelly.

"Hell, who knows? Who can say? We got two transports through. McClernand got some of his people down to New Carthage. More comin' . . . more transports comin' too . . . least I hope so. Who knows . . . maybe."

Spalding remained skeptical, his folded arms reflecting the attitude. The oarsman uttered a nervous grunt and glanced away.

"It seems to me a few more 'for sures' and a few less 'maybes' would be a big improvement to this grand strategy," Spalding said.

The remark annoyed the oarsman. His face twisted into a scowl and he grabbed the deckhand's arm, leading him toward a boulder that had been extracted from the canal. Then he placed his beefy hands on Spalding's shoulders and forced him to sit.

"Let me tell you somethin', son," the oarsman began. "First thing is my name. It's Sergeant Adam Cahill of Sherman's Corps. So if you want to repeat what I have to say, you have somebody to blame."

As he talked, Cahill raised a scolding finger directly in front of Spalding's face. This and the tremulous quality of the sergeant's voice let Spalding know it would be a good idea to listen.

"The second thing is, General Grant lives on 'maybes.' That's how he wins battles."

"But that makes no sense. Wouldn't it be better to have a solid plan? What's going to happen when we get to the Vicksburg side of the river? We'll have Pemberton on our left in Vicksburg, Johnston on our right in Jackson and the rest of the Reb army in between. And if we make any decent penetration we'll have to maintain a supply line all the way back to Young's Point . . ."

Cahill's head vacillated between a negative shake and a vigorous nod, shifting gears every time Spalding began a fresh sentence. Eventually finding his voice, or, perhaps, dizzy from the oscillations of his head, he straightened and said, "No, no, you've got it all wrong. General Grant has a plan. It's just not a hard and fast plan. It's flexible."

"What is it, this plan?"

"How the hell would I know?" said Cahill, throwing his arms up in frustration. "I'm just a sergeant."

"But you said Grant didn't have a plan."

"I most certainly did not."

"You said he lived on 'maybes.' That's not what I call a plan."

The big soldier was momentarily at a loss for words. Rather than react, he seated himself on the boulder next to Spalding, thrust his hands onto his knees and fumed. In two minutes he was breathing normally and was again capable of normal speech. He looked sideways at his companion.

"For a sailor, you have a lot of opinion about the army way of doing things."

Spalding shrugged and replied, "I'd like to get out of this war alive."

Cahill nodded, appreciating the sentiment.

"So would we all," he offered, glancing away. When his gaze returned to Spalding, it had a conciliatory glimmer. "Tell you what. Why don't we ask Sherman?"

"Ask him what?"

"Your questions. What's Grant's plan, how does he intend to supply the army, all that."

Spalding's initial reaction was to laugh out loud, but he restrained the impulse. Then he looked toward the mound over which Sherman had disappeared and brought his gaze back to Cahill.

"Nah . . . Sherman's got better things to do."

"Tonight he's the captain of a rowboat squadron. It's not exactly a challenging assignment," Cahill said, taking Spalding by one arm and urging him forward. "Come on, let's find him."

Reluctantly, the deckhand followed the sergeant over a small hill and down to a campfire, where Sherman and several officers were eating baked beans and drinking coffee. Sherman was seated in what looked like an old kitchen chair with his legs crossed.

"Sir!" said Cahill, snapping a salute.

Sherman lazily sipped at his coffee and looked up at the two men. Cahill still had Spalding by the arm, a fact that did not provoke a response from the general.

"Yes, Sergeant?"

"Sir, Mr. Spalding has some concerns about the conduct of the Vicksburg campaign."

Spalding squirmed in embarrassment, tossing his head from side to side and repeating, "That's not . . ." He seemed unable to find a way to complete the sentence and was eventually beaten to the punch by Sherman.

"Really?" the general challenged. "You're the civilian we picked up, aren't you? Mr. Spalding? Maybe I should have let you float out there a while longer, let you meditate on your concerns."

The flames of the campfire masked the scarlet of Spalding's face. He wrenched his arm from Cahill's grasp and peevishly grumbled, "That's not the way I would . . ."

"Mr. Spalding thinks General Grant's plan has some flaws," Cahill asserted.

"That is *not* what I said!" Cahill shouted.

Sherman calmly signaled for silence with a raised hand, ingested a mouthful of beans, and took another sip of coffee. Then he presented a blank stare to Spalding.

"What is it you find inadequate in our plan?"

Our plan, Spalding thought. *Not Grant's plan.*

Settling himself, Spalding said, "I was just wondering out loud, that's all. No criticism intended."

"You were wondering how we should deal with Pemberton?"

"Yes."

"And Johnston in Jackson?"

"Yes."

"And the Reb army?"

"Yes."

"And you were wondering how we can maintain a supply train across the Mississippi without having it cut to pieces by the Confederates?"

Encouraged by Sherman's comprehension of his apprehension, Spalding sputtered, "I was curious about what General Grant has in mind . . ."

"So am I," Sherman stoically announced. Neither humor nor anxiety was evident in his face.

Spalding waited for more, but no further explanation was forthcoming. Sherman extracted a cigar from a knapsack next to his chair, lighted it, and puffed contentedly.

"So are you what?" Spalding asked, adding a meek, "Sir."

"So am I concerned, Mr. Spalding. Everyone is, and should be," Sherman answered, then fell silent again.

"I don't understand," a confused Spalding admitted.

Sherman removed the cigar from his lips and sighed. He stared up at the befuddled deckhand.

"Let me tell you what a Ulysses S. Grant battle plan is *not*, Mr. Spalding. It is *not* Wellington at Waterloo. It is *not* even Washington at Yorktown. It is *not* a work of art . . ."

"But it must be a plan of some kind . . ." Spalding interjected.

"It is and it isn't," Sherman quickly shot back, then took a short drag on the cigar and slowly exhaled. "Consider the other projects the general has blessed us with. How many have there been, seven, eight?"

"Seven," Sergeant Cahill replied.

"Right, seven. We've spent several months digging canals and exploring swamps trying to find a way to attack Vicksburg. We haven't yet found one that shows much promise of success. That doesn't mean there's been no planning. There has. Are they well thought out plans? Maybe not. Do some of them look a little silly on sober reflection? They probably do. But I'll tell you one thing, Mr. Spalding . . ."

Before fulfilling his promise, Sherman drank deeply from his coffee mug. After swallowing, he held the cigar poised for action, but did not return it to its place of honor between his lips.

"I'll tell you one thing, Mr. Spalding. If any one of these seven adventures had shown even the slightest prospect of success, General Grant would have pounced."

"Pounced?"

"Yes, pounced! That's what he does. That's what sets him apart from the dilettantes like George McClellan. He pounces on the enemy, seizes him by the throat, and chokes the life out of him. You don't need a grand battle plan if you're willing and able to commit your forces to the destruction of the enemy."

Which also means committing a good many of your own troops to destruction, Spalding thought, but did not transform into words.

"I think I understand, sir, but what exactly will be accomplished by tonight's activities?"

"I can't tell you."

"Why not?"

"Because you're a damned civilian and it's a military secret," Sherman said, smiling through a cloud of cigar smoke that had drifted his way.

Spalding snorted in frustration and muttered, "Does this eighth . . . plan . . . show any more promise than the other seven did?"

"Be damned if I know. Too early to tell."

"Will your troops be involved?"

"Yes."

"How?"

"Can't say. Military secret."

"So there is a plan?"

"Never said there wasn't."

Spalding knew Sherman was enjoying himself and was ready to conclude the conversation. But Sherman, perhaps noticing his companion's consternation, had a final word.

"War time is not peace time, Mr. Spalding. As warriors, we do things we would never do, would never be allowed to do, in peace time. To put it simply: War is Hell. It is in fact worse than Hell because we do not understand why we are being punished. In Hell, a man knows his sins; at a battlefront he does not. A virtuous man is as likely to suffer a horrible death as a sinful one . . ."

Sherman snarled and waved an arm in a dismissive gesture.

"We need secrets, Mr. Spalding. We must maintain absolute secrecy in some matters. Plans of battle are one of these."

"But you and I have been discussing the plan of *this* battle for fifteen minutes . . ."

"No, we haven't," Sherman interjected. His narrowed eyes bored into Spalding's.

"Think about it. What do you know about the coming campaign that you learned from me? That you didn't learn by observation?"

Spalding reviewed the tidbits of his recent education. He knew that the transports, one of which had been blown out from under him, were to be used to transfer troops across the Mississippi downstream of Vicksburg. He knew that some of those troops, mostly from McClernand's Corps, had already arrived in New Carthage and more would be coming. That was all he knew.

"We must have secrets, Mr. Spalding, because if we are unable to keep the enemy in a state of ignorance as to our actions and whereabouts, men will die. It's that simple," Sherman said.

Had the remark been made contentiously, as some had been this night, Spalding might have given an argument. But the normally cantankerous Sherman had spoken with humility, almost reverence. He tossed the cigar on the ground and stomped it out.

"Will you and your Corps be joining the invasion?" Spalding tried one last time.

"Mr. Spalding, I told you . . ."

". . . that you can't tell me," Spalding finished.

The general shrugged.

"Good night, General Sherman."

"Good night, Mr. Spalding."

The deckhand turned and walked away, looking for some indication of where his fellow crewmembers who had been fished from the Mississippi might be.

"Mr. Spalding!" Sherman's gravelly voice called.

Spalding turned to see Sherman standing by his chair. He had donned a slouch hat and appeared to be preparing himself to depart the premises for the night. The expression on his face was masked by the flickering firelight but seemed calm, even affable.

"My Corps and I will not be going east. We will be engaging the enemy in another direction."

Sherman snapped a salute and strolled off. Spalding was not sure, but he thought he detected a slight grin on the general's rough-hewn face.

★ TWENTY ★

April 16, 1863, McClernand's Road

It was not a good road but it was a road, and that was one of the two things Grant needed. The other was moonlight to let him see the potholes before the horse stepped into one and broke a leg. John McClernand had done a decent job on the road, and for that Grant was grateful.

"Thank you, General McClernand," he said aloud, knowing he would not be heard. What would his friends and colleagues think if they heard him speaking favorably of his nemesis? McClernand was, in fact, the only one of his corps commanders who was enthusiastic about this, the latest and possibly the greatest of Grant's follies. Sensible officers like Sherman, McPherson, and Dana, probably "Old Brains" himself, if he knew the details, would never have conceived an expedition whose first phase was running boats filled with supplies and equipment past the Vicksburg batteries, then marching troops across thirty miles of swampland between Young's Point and New Carthage.

But John McClernand was a little short on common *military* sense. For that limitation, Grant once more expressed his thanks.

Coming upon a corduroy road that McClernand's engineers had built across a flat expanse of swampland, Grant slowed the horse, gently patted her neck, and whispered sweet nothings in her ear. The horse wanted to balk at the hard and irregular terrain beneath its hooves, but the General coaxed her to a trot. Anything more would have been out of the question. When, finally, horse and rider put the corduroy road behind them, Grant reined up and dismounted. It had been an hour since they'd set off at a gallop. A respite was needed.

Immersing himself in a patch of swamp grass, he removed his slouch hat and wiped his brow with one coat sleeve. Then he snatched a cigar from a breast pocket and lighted it, puffing with hungry certitude. Except for brief moments with Julia and their children, this was about as much happiness as he was capable of achieving under the circumstances—circumstances that might even be favorable if Porter and McClernand had made it to New

Carthage unscathed. Even slightly scathed would do. If not, well, then he'd try something else. There was always something else.

Gazing through the fog and cigar smoke at a blurred moon, Grant wondered what fate, or God, had in mind for him. He did not judge himself heroic. At most things he had failed: as a farmer, as a partner in a general store, in virtually all of his academic pursuits at West Point except horsemanship. What was it that lent his generalship a modicum of success? A keen sense of reality? The occasional willingness to interpret orders to suit his own purposes? A vivid but practical imagination? A stoic disregard for failure? It could have been any of these that served as the Praetorian Guard of his destiny.

But it was really much simpler than any symbiosis of personal qualities. Unlike many of his colleagues, he understood what needed to be done and was not squeamish about doing it. The armchair generals in Washington be damned.

"Come on, girl, let's get going," he said, tossing the cigar and re-donning his slouch hat. After mounting the horse, he added, "We've got a long way to go, and you'll be doing most of the work."

April 16, 1863, Downstream of Vicksburg

Gazing on Porter's motley fleet, Grant could not help but wonder if his earlier musings about fate and God had any truth in them. This did not look like success. The boats were at anchor, steam hissing from damaged boilers and merging with the fog to add to the already oppressive humidity. The sounds of cranking and groaning machinery were a pervasive fugue in no particular key. Sailors were everywhere, plugging hulls, repairing leaks, turning valves and securing boats to the shore with thick hemp ropes. Grant felt what he thought were droplets of rain on his bare hands, only to discover on closer inspection that the "droplets" were pieces of soot, sometimes sparks from the numerous, tightly packed smokestacks.

Spotting a sailor rushing by with a bucket of water, he dismounted and grabbed an arm. The man turned, annoyed by the interruption in his frantic activity. When he saw the source of his annoyance, his coal-dusted face assumed a humbler mien.

"Son, I'm looking for Admiral Porter. Do you know where I can find him?"

Nervously, the sailor saluted—a feeble, Navy salute, Grant thought—and said, "Yes, sir, I'll go get him."

The sailor sat his bucket down and scurried off while Grant continued his visual inspection of Porter's command. He noted that many of the boats had coal barges lashed to their starboard sides to permit port side weapons a free field of fire. There was a profusion of water-soaked haystacks on board to shield the boilers. They had not completely fulfilled that purpose. Some were charred and burned, leaving the boilers unprotected.

His meditations were interrupted by a crisp "General."

It was David Porter, his coal black beard disheveled and his uniform soiled with coal and sundry other dusts.

"Admiral, I'm glad to see you looking well," Grant said with a handshake, then turned his gaze to Porter's small fleet. "I'm not as sure about the health of your . . . boats."

Boats, not ships, Grant mentally verified.

Porter's laugh was strained, but it was a laugh.

"It's mostly housekeeping. They must have fired four hundred to six hundred rounds at us, but managed to sink only the *Henry Clay*. The *Lafayette* went aground in front of a Rebel battery and took some serious hits but her captain managed to extricate her. She's still afloat."

"What kinds of sh . . . boats are they?"

"*Henry Clay* is a transport. The *Lafayette* is one of the turtles."

The turtles were ironclad gunboats that rode so low in the water that they resembled the slow-moving reptiles.

At the news of the losses, Grant asked, "Anyone hurt?"

Porter laughed again, this time with more of a chuckle. He wasn't sure, but it appeared to Grant that, beneath his unkempt beard, a smile graced Porter's lips.

"Twelve casualties in all. General Sherman, or, should I say, *Admiral* Sherman helped us. He sent out a squadron of rowboats looking for survivors. Among others, he saved the *Henry Clay's* pilot."

"And the *Lafayette*?"

"Has nine holes in her superstructure but there was no damage to her engines or cannon."

"And the two transports that did make it through?

"The *Silver Wave* and the *Forest Queen*. We haven't completed our inspections, but any damage they might have suffered appears to be tolerable. See for yourself."

As he spoke, Porter swept an arm in the general direction of his two relatively unblemished transports, each secured by two heavy lines to the shore. They were indeed afloat and did not appear to suffer any fore-aft or port-starboard listing.

"We'll need more than two transports," Grant said, walking along the shore to get a more comprehensive view. His voice resonated with concern.

"General Grant, you'll need more than *three* transports," Porter said sardonically. "We both know that."

Wringing his hands behind his back, Grant anxiously broached the inevitable subject.

"Then you know what I'm going to ask you to do."

"Of course. You're going to ask us to make another run past Vicksburg," Porter replied, almost pleasantly. "You have to. There's no choice."

Relieved that he did not have to exercise his limited powers of persuasion to convince Porter that another run past Vicksburg would be necessary, Grant straightened and faced his colleague.

"Good, good, I'm glad I didn't have to make it an order."

Which provoked a hefty guffaw from Porter. Both men were all too well aware that their two commands were entirely separate. Grant could not command Porter any more than Porter could command Grant. That they got the job done anyway was a testament to the spirit of cooperation between them and their services.

"When?" Grant wanted to know.

"Two days, maybe three," Porter answered.

"Good, good. We'll need some time to march the rest of General McClernand's troops to New Carthage. Where is he, by the way?"

"I have reports that he's *at* New Carthage."

Which heartened Grant. It was exactly where McClernand was supposed to be.

"Good. How long will it take your boats to reach there?"

"We can make some quick repairs and steam all night. Should get there by daybreak."

Grant allowed himself a brief grin of satisfaction. Things seemed to be going well, very well. But as soon as the rosy outlook appeared in his head, he quashed it. Nothing ever went perfectly and an operation as complex as the one he envisioned stood no chance of achieving perfection. He mounted his horse and reached down to shake Porter's hand.

"Admiral, you've done a fine job, and you don't need me around to finish it up. We agree on the need for a second run past Vicksburg?"

"We do."

"Good. Let me know when it happens and your entire fleet reaches New Carthage."

"I will."

Grant nodded, nudged his horse into motion, then reined it up again.

"Oh, we must discuss how to handle the crossing. I'll need you back at Young's Point after your boats and your people have settled in."

"Of course, General. Just don't expect us to come by boat."

Porter was, at least in part, joking. More than once, the Admiral had made the point that "when the gunboats go below Vicksburg, we give up all hopes of ever getting them up again."

Grant squeezed Porter's hand one more time and headed north along the crude road McClernand's men had constructed.

So be it, he thought.

April 29, 1863, Chickasaw Bayou, Mississippi

From the deck of the *Choctaw*, the lead gunboat, General William Tecumseh Sherman lifted his head to view the scenery. It was not like anything he had been brought up with in Lancaster, Ohio. Though Lancaster was well north of the Ohio River, he had visited it often enough to appreciate its clear, open water. The Ohio did not have legions of cypress trees, or an abundance of strange reptiles and flying things, or the overwhelming heat and humidity of the Yazoo. The only large creatures the Yazoo was suited for were alligators and Confederates.

"Is the band ready?" he asked Francis Blair.

"Yes, they're ready," Blair replied without comment. Major General Blair was a stoic Kentuckian with a long, bushy beard of a type favored by many Union and Confederate military officers. His was neatly trimmed and lacked the post-lightning strike appearance of many such growths.

"Remember, this is a feint," Sherman cautioned. "Don't get excited and don't try to win. All we're trying to do is deflect attention away from Grant's operations in Grand Gulf. Don't get anyone killed."

Blair grunted his concurrence but said, "With eight gunboats and ten loaded transports it's going to be difficult to avoid casualties entirely."

"I know, I know. But try."

"What do you want them to play?"

Sherman glanced back at the band members mulling around on the fore deck of the lead transport. As if preparing to do musical battle, they had their instruments at the ready.

"Oh, I don't know. Something loud and obnoxious."

"Obnoxious?" Blair asked.

Sherman studied his subordinate, who had obviously taken offense at the suggestion that an army band could play "obnoxious" music.

"All right, then. *Loud* will be satisfactory," Sherman conceded. "Just make sure the Rebels hear us coming."

"Will the band be going ashore, sir?"

Sherman considered the question. Depositing a band in a swamp to play loud music did not seem like a good idea. However, the band had to be near enough to the Confederates to be heard.

"We'll wait until all the fighting men have disembarked and are formed up. When the attack pushes off, the band can form themselves up and . . . play. They will not, however, follow the army into battle. I do not want to see men engaging in hand-to-hand combat wielding trumpets and drumsticks."

That settled the matter, at least in Sherman's mind. His orders given and understood, he withdrew a pair of binoculars and studied the terrain. While he silently cursed the absence of dry land, a voice next to him said, "That's it, sir."

Sherman looked up to find the Navy's chief officer on the expedition, Lieutenant Commander Randolph K. Breese, pointing at a high promontory to the northeast. Breese's youthful face sported the "mutton chop" beard popularized by Ambrose Burnside. Because it covered the corners of the mouth but left the chin naked, Sherman thought the "mutton chop" tended to conceal smiles of good cheer on the faces of its devotees.

"That's where we're going, the little one called Drumgould's Bluff," said Breese, lowering his pointing finger toward a relatively flat clearing on the east bank of the Yazoo. "And that looks like a good place to disembark."

Sherman took up his binoculars again and looked at the landing. It seemed too small to accommodate ten transports and eight gunboats, but there did not appear to be anything larger available. He looked first at Breese, then at Blair and said, "All right. Get them off as quickly as possible. The band goes last."

Blair and Breese departed to carry out Sherman's orders. Within a half-hour, the first transport was docked and its troops deposited onshore. The band disembarked after the troops and moved away from the landing to make room for the next transport's load of men and equipment. To the consternation of their officers, some of the musicians thoughtlessly discharged their weapons. They were promptly shushed to silence.

When all the troops were safely ashore, Sherman summoned Blair and the other subordinate army commanders for a brief war council. It was already 6:00 PM and he wanted to get the charade underway as soon as possible.

"The gunboats will continue upriver while we follow on foot. When the Rebel batteries open fire on the gunboats, we will attack," he instructed, then immediately raised his hands in a cautionary stance and added, "But do not get yourselves in trouble. We do not seek a victory. Is that understood?"

It was, but a grumble of disquietude propagated through the assembled ranks.

Blair, his officers, and his corps moved forward in the general direction of the Haynes' Bluff and Walnut Hills fortifications, of which Drumgould's Bluff was a part. Sherman rejoined Breese aboard the *Choctaw*, and the gunboat made what seemed like a painfully slow disengagement from the shore. Breese's officers signaled the remaining gunboats and transports to follow his lead. They obeyed with as little haste as possible, to avoid getting ahead or Sherman's soldiers.

Suddenly, unsteadily at first, the evangelical strains of *The Battle Hymn of the Republic* resounded through the swamp. Some unsteadiness persisted, probably musicians ducking under branches or avoiding mud holes, Sherman thought.

"Very impressive," Breese said, grinning. "And very appropriate."

"Glory, glory, Hallelujah. His truth is marching on," Sherman offered sardonically.

"Whose truth, Grant's?"

"At least. We'll find out shortly if God really wants to be involved."

His words became prophetic sooner than expected. Musket and artillery fire rained down on the *Choctaw,* splintering wooden decks and twisting metal machinery and boilerplate. Breese and Sherman instantly dropped to the deck.

"Let's try not to get killed. My men will take me to task if I disobey my own orders," Sherman said.

"I'll do my best."

Hunched over, Breese quickly made his way to the pilothouse and ordered the captain to turn the *Choctaw* into the enemy fire. Sherman understood—Breese wanted to protect the engine and propulsion system as best he could—but it placed Sherman up front in a more vulnerable position. While Breese made his way back, Sherman noted an increase in the rate of fire of the *Choctaw's* forward gun. Her commander had put the fear of God into his gunners.

"Did you see how many holes they've put in us?" Breese asked, crawling beside Sherman.

"No, I've been too busy trying to avoid having one put through me."

Ignoring the sarcasm, Breese shook his head and, with some pride, said, "They won't sink her. Not the *Choctaw*. Not today."

Sherman wanted to ask Breese about the basis for this conclusion, but the din of exploding gunpowder was suddenly interrupted by the imprecation, "Charge!" and the random cheers of men going into battle. Blair and his corps were on the way.

Despite the deafening cacophony of battle, Sherman noticed the close of *The Battle Hymn of the Republic* and heard the opening chords of *A Mighty Fortress is Our God*. Well, God was definitely here, if only through His surrogates. Apparently, the bandleader's musical selections would emphasize God, righteousness, and sound intensity. Sherman was especially grateful for the latter.

After an hour, the assault force had reached the fortifications and, based on the magnitude of the clamor reaching back to the flotilla, was engaged in heavy fighting. Even the band could not compete with the racket, so the bandleader ordered a musical stand down. The *Choctaw* and the other gunboats continued their barrage of the Confederate bastions but were no match for the higher emplacements on the Walnut Hills. Ultimately, a corporal from Blair returned with a message.

"Sir, General Blair requests orders," he reported in a meek but controlled voice.

"What's the situation?"

"We're holding our own but no more."

"Casualties?"

"Yes."

That was enough for Sherman. He had not wanted men wounded or killed for a diversion, but now that it had happened, it was time to bring a halt to the proceedings.

"Tell General Blair to order the withdrawal," he told the messenger. The corporal was promptly on his way.

Breese gave the order to the *Choctaw*'s captain and the other boat captains to return to the pickup point and await the arrival of Blair's corps. The band, which had halted well short of the shooting war, boarded the first transport to dock. The *Choctaw* did not dock but remained operational with the gunboats in case covering fire was needed when the troops returned.

While the naval units were maneuvering for the pickup, Breese said, "Come with me, General. I want to show you something."

Sherman did as he was directed, following Breese toward the stern. Breese pointed up at the *Choctaw*'s tall smokestacks and then toward the pontoons enclosing the sidewheels, saying, "There," and, "See that?"

With his minimal knowledge of marine architecture, Sherman could see that not all was as the designers had intended. The smokestacks had two huge dents each, and the sidewheel pontoons looked like a general collapse was imminent.

"They did some damage," said Sherman for lack of a more astute observation.

"They did indeed," Breese agreed, a note of pride.

The next inspection point was the starboard bow. Breese leaned over the rail and beckoned Sherman to do the same.

"See those dents in the ironclad?" he asked.

"I do."

"I just hope there are none below the waterline. I don't think there are, or we'd have sunk by now."

While he was completing his visual inspection, Sherman noticed the boat's name *Choctaw* painted on its bow. He lifted himself to a standing position and faced Breese.

"The name, *Choctaw*."

"What about it? Breese inquired.

"It's an Indian name."

"It is indeed."

Sherman leaned back, folded his arms, and gazed wistfully into Breese's eyes.

"Did you know my middle name is Tecumseh?"

"No, what's *Tecumseh?*"

Sherman grasped the railing as the gunboat lurched to port.

"*Tecumseh* is actually my given name. *William* came later. To answer your question, *Tecumseh* was a Shawnee chief from Ohio who fought to save his people."

"Who did this *Tecum-seh* fight against?" sputtered Breese, struggling with the pronunciation.

"Us. The United States."

"Then why were you given the name?"

Sherman smiled artfully, pausing while he scanned the area for signs of returning troops. There was nothing yet.

"The people of Ohio came to realize that *Tecumseh's* cause was a noble one. After his death, he became an icon, and I got his name. I'm sure other children did as well."

"That's an interesting story," Breese said, nodding.

"That's not my point. What I'm trying to say is that we tend to honor Indians, who have historically tried to do us in, while we enslave Negroes, who have never attacked us and who, in their native Africa, live very much like the Indians. There's a certain irony in that."

Still puzzled, the navy man asked, "So . . . what's the point again?"

Rubbing his fingers over his chin, Sherman replied, "Well, I'm not sure. Maybe all it means is that the white man is a sonofabitch."

Breese laughed aloud, then said, "But we already knew that, didn't we?"

The irascible, complaining voices of many men suddenly filled the air, and Sherman realized it was Blair and his men returning. The diminished roar of battle accentuated the buzz, which carried with it a predominant overtone of profanity. Sherman welcomed the cussing, interpreting it as a sign of healthy, and more importantly, unharmed soldiers. While generally correct, this conclusion was premature.

Francis Blair presented himself to Sherman while his corps boarded the transports or mulled around while others did.

"What were the casualties?"

Blair sighed, keenly aware that Sherman had wanted zero casualties.

"Several. I don't have a precise count. Only a few killed."

"Get the wounded aboard and tended to first."

"I've already given that order."

He felt like returning to his quarters, but Sherman made it a point to meet and reassure every wounded man he saw. A few had limbs blown off from artillery fire or had intercepted musket balls with their flesh. Head wounds were rare; they tended not to leave their recipients walking around. There was no comfort for these men. They came aboard on stretchers covered by burlap or woolen blankets.

"This . . . is hateful. Killing men for a damned diversion," Sherman grumbled.

Blair gave no response.

Staring with what might have been interpreted as hostility, Sherman said, "Have I ever told you war is Hell?"

"I might have heard it once or twice."

Sherman ploughed on.

"Some day I'm going to write it down. It will be a maxim of my military philosophy."

★ TWENTY-ONE ★

The Willis-Cowan House, Pemberton Headquarters, Vicksburg

Brigadier General John Bowen, who had only that afternoon returned from Grand Gulf, could see John Pemberton was upset. His commander had good reason to be in such a state. He had just received much bad news from Bowen and was unsuccessfully trying to sort it out.

"But Sherman attacked the Walnut Hills emplacements yesterday, and I can tell you it was no minor effort," Pemberton said, pounding a balled fist on the mahogany desk in front of him.

Bowen, who was standing at ease, answered, "Sir, all I can tell *you* is that Grant is crossing somewhere near Hard Times or Grand Gulf. McClernand's corps and at least part of McPherson's. If we don't stop them, they'll be in our rear."

Pemberton slammed two balled fists on the desk and abruptly rose to his feet.

"I know, I know! You don't think he is attacking on two fronts, do you?"

"I believe Sherman's attack is a deception."

"But how do we know McClernand and McPherson aren't bluffing?" Pemberton nearly shouted, halting in his journey to the window.

"We don't," Bowen said stiffly. "But my best judgment tells me their presence south of Vicksburg is not a bluff."

Pemberton paused to study his subordinate's demeanor and then resumed his trek to the window. He looked out on what appeared to be a magnificent day.

"That's essentially the same message I got from Walnut Hills. You see my dilemma, don't you, General?"

Bowen did and said so. Pemberton continued in what was not quite, but almost, a tirade.

"I've got Sherman on my northern flank, Grant on my southern flank, and General Johnston is somewhere in Jackson and of absolutely no use to us. To boot, I've been hearing reports about some fellow named Grierson conducting cavalry raids down river. What's that all about?"

"Probably another diversion."

"Are you sure?"

"No, sir. I have no information on this Grierson. My attention is focused on what's happening at Grand Gulf."

Which was, Pemberton had to admit, as it should be. Bowen could not be expected to spend his time formulating strategies for the defense of Vicksburg. That was Pemberton's responsibility. Nevertheless, he felt a need, even a compulsion, to share what he knew with someone. Bowen was available.

"As you know, we no longer have the services of General Forrest. He is now in Georgia, having successfully assisted General Bragg against an attempt by the Yankees to sever our lines of communication in Tennessee. While General Forrest and his men have saved Bragg's army, they have also exhausted themselves in the process. They will not be back soon."

Vigorously nodding his understanding, Pemberton said, "Sir, I'm aware of General Forrest's predicament and its impact on us, but what does it have to do with Grierson?"

Before turning to answer, Pemberton parted the curtains of a front window and stared southward across the Mississippi toward De Soto Point. He could just make out the canal Grant had cut across the finger of land enveloped by the Mississippi. The huge dipper dredges that had done much of the work were easier to spot. However, there appeared to be no activity, which probably meant that Grant had probably given up on that scheme. In Pemberton's mind, it was also confirmation that Grant must be trying something else.

Returning his attention to Bowen, Pemberton said, "Two weeks ago, Colonel Benjamin Grierson and seventeen hundred United States cavalrymen left La Grange, Tennessee heading south. They passed directly through the gap Forrest left when he went to assist Bragg."

"So the Yankee attack on our communications was a diversion?"

"Maybe, maybe not. Whatever it was, it lost us the best cavalry commander in the west and replaced him with a Yankee cavalry officer who has been tearing up railroad track, telegraph lines, bridges and water towers ever since leaving Tennessee. What Bedford Forrest gained in Tennessee has been lost in Mississippi. Our lines of communication are severely threatened by Grierson. We cannot ignore him."

Bowen fidgeted uncomfortably, struggling to contain his growing irritation. To Pemberton, it was obvious that his subordinate remained convinced that Grant's crossing at Grand Gulf was the main Union thrust. Despite his own gnawing uncertainties on the subject, he decided to order Bowen back.

"General, I thank you for promptly reporting the Grand Gulf situation to me. I believe it is time you returned to your post. Please keep me apprised of developments."

"Yes, sir," Bowen snapped, obviously relieved. After salutes had been exchanged, he turned and left the room.

With foreboding thoughts racing through his mind, Pemberton immersed himself in an overstuffed chair and rested his head in his hands. What was he to do? What was the most effective course of action? Was there, in fact, a course of action that could check all the Yankee threats: Grant, Sherman, and, now, Grierson? After a half-hour of mental and emotional torment, Pemberton concluded he was getting nowhere and was, perhaps, taking too much on himself. He strode to the door of the sitting room, where a pale, thin sergeant snapped to attention.

"Mr. Dunn, I need you to send a message to President Jefferson Davis."

While Pemberton seated himself at Dunn's working table, the sergeant retrieved a pencil and paper and took up a position on his commander's right.

Pemberton began, "As a result of recent attacks, I regard navigation of the Mississippi to be closed to us. No further supplies will be able to reach us from the Trans-Mississippi Department. Please notify me of my orders."

Dunn waited patiently for more, his gaunt face betraying his anxiety.

"Is that all, sir?" he asked.

"Yes."

"What about General Johnston, sir?"

"Yes, yes, of course," Pemberton hastily replied, berating himself for the oversight. Joseph Johnston was his immediate superior and needed to be notified of the threat to Vicksburg. As often as not, however, President Jefferson Davis gave Pemberton his marching orders. Davis had, in fact, appointed Pemberton commander of the Mississippi and East Louisiana Departments, of which Vicksburg and its military defense were a vital part. For that promotion, he owed Davis a debt of gratitude. Which of his two superiors Pemberton actually reported to was not clear.

"Is it really as bad as it sounds, sir?" Sergeant Dunn inquired, his concern deflating his cheeks so severely that he looked half-starved.

"It could very well be, but we don't know that yet."

"But your message sounded . . . urgent."

"It was," Pemberton conceded. "And is. It is better to offer up a little pessimism than to risk having a superior officer underestimate the gravity of the circumstances."

To Pemberton's chagrin, the words came out churlish and censorious. Dunn reacted by bowing his head and murmuring, "Yes, sir."

As he departed, Pemberton gave a curt salute and a cheery, "Goodbye," to upgrade the mood in the room. Dunn returned the salute and offered a weak smile.

Damned impatience! Pemberton silently cursed. He was responsible for this post and the welfare of its garrison. He could not yield to defeatism! But neither could he repress his legitimate fears. There had been times when he thought Vicksburg virtually impregnable. Not now. Not against a Union commander who was prepared to come at him from all directions all the time.

John Pemberton walked to the window and gazed out. It would indeed be a glorious day.

He was beginning to feel like a very lonely man.

* * *

April 30, 1863, Grand Gulf, Mississippi

From the deck of a tugboat, Ulysses S. Grant watched as David Porter's flotilla approached Grand Gulf. There were seven boats in all: the flagship *Benton* plus the gunboats *Carondolet, Lafayette, Louisville, Mound City, Pittsburg,* and *Tuscumbia.* The objective was to silence the Rebel batteries at Grand Gulf or at least distract them so the transports could bring the army across. On paper, Grand Gulf had looked like a good place to do it, although David Porter had never been happy with the prospect of lofting shells upwards and over the seventy-five-foot bluffs while the Confederates showered him with destruction. It was almost as dangerous as attacking Vicksburg from the river. In the diffuse maize glow of dawn, Grant was beginning to appreciate Porter's reservations.

"What time is it?" he asked his companion, Charles Dana.

Dana checked his watch and said, "Seven fifty-five."

"It won't be long now," Grant said, trying his field glasses once more. "We should know pretty soon."

Through the morning fog, Grant could discern only the outlines of Porter's flotilla. The *Benton* was the easiest to find, having the largest profile with its decks well above the waterline. By contrast, the low profile, nearly submerged gunboats were difficult to find. All were moving slowly, fearful of bumping into one another or becoming grounded. Grant suspected some of this anxiety was due to the fact that many of the officers and men had prior experience under the guns of Vicksburg. It was not an experience any wanted to repeat.

"There's the flare," Dana said, pointing skyward.

The signal for the attack had barely reached its apogee when the guns of the flotilla opened up in a symphony of savage thunder. This was soon joined by a counter-symphony from the Grand Gulf fortifications. As the two clamorous orchestras dueled in the skies above the city and their debris rained down on the men and machines below, Grant could see in the frequent flashes of brilliance the faces of McClernand's troops lined up along the railings of the transports. None looked anxious to enter the fray, but most appeared ready to go.

The captains of the *Benton, Tuscumbia, Lafayette,* and *Pittsburg* boldly directed their vessels in close, to inflict maximum damage; the *Carondolet, Louisville,* and *Mound City* stayed at a safer, but less effective, distance. It was soon clear to Grant that, far from inflicting maximum damage, the four valiant boats were having it inflicted on them. It seemed the Grand Gulf batteries had only to lob shells in the general direction of the hapless boats and gravity would take care of the rest. In this war, Grant concluded, possessing the high ground had meaning for the navy as well as the army.

When the *Tuscumbia* drifted by somewhere around noon, listing in the water, fires raging on her decks and in her propulsion machinery, Grant knew the attack would not be successful. Facing the seventy-five-foot bluffs, he now wondered why he had ever thought it would. At 12:30 PM the Union guns fell silent. Shortly thereafter, so did those of the Grand Gulf batteries. Within the hour, Charles Dana spotted David Porter in a rowboat accompanied by two of his sailors. When they reached the tugboat, Dana helped a gloomy Porter aboard. After formal salutes, Grant said stoically, "Not a good night then, Admiral?"

"No. By no means."

Grant was pleased that Porter was not brandishing an "I told you so" attitude. It would have been justified.

Grant directed his navy colleague to a table where Dana had already seated himself.

"Any damage reports yet?" Grant asked. "We saw the *Tuscumbia* float by. It was not a pretty sight."

"She's beached on the Louisiana side. I don't know how many hits she received, but it was a lot. More than sixty and less than a hundred, I'd say. I'm not sure she's salvageable."

"Did *we* do much damage?"

"I don't know, but I doubt it. To hit anything on that bluff, we have to elevate the cannons like mortars. It's hard to get any accuracy that way."

Grant moved to the tugboat's railing, lost in thought, leaving his two colleagues to find their own conversation. He did not appear to be angry or emotional, merely preoccupied. When he returned, his visage revealed little.

"Do you know where De Shroon's plantation is?" he asked, directing the question at Porter but glancing hastily at Dana as well.

"I've seen it on the map, but . . ." Porter began.

Rather than wait on Porter's powers of recall, Grant pulled a map from his breast pocket and spread it on the table. He laid a finger on the west bank of the Mississippi.

"It's right there, below Grand Gulf. I'm going to have McClernand and McPherson march their men down from Hard Times . . ."

"Tonight?" Dana asked.

"Tonight, yes. We can't afford to wait, and we need as much night as we can get so you can bring the transports south to De Shroon's."

Instinctively, Porter raised a hand. He had just returned from a failed attack on a Rebel stronghold, during which one of his boats had been rendered inoperable, and three of the remaining six were peppered with shell holes and the afterbirth of their detonations.

"Wait, wait a minute, General. You want us to sail the flotilla *with* the transports, down to this plantation *tonight?*"

"Yes, said Grant. For a brief moment, a spark of irritation flashed through the stoic façade, but it was gone as quickly as it had come.

"Yes," he repeated calmly, moving his finger south along the Mississippi's west bank. "Have the boats hug the shoreline as they pass Grand Gulf. We already know the Rebel batteries can't reach us if we stay on that side."

Porter knew Grant was basing this conclusion on the absence of damage to the *Carondolet, Mound City*, and *Louisville*. They had been at the greater distance from the Grand Gulf batteries and had gotten through the attack relatively unscathed. *Ergo*—Porter mimicked Grant's reasoning—Grand Gulf could be safely passed by sticking to the western shore. It was a logical deduction but may have overlooked important particulars, like the fact that the big transports made excellent targets, whether distant or not.

Porter sent a beseeching look towards Dana, but there was nothing in Dana's eyes to lend him comfort.

Turning back to Grant, Porter inquired, "Are you sure McClernand and McPherson can get their men down here tonight?"

"If they don't get here, it won't be your fault. It will be mine."

"Where are we crossing?"

"I don't know yet, but it will be well downstream of Grand Gulf. There's a town called Rodney that might do. We'll have to reconnoiter . . ."

Grant outlined his plan, which was not much more complex than he'd already outlined. Once the army and Porter's navy were below Grand Gulf, McClernand's corps and McPherson's three divisions would cross to the east bank. To find an acceptable crossing point, Grant sent a squad out to cross the river and report back. Meanwhile, Grant and Dana disembarked from the tugboat and met an *ad hoc* praetorian guard to accompany them on the road to De Shroon's plantation. They arrived before midnight.

De Shroon's Plantation, Mississippi

At De Shroon's, a delegation of McClernand's officers had arrived and was poring over a map inside Grant's headquarters tent. Four lanterns served the dual purpose of illuminating the sometimes-illegible script on the map and securing its corners. Two scouts from McPherson's divisions had also arrived, their objective being to keep tabs on Grant so that McPherson would be able to find him when the time came. Given the night's previous and ongoing activities, this was not a small task. Having located Grant, the scouts were enjoying coffee with Charles Dana outside the tent.

"Sir," said the taller scout with a provocative sense of irony, looking around as if lost. "Mr. Dana, sir, can you tell me exactly where we are?"

"We're at De Shroon's plantation. But you knew that. De Shroon's is four miles downstream of Hard Times."

"Ah, Hard Times," the tall scout said. "Let's hope the name is not prophetic."

Dana and the shorter, more taciturn scout dutifully chuckled at the joke, which had been inflicted numerous times by would-be jesters during the campaign. The short man, serious intent evident in his features, pointed across the river.

"Do we know what's over there, sir?"

"In a broad sense, we do. Grand Gulf, of course, and a town called Rodney. But we don't know exactly where Rodney is . . ."

"I assume we will not be crossing at Rodney until we find it?" the tall scout queried with enough sarcasm to annoy Dana.

"I can assure you there will be no crossing until it is clear a beachhead can be established on the other side," Dana said, surprised at his own audacity and the ease with which he was now accepting Grant's orders. The two men fixed eyes on one another, Dana's stare the more glaring. The scout's face revealed mostly embarrassment and a desire to render himself invisible.

His wish was almost granted when the contingent Grant had sent out returned, their horses drenched in sweat and river water and breathing heavily. With them was an additional member of the party, a middle-aged black man mounted behind one of the soldiers. That he was black was an assumption; the firelight was not bright enough to clarify skin color, but his features and the tight black spirals of his hair exposed him as a Negro.

Dana and the two scouts looked quizzically at one another and followed the procession toward Grant's tent to watch and listen. By the time they reached the entrance—they could go no further because of the crowd inside—the black man was seated next to Grant. His riding companion, a young sergeant with extensive acne, stood to one side, allowing the lamplight to bathe the Negro. The stranger's darting, cue ball eyes moved from one soldier to the next, as if he were recording their faces in his mind. He did not look afraid but was clearly nervous, whether out of fear or simply because he was the center of attention was not clear. He wore a faded cotton hat with a wrinkled brim on the back of his skull, boots with leather laces, and woolen trousers held up by suspenders that looked too thin and frayed for the task they were being asked to perform. His torso was not covered by a shirt; only long red underwear served as a buffer between his skin and the overstressed suspenders. As Grant spoke, the black man nodded, but only to show he understood.

"I want you to look at a map," Grant was saying. "The one in front of us."

"A map?"

"A picture of the land," Grant explained, pressing his hands against the map. The man followed the movement with his eyes, as did everyone in the audience. "It shows where the towns and roads are, and which side of the river they are on."

"What's dat?" the man asked, pointing to a circle with the words 'Grand Gulf' beside it.

"That's Grand Gulf," Grant replied, then pointed to an area designated 'De Shroon's Plantation.' "And this is where we are."

"And . . . dis mus' be de Miss'ippi in between," said the black man, laying a finger on the fat, serpentine line wriggling north to south across the rendered landscape.

"Yes, what we are looking for is a good place to cross," Grant said, putting the question on his face rather than his lips. "We've already determined that Grand Gulf is not that place. But there's a town called Rodney . . ."

The black man shook his head gloomily as if he were about to tell the saddest tale he had ever heard.

"If you don' mind me sayin' so, suh, I don' think dat goin' be a good place to cross either. It way down here."

Grant and the black man were on opposite sides of the map's rendering of the Mississippi—Grant on the east bank and his guest on the west bank. The black man set his finger between them and traced the flow of the river until it dropped off the bottom of the map. He brought his finger to a halt a foot beyond the table's edge.

"Dis where Rodney be," he said, gazing steadfastly at Grant.

"That far, is it?" Grant muttered, straightening himself.

"Uh-huh. Dat where it be."

Grant studied the map, searching for other possibilities while the black man and his officers studied him. He lit a cigar, drew in a few puffs, and strolled to the rear of the tent, his back to the assemblage. Then he withdrew the cigar, returned and looked afresh at the map.

"Tell me what this leads to," he said, using the cigar to point to a road that appeared to connect the Mississippi with points east and north.

The Negro's head was shaking again as he said, "Dat road get up to Bayou Pierre, but you can't go dat way cause it got too much backwater."

Clearly disappointed, Grant looked as if he were about to smash the cigar on the wretched stream called Bayou Pierre. The black man recognized the reaction as anger and, thinking Grant might take it out on him, backed away. Sensing the man's fear, Grant regained control and offered his hand.

"Thank you for your help, sir," he said, smiling. "We'll give you a good meal before taking you back home."

Unaccustomed to shaking the hands of white men, the Negro hesitated at first, then tentatively took Grant's hand in his. That was as far as he cared to commit himself. Grant, however, had no

such reservations. He grasped his guest's hand and shook it vigorously, then released it and resumed his mental machinations.

"Gen'l . . ." the black man whispered. "Gen'l, if it be all right, I
has a idea."

"Oh?"

"Yeah, yeah. Lemme show you," the black man said, laying an
index finger on a point halfway between Grand Gulf and Rodney.
There was no circle indicating a town. "Dat be Bru-insburg. It don'
show on yo' map, but it surely be there."

Grant visibly brightened, expanding the smile on the black
man's ample lips. It was nearly an ideal spot for a crossing. Once
on the left bank of the Mississippi, the army could locate Bayou
Pierre and follow it upstream until they found a workable crossing
point. The only other natural impediment, other than swampland,
was the Big Black River, which flowed southwest and spilled into
the Mississippi near Grand Gulf. *If we can cross the Mississippi,
Grant mused, we can surely cross the Big Black.*

But his black guest was wearing a full grin and had more good
news.

"Suh, look here," he said.

Grant watched the callused finger trace its way across the
map once more, this time moving east from the invisible town of
Bruinsburg.

"They a road here. It go to Port Gibson and then up to Grand
Gulf," said the Negro, sensing the import of the intelligence he
was providing. "Once you on dat road, you don' have to march in
no swamps, and you don' need no boats. Best houses in the whole
South on dat road, sir. All you got to do is walk. It high ground all
the way."

Grant was ecstatic. He now had a way to get behind the
enemy's defenses. After effusively thanking the black man one more
time and ordering that he be given a good meal before being taken
home, Grant ordered his tent cleared of all personnel but staff and
corps officers. When that was done, he reached into a rucksack
behind his traveling desk and removed a bottled labeled simply:
"Tennessee Whisky." Pouring a couple of shots into a drinking cup,
he downed it in one swallow and held the bottle up for viewing.

"Anyone else?" he asked.

There were no takers. The officers were keenly aware of
Charles Dana's presence and the assignment with which Secretary of War Stanton had charged him. Grant moved the bottle directly in front of Dana.

"What about you, sir? Will you have some?" he inquired
mischievously.

"No, I would be putting myself in an untenable position."

Shaking the glass out and re-corking the bottle, Grant then stowed them away and asked, "Are you going to report me?"

Feeling not only Grant's but all eyes boring into him, Dana said, "No. I've come to believe you do your best work when you are slightly drunk."

"Perhaps I should get the bottle out again."

"The key word, sir, is *slightly*. I think two of your usual drinks might exceed that limitation."

Disappointed, but acknowledging Dana's words with an awkward grin, Grant rearranged the candles to better illuminate the area around the hypothetical Bruinsburg and motioned for the officers to gather round. He stuffed a half-smoked cigar back into its place of prominence between his lips.

"Gentlemen, if we can cross here at Bruinsburg," he said, indicating the spot on the map identified by the black man, "we are definitely in business. I don't have to tell you what it means to secure a dry base of operations in the enemy's territory."

They did not have to be told.

Lifting his eyes from the map, Grant scanned the room and said, "But, we *will* be in the enemy's territory with Vicksburg and the Mississippi River between us and our base of supply. Does that concern anyone?"

The words were not spoken harshly but did have an element of challenge in them. The congregation was at first intimidated into silence but quickly recovered.

"We expect you've already figured that out, sir," came a voice from the rear. "Whatever you have in mind, it can't be any worse that digging ditches and slogging through vermin-infested swamps."

For the sharpness of his wit, the speaker received a collective chortle. Grant, however, was neither amused nor bemused. His silence prompted another query from a lieutenant safely hidden in the middle of the crowd.

"You *do* have something in mind, don't you, sir?" the lieutenant asked meekly.

"I do."

"Could you tell us?"

"Not now," Grant said curtly, then shifted his gaze toward the source of the question. "You'll know when the time comes if you haven't puzzled it out already. For now, there's no need to telegraph our intentions. At the moment, I'm more concerned with coordination. We've got four of General McClernand's divisions and one of General McPherson's here, but we need to get General

Sherman and his men down here as soon as he's persuaded Pemberton that the main Union attack will be in the north. Once we're established in Bruinsburg, Sherman must be told to break off his attack immediately and join us. Are any of Sherman's officers here?"

"I am, sir," a high tenor voice said. When the officer stepped forward, Grant was surprised to see a big man sporting a bushy red beard and a gray slouch hat. The officer snapped a quick salute.

"And you are . . ." Grant said, returning the salute.

"Major Rowley, sir."

"At ease, Major. Just tell me about Sherman's diversion. Is it working?"

Rowley failed to assume the *at ease* stance but did relax a bit.

"General Blair's *attack* seems to have been successful. As you know, the object was not to win the engagement . . ."

"I know, Major. I planned the mission. No need to explain why we didn't win."

"Yes, sir, yes, sir, of course," Rowley chattered, then regained his equanimity and said, "The diversion was . . . quite successful. I myself observed the goings-on at Vicksburg. A substantial number of Rebel troops have been sent north. The only explanation for such focused activity would be the defense of Haynes' Bluff against an assault by General Sherman."

"Is that all?"

"It's all I know, sir, at the present time."

Grant rubbed his chin thoughtfully and peered up at his taller subordinate.

"Major, I would like you to return to General Sherman and find out what has actually transpired and whether or not he is ready to join us."

"When, sir?"

"Now."

Unhappy to be sent packing through swampland in the middle of the night, Rowley knew better than to object. He saluted and said, "Yes, sir," trying to keep the chagrin out of his voice.

When Rowley was on his way, Grant had another query.

"Does anyone know Colonel Grierson's status?"

Apparently no one did, for no hands were raised, no voices heard.

"Damn!" Grant muttered, striding briskly from his tent in search of an aide. He found two sitting by a campfire, both with coffee mugs.

"You two, what are you drinking?" he snapped at the privates.

"Coffee," the nearest one said.

More sheepishly, the other one replied, "Whisky, sir, but not much."

Grant gazed directly at the coffee drinker and said, "Son, I want you to find Colonel Grierson. Are you up for that?"

The private choked on his coffee.

"Find Colonel Grierson? But he's liable to be anywhere."

"That's why I need you to find him. I want to know if he's close enough to support us if we need him," Grant said with a stern scowl. "We'll get you a good horse, but don't ride out just yet. Wait until morning. You'll have a better chance of finding him in the daylight. Like you said, he's liable to be anywhere."

Grant gave the soldier a hefty pat on the back and returned to his tent, strolling directly to Charles Dana. With a look of concern on his face, he inquired, "Dana, do you know that Negro's name?"

Charles Dana shook his head. "No, sir. Why?"

"I just realized I didn't know it."

Frustrated, Grant asked the same question of several members of the contingent that had brought the black man in. None knew his name. Apparently, no one had asked.

Snorting and fuming, Grant turned back to Charles Dana and said, "By God, this is uncalled for. The man goes out of his way to help us, and we don't even know his name. It's a hell of a note!"

*   *   *

From David Porter's pilothouse aboard the flagship *Benton*, Ulysses S. Grant watched the paddlewheels churning up the Mississippi mud and propelling the boat to Bruinsburg, Mississippi on the east bank. Behind them was a steady parade of gunboats and transports, some with barges, all filled with men and supplies for the final push to Vicksburg. McClernand's Thirteenth Corps landed first, then McPherson's Seventeenth Corps. When the *Benton* pulled up to the Bruinsburg landing, the military band marked the occasion by playing patriotic songs. This provoked the inevitable hoots and cheers reserved for such occasions. They were on Mississippi soil and below Vicksburg. Just where Grant wanted to be.

"Does it ever strike you, General, that a war is a very odd place for a band?" Porter asked.

Grant, who was gripping a handrail, looked at him quizzically and said, "I would have to disagree. A band is a necessary military institution. It lifts the spirits; it prepares one for the attack or the defense. Haven't you heard the Scots brag of how a steady drone of bagpipes can frighten the bejesus out of an enemy?"

Porter chortled and said, "I have heard it, and I believe it. The sound of a bagpipe on a battlefield would certainly frighten me. But a trombone or a tuba? I don't think so."

When everything that was going ashore was ashore, Grant and Porter met for a final handshake.

"Good luck, General."

"Good luck, Commodore."

"Maybe I'll see you on the heights soon."

"Maybe I'll see you *from* the heights soon."

The handshake was severed and each man retreated to his post, Porter to his flotilla and Grant to the Army of the Tennessee.

★ TWENTY-TWO ★

May 1, 1863, Pemberton
Headquarters, Vicksburg, Mississippi

Standing on the front porch of the Willis-Cowan House, General John Pemberton gazed hopefully toward the river. It was another pleasant day with a bright morning sun overhead, and Vicksburg was remarkably still. But Pemberton knew the city would soon be under siege from the north or the south, or both. It was in the air, some invisible disquietude. In his hand was the telegram his aide had brought just fifteen minutes earlier. It was from General Joseph Johnston, who was somewhere east of Vicksburg, probably in or near Jackson. He opened the telegram and read:

"If Grant's army lands on this side of the river, the safety of the Mississippi depends on beating it. For that object, you should unite your whole force."

Unite his whole force? Where? Haynes' Bluff? Grand Gulf? Should he send cavalry to pursue Grierson and his raiders? Jefferson Davis had telegraphed him the day before that he would do all he could to send troops from Alabama. Secretary of the Army Seddon had recently informed him that reinforcements would soon arrive by rail. But when was *soon* and would it be *soon enough*?

"Sir, would you like to reply?" the aide asked cautiously, sensing Pemberton's consternation.

"Yes, I certainly would," Pemberton said, preparing to magnify his voice to a bellow as he turned to face the young man. But there was such a look of vulnerability on the private's face that he could not do it. Instead, he exhaled and said, "Just tell the General his message was received."

The aide snapped to attention, barked the mandatory, "Yes, sir!" and departed with a crisp salute.

Discouraged, Pemberton crumpled the message in his hand and lifted his arm to throw it away. Thinking better of the impulse, he stowed it in his breast pocket. In the army, one never knew. As a northerner, he had plenty of enemies who would love to charge him with insubordination. He might need the telegram for his court-martial.

He couldn't help laughing. A court-martial was at once a ludicrous and a thoroughly realistic possibility.

Somewhat calmed by his acceptance of personal catastrophe, Pemberton found himself a chair at the south end of the porch, turned it to face the same way, then seated himself. John Bowen was in that direction, he knew, trying to prevent the enemy from gaining a foothold on the east bank. The last time he'd heard, Union soldiers were coming ashore at Bruinsburg, a small town ten to fifteen miles below Grand Gulf. To be specific, twenty thousand soldiers had landed, four times as many as many as Bowen commanded.

As if he could see what was happening fifty miles downstream, Pemberton steadied his gaze southward and brought his palms together.

"Come on, John, stop them. I need you to win."

He briefly maintained the prayerful pose, then plunged his face into his hands.

"Please," he murmured, thankful there was no one to view his despair.

*   *   *

Port Gibson, Mississippi

Four-to-one odds, thought John Bowen as he inspected the defensive position he had established to prevent the Union Army from taking Port Gibson and heading north. Four-to-one. My five thousand against Grant's twenty thousand. It was not a fair fight, but it rarely was in this war.

The position was a good one, high ground and lots of trees overlooking the only road open to the north. Grant had no choice but to take it if he wanted Vicksburg. There was a fork in the road that Bowen thought might confuse the Yankees, hopefully long enough for his men to do some serious damage. The atmosphere was tense with anticipation. There had been some sporadic artillery exchanges during the night, but all was quiet now. Even the morning songbirds were mute. Bowen reflected on Pemberton's dispatch of the night before, congratulating him on his defense against the Union ironclads:

In the name of the army, I wish to thank you and your men for your gallant conduct today. Keep up the good work. . . ."

The rest of the message dealt with Pemberton's announcement that he was recommending Bowen be promoted to major general. It was good news, of course, but Bowen was not in a position to rest on such laurels. He had four-to-one odds confronting him. He hunkered down behind a boulder and waited for something to happen. He did not have to wait long. The forest was soon aflame with the flash and roar of Federal cannon.

Union Army approaching Port Gibson, Mississippi

In an attempt to override the din, the lieutenant from Smith's division shouted, "Sir, we need to know which road to take." Representatives from Osterhaus's and Carr's divisions were also present, but McClernand could tell from the expressions on their faces that they had the same question. It was a critical decision he would have to make.

"Let me look at the map again," he said, scratching the rash under his beard.

He looked and, as it had done on three previous occasions, the map showed no fork in the road.

"Damn, sonofabitching map makers," he cursed. "Put the damn thing away. It's useless. We'll have to reconnoiter both roads."

Smith's lieutenant was folding the map to stuff it into a pouch he carried over his shoulder when two men appeared from the rear. McClernand recognized the one riding a horse as one of Hovey's officers. The other one was walking and was a gray-haired Negro in a cotton blouse, burlap trousers, and well-worn shoes.

"Is this the same . . ." McClernand began.

"No," said Smith's lieutenant. "He was younger."

McClernand and the lieutenant exchanged nods, agreeing that this black man was not the one who had told Grant about Bruinsburg.

"There must be a lot of them coming over to our side," the lieutenant said.

"They damned well better be. That's why Lincoln sent us down here, isn't it?"

The lieutenant bridled at the remark. He did not know that John McClernand was a Democrat and had sought a commission in the army only to help in the saving of the Union. The Emancipation Proclamation annoyed him nearly as much as it did the average slave owner. He was not enthusiastic about sacrificing America lives for the lives of southern Negroes.

"Let's hear what he has to say," McClernand declared. He turned to the black man, whose skin was light and close to the bone. He faced McClernand with a nondescript expression, his posture and stance equally ambiguous. "Sir, do you know the roads hereabouts?"

The man nodded, exposing several missing teeth as he said, "Yessuh, I do."

Pleased by the positive response, McClernand asked, "Can you tell me which of these roads leads to Port Gibson?"

The man nodded again and replied, "Both do. They comes back together a ways on, befo' you gets to Port Gibson."

Having been asked and answered the question, the black man lowered his eyes and assumed a deferential posture. The response having solved his immediate problem, McClernand was feeling magnanimous.

"Sir, could I ask your name?"

The man lifted heavy eyelids to stare at the unfamiliar white man in the dark blue uniform and said, "My name Jacob."

McClernand waited for more, but there was none. "Jacob, just *Jacob?*"

Thrusting his hand out, McClernand said, "*Jacob*, now that's a fine name. Please accept my thanks, Jacob. You've been of great assistance."

Jacob placed his hand in McClernand's and allowed the General to shake it vigorously. A smile appeared on the black man's lips, which he kept pressed together so his teeth and the absences thereof could not be seen.

Jacob was returned to where he had been found walking along the road. McClernand assigned the left fork in the road to Osterhaus's division, and all three remaining divisions took the right fork. McClernand was left to reflect on his generalship, which, his having been a political appointee, came from a different perspective than those of his colleagues. Lincoln was pleased to have a Democrat on board, even if he was, militarily, an amateur. Still, he had not performed badly. There had been successes, many of which he could call his own, but he could not get over the feeling that the West Pointers—Grant, Sherman, and McPherson—were overly critical of his decisions.

Climbing aboard his horse, McClernand gazed warily at the two roads, keenly aware he had committed men to battle and hoping it was the right battle. Amidst the thundering of howitzers and the incessant yapping of small arms fire, he waited patiently for the next development to rear its ugly head. It always did. War, he thought, was so messy and uncertain. It was nothing at all like newspaper editing or serving as a representative to the United States Congress, two of his previous occupations. In war, you never knew what would happen next.

Above the cacophony of battle, McClernand heard hoof beats approaching.

Like now, he thought.

He glanced toward the source of the sound and saw a solitary figure on horseback emerging from a bend in the right fork—a messenger.

"Sir, there's a problem," said the soldier as he halted before McClernand.

There always was.

"What kind of problem?"

"The roads . . ."

"Don't come together like the Negro told us?"

"Maybe, maybe not. We ain't got that far. Both of the roads ride along high ridges, with a deep ravine in between."

"I still don't understand the problem."

The soldier gave a brief snort of frustration, then tried again.

"We can't communicate with General Osterhaus. There's too much undergrowth and too many trees in the ravine. It's too thick for anyone to get through, on foot or horseback."

McClernand told the messenger to dismount and show him where the problem was. Along with two aides, they unfolded the map again, and McClernand told the messenger to sketch in as best he could the juxtaposition of the two roads. The messenger studied the indicated terrain, then drew two diverging roads starting from their present position. Then he lifted the charcoal marker from the paper and turned to his commander.

"That's about it. Ain't got no farther," he said.

McClernand looked at the two lines. They were anything but parallel, and if the sketch were even close to being accurate, the roads might never come together again.

"Damn . . . damn!" he cursed, bemoaning the imponderables of war.

After several minutes of contemplation, he sent the messenger back with orders to the commanding officers on both roads to establish communications by whatever means they found necessary and to keep him informed of their progress. He knew it was a pointless order, but it would give him time to think of something more concrete. If nothing else, he could always call a council of war, but he hated councils of war. They had a tendency to expose his military shortcomings and then disseminate them to an expanded audience.

After an hour of continued bombardment without notable progress, Grant arrived with his entourage. Feeling small and inadequate, but reluctant to show it, McClernand stood stiff and confident as Grant approached.

"General McClernand, why are you standing still?" Grant demanded coolly.

"We've run into some difficulty, sir," McClernand began, as calmly as his nerves would permit. He explained the map error, the Negro's revelation, and the lack of communications between the two appendages of his army.

Grant nodded, scanned what he could see of the bifurcated road, and said, "We'll bring up some of McPherson's men. You should have called for help."

Without further discussion, Grant dispatched an aide for McPherson to send him a brigade or two. He did not bother to mollify McClernand. In fact, McClernand detected annoyance in his commander's manner. As Grant steered his horse toward the fork in the road, his eyes caught McClernand's. For an instant, McClernand thought he sensed hostility, even rage in them. It was an unnerving moment. Whatever his stoic demeanor suggested, Ulysses S. Grant was a powerful man. He was not a natural politician like McClernand, but he had been around long enough to learn military politics, which were every bit as vicious as the civilian variety. McClernand barely suppressed a shudder.

Whooping and shouting, a group of Union soldiers emerged from the main road. It was John Logan's division.

"You men over there!" Grant shouted, waving with his slouch hat in one hand.

Shocked to hear Grant himself yelling commands, the lead group of soldiers scurried toward him.

Pointing his hat at them, Grant said, "This brigade go that way," then made a broad sweep with the hat toward the left.

When that was done, he pointed at the second brigade and said, "And you gentlemen go this way," completing the order with another sweeping gesture.

McClernand looked on in amazement as Grant sat firmly astride his horse directing the flow of men and materiel like a policeman directing traffic at the intersection of two heavily traveled city streets. On one hand, he was appalled that the commander of the Army of the Tennessee was performing a task better suited to a sergeant. On the other hand, he grudgingly admired Grant's willingness to do the job himself. The dichotomy evoked emotions in McClernand to which he was unaccustomed.

Shaking himself free of the unwelcome reverie, he mounted his horse and headed toward the right fork.

"General!" Grant called.

Halting, McClernand redirected his horse back toward Grant. "Yes, sir?"

Before answering, Grant barked a few more commands at passing soldiers and then brought his attention back to McClernand.

"General, when you get back to your corps, send me a man or two."

Not quite comprehending, McClernand sputtered, "A man or two?"

"Yes, yes," Grant snapped as he waved an especially slow-moving group of soldiers down the left fork. "I can't do this all day. I've got other matters to attend to."

McClernand mouthed his understanding with a small, "oh," and then took command of himself and said, "Yes, sir. Of course. I'll do that."

McClernand saluted and, after Grant gave a wave of dismissal, returned to the right fork. Before reaching the first bend in the road, he stopped to gaze back at Grant. The commander was still vigorously directing the advance.

McClernand smiled with satisfaction, Ulysses S, Grant was a mere mortal after all.

*   *   *

As was his habit, John Bowen read Pemberton's dispatch a second time:

Is it not possible that the enemy himself will retire tonight? It is very important, as you know, to retain your present position.

The message went on to say that Bowen should use his own judgment and complimented Bowen and his men on their *noble* performance.

Bowen crumpled the message in his hand. It was totally irrelevant now. The Federals and their ever-expanding numbers seemed to be everywhere. There was no way he could hold a defensive position outside Port Gibson. He had to withdraw.

"Sir, we are being pushed back. Everyone is being pushed back," said the nervous young lieutenant at his side.

"I know that, lieutenant. I'm not a fool."

As if to punctuate the statement, a howitzer shell blasted apart a copse of trees no more than fifty yards distant. Bowen and his lieutenant reflexively ducked their heads.

Cautiously returning to an upright stance, Bowen said, "Give the order. We will fall back across Bayou Pierre and set up a new defensive position."

Bayou Pierre was north of Port Gibson, running nearly east to west and flowing into the Mississippi at Bruinsburg.

"Now, sir?" asked the hopeful lieutenant.

"No, we'll wait until dark. There'll be a moon, I think. If not, well, we'll make do. Can't leave now. It would be suicide."

At the word "suicide" the lieutenant gulped, but managed a shaky salute and went on his way to inform the field commanders. Bowen leaned against a nearby boulder, trying to settle his mind and think his way through the situation. They would have to destroy the bridges across Bayou Pierre, of course, and set up defensive positions on the north side of the bayou. What else?

While he was meditating, he realized Pemberton's message was still in his hand. He uncrumpled it and read it again, focusing on the clause "be guided by your own judgment."

Of course I'll be guided by my own judgment, he thought. *There is no other judgment to be guided by.*

He hastily re-crumpled the message and tossed it aside.

★ TWENTY-THREE ★

May 1, 1863, Bruinsburg, Mississippi

As a member of the Thirteenth Illinois, Charlie Johnson usually marched along stoically, sometimes cheerfully. It was a nice day and a pleasant walk if the marching pace of an army on the move could ever be called "pleasant." And the scenery was comforting: farmhouses, cultivated fields, woods, and silence. Except for the occasional swamp, it could have been Illinois.

As if to purposely shatter Charlie's illusions, the man beside him, a red-faced farm boy named Darren McGlover, complained, "Charlie, why're you so cheerful? I'm as hot as a boiled pig, and the dust is cloggin' me up somethin' awful."

Charlie had noticed the heat but had not allowed it to dim his spirits.

"It ain't that hot, Darren! Do like me. Tie a han-kerchief over your nose so the dust don't get up your nostrils."

McGlover groaned in protest but did as Charlie had instructed.

"How's that?" Charlie asked.

"It's better, but now the han-kerchief is gettin' all full of snot."

Charlie declined to comment. There was no satisfying some people and Darren was among the most unsatisfiable person he had ever met. And he didn't want to encourage a conversation that had *snot* in it.

Five minutes later, McGlover broke the silence.

"How's your meat holdin' up, Charlie?"

Charlie glanced at the slab of meat adorning his bayonet. To make room in their haversacks for as many rounds of ammunition and as many rations as possible, bayonets had been affixed to infantry rifles and used to spear and carry slabs of beef. At first, rivers of blood had run down the gun barrels, but now enough blood had run off that the stocks were, if stained, at least relatively dry.

"It's fine, except for a family of flies I keep tryin' to chase off."

"Me, too," McGlover retorted. "Sons of bitches are big. Might have to shoot one or two to teach 'em a lesson."

McGlover hoisted the butt of the musket to his shoulder and sighted along the barrel as if aiming to shoot one of the flies buzzing around his slab of beef. On several occasions, the gun barrel was aligned, however briefly, with the heads of marching soldiers.

"Darren, don't do that. You're gonna kill someone," Charlie scolded.

McGlover howled, popped a smile on his face, and said, "Just jokin', Charlie. Just jokin'.'" Then he rested the gun on his right shoulder and resumed a marching pace. Soon, the expression on his face was as dour as ever.

Charlie was not only content with the relative silence, he cherished it. The road proceeded up a shallow but persistent incline, causing his thighs to burn. But he couldn't complain. Every once in a while, there was a break in the forest, and he could glimpse the army moving forward, its bayonets gleaming with an amber or silver glow, depending on the amount of surface beef blood present. At the top of the rise, the column halted. Everyone but Charlie lowered himself to the ground, many assuming prone positions. Charlie made his way past the edge of the road, through the trees, to the berm of the road where the land fell abruptly to the Mississippi Valley. He saw the broad expanse of the Mississippi River. He saw endless fields. He saw a brilliant white mansion with Corinthian columns that he took to be a plantation house. The setting was more beautiful than anything he had ever seen, even in Illinois.

A wave of chatter emanated from the front of the column and sped rearward. Charlie returned to his position to find McGlover talking to the two men immediately in front of them in the marching order. McGlover waved him over.

"Looks like we're settin' up camp," he announced.

"Why are we stopping?" Charlie asked, gazing skyward. "There's plenty of daylight left."

McGlover groaned and said, "How would I know? I'm just glad to get off my feet. They're hurtin' somethin' awful."

Charlie pretended to listen while his companion complained, listing a series of ailments which, if he actually suffered from them all, would have gotten him a medical discharge. It was a ritual to which Charlie had become accustomed.

But he was still curious. Rather than immediately set up his pup tent, Charlie made his way up the line, looking for an officer who might be able to explain what was happening. He found a sergeant squatting over a fresh campfire with his bayonet and meat inserted into the flames. The sergeant, a wiry athletic man with a dark tan and a flat profile, glanced up at him and said, "What do you need, soldier?"

"Sir, Charlie Johnson is my name."

"And mine is Smith, Patterson Smith," said the sergeant, rising to offer his hand.

Charlie shook it, noting that the sergeant did not seem as tall standing as he did squatting. *Short legs*, Charlie concluded.

"Sir, I was just wondering why we stopped."

"Why don't you stick that beef in the fire, son?" said the sergeant.

"What?"

"The beef. Might as well cook it now and eat as much as you can, save the rest for later. Flies'll make a mess of it if you wait too long."

Charlie took the suggestion and soon downed a third of his beef while he waited for an answer. He took a foul-smelling cloth from his haversack, wrapped the remaining—now cooked—beef in it, and stuffed it back into the haversack. Then he waited for the sergeant to finish eating.

Finally, noting Charlie's obvious interest in what he had to say, Smith wiped the grease from his lips and said, "We ran into a crossroads. The general is tryin' to figure out which way to go."

"General McClernand?"

"Yep, that's the one. You know the army. Everybody waits for the generals to make up their minds and when they finally do, the rest of us have to make up for lost time."

It was true enough, but Charlie's attitude was not cynical. He accepted the dithering and uncertainty of officers as a fact of military life and was content not to be one of them. But he would enjoy the opportunity to spend more time in such a pleasant place.

"Do you think we'll be here long, sir?"

Smith speared the remaining beef with his bayonet and wrapped it in a rag like the one Charlie had used.

"No way to know. We'll just have to wait and see. Overnight, maybe."

Charlie considered that. Overnight might not be too bad. It would give him a chance to explore the area and relax. He studied the plantation house, wishing he could spend the night within its no doubt luxurious confines. But that would be impossible, he knew, because General McClernand and his staff would make the house into a center of operations. He was heading back to talk further with Smith when a horde of Union officers rode by, kicking up dust and pebbles in their wake. They seemed to be in a hurry. Charlie would have thought nothing of it except for the short rider with the dark beard sandwiched between two outer ranks of cavalry. It was General U.S. Grant!

Excited, Charlie hurried to meet Sergeant Patterson Smith

"Sir, that . . . I think that was General Grant," he stammered.

"It was."

Puzzled, Charlie glanced again at the horsemen and then back at Smith.

"What does it mean?"

Patterson Smith rubbed the dirt from his eyes that the horses had kicked up. Straightening, he placed his hands on his hips, squinted, and said, "It probably means we won't be here long. The general does not like delays. My guess is he's on his way back from clearin' up McClernand's *crossroads* quandary . . . personally."

"Oh," Charlie mumbled, lamenting the loss of the rest and relaxation he had been looking forward to. Excusing himself, he trudged back to his position in line where Darren McGlover was trying to cook his beef. McGlover's fire was not as robust as Patterson Smith's had been, and he was having difficulty. After vigorously poking the small pile of wood that was the intended fuel for his fire, he glanced at Charlie.

"What's happening, Charlie? I saw you talking to some officer."

"We may be moving out."

Distressed at the possibility of not having enough time to cook his meat, McGlover said, "Why? We just got here."

"You saw General Grant pass by?"

"I saw a bunch of horses . . ." McGlover replied, his eyebrows rising. "Was that Grant?"

"Yeah."

"Well, I'll be damned," McGlover sighed, squinting his eyes in the direction of Grant's receding entourage.

"Won't we all," Charlie opined, more cynically than was his habit.

April 30, 1863, Port Gibson, Mississippi

It was a race, a race that John Bowen had to win to prevent the turning of his flank. The Federals were advancing eastward along the Bruinsburg and Rodney Roads. The Yankees had been stalled for a while, but the hiatus was over. McClernand's Thirteenth and McPherson's Seventeenth were on the march, twenty thousand against Bowen's twenty-five hundred. Marching southeast from Grand Gulf, Brigadier General Edward Tracy of the Alabama Brigade and Brigadier General Martin Green with his Mississippians and Arkansans were hastening to block the Union juggernaut.

The scout sent by Green and Tracy was facing Bowen and his immediate staff, all on horseback. The scout was perspiring, a fact which spoke favorably of the young man in Bowen's eyes. Sweat meant commitment and exertion in the pursuit of the enemy.

"General Tracy's brigade is a few miles west of Port Gibson on the Bruinsburg Road and General Green is, I'd say, a mile southwest of that on the Rodney Road," the young man said.

"What's the terrain like?" Bowen inquired.

A bemused grin appeared on the scout's lips.

"Good for us. Hills, ridges, ravines, even caves. Ideal for defense."

Bowen nodded. It was indeed good ground for defense, but he was getting tired of defense and strategic retreat. The trouble with strategic retreat was that if it happened often enough, it could turn into a reflex.

"Good, good, good," Bowen mumbled as he nodded approvingly. "What else?"

"Lots of cane and trees stuffing the ravines. If the Yankees come that way, they won't be able to see more'n a few yards, and they surely won't be able to make it through without cuttin' a path. Meanwhile, we can shoot at 'em all day long."

Bowen continued nodding and said, "Let me look at the map again."

One of his aides, a red-haired boy with an apoplectic complexion, produced the map and laid it across Bowen's lap. Bowen, the red-haired aide, and another aide whose hairline was not visible beneath his slouch hat studied the myriad wiggles that represented roads, creeks, and bayous that lay between the Bruinsburg and Rodney Roads.

"What's this?" Bowen asked, pointing to a brown square beside the Rodney Road.

"Magnolia Church. General Green's headquarters."

"Where's Tracy?"

"Here, sir," said the aide, pointing to a position along the Bruinsburg Road.

"You say the terrain between these two roads helps us?"

"Yes, sir."

Bowen stared into the faces of the two aides, one after the other, and said, "I want to see. Take me there."

The red-haired aide withdrew the map and put it away while the balding aide directed the remainder of Bowen's entourage eastward. Approaching from the northwest, they reached the Bruinsburg Road first, checked in with Tracy, and continued cross-country south to the Rodney Road. The terrain between the roads was as the red-haired aide had described it: steep ravines filled with impenetrable forests, and topped by flat ridges peppered with homes and farm buildings, all connected by serpentine country roads.

"Magnolia Church. Where is it?" Bowen demanded.

The red-haired aide did not answer but responded by waving an arm and heading for the Rodney Road. Bowen and his staff followed. From a valley through which a stream called Centers Creek flowed, the aide held up the flat of his hand and the procession came to an abrupt halt. At the top of a gentle rise stood the Magnolia Church, peaceful and inviolate, its white steeple brilliant in the sunlight. But the flat crack of muskets and the roar of cannon fire were unmistakable. Martin Green was under attack. As Bowen observed, the scenes of battle progressed from skirmishing between long lines of blue and shorter lines of gray to full-fledged artillery salvos that scattered men, flesh and blood in all directions.

"Damn," Bowen murmured.

"What should we do, sir?" the balding aide asked.

Bowen removed his slouch hat, wiped his brow, and shot the aide a penetrating stare. Reflexively, the aide recoiled. Bowen would like to have said, "How the hell do I know?" But that would have been ignoble and smacked of defeatism. Such traits were not in his repertoire.

Instead, he said, "Get up to General Green. Tell him to re . . ."

Suddenly, a Rebel yell, then a chorus of Rebel yells resounded from the northeast. A rider had his horse at a full gallop and was headed straight for Bowen. When he arrived, greetings and salutations were brief. The rider, a middle-aged corporal with a disheveled beard and a matching kepi, grinned happily.

"We're here, sir," he announced in a crusty tenor voice.

"Who is?"

"General Baldwin and Colonel Cockrell, sir. At your service."

Chiding himself for not immediately recognizing the reinforcements, Bowen snapped a salute at the messenger and said, "Tell General Baldwin and Colonel Cockrell to establish a defensive line on the other side of that creek."

Bowen pointed to a ridgeline on the northern bank of Centers Creek.

The rider acknowledged the order and asked, "Do we still hold the Rodney Road?"

Bowen turned his gaze back to Green's predicament. The waves of retreating gray uniforms confirmed his suspicions.

"Yes, but not for long," he groaned.

Bolstered by the reinforcements, Bowen gave further orders to them and whatever delinquents he could find fleeing from Magnolia Church to fall back a half-mile and dig in. This strengthened the left wing of the Confederate line enough that Bowen ordered Green to join Tracy on the Bruinsburg Road. That done, he counted his blessings—meager as they were—and waited.

As he waited, Bowen remembered the period when he and Grant had been neighbors in Missouri. The irony of it percolated through his mind. *Sam Grant,* he thought. Who would ever have thought him capable of commanding an entire Union army? Mild-mannered, unassuming, friendly *Sam Grant* the conqueror. Bowen nearly smiled, but then remembered his duty and the thousands of Confederate soldiers whose deaths could be directly attributed to the army of Sam Grant. For a moment or two, he tried hating his old friend, but found he could not. The best he could do was direct his frustrations to the job at hand. Carefully, meticulously, he inspected his defensive line, correcting its flaws and augmenting its strength where needed. Then he took a long look at the battleground-to-be.

Well, Sam, come on in, he thought. *It'll be good to see you again.*

* * *

"My God, this ground is awful!" exclaimed Ulysses S. Grant as he directed his gaze toward Bowen's defensive line. All around him were tall, steep hills, and vertigo-inducing ravines filled with canebrakes and underbrush.

The two generals, Grant and his lieutenant John McClernand, were inspecting the battlefield between Magnolia Church and a homestead northwest of it called the Shaifer house. On and beside the Rodney Road lay Confederate howitzers, caissons and ammunition wagons. Grant's forces had also taken several hundred prisoners. All in all, a good day for the Union—so far.

"A great victory, General Grant," McClernand boasted.

"I understand there was a problem with rations," Grant said, hoping to put a damper on McClernand's bombast. Before the Union assault, McClernand had forgotten to feed his men.

"An unfortunate oversight, General, a consequence of rapid deployment and the numerous dislocations it engenders. An oversight, but not one to be repeated."

Grant watched McClernand squirm, a state of being to which he was unaccustomed. It was an entertaining phenomenon. Perhaps sensing Grant's amusement, McClernand excused himself and rode off to the Shaifer house to practice his oratorical skills among men who might be more appreciative.

Grant pulled his horse off the road for coffee and a cigar with his staff and to compose his thoughts. Leaning his back against a tree stump and removing his hat, he reviewed what he knew of the day's events. It had started when General Eugene Carr and the Fourteenth Division had run into Confederate pickets at the Shaifer house. They had been promptly chased off and Carr had gone in pursuit. Because of the terrain and the smothering vegetation, it had not, except for the weather, been a hot pursuit. Instead, Carr had sent one brigade at a time through the thick brush while a second brigade struck the Confederate left flank. He had been joined by General Alvin Hovey's Twelfth Division, and together they had enveloped both Confederate flanks.

His cigar half-smoked, Grant spotted Charles Dana meandering over from the Shaifer house. When he was within hailing distance, Grant held up his mug and said, "It's coffee."

Smiling, Dana seated himself next to Grant and remarked, "You don't drink at times like this."

"How can you be sure?" Grant challenged, thrusting his mug toward Dana. "This could be fine Tennessee whisky for all you know."

With a benign smirk on his face, Dana seized the mug and took a deep swallow. Then he choked and spat it violently to the ground.

"God, that is awful stuff," he croaked "It's hot so it must be coffee, but it tastes like dishwater."

"You've drunk dishwater?"

"No, but if I had, it would taste like this."

Grant pointed at the mug in Dana's hand.

"That's only *approximate* coffee," he said.

"*Approximate* coffee?"

"Yes. We're low on real coffee. There are a few coffee-*like* ingredients in it as well."

Dana did not ask what the coffee-like ingredients were. He was satisfied that one of them was not Tennessee whisky.

Flipping a thumb in the direction of the Shaifer house, Dana said, "Did you know General McClernand and another fellow from Illinois . . ."

"Yates. Richard Yates, Governor of Illinois."

"Yes, McClernand and Yates are in there claiming a great victory."

"That's what politicians do: *speechify*. I've tried to break them of the habit but have not yet been successful."

"Is it?"

"Is it what?"

"A great victory."

Grant inhaled and blew cigar smoke out his nose. He offered a cigar to Dana, who declined.

"Not yet it isn't. Bowen is still out there fighting, and he's still getting reinforcements. Don't forget we are in the South. He can get reinforcements from any direction. We have to ferry them across the Mississippi at one place: Bruinsburg."

"You *know* Bowen," Dana said tentatively.

Grant lifted himself to a standing position and brushed off his pants.

"I knew him in Missouri. He was a neighbor, a good man. A good soldier. He knows what he's doing."

Grant's eyes bored into Dana's, seeking enlightenment, but Charles Dana did not reveal the source of his information about Grant's former relationship with Bowen. The awkward moment—it did not rise to the level of impasse—vanished with the pounding of multiple horse hooves beating on the Rodney Road. Grant was the first to turn his head toward the sound, then Dana did the same.

"Who are they?" Dana wanted to know.

Grant did not immediately respond but walked toward the approaching armed force, his eyes squinting.

"It's . . . McPherson's Corps, or portions of it at least."

The reinforcements turned out to be A.J. Smith's Tenth Division and Stevenson's brigade of the Seventeenth. Grant was continuing toward them when he spotted a hollow-eyed, gaunt-faced man with two projectiles of gray hair shooting from both sides of his chin and a ring of the same hair surrounding a balding pate. It was Brigadier General Andrew Jackson Smith. Except for the shortage of skull hair, he maintained the same aura of harsh dignity as his namesake.

"General Grant," Smith barked in an aging baritone. He saluted and dismounted.

"General Smith," Grant acknowledged with a proper but somewhat less crisp salute. He swung an arm toward Dana and said, "You know Mr. Dana, don't you?"

Smith offered his hand and said, "Of course, everyone knows who Mr. Dana is."

Smith smiled.

Dana smiled. Smith's reaction was a familiar one. Grant's staff was quite protective. They did not appreciate the War Department sending a spy to keep an eye on their commander's drinking habits. Grant ignored the interplay.

"General Smith, do you know the situation?" he asked.

"We're winning, aren't we?"

"Yes, we are, but we're stuck," Grant replied, then pointed east. "John Bowen is somewhere in those weeds over there. We need to kick him out."

At first, Smith's face broke into a wide grin, giving him the appearance of a cheerful specter. When he saw the terrain he and his men would have to cover, the smile vanished.

"That's the most god-awful ground I've ever seen," he declared.

"My sentiments . . . approximately."

Smith glared at the hideous obstacles in what was destined to be his path, shook his head, and turned to face Grant again. He looked as if he might say something but declined. There was nothing to say. It had to be done.

By this time, McClernand had been informed of Smith's arrival. He was strolling across the road toward Grant when McPherson arrived, dismounted, and approached the *ad hoc* council of war. McClernand brought a small following with him, one of whom was Governor Richard Yates, who had plenty of dark hair but, unlike most of the others, not on his face. Grant liked Yates, having been appointed by him as mustering officer for Illinois in the initial stages of the war. Although both were political animals, Grant found himself able to get along with Yates but not McClernand. Maybe the old saw was true: familiarity breeds contempt.

"General McClernand, place your men in battle order. The fighting is not quite over," Grant said abruptly.

"Where?" a startled McClernand asked.

"Down there," Grant said, pointing to the natural abatis of canebrake and underbrush. "Bowen is dug in. I would appreciate it if you would remove him."

McClernand sent Grant a look that might be interpreted as 'easy for you to say,' but was, in fact, a reaction to the news that the victory about which he had freely boasted was not yet in hand.

"Sir," McClernand said, snapping an abbreviated salute. "He'll be out of there within the hour."

Grant returned the salute and McClernand rode off to form up Carr's, Smith's and Hovey's divisions for the impending assault. Grant turned to McPherson.

"General, I don't think you'll be needed here. You will be of more use to General Osterhaus farther north."

"The Bruinsburg Road? We heard artillery and rifle fire on the way in."

Grant nodded and said, "Osterhaus has sharpshooters and artillery keeping the enemy at bay, but he's been unable to sustain an offensive. With your people in place, that situation should change."

McPherson and his entourage swiftly departed, creating a cloud of dust in their wake. A half-hour later, he reached Oster-haus's line. McPherson halted the march and made an immediate inspection of the Confederate line, searching for vulnerabilities.

South and east of Magnolia Church, McClernand formed his army along a north-south front, straddling the Rodney Road with Carr in the north, Smith in the center and Hovey at the southern end. The battlefield had evolved two fronts, one pitting Bowen against McPherson across the Bruinsburg Road, and the other pitting McClernand against Cockrell's and Baldwin's brigades on the Rodney Road. The Federals enjoyed the numerical advantage; the Confederates had a capable but concerned John Bowen.

★ TWENTY-FOUR ★

May 1, 1963, The Battle of Port Gibson

John Bowen saw them coming a half-mile away: McClernand's Corps and McClernand himself marching slowly but inevitably at him. He lowered his field glasses when the Union artillery rolled into position.

"We have to stop them *now*," he said to General William Baldwin and Colonel Francis Cockrell, both brigade commanders. "If we don't, they'll be in Port Gibson by sundown."

With grim expressions on their faces, Baldwin and Cockrell nodded.

"Well, can we?" Bowen demanded.

Cockrell offered, "We might be able to hold. We need reinforcements . . ."

"You *are* my reinforcements!" Bowen growled, then said in a more moderate tone, "General Baldwin, I want you to hold the line right here. Colonel Cockrell, I want you to envelop their right flank."

The two officers stared at each other in shock, then looked back at Bowen.

"Sir, how am I supposed to do that?" Cockrell pleaded. "They have a five-to-one advantage over us. And both Union flanks extend beyond ours by at least half a mile."

"I know that, Francis. I'm counting on you," Bowen said, clamping a hand on Cockrell's shoulder.

The sincerity in Bowen's plea and in the lines of his troubled countenance melted away Cockrell's resistance.

"All right, all right," he murmured unconvincingly. He flashed Baldwin a fatalistic glance, moved away from Bowen's grasp and gave a crisp salute before departing. Baldwin followed, then broke off to join his brigade. Within the hour fighting along the line was furious; on the Confederate left flank it was especially deadly.

The offensive was seized by Cockrell's brigade, who, to everyone's surprise, nearly succeeded in enveloping the Union right flank. Cockrell's Missouri troops fought vigorously through the stiff but hesitant opposition of their mid-western brethren from Ohio and Wisconsin. But the Federals finally remembered that they had the numbers, and they had something else: artillery. Confederate survivors of the attack would later compare the profusion of Minie balls and grapeshot suffusing the atmosphere to a thundercloud of leaden rain and iron hailstones. Some even claimed that the buzzing swarm of killer bees was so dense it shut out the sunlight, but that wasn't quite true; there was enough light for effective killing. By mid-afternoon, it was clear that the Confederate ranks were too thin to sustain the offensive, were too thin even to hold the ground they had just captured. Reluctantly, Cockrell ordered a retreat.

Bowen was standing by his horse, a chestnut gelding, at the rear of the line. Cockrell pulled his horse alongside.

"How is Baldwin coming along?" he asked solemnly.

"He's holding," Bowen replied.

Cockrell bowed his head and said, "I'm sorry, sir. We beat them back but couldn't hold."

"I know, I know," Bowen sighed, patting Cockrell's horse on the flank. "I was afraid none of you would make it back. But you did, and we have that to be grateful for."

Cockrell was silent. His gaze drifted to Bowen's left. His lips were clamped tightly together.

"You do understand the attack had to be made," Bowen asserted. "Doing nothing was not an option."

With a loud sigh, Cockrell exhaled through his nostrils. Then he glanced sharply at his commander.

"'Course I understand, sir. I'm a soldier."

Bowen waited for more, but no further commentary was forthcoming.

"Why don't you and your men get some coffee, Colonel? Some food too."

"Yes, sir. Thank you."

Cockrell dismounted and told his officers to assemble the brigade for a meal. For once, the men were happy to obey an order. While a thousand conversations were breaking out, Bowen steered his horse toward Cockrell, who had promptly poured himself a cup of coffee and was ferociously ingesting it.

"Francis, when you're done eating, send someone to General Baldwin and apprise him of the situation. But let him know I need him to hold for the time being."

Cockrell took a final bold swallow of his coffee and asked, "Where will you be, sir?"

"I need to determine how Green and Tracy are doing on our right flank. If they can hold, maybe we can salvage some ground, keep the Yankees bottled up until relief arrives.

"Relief, sir? We have relief coming?"

The question caught Bowen by surprise. He had not intended to suggest that relief was on the way. For all he knew, Generals Pemberton and Johnston remained hidebound in their respective bastions of Vicksburg and Jackson. But he was hopeful that one of them would recognize the seriousness of his plight and come running to the rescue.

"Nothing definite, Francis. But General Pemberton knows what we're up against. He won't let us down."

Bowen and Cockrell exchanged salutes and Bowen nudged his horse to the northwest. As he made his way through the marshy terrain, he could not help wondering if his optimism was little more than wishful thinking. But he had no choice. Pessimism was not the proper philosophy for a general.

* * *

Like their counterparts Baldwin and Cockrell on the Rodney Road, Generals Green and Tracy achieved a degree of initial success along the Bruinsburg Road against Union Brigadier General Osterhaus. The terrain and the thick underbrush covering it made an attack by either side a risky proposition. The depleted Confederates were not about to launch another futile attack against an enemy with far superior numbers. So the offense was left to the Federals, and they took it.

General Edward Tracy was struck down early in the action with a ball through the back of the neck. He died instantly. His brigade was taken over by Colonel Isham Garrott of Alabama, who held his ground throughout most of the day. Osterhaus eventually took the ground above Centers Creek. That was when McPherson arrived, bringing not only reinforcements but a plan to turn the Confederate right flank. For the most part, the flanking maneuver worked. Where it didn't work, McPherson used his numerical superiority to wear down his enemy; drive him back one inch at a time, kill him one man at a time. Then the Union artillery found the range and began mowing down guns, men and horses as if they were nothing more than tall grass. In desperation, Martin Green counterattacked with the Sixth Missouri to relieve Garrott and his men. They were driven back with heavy losses.

John Bowen had had enough. He ordered a withdrawal to the north, across Bayou Pierre.

"Can I ask, sir, where are we going?" asked one of the aides with whom he was entrusting the withdrawal order to his officers.

"We'll be joining General Pemberton."

"Where's he, sir?"

Bowen suppressed a snort of frustration as he said, "Son, I'll be damned if I know. But we'll find him. He won't be moving very fast."

The Battle of Port Gibson was over.

★ TWENTY-FIVE ★

May 2, 1863, Baton Rouge, Louisiana

As he watched the Mississippi drift by, Colonel Benjamin Grierson thought he'd done pretty well for a Pittsburgh-born music teacher who, as a boy, had been kicked in the head by a horse. He still didn't like horses, even the bay he was mounted on, but one could not be a cavalryman without riding a horse; it was part of the job description. To steady himself, he took a Jew's harp from his breast pocket and played a few strains of "Dixie," but stopped when he detected the silent disapproval of the Second Iowa, Sixth Illinois, and Seventh Illinois Cavalry officers beside him.

"So, that's the Mississippi River, is it?" he said with blithe indifference. "Doesn't look that formidable."

"You have to be in it to feel its power," said Grierson's adjutant, Lieutenant Samuel Woodward. Woodward was on his immediate left, and, like Grierson, had a spade beard that lent him a devilish air. "If you catch one of its whirlpools it can suck you under and hold you there until you drown."

"Well, I don't plan to do that," Grierson said, returning the Jew's harp to his pocket and retrieving a map from another inside pocket. "Where are we, anyway? Have all the men come up yet?"

As he asked the question, Grierson turned to view the double line of blue-coated, mounted cavalry stretching eastward. It was hard to believe that, after leaving Tennessee, they had ridden six hundred miles, destroyed sixty miles of railroad track, captured five hundred prisoners, and seized five hundred mules, all while suffering only a dozen casualties. The amazement he felt completely overshadowed any sense of pride.

Woodward took the map and unfolded it.

"Where are we?" Grierson repeated.

"Right here. River Road," Woodward said, pointing to the map.

Grierson looked at the spot on which his subordinate had laid his finger. River Road was on the eastern side of the Mississippi next to a stretch of river that flowed almost directly south from one of its numerous, greater-than-ninety-degree bends.

"What do you think, Sam? Is this far enough?" he asked, not entirely frivolous.

"That's up to you, Colonel," Woodward said. "If it were up to me, we'd burn the town."

Had he not been familiar with Woodward's background, Grierson might have been shocked. But he knew Woodward and his family had been harassed by Rebel sympathizers in Kentucky before the young man had joined the Sixth Illinois Cavalry in 1862. The harassment had included death threats and being mobbed in the streets. To escape it, the family had moved to Illinois, leaving the cavalryman-to-be with a permanent emotional scar.

"We already own Baton Rouge. Why would we burn it?" Grierson said, hoping to mitigate his adjutant's hatred. "I think this is far enough. Let's find a place where I can be heard without shouting."

There was, of course, no such place. Besides the Second Iowa and the Sixth and Seventh Illinois Cavalry, Grierson's entourage included a motley parade of poor southern whites and Negroes who, having become disenfranchised by the cavalry raids, or, simply out of hunger and curiosity, stretched behind the mounted soldiers for several miles. There were also the members of the Union garrison from Baton Rouge who had come out to meet the "brigade of General Grant's army" that had cut its way southward from Tennessee to Louisiana.

Woodward managed to find a Baton Rouge resident who gave him oral directions to a large magnolia grove five miles south of town. Weaving its way through the city streets and around the public square, the long procession followed the dusty road to its destination, losing a few stragglers on the way, but replacing them with fresh curiosity-seekers. The men of the three Union cavalry units took advantage of the lethargic pace to nap in their saddles. It was a skill they had learned on the way down during the all too infrequent and far too brief respites between raids.

A colonel from the Baton Rouge garrison rode up and inserted his horse between Grierson's and Woodward's. He was tall, straight in the saddle, and clean, the latter virtue inspiring a certain envy in Grierson, who thought he could feel grime deep in his bones. The difference between a garrison soldier and a cavalryman, he concluded.

"Do you know where you're going?" asked the officer.

Grierson slowly lifted his head, his eyelids heavy with sleeplessness.

"More or less," he said with a yawn. "Can't be far now. Some grove of magnolia trees or the like."

"I know where that is," the colonel said with what seemed to Grierson more enthusiasm than he could stand.

With the colonel as point man, they arrived at the magnolia grove sooner than Grierson would have preferred. It was a spacious lowland pasture with magnolia trees every thirty or forty feet, enough to provide a continuous roof of rich green, oval-shaped leaves over the spectators. Interspersed among the leaves was an array of white, pink and lavender flowers.

The garrison officer dismounted and strode toward Grierson, offering an arm.

"Let me help you down, sir."

"Nope. Thanks, but I have something I need to say. I'll stay here," said Grierson. He turned to Woodward, adding, "Have all three units dismount and form into a circle, around me."

When Woodward's parted lips conveyed incomprehension, Grierson explained, "I have to make a speech and I don't want to yell."

The adjutant nodded his understanding and separated himself from Grierson, then busied himself forming up the men into the requested formation. No one resisted and no one promptly obeyed. It was like a cattle roundup with officers prodding the lethargic beasts with curses instead of sticks and directing them to open stalls in the ring. Most seated themselves on the ground, some stood around the outside of the crowd and nearly all removed their kepis or slouch hats. There was a sense that this was to be more of a social gathering than a council of war, and a steady murmur of good cheer resonated beneath the leafy umbrella of the magnolias. When the packed circle was finally stationary, Grierson steered his bay into an empty space around one of the larger trees and turned to face the soldiers under his command. To give him more room, soldiers of the innermost circle moved back, or, if that was not possible, out of the way.

"Gentlemen," he said, raising his hands for silence. He briefly considered adding, "and ladies," to recognize the fact that some members of the non-military entourage who were milling about beyond the circle of blue were women. But he rejected the notion. His address was strictly for the men who had followed him into battle.

"I'm sure many of you already know, or at least suspect, the truth, but I wanted to tell you myself: We have reached the end of our mission and are completely victorious!"

As he knew they would, the throng of soldiers rose to their feet, uttered a series of bellicose cheers, and threw their hats and kepis into the air. Many of the headpieces did not get any farther than the nearest magnolia branch and, along with the blossoms they dislodged, promptly fell to the ground. Grierson did not remove his hat but waited for the noise to quell, then raised his hands again.

"Boys, I want to take this moment to congratulate you and to thank you for a job well done," he said with a solemnity that, except for a brief buzz of appreciation, discouraged further uproar.

"I believe . . . No, I am convinced that our Mississippi campaign will go down in the annals of military history as the greatest, most successful, campaign of the war, far and away eclipsing anything our Rebel counterparts—Nathan Bedford Forrest and Jeb Stuart—have achieved."

Another ovation erupted, louder than before, with howling cries and abrupt hoots, many sounding like imitations of the famed "Rebel yell." To Grierson, it was an exhilarating cacophony of sounds, expressing both animosity and a profound respect for the cavalry led by the two Rebel generals.

Grierson pulled a leather-bound notebook from his pocket, opened it to a prearranged page, and held it over his head for viewing. Then he said, "For your edification and appreciation, gentlemen, I have asked Colonel Woodward to compile some statistics, which I would like now to share with you . . ."

A hum of annoyance coursed through the assemblage.

"No, no, you misunderstand me," Grierson exhorted with a grin. "These are not the kind of statistics you hear every day from our quartermaster: lists of supplies, shortfalls, and so forth. Let me give you some examples."

A hush fell over the gathering. They would give their commander the opportunity not to bore them. Grierson lowered the notebook to reading level.

"April 24, 1863. Newton Station, Mississippi. Two locomotives and three-dozen freight cars destroyed, along with their contents.

Light applause and laughter.

"Thirty miles a day through Ripley, New Albany, and Pontococ. Even the Quinine Brigade did their part . . ."

This time the applause was more intense, and was accompanied by an audible undercurrent of pride. The Quinine Brigade consisted of sick and saddle sore cavalrymen whom Grierson had ordered home, with instructions to obliterate railroad track and generally wreak havoc with enough enthusiasm to delude the Confederates into thinking they comprised the entire raiding party. They had done an excellent job, mostly at night, when it was more difficult to count heads. When the applause subsided, Grierson resumed his oration.

"Cotton warehouses burned in Okolana, a thousand horses and mules seized, trestles and bridges destroyed, telegraph wires cut at Chunky River, boxcars set ablaze in Hazelhurst, et-cetera, et-cetera, et-cetera! All in all, I'd say you boys have generally had more fun than a herd of country boys on a possum hunt."

The joke went over reasonably well, though Grierson had been worried that the reference to "country boys on a possum hunt" might be taken the wrong way by the former Iowa and Illinois farmers present. If it had been, there was no indication of it in the prevailing mood. No one was going to be unhappy this day.

"But far be it from me to celebrate the devastation of the Rebel homeland," Grierson went on, provoking puzzlement in a number of faces. "By God, we performed some creditable rescue work as well! Why, what would have happened to that Rebel whisky we found at Newton station, or those fifty gallon barrels of rum at Brookhaven if we hadn't liberated it and put it to good use?"

The puzzled expressions disappeared, replaced by hefty back-slapping and bellows of laughter. Grierson breathed another sigh of relief. At the time, the rum and its consumption had presented a serious problem. The sheer volume of the stuff had been so great and the number of affected revelers so comprehensive that it seemed the entire cavalry had gone on a drunken binge. It had been touch and go, forcing them into a night march to dissipate the effects of the Rebel spirits. The next morning brought an abundance of hangovers but precious little revelry.

"Well, that's about all I have to say, unless you boys want me to bore you with more statistics. Anyone have anything they want to ask?"

The crowd offered respectful applause, fell silent for a moment, then found its spokesmen. A sergeant two or three rows from Grierson went first.

"Sir, if this is the end of the campaign, what was the point of it? Is General Grant launching a new offensive?"

It was a better question than Grierson had anticipated. He wondered if asking for questions had been a wise move.

"The point of the campaign was to destroy the will and the ability of the Confederates to wage war. We accomplished that," Grierson said, took a breath, and steeled himself for the hard part. "And, yes, General Grant has launched a new offensive."

It was a pithy, to-the-point response and Grierson knew it would only provoke more questions. In itself, his announcement should not have surprised anyone. Grant seemed always to be launching offensives, seven to date. But Grierson, and perhaps his men, sensed that something different, something more conse-quential, was about to happen.

"Sir, will General Sherman's army have the main thrust?" asked a red-faced, red-haired man with fat freckles covering his face and neck.

"All I can tell you, Billy, is that General Sherman will certainly be involved in any major offensive operation."

"Is it Haynes' Bluff? Is that where they're goin' in?" the red-haired soldier somewhat irritably inquired.

Annoyed by the soldier's persistence, Grierson replied, "I can't get into that, Billy. You know I can't."

"How about us, Colonel? Are we goin' in?" Billy wanted to know.

From the silent anticipation that followed the remark, Grierson knew this was not only Billy's concern but the singular concern of his entire cavalry. He allowed a smile to creep into his features. It was a crooked smile because of the cheekbones the horse had crushed when it kicked him as a boy, but it was genuine. He smiled because, at least in this one instance, he had good news.

"No, we aren't staying. We've done our job. Back to Tennessee for us," he replied. "After a decent rest, that is."

The cheering and backslapping were as raucous as before and more heartfelt. Regardless of which side you were on, when the opportunity to do nothing presented itself, you took it.

Grierson gazed around, found Woodward, and motioned him over. The adjutant obeyed, stationed his horse next to Grierson's and waited for his commander to speak.

Gesturing with a wide sweep of his arm, Grierson said, "These boys are in pretty much an uproar now, but I don't think they have much noise left in them. After a good meal, I think they might just nod off."

Understanding that he'd been given an order to have a meal prepared, Woodward sniffed the magnolias, admired the blue sky, and said, "It's a beautiful day. You may be right."

After he had broken off and arranged matters with the cook, Woodward returned wearing a dour expression.

"What is it, Sam? You look like Nathan Bedford Forrest just galloped over your grave."

"It's nothing much, sir. But I wonder if celebrating the destruction of an enemy is an appropriate Christian viewpoint."

"What would you have us do, turn the other cheek?"

"No, no, of course not," Woodward said, shaking his head. "I just think celebration is not the proper Christian attitude. If we weren't at war, we'd be arrested for what we've done."

"But we *are* at war."

"I know. At least in my head I know. But I can't help thinking that, once the war is over, Northerners and Southerners will take a long time getting over what they've done to each other. They may never get over it."

"All the more reason to get it over with as quickly as possible—to keep the bad memories to a minimum," Grierson said, hoping to lighten his subordinate's dreary mood. Woodward seemed to understand Grierson's intent and figuratively clamped his mouth shut.

Many of the weary, grimy soldiers did not make it for dinner and lay exhausted on the ground, where they slept more soundly than they had in weeks. Their collective snore rose above the animated chorus of those still awake like a somnolent descant. Woodward steered his horse back to where the cook and his staff were working feverishly. Grierson watched while the two men spoke, the cook with some irritation. Woodward returned, apparently chastised.

"What's wrong with him?" Grierson asked.

"He's unhappy that he has to work while everyone else has a good time."

"That's what cooks are for."

"He knows that. He just wanted to complain to someone, and I was available."

"Sam, I want you to lead the corps back to Tennessee," Grierson announced as he turned and headed his horse back toward Baton Rouge.

"Sir?" Woodward asked, following.

"I'm going to enjoy myself. Take a steamboat down to New Orleans and spend some time there. I hear it's a magnificent city."

"I wouldn't know. I'm from Illinois," Woodward replied somberly. "Have we heard anything about the situation at Grand Gulf?"

The "situation" was the attempted crossing of the Mississippi by Grant's invasion force, consisting of McClernand's divisions and elements of McPherson's corps. Sherman would also participate after putting the final touches on his deception at Haynes' Bluff. Whether Grierson had received news that any of this had happened was the question Woodward was asking.

"I have not," Grierson replied.

"How close did we get to them?"

Grierson glanced uncomfortably at his adjutant, then said, "Forty miles—just before we turned east from Union Church. The distance from there to Grand Gulf is about forty miles."

"So we don't know if the crossing was successful?"

"No, we don't. If it had been, General Grant would have let us know. But even if it hasn't happened doesn't mean it won't."

Neither man offered further comment, both fearful of dampening the euphoria generated by the completion of their historic mission. Finally, Woodward spoke.

"Maybe we could've helped more by being there."

Grierson shook his head and upwardly adjusted the brim of his slouch hat to allow an unobstructed view of the horizon.

"Maybe, but not much. What can cavalry do to help infantry cross the Mississippi, lend them their horses to swim across? Our orders were to proceed according to plan if no word was forthcoming. That's what we did."

That was the end of the discussion, and Woodward recognized it as such.

"I hope your stay in New Orleans is a pleasurable one, sir," he offered.

"It will be, Grierson said confidently, flashing his colleague a sly smile. "And I hope your journey back to LaGrange will be a pleasant one."

Woodward declined to take the bait, instead said, "How will you get around in New Orleans?"

"We-e-ell, I'll think of something. It is a Union city now. Civilized citizenry. No Rebel sharpshooters trying to blow the heads off Union soldiers and sympathizers."

"Maybe the civilized citizens of New Orleans will give you a horse."

Grierson stiffened in the saddle and instinctively pressed a finger to the spot on his jaw where he'd been kicked as a boy.

"God, I hope not. A carriage would be satisfactory and . . ."

He looked at the horse he was riding and glanced furtively at Woodward. Raising a hand to one side of his mouth as if to prevent the horse from hearing, he whispered, ". . . I hate these damn beasts. I really do."

★ TWENTY-SIX ★

May 3, 1863, Grand Gulf, Mississippi

Ulysses S. Grant had a really sore posterior. For nearly every waking hour over the past four days he had been in the saddle, often on borrowed and unfamiliar horses. Although he could still laugh at his condition, it did not help the discomfort one bit. He remembered hearing that Napoleon had suffered from hemorrhoids, and wondered if he was doomed to suffer the same humiliating fate. Carefully, he dismounted from his latest horse, a chestnut mare, and started toward the bluff overlooking the Mississippi and Grand Gulf.

"May I help you, sir?" asked an aide offering an arm.

"No, I'll be all right," Grant said, his slightly bow-legged gait propelling him across the soft turf of the bluff. He scanned the scene and found most of his staff gazing out over the Mississippi. McPherson, McClernand, and Sherman were there, as was Porter: a clear quorum. Grant strode awkwardly toward Porter. The Admiral turned, looked at him and struggled to suppress a grin.

"General Grant, you seem to be walking . . . oddly," he said.

"Saddle sores," Grant admitted, then shifted his gaze to Porter's flotilla docked on the eastern shore. "When did we take Grand Gulf?"

"This morning. We heard them spiking the guns and blowing up the magazines."

"No casualties?"

"No fighting. We just took over."

Grant nodded his approval.

"That's the best way," he said.

Porter remained silent.

"Let's go," Grant said, tossing a glance in the direction of the headquarters tent. Inside the tent were a long table with a large map of Mississippi and Louisiana laid out on it, James McPherson, William Sherman, John McClernand, and junior officers of their staffs. James Wilson and John Rawlins were among the latter. Charles Dana hovered in the background.

"All right, gentlemen, what's our status and what do we do next?" Grant asked as he stared down at the map. "I have my own ideas, but I want to hear yours."

"Bowen is retreating. He doesn't have the manpower," McClernand said forcefully. He was still embarrassed because of Bowen's nearly successful offensive at Magnolia Church.

"Where's he going, back to Vicksburg?"

"He's joining Pemberton," McPherson said.

"Almost the same thing," Grant noted. "Both of them will need reinforcements before they can do anything but retreat.

There was a general murmur of agreement. Grant pounded a finger on the word "Vicksburg" on the map. "What I want to do is drive them back there. But there are problems."

He paused to let his words sink in. Then he said, "The first is that General Halleck still wants us to support General Banks at Port Hudson. We can't do both."

A collective groan filled the humid atmosphere inside the tent. For several months, Halleck had been urging Grant to send a portion of his army to Banks. Grant had even drawn up a plan to float McPherson's or McClernand's corps south to Port Hudson, where Nathaniel Banks would fling the weight of the combined forces at that city. But now that a beachhead had been established at Grand Gulf, no one in the Army of the Tennessee wanted to play second fiddle.

"I don't want to do that," Grant firmly declared. "It's not that General Banks doesn't need our assistance. He's a good man. But I think we have a better opportunity here."

Grant glanced up from the map to see if he had their attention. In fact, all eyes were riveted on him.

"Our problem is Joe Johnston," he said, using his finger as a gavel. Then he started moving the finger across the map. "He's here in Jackson, or somewhere nearby."

He dragged his finger eastward to Jackson and stopped.

"If we attack Vicksburg, Johnston will probably decide to leave Jackson and boot us in our rear. If we attack Johnston while he's still in Jackson, Pemberton could come east and do the same thing. Does everyone see that?"

Murmurs of agreement told Grant they understood.

"All right. Good. You must also know that we can't attack directly north. The ground south of Vicksburg is not suitable for an invading army. It's eroded, it's treacherous, and it supports acres of an iniquitous vegetation that has no place in civilized warfare."

A refreshing undercurrent of amusement echoed in the tent.

"What we are *not* going to do is get trapped on that land," Grant said, indicating the terrain between the Big Black and Mississippi Rivers. "What we *are* going to do is march northeast instead of directly north, keeping the Big Black on our left. That way, we'll have that river between us and the Mississippi and we can keep an eye out for Johnston."

"If we're not attacking Vicksburg, what are we attacking?" a skeptical Sherman asked.

"The Southern Railroad. If we can cut it somewhere between Vicksburg and Jackson, the Rebels won't be able to ferry supplies and reinforcements between the two."

There was a collective murmur of acceptance, except for the ever-scowling Sherman.

"But to do that we'll have to march pretty far inland, away from naval support. Aren't you a little worried about over-extending our supply line?"

"No, Sherman, I am not," Grant said firmly. His tone was amiable, almost buoyant. He had no intention of dressing down his friend and colleague; he was merely stating what, in his mind, was a fact.

Despite Grant's easy manner, Sherman could not help being startled. His puzzlement left his expression hard and grizzled. Grant immediately recognized the familiar visage and laughed.

"I'll explain," he said. "Of course, we'll need a supply line for weapons and equipment, but we don't need a supply line for food and drink."

The only one who did not greet Grant's proposal with a blank stare was Charles Dana, who obviously failed to appreciate the ramifications of what he had heard.

Amused by the dearth of comprehension, Grant stretched his arms out and said, "Gentlemen, where are we?"

It was a few moments before a hesitant voice replied, "Mississippi."

Smiling broadly, Grant said, "Exactly. We do not need to supply the Army of the Tennessee with full rations through Grand Gulf. What we do need to do is make this country furnish the balance of our needs. This is Mississippi, gentlemen! Magnificent farm country—pigs, cattle, chickens, corn, vegetables, fruit trees virtually everywhere. All we need to do is confiscate whatever is necessary for the successful conclusion of this campaign."

He paused to let his words stew in their minds and lit up a cigar. It was Sherman who reacted first.

"Is this the 'something in mind' strategy you mentioned a few days ago but didn't elaborate upon?"

"Yes."

"It's unorthodox."

"It is."

"It may even be immoral."

Grant blew a cloud of smoke over one shoulder and said, "Some might see it that way, but this is a war against an enemy who fights to destroy the union and to continue enslaving his fellow man. I do not intend to starve Mississippi, only to leave it with a little less abundance than it would otherwise have."

"That will be hard to measure or control. What about looting? How will we control that?"

"By keeping a keen eye out for looters. Sherman, we did the same thing when we marched south from Corinth. I don't recall suffering any insurmountable supply problems."

"Anything works over the short term. How can you be sure there will be enough?"

"I can't. We'll just have to find out. If we can't get enough, we'll do something else. But I do not want to guard every inch of a supply line that stretches all the way back to Milliken's Bend if I don't have to."

There were several more comments and questions from the officers. Most saw the inherent logic in Grant's "live-off-the-land" strategy, but few embraced it with any enthusiasm. Soldiers preferred a guaranteed source of sustenance.

When a lull in the conversation presented itself, Grant changed the subject.

"Gentlemen, we need to get back to the business at hand. Let's discuss how we're going to get on with this campaign."

He swept a hand west to east across the map, encompassing every settlement from Grand Gulf to Jackson.

"General McClernand, your boys have done a fine job so far, so you'll have the left flank, closest to the Big Black River and Pemberton. I imagine he'll be watching us from the other side."

"I suspect he will," McClernand agreed.

"Sherman, you'll be in the center and will lead the advance with the Fifteenth Corps."

Sherman nodded grimly.

"Will we be taking off from our position east of Grand Gulf?"

"Yes.

General McPherson, you'll be making a demonstration against Hankinson's Ferry on the Big Black. If you can, try to keep Pemberton occupied. I'd prefer he didn't know what we're up to."

"Yes, sir!" McPherson snapped smartly.

With basic troop dispositions decided upon, Grant and his staff began the serious business of establishing when and how swiftly the campaign should proceed. Too fast and there might be severe dislocations the Confederates could use to their advantage. Too slow and even the overcautious Pemberton would be able to harass them. Grant needed deliberate speed for another reason: so that Halleck could not order him to support General Nathaniel Banks against Port Hudson.

"May 7, that's when we'll go," he announced after several hours of planning and debate.

There were no objections. The staff officers filtered out of the headquarters tent to meet with their men and acquaint them with the coming events. Grant waited until all but one had departed. The lone soldier was an aide whose shoulder he had grasped while the others were departing. The aide knew this meant he was to stay.

For a minute following the exodus, Grant said nothing. Into this void, the aide inserted, "Sir?"

Grant remained silent, paced toward the open tent flap and back again. He gazed lazily up at his aide.

"I need you to send a message to General Halleck."

"Of course, sir."

"Tell him . . ." Grant paused. "Tell him we're going after the Southern Railroad and . . . that he may not hear from me again for several days."

Pulling a pencil and pad from his breast pocket, the aide scribbled the message onto it and returned his complete attention to his commander.

"Anything else, sir?"

"No, nothing," Grant responded, tempted to add, "That's all General Halleck needs to know."

But he restrained himself and regained his silence.

* * *

May 7, 1863, Big Black River, Mississippi

Charlie Johnson of the Thirteenth Illinois, a part of Sherman's Fifteenth Corps, was sweating profusely and had been since the march began. The Mississippi Valley felt like it was turning into a desert. There had been no rain for several weeks and, far from being bogged down in muck and mire as had been the case during winter and early spring, the Army of the Tennessee was actually short on water. There was still plenty in the Mississippi River, but the creek beds were drying up, and the Big Black was getting low.

"We shoulda stayed in Willow Springs," said Darren McGlover, the red-faced farm boy who was Charlie's marching partner, "Shoulda waited for rain."

"Then you'd be complainin' about the wet," Charlie said. "Armies don't wait on the weather."

"Hell they don't," Darren declared. "If we have to march much longer in this heat, we're all gonna keel over from heat prostru . . . prostiro . . ."

"Prostration," Charlie said.

"Yeah, heat prostration," McGlover crowed.

It was possible, but Charlie didn't think death by heat prostration was likely for most of the hearty souls he knew, himself included. True, the heat could overwhelm the senses, and the pervasive dust kicked up by horses, wagons and plodding footsteps did sting the eyes and create a ravenous thirst. But Charlie remembered the march from the Mississippi via Bruinsburg: pleasant grasslands, pretty trees and flowers, blue skies laden with puffy clouds. If you ignored the heat, humidity, and dust, and could focus your eyes before the tears came, this country looked much as it had then.

"Look at that sonofabitch, Charlie!" McGlover cried, pointing across the river.

Charlie looked and saw a lone Rebel soldier aiming his musket at the Union column.

"He ain't serious. Too far away. Can't hit nothin' with a musket from that distance."

Charlie was proven right a moment later when the Rebel soldier mimicked a trigger pull followed by a faked kickback of his musket. When he looked up and dropped the weapon to his side, there was a mischievous, though hardly malicious, grin, which displayed his reasonably well formed but greasy yellow teeth.

"I guess he ain't serious," McGlover acknowledged.

"Couldn't be, too far away," Charlie muttered, letting the words fade away as he spoke them. He derived no pleasure in being proven right. Darren was not a great thinker. And Charlie was more concerned with the fact that the Confederates under Pemberton were still shadowing them. The Seventeenth Corps was supposed to have created a diversion at Hankinson's Ferry and drawn Pemberton off. Obviously, it had not done the job.

Anxious to find something else to complain about, McGlover stepped out of line, wiped the perspiration from his brow, then resumed his place and said, "Where in blazes are we, anyway? We been marchin' a long time."

Remembering the map Sergeant Patterson Smith had taken from a saddlebag and laid out before a campfire six days before, Charlie said, "I would reckon we'd be comin' up on a town called Raymond pretty soon."

"Raymond! Funny name. Where is it 'zactly?"

"A little west of Jackson."

"Jackson! Why are we goin' to Jackson? I thought we was attackin' Vicksburg."

Charlie pointed to Pemberton's column marching on the opposite shore of the Big Black.

"See those boys over there? They ain't just gonna let us walk into Vicksburg and take over. Didn't you listen to Sergeant Smith explain it to us?"

It was clear from the dumbfounded expression on McGlover's face that he had not.

Heaving a heavy sigh, Charlie said, "We're gonna go after a piece of the Southern Railroad, probably in Raymond, since we're headed that way. When we do that, we can starve Vicksburg out."

"Pemberton ain't gonna let us do that either, is he?"

"No, but it ain't as easy to defend a small town like Raymond as it is Vicksburg. And Pemberton ain't got a big army like we do. He's gotta be careful how he uses his people."

"It looks pretty big from here," McGlover said with a nod toward the opposite shore.

Charlie had to concede the point. Pemberton's forces did appear to be substantial, perhaps twenty or thirty thousand. He tried another tack.

"Pemberton's gotta get across the Big Black first, then he's gotta get past us before he can even establish a defensive perimeter around Raymond. That ain't gonna be easy."

"No. I guess it ain't," Said McGlover, bowing to his companion on matters tactical and strategic. "But maybe there's already some Rebs in the place."

"Where would they come from? They ain't from Pemberton's army, couldn't be. We'd have spotted them movin' east."

But this time, Darren McGlover was ready. With a freckle-faced grin poised on his pink features, he exclaimed, "You said it yourself, Charlie! We're closer to Jackson than we are to Vicksburg. They could've come from there."

The point was a valid one. Charlie was not a little surprised by McGlover's understanding of the larger battlefield.

"You're right, Darren, there could be a Reb army in Raymond. Not a big one; they still have to take care of Jackson. But bringin' some of Johnston's boys into Raymond would be the smart move.

Pleased by Charlie's concession, McGlover said, "So . . . what do you think Grant will do?"

Charlie shrugged and shook his head.

"Don't know. Pray the Rebs ain't too smart, I guess.

*   *   *

Brigadier General John Gregg of Walker's Division, Confederate Department of the West, was a bit rankled by Pemberton's order that he take on Grant's army as it descended upon or passed by the town of Raymond. His resentment derived from the fact that Pemberton's defense force was thirty-eight thousand strong while his own brigade comprised a meager three thousand. Gregg understood the difficulties Pemberton would have transferring any of his forces with Grant nipping at his heels. Even so, he would have liked a few more men, say, ten or twenty thousand. But, he shrugged to himself, it was not to be. Live with it.

Turning to his aide, a middle-aged former blacksmith from one of the northern suburbs of Jackson, Gregg said, "Is everyone and everything here?"

"They are, sir."

"Any action yet?"

"No, but they're comin'."

The aide spoke with a quiver in his speech. Gregg couldn't fault him. The rough count of Union soldiers who had crossed at Bruinsburg and Grand Gulf was upwards of fifty thousand. Gregg wondered if his own voice wavered when he spoke. Fifty thousand was a lot of Yankees.

"Let's hope they're not all coming at us," he joked, hoping to stabilize his vocal cords with cheerful words.

The aide offered a weak smile.

"All right, what's our status? What kind of shape are we in?" Gregg demanded, getting down to business.

"Not so good, sir. Lots of men are still sick from the march."

The "march" was the largely overland, feet-on-the-ground journey the brigade had begun a week ago at Port Hudson. The plan had been to transport Gregg's brigade and several others by rail to Jackson. But Grierson's raids had demonstrated their effectiveness by rendering the railroads unreliable as a means of travel. As a result, Gregg's brigade was forced to march more than half the two-hundred-mile distance from Port Hudson to Jackson. They enjoyed one day of rest and had then been ordered by Pemberton to harass any Federal forces crossing their path.

"How many are disabled and how many are just sick? Sick men can still fight."

"Yes, sir, I'll find out."

"Don't go, not yet. Show me what we've got."

The aide searched in his pocket for a map and, finding none, withdrew a notepad and began scribbling on it. When finished, he thrust it before Gregg's eyes.

"This here is Fourteenmile Creek," he said, tracing a forefinger along a line snaking southeast to northwest. "We have men and artillery dug in all along here. Creek ain't much help, though. Nearly dried up."

"How many Yankees headed our way?"

"Don't know."

"Where are they coming from?"

"South. Maybe Utica."

Utica would be a logical jumping off point for the Union forces, but one that was not particularly close to Raymond. Could the entire Union army be lurking somewhere southwest of Raymond? Gregg didn't think so.

"Tell the officers to prepare a line of battle," he said. "Then get me an exact fix on the approaching Federals."

"Yes, sir," said the aide.

"We might as well get the jump on them if we can," Gregg said with a grin, although it was lost from sight inside his voluminous black beard. "No sense in waiting."

Looking somewhere between sheepish and enthusiastic, the aide flung a hasty salute and made his exit.

Gregg looked up at the sky. The sun was hot, white and high overhead. Mississippi in July was truly miserable and this day fit the template. The sun was so bright that Gregg had to lower his line of sight. When he did, he spotted a line of blue infantry atop the hill on the far side of Fourteenmile Creek.

★ TWENTY-SEVEN ★

May 12, 1863, The Battle of Raymond

Major General John A. Logan of McPherson's Third Division, Seventeenth Corps tried mightily to control his mount, a gray gelding, as the artillery and musket fire erupted on the opposite side of the ridge.

"Damn," he muttered. "Damn, damn!"

His momentary descent into profanity was only partly due to his horse's skittishness. The other part had to do with his distaste for being attacked by Confederates. Like most commanders and lawyers—both of which he was—Logan liked surprises only when he sprung them on the enemy.

"Damn!" he bellowed in a final fit of pique.

As he struggled to control the gelding, Logan saw most of the blue infantry in front of him reach and then disappear over the crest of the hill. But one of them was running the wrong way. Thinking the man might be a deserter, Logan dug his heels into the Gelding's flanks and went after him.

"You there . . ." he shouted, then stopped when he recognized the man as his sergeant, Alonzo Crowley. Up close, Crowley's salient features—a handlebar mustache like his own, red suspenders and a gray slouch hat with its brim pinned up in front—were hard to mistake.

"Sir, we're under attack," said Crowley, rushing to Logan's side.

"I gathered that," said Logan. "Where are they and how many are there?"

"Don't know how many. They're down in the valley. Looks like a creek bed."

"Creek bed?"

"Dried up. No water."

"How many?" Logan repeated.

"We don't know, sir. It could be a division, it could be a brigade."

"Why don't we know?"

The sergeant turned suddenly sheepish.

"The roads weren't properly posted, sir."

Angry and beset by a panicky feeling that he might have run into a sizable Confederate force, Logan snorted and focused on settling his horse and, to a lesser extent, himself. When the horse was finally under a modicum of control, Logan urged it to the top of the ridge and gazed down. He saw musket flashes and wispy donuts of cannon smoke. But he could not see the muskets, the cannon, or the men firing them. They were all in the woods on the opposite side of the valley. There was no easy way to determine how many Rebs he was dealing with.

Turning, he steered his horse back down the slope to meet Sergeant Crowley, who was striding purposefully toward him.

"Sergeant, we need to establish a skirmish line. Send a man to inform the brigade commanders. A skirmish line. Is that clear? No unnecessary heroics, just a skirmish line. We need to assess what's in front of us."

The sergeant departed to do his duty while Logan dismounted and stroked the gelding's neck, still attempting to calm it down. It was difficult because his own nerves were on edge from the artillery bombardment the Confederates were raining down on them. God, he hated being on the receiving end of artillery fire. Hell itself could not inspire greater terror.

He returned to the ridge and watched as the troops of the Twentieth Ohio Infantry—the first to respond to his orders—formed into a skirmish line on the descending slope and cautiously moved through an ugly tangle of bushes and coarse vegetation. He drifted slightly rearward so his view could encompass as much of the battlefield as possible. For the most part, what he saw were his own men being picked off by musket fire or being blown to bits by Rebel cannon. Searching for some kind of advantage, he spotted a bridge spanning the waterless creek. If only he could get enough men across . . .

Then the Rebels came at him.

* * *

En Echelon was the military term for the Confederate attack formation. It meant that rather than charging in a straight line of battle—thus exposing the entire line to enemy fire—each member of the formation would be staggered behind and to the right or left of the man preceding him. Like a flock of geese. It was a formation that maximized the field of vision for each member and reduced the enemy's choice of targets.

"Let's go, go, go . . .!" shouted General John Gregg, trying to stir up some enthusiasm in the troops under his command. He could hear the officers barking similar entreaties as well as imaginative epithets all along the line. One notable disadvantage of the *en echelon* attack was that the point men—the ones who led the charge—were often hesitant to be the only exposed members of the formation, if only for a brief interval. They frequently needed "encouragement."

Finally, all members of the Confederate assault line were on the field of battle and working their way up the difficult terrain toward the Yankees. For their part, the Federal forces dug in, except for an artillery battery setting up near the bridge, on the right side of the Confederate line. That worried Gregg because the presence of artillery meant he was facing at least a brigade. As he was mulling over this development the Yankee cannon began clearing the bridge with canister shot. Hastily, Gregg called to the long-haired, blond, young Georgian who was serving him as adjutant.

"Jacob, come here," he called.

Jacob Greenwalt swilled down the coffee he was drinking and abandoned the company of several other officers who were doing the same. He brushed the lengthy strands of hair from his eyes before saluting.

"Yes, sir."

"Jacob, inform the regimental commanders I want them here immediately."

"What shall I tell them is the reason, sir?"

"A war council. We need to get rid of that damn cannon."

Gregg thrust a fist and a finger in the direction of the Federal artillery battery. Greenwalt immediately understood and hurried off with the message. Within ten minutes all the officers or their surrogates were gathered at Gregg's headquarters tent.

"Gentlemen, I think you may have noticed that Yankee cannon over there. Here's what we're going to do about it."

Bending over a map laid out on a battered folding table beneath the raised flap of the tent, Gregg outlined his plan.

"First, we move all regiments to the left," he said, moving a cupped hand like a broom from right to left over the map, away from the cannon. The gesture met with murmurs of approval. Such a movement was in the interest of anyone who valued his life.

"Every regiment but four, that is," he added, directing his gaze to observe the reactions of his officers. He was pleased to see he had their rapt attention.

"We'll wait until the Yankees cross the bridge—which they will try to do. When they do, two of our regiments will take the bridge and whatever Yankees are on or near it. The other two regiments will make their way through the woods and capture the artillery battery in a surprise attack. Got it?"

Gregg waited a full minute for a reply while the officers stood mute, lowered their heads, or grinned silently. He always worried about the happy warriors, the ones who looked forward to battle. They could, and often did, get themselves and other men killed with their careless enthusiasm.

"Sir, do we know how many Yankees we're facing?" came a voice from the rear of the captive audience.

It was a question Gregg himself had been rolling around in his head.

"We don't know how many," he said cautiously. "But we do know that Yankee brigades are smaller than ours, especially now that we're being reinforced by the local militia. That could be nothing more than a raiding party over there."

"What if it's not, sir? You said yourself it was at least a brigade. What if it's the main body?" the same officer asserted.

Gregg shook his head and slapped the table with an open palm.

"It's not. The main body is further north, up around Edwards. That's the latest report."

"That's just what it is, a report," said Colonel Hiram Granbury of the Seventh Texas Infantry. "The Yankees could be anywhere. They've got enough men to stampede all over us if they want to. And I believe General Pemberton's orders were that we should *not engage the enemy in the face of overwhelming odds.*"

Gregg nearly permitted himself a smile. Hiram Granbury was a Texan, who looked like a young Abe Lincoln with a mustache and loved nothing more than being contrary. Thin and lanky to begin with, his physique had actually shrunken while he had been a prisoner of war at Fort Warren in Boston Harbor. Freed in an exchange of prisoners, he had immediately joined up again as a colonel in the Seventh Texas Infantry.

Even as he looked at the man, Gregg thought he saw a twinkle in the eyes partially shadowed by the brim of his black slouch hat.

". . . *but to retreat to Jackson,* I believe was how General Pemberton's order concluded," Gregg said, putting some fire into his tone. Then he pointed to the Federal soldiers holding their tiny plots of ground on the opposite slope. "Now I ask you, does that look like overwhelming odds?"

Gregg placed both hands palm down on the map and directed his gaze individually to each officer, ending at Granbury. The Texan locked eyes with his commanding officer, but after a heartbeat, gave a silent shrug and turned away.

"Well, if it doesn't, let's go after the sons of bitches!"
And they did.

* * *

To say that John Logan was impressed by his counterpart's
generalship would have been to understate his admiration.
Gregg's deployment of his brigade was a thing of beauty. While the
bulk of the brigade shifted five hundred yards in good military order to their left, the remainder marched assertively toward the
cannon that was clearing the bridge. They obviously intended to
put the cannon out of action. As he was considering what to do
about the situation, Logan saw the Twentieth Ohio Regiment
move forward on his right. Or was it the Rebels moving past them
up the slope? Either way, it was a breach of orders. He spurred
his horse into action and found Sergeant Crowley looking dis-
mayed.

"Sergeant, what in the name of everything holy does Colonel
Force think he's doing?"

More confused than Logan, Crowley said, "I don't know, sir.
We heard that God-awful Rebel yell and the colonel ordered an
advance. I seen three or four of his boys jumpin' into the creek
bed."

"I did *not* give the order to advance!"

"I know, sir. I think the colonel had a mind to take advantage
of an opportunity."

"What opportunity? There is nothing but Rebels in the creek
bed, and now Colonel Force is down there with them. How can
that be an *opportunity*?"

The roar of battle suddenly increased as Confederate fire on
the Union right exploded. Logan's eyes were instantly drawn in
that direction. The Union cavalry and infantry over there were
withdrawing up the slope and there were no signs of the regiment
he had sent to guard the right flank.

"What the hell . . ." he muttered in fear and exasperation.

"Sir, Colonel Force seems to be in trouble," Crowley announced.

Logan glanced toward the creek bed and saw a huge cloud of
smoke and dust hovering over it at the point where Force's salient
had entered. The rapidity of the musket fire coming from that direction told him a hot and heavy battle was being waged there.

"So he does," Logan said angrily. "Call him back. For God's
sake, call him back!"

Crowley stood numbly, glancing back and forth between Logan and the creek.

"Sir, I don't know how to do that," he murmured meekly, then steadied his gaze on the dust and smoke hanging over the battle-field like a pregnant thundercloud. "How can we order Colonel Force to do anything right now?"

The remark aggravated Logan's already expanding rage. Force needed to get out of his precarious situation. If he didn't have the good sense to make the decision himself, Logan would order him to.

But then he realized what Crowley was saying: With matters as they stood, no one could reach the men who had flung them-selves into the creek bed and expect to live.

*   *   *

Privates Aaron Ferguson and Salvadore Zemprelli lay petrified, filthy and thirsty in the mud of the not quite completely dry bed of Fourteenmile Creek. Ferguson was a tall, light-skinned scarecrow from Canton, who, at the age of seventeen, was not yet capable of growing facial hair. Zemprelli was a short, dark, stump of Italian extraction from Cincinnati who frequently shaved twice a day to keep the tight spirals of jet-black hair from chafing his neck. To avoid the maelstrom happening all around them, both men were playing dead. They were assisted in this deception by two things: Each man was covered with a copious amount of blood and had his face planted firmly in the clay and silt of the creek bottom. They *looked* dead. The blood covering Ferguson's torso and neck was due to a bloody but superficial wound to his left bicep. But Zemprelli's crimson décor came from a Rebel he had bayoneted in the opening stages of the conflict. The bayonet had cut an artery in the man's chest and hosed the blood directly at Zemprelli. It had been an unpleasant experience, but one he now realized had probably saved his life.

For an instant, the hue and cry of battle seemed to subside. Initially, the two men stayed put, fearing the Confederates might have prevailed. When six minutes had passed without a blood-curdling scream or a musket blast in their immediate vicinity, Zemprelli decided to speak.

"Aaron, you all right?" he asked, working the mud away from his lips.

"Almost. I got a hole in my arm, though."

"A hole?"

"A wound. It was bleedin' pretty good, but I think it slowed down considerable."

To Zemprelli, that did not sound healthy. "Bleedin' pretty good" could mean a severed artery. Maybe his friend was on the edge of bleeding out and didn't know it. He lifted his face from the mud and looked around. There were a few dead soldiers from both sides lying nearby, but, as far as he could tell, no living ones. The cacophony of battle still resonated in the air, but its source had moved farther up the hill. Cautiously, he lifted himself and moved to Ferguson.

"Aaron, let me see that hole you got."

Slowly, his eyes darting to and fro, Ferguson turned over and took off his coat. Zemprelli examined the left arm where the Minie ball had entered and lodged. It and the shirtsleeve were soaked, but there was only a trickle of blood from the wound.

"You're all right," Zemprelli said, ripping off the lower end of Ferguson's right sleeve and using it as a bandage.

"You're bleedin' pretty good yourself," said Ferguson in shock.

"No, I ain't. He is," Zemprelli said, pointing to the body of the Rebel he had killed.

"Oh," Ferguson said sheepishly, seeing the dead man for the first time. He had seen dead men before, but usually at a distance. This dead man's face was imprinted with abject terror; it seemed to ooze out through his bulging eyes and the maw of his gaping mouth. Aaron could appreciate what the man had felt. He had felt it himself until finally realizing his wound was not that serious.

"Stand up, Aaron," Zemprelli said, putting the finishing touches on the bandage. He checked it, tied a tourniquet farther up the arm using another piece of sleeve and a wooden stick, then asked, "How's that?"

Ferguson tried the arm. The movement was painful, but everything appeared to work. He nodded.

"Good. Now we have to get out of here. Get your musket."

Ferguson found the musket three feet from where he had fallen. He slung it over the shoulder of his good arm and said, "Which way is out?"

Snickering, Zemprelli said, "Good question. The Rebs passed us and charged up the hill. We are what is known as *behind enemy lines.*"

Ferguson nodded his agreement and said, "I don't see we have any choice. We have to get back to wherever our line is."

Zemprelli did not bother acknowledging the statement, but he did rush up the rocky bank of the creek, turn, and offer a hand to his friend. When both men had extracted themselves from the creek bed, Zemprelli faced west and started up the hill. He immediately tripped over something.

"O-o-o-oh!"

"Are you all r . . ." Ferguson began, thinking the moan had come from his companion. He realized his mistake when he saw Zemprelli standing over the prone figure of a Confederate soldier with his musket aimed at the man's chest.

"No, no, don't, please!" the man pleaded, raising his arms defensively.

Ferguson stepped forward and gently brushed aside his colleague's musket. Performing a hasty visual inspection, he observed that the man was a boy with lots of sandy hair, most on his head but a superficial amount on his cheeks and chin. He was in obvious pain.

"Who are you, Reb?" Ferguson inquired.

"Jasper Bennett," the boy said between gasping breaths. "Private, Seventh Texas."

"You hurt?" Zemprelli asked with little sympathy in his tone.

"Well, *yeah* . . ." Bennett replied. "It's my leg."

The soldier's right leg looked like Ferguson's injury: thoroughly bloodied but with congealed blood, not the fresh stuff. Ferguson saw the boy's expression tighten in terror, then felt Zemprelli's musket brush his arm in an upward sweep. Once again, he deflected the weapon.

"We don't need to do that, Sal. Mr. Bennett ain't gonna hurt us," Ferguson said, staring directly at the young Rebel. "Are you, Mr. Bennett?"

Relief shone brightly and immediately on Bennett's smooth face.

"No, I ain't. I can't," he stammered and took a wide-angle sweep with his eyes. "Ain't nobody else gonna hurt you, either. They're all . . . dead."

Bennett sobbed, then tried mightily to restrain himself, partially succeeding.

"Well, just so you ain't tempted, I'm gonna take your gun so you can't shoot us," Ferguson said, grabbing the musket that lay a foot in front of the wounded Rebel.

"Sure, sure, I understand," Bennett murmured meekly.

Ferguson and Zemprelli turned to go, but Ferguson had a second thought, turned, and strolled back to the wounded man on the ground. Unsure what was happening, some of the apprehension returned to Bennett's face.

"Here," Ferguson said, removing the canteen from his belt and tossing it to Bennett.

The Confederate opened the canteen and looked up.

"Thanks."

Bennett guzzled thirstily, considered guzzling further and, deciding he did not want to risk offending a Yankee with a gun trained on him, tossed back the partially empty canteen.

"Thanks again."

"You're wel . . ." Ferguson began.

"I really appreciate it," said the wounded Confederate before Ferguson had a chance to reconsider his action.

"Let's go, Aaron," a fitful Zemprelli insisted.

"Yeah . . . yeah," Ferguson said, returning the canteen to his belt and gazing down at Bennett. "Somebody'll be along pretty soon to get you, Reb. Maybe you and I'll get to jawbone some after we take Vicksburg."

"Ha!" Bennett laughed, shaking his head. "Ain't gonna happen, Yank. The lady's defenders are determined. They won't let you bring her down."

Ferguson grinned at the bravado and decided to let Bennett have the last hurrah. Grasping the Confederate rifle with his good hand, he joined Zemprelli, who was ten yards ahead of him up the hill. Zemprelli paused to let him catch up; then both men scurried up the slope toward what they hoped was the Union line. With their path covered by random blue and gray bodies, it was not an easy task.

"Why'd you do that?" Zemprelli challenged, clearly peeved.

"Do what?"

"Give him a drink. He's the enemy. We should've shot him."

"Can't shoot him. He's wounded. It's against the rules of war, and it ain't the Christian thing to do."

"The rules of war be damned!" Zemprelli spat, dodging a shin and foot that had been separated from an unknown leg. "There ain't no such thing as war rules. You just kill the other fool before he kills you."

The crescendo of battle picked up and with it the density of smoke and dust permeating the atmosphere. Already in oxygen debt, Ferguson and Zemprelli coughed and spat and tried unsuccessfully to rub the sting from their eyes.

"Does it strike you, Aaron, that we might want to reconsider our escape plan," Zemprelli shouted above the din. "I mean, we can't hear each other, we can't see anything, and we don't know where we're goin'."

The roar of a cannon momentarily jolted the two men into silence.

"It strikes me, Sal. It surely does, but we got no choice," Ferguson said, waving his companion forward. He had seen the muzzle flash of the cannon and prayed to God it was a Yankee weapon.

* * *

John Gregg was encouraged. The defeat of the Federals had been a simple matter after they had been drawn into and across Fourteenmile Creek. That accomplished, he had sent his men across the creek and up the hill after Yankees and Yankee artillery. He wasn't sure which units they belonged to, but the sketchy intelligence he had received pointed to the presence of McPherson's Ohio, Indiana, and Illinois infantry. Now his forces were scattered throughout the woods topping the hill, fighting from tree to tree as his skirmishers engaged the lead elements of whatever Union brigade he was facing. He called to Jacob Greenwalt, who was walking behind and to the left of Gregg's horse.

"Jacob, run ahead and find out what's happening in our front. I can't see a blasted thing," he said, then aimed a curse at the thick haze surrounding him.

"Yes, sir," Greenwalt said and departed. Gregg used the slow pace of the advance to observe the groups under his command. Most were in good order, staying tight, periodically pulling in the chronic stragglers like fish on a line. Whether from fear or physical ineptitude, some men always seemed to lag behind.

Gregg and his men were exhausted. Everything had happened so quickly and yet, paradoxically, so slowly. The march from Port Hudson to Jackson had consumed time and energy, sapping the strength of the brigade. They had hoped for a long respite but had received only a day's worth at Pearl River before being called back into action at Raymond, Mississippi. Silently, Gregg leveled a curse at the Yankee cavalry officer named Grierson for destroying the railroad track south of Jackson, forcing his men to make the hundred-mile march. A train ride would have been nice. Still, he was confident his over-strength brigade could beat back whatever the Federals could throw at him. Exhaustion had yielded to euphoria when his troops had marched through the streets of Raymond to the sounds of cheers and crude Rebel yells from the citizenry. Many of the male revelers had volunteered for service, swelling Gregg's ranks even more. What did he estimate his advantage to be: 1.5-to-1, 2-to-1? He had plenty of man- and firepower to teach the Yankees a lesson.

Fifteen minutes after leaving, Jacob Greenwalt was back, running alongside another, shorter and more agile soldier holding a musket in one hand. Gregg recognized the man as one of the pickets he had sent out that morning, though he couldn't remember the man's name.

When Greenwalt was within shouting distance, he bellowed, "General, sir, John here needs to tell you somethin'."

John Smith—*how could he forget that*—was the man's name. Smith stepped forward and saluted.

"Sir, there's a substantial Yankee force approaching."

"From where?" Gregg demanded. "I don't see anything."

John Smith said, "Follow me," and started walking to the southwest. Gregg and Greenwalt did as instructed. Soon they emerged from the woods on the west side of Fourteenmile Creek. Though the haze still suffused the atmosphere, it was not as dense as it had been in the woods, improving visibility.

"There," Smith said, punctuating the statement with an extended arm.

Gregg squinted, made out a man, then another, then a horse, then a continuous line of blue stretching in both directions. He tried to judge how far the line stretched but found he could not; the flanks were beyond his range of vision.

"My God," he murmured under his breath. "It's not a brigade. It's a damned Yankee division!"

* * *

It was McPherson's Third Division that was disrupting Gregg's sensibilities. In a sense, it was a covert action that used the fog of battle for visual cover and drum and bugle silence to minimize the audible signs of a large military presence. Moving forward, they had finally arrived *en masse* and in good order. McPherson's Federals outnumbered the Confederates by 2-to-1.

Bringing his horse to a hurried halt, Hiram Granbury launched himself from it and rushed to find his adjutant. After conferring with several of his staff, he found Major Jeffrey Meyer near an artillery emplacement.

"Major Meyer!" he shouted, trying to make his voice heard above the thunder of sequentially firing Parrott field rifles. Despite the noise, Meyer heard the call and hastened toward his commander.

"Jeff, get a message to all units of the Seventh Texas and Tenth Tennessee Regiments to withdraw across Fourteenmile Creek."

"Sir, we're doing pretty well here."

"We won't be for long. There's a whole Yankee division coming at us. I said they were everywhere and by God they are," Granbury barked irritably. "The Third Tennessee is already under enfilading fire."

Granbury dismounted and seated himself twenty yards from one of the field pieces. Men were already spiking some Parrotts and preparing others for the withdrawal. Although they were clearly hurrying, the process of moving a field piece—even a small Parrott—from a battlefield was a complex operation. To do so in the face of a likely defeat was doubly difficult. Granbury could see, even feel the dejection in the faces and mannerisms of his men. Texans were not supposed to lose.

However desperate he might feel, Granbury could not afford to show it. Emotions were for those who didn't have to use their heads. With much concern, he watched the remnants of the proud regiments he had sent into battle fleeing the field. It was not a rout, but neither was it a strategic retreat. He did not approve. Raising himself to a standing position, he drank from his canteen and searched for his officers. He found an artillery lieutenant named Blaine.

"Lieutenant," he said. "Don't be in such a hurry. Have your colleagues man every other good Parrott and keep the Yankees at bay while the rest beat it back across Fourteenmile Creek."

He found an infantry officer and told him to spread the word that half the infantry should remain to cover the retreat of the other half. The consequence of this action was that the Seventh Texas Regiment held off McPherson's Third Division long enough for a multitude of Rebel infantrymen to depart the field of battle with their lives. When the last wave began their retreat across Fourteenmile Creek, Granbury halted his horse and turned to observe what was now a semi-orderly procession. Men, horses, and wagons were struggling to negotiate the rugged and soggy terrain of the creek bed.

"Sir, it looks like we made it," a voice said. He turned to find Jacob Greenwalt, one of his hands gripping his horse's bridle.

"It's still a retreat, Jacob," Granbury said, determined not to find satisfaction at the sight of so many fleeing sons of the Confederacy.

Accepting the rebuke, Greenwalt smiled up at his commander and said, "It surely beats dyin'."

Granbury leaned forward on the horse's neck and gazed down at Greenwalt.

"It does that," he admitted.

*   *   *

The outcome of the Battle of Raymond was a foregone conclusion. There were simply too many Yankees and too much indecision on the part of the Rebel commanding officers—Pemberton and Johnston. Heroism was rampant on both sides, but more of it from the side that lost the battle, the Confederacy: Manning Force's bold but ill-advised advance across Fourteenmile Creek, the uphill attack of the Seventh Texas and Third Tennessee Infantry Regiments against the Twenty-Third Indiana, the Third Tennessee's stubborn tolerance of a persistent Yankee enfilading fire decimating its ranks and the patience of the Seventh Texas in holding back McPherson's Third Division while fellow Confederates withdrew from the field of battle. There was plenty of courage to go around—perhaps too much.

Grant had wanted not only to destroy the railroads and defeat the Confederates but to split the forces of Pemberton in Vicksburg and Johnston in Jackson. He did not quite accomplish that objective. The left wing of Pemberton's army escaped to Jackson, leaving an unacceptably large Rebel army on his right flank. Grant had little choice. He would have to launch a major assault on Jackson, Mississippi.

★ TWENTY-EIGHT ★

May 14, 1863, Jackson, Mississippi

The sight of the huge Confederate flag beckoning to him from its flagpole atop the golden dome of capitol building was more than twelve-year-old Frederick Dent Grant could stand. He wanted it. Having been essentially an observer in many of his father's campaigns, he longed for more, to be a participant in a great battle. But, despite his tender age and adolescent compulsions, Fred did not deceive himself. He knew he was too young and too small to be a real soldier and was not anxious to kill anyone, even a cursed Rebel soldier. But he was capable of capturing a flag.

"Let's get it. Let's go get that flag!" Fred cried to the journalist who was sitting astride the horse next to him, and whom he knew only as "Bob." Bob was squinting his eyes in the direction of Jackson.

"Fred, the army hasn't cleared the streets yet," Bob appealed. "It's too dangerous."

"Are you afraid?"

"Of course I am," Bob said as he massaged his eyebrows, which always seemed to develop an ache when Fred Grant wanted him to engage in some outlandish activity. He was beginning to regret his decision to befriend the boy to gain access to his father, the commander of the Union forces. "Who wouldn't be?"

"What do you have to be afraid of, Bob? You're not even wearing a soldier uniform like I am. You're wearing a suit. If we get caught, all you have to do is tell the Rebels you're writing stories for a newspaper, and they'll let you alone."

Bob looked quizzically at the youngster, who was dressed in a specially designed uniform that included his father's dress sash and sword. He shook his head.

"I'm afraid they might shoot first and ask questions later, especially if you start wielding that thing," he said, pointing to the sword.

"I won't," Fred said, withdrawing the sword and cupping it in his hands at both ends. "I'm not dumb. I know swords are obsolete. My Dad's told me often enough. It is pretty, though, isn't it?"

"It is," Bob acknowledged, blinking his eyes as the sunlight reflected from the mirrored steel finish of the blade.

Fred put the sword away and shouted, "Giddy-up," to his sorrel mare. The horse quickly responded, surging forward on the muddy street leading into town.

"No, no, Fred. Wait!" a panicked Bob called, steering his piebald mare toward the other horse. When he caught up, Bob said, "Fred, we can't. Your father will have my hide."

"But it's not dangerous. Look at all the soldiers around us."

Bob was already aware of the Union infantrymen making their way toward town and was, to a degree, comforted by their presence. But he knew they were not the main body, which had not arrived yet. Neither had Ulysses S. Grant and his staff. Bob guessed these scattered lead elements were either scouts or skirmishers sent to probe the strength of the enemy. Surely there were no deserters among them; they were headed in the wrong direction. Deserters fled to the rear, didn't they?

"I'm not sure they have our best interests at heart, Fred. They seem to be focused on other matters," Bob said.

Fred waited a beat before answering.

"Like winning the battle," he concluded.

"Maybe, maybe not," Bob said, staring back at an infantry soldier, whose dirty face and sour expression seemed to project a silent criticism. "They might be souvenir hunters like us, in which case I wouldn't give two hoots in . . . I wouldn't necessarily rely on them helping us out of a difficult situation if one should arise."

The soldier with the dirty face scowled and averted his gaze.

As they entered Jackson proper, the soldiers Bob had thought of as "lead elements" were coalescing into groups, most for nothing more than conversation and common defense, but some who were actively confiscating food and goods. Bob was aware of Grant's "live off the land" strategy but thought some of these incidents were more akin to theft than procurement. At one intersection, a group of Union infantrymen was hastily exiting a tavern, each with two full bottles of whisky in hand. The saloonkeeper, a balding, middle-aged man in a black leather apron, was chasing them into the street with an empty bottle in one hand. As Fred and Bob watched, he raised the bottle over his head and brought it down on the kepi of one of the soldiers. The bottle did not break but caused the solder obvious pain because, after recovering from the blow, he turned and grabbed the saloonkeeper by his collar.

"Fred, let's go. This is not for you," Bob said urgently.

Puzzled, Fred could not keep his eyes off the action, which had broadened to a three against one *melee*.

"But he's a Rebel, isn't he?" Fred said, looking at Bob but pointing to the saloonkeeper.

"He's just a storekeeper. He doesn't deserve a beating."

Fred appeared to understand, but the expression on his face betrayed his Union sympathies. Then his expression softened, and he spurred his horse toward the fray.

"Fred . . ." Bob called too late.

The youngster halted his mare directly in front of the belligerents and shouted, "Stop doing that. Stop!"

The three Union men snarled and bellowed curses until their heads were turned, and they found themselves facing the son of their commander.

"Why, Master Fred, we were just doing what your father ordered," said one soldier in an unctuous Irish accent.

Fred gave him a hard stare. Bob moved beside Fred and said, "Whisky? That's what you're supposed to bring back, nothing but whisky? It'll be a hard march to Vicksburg."

The Irishman, whose upper incisors were broken off halfway to the gum, sat his whisky bottles on the ground. He glanced first at his companions, then at the saloonkeeper, then back at Fred.

"We keep three, and the Johnny Reb can keep three," he proffered.

Fred considered the compromise and nodded shyly.

"That would be fine," he said, his small eyes darting nervously in their sockets as the soldiers handed one bottle each to the saloonkeeper. For his part, the only sign of appreciation shown by the saloonkeeper was a stiff nod to Fred, who returned the gesture.

Turning his horse to face the city again, Fred smiled and said, "That was fun!"

"It certainly was not," Bob replied sternly.

Digging his heels into his horse's flanks, Fred pointed upward at the prize overhead and cried, "There it is!"

The sorrel was off in a flash. Bob struggled to keep up on his piebald, but it was hopeless. Fred disappeared around a corner, momentarily generating a surge of panic in Bob's breast. Scanning the neighborhood, he saw only Union army personnel, most of them engaged in acts of confiscation, legitimate or otherwise. He turned the corner in time to see Fred dismount, tie his horse to a hitching post, and hasten up the wide staircase and onto the portico of the capitol. Bob hurried and joined Fred at the entrance.

"Fred, slow down," Bob said, laying a hand on Fred's shoulder.

"Can't slow down," Fred puffed. "Or someone else will take the flag."

Bob looked around and confirmed Fred's conclusion. There were a considerable number of Union soldiers whose movements were directed toward the golden dome. A traffic jam had formed on the stairway leading to the upper floors. All motion on the stairs was upward; anyone wanting to descend would have to wait or risk being trampled.

"You can't go up there. You're not an adult. You'll be crushed."

But Fred was not to be dissuaded by Bob's protestations. He offered no argument, but rushed headlong into the crowd, quickly disappearing among the taller figures jostling for position. Once more, Bob fell into a panic. Hurling himself into the chaos, he pushed and pulled at the bodies blocking his passage, hoping to find an intact Fred sandwiched somewhere between. His apprehension grew as he repeatedly found nothing but buttocks and thighs clad in blue.

Then an enormous cheer erupted from the floor above.

What on Earth was that?

Fearing the worst, Bob accelerated his pace, knocking down several artillerymen in the process. Fortunately, he was moving with such speed that the threats they flung at him could not promptly be fulfilled. He reached the upper floor and made a wide scan of the area. Toward the far side of the room was a group of cavalrymen, holding the Rebel flag that had adorned the dome of the capitol. The men were distributed around the edges of the flag and had raised it like a canopy above one of their members, shouting *hoo-rahs* as they pumped their arms up and down to create a ripple in the flag's otherwise flat expanse. From what Bob could discern, the man in the middle, a dirty, disheveled, unshaven but nevertheless happy man was the one who had captured the prize.

Remembering his mission, Bob tore his eyes from the celebration and searched for Fred. He found the youngster seated on the floor against the stone balustrade next to the stairs. Fred was bent over, head in hands, hiding his face. Bob walked over and again laid a hand on the boy's shoulder.

"You can't always win," he said.

After a moment, Fred removed his hands, revealing a face filled with emotions ranging from anger to disappointment. He looked as if he were about to cry, but didn't.

"I know that!" he whimpered, then redirected his gaze to the hero of the hour. "Look at him! He's dirty, and . . . he's ugly."

It was not an appropriate remark but Bob let it pass. Instead, he looked at the man and concluded that, inappropriate or not, Fred's description was accurate.

"He probably deserves it, don't you think? He's probably laid his life on the line many times over."

At twelve years of age, Fred's sulking time was less than that of a younger child and greater than that of an adult. *In toto*, it lasted about three minutes.

"I guess so," he finally conceded, casting his eyes toward the ongoing festivities.

"But he is not a handsome man. I'll give you that," Bob joked.

Fred snickered and rose to his feet. Although he was not crying, he found it necessary to wipe droplets of water from the inside corners of his eyes. Quietly, he composed himself and stood erect, then looked to Bob for guidance.

"Let's go meet him," Bob suggested.

The man's name was Josh Theuret. He was from a small town on the west bank of the Ohio River, upstream of Wheeling. He was not so much ugly as grotesque, a bulbous nose and cleft chin lending him a clownish air that was accentuated by the spasmodic movements of his arms and legs. His smile was broad and filled with misaligned teeth. When Fred and Bob had made their way through the crowd to him, Bob said, "Mr. Theuret, Master Fred Grant and I are pleased to meet you."

Fred was the first to extend his hand and, despite Theuret's grimy fingers, squeezed it firmly.

"Pleased to meet you, sir," Fred said.

Disoriented by the presence of a celebrity, Theuret hastily snapped his lips over his crooked teeth and mumbled, "Uh, yeah . . . why . . . yeah . . . I'm pleased to meet you too, Mr. Grant."

Theuret could not easily form coherent words with his semi-sealed mouth, but he executed a series of gestures, bobbing and weaving, spreading his fingers and waving, all of which were uninterpretable.

Fred pointed to the flag and said, "Could I get under it with you?"

Theuret managed a grunt of acquiescence and led Fred to a spot directly beneath the flag. In awe, Fred looked up at it. Even though the flag's colors were somewhat faded from weathering, it was a magnificent creation. Fred found himself admiring the design—the blue St. Andrews Cross emblazoned with white stars on a red field. It was like the British Union Jack with stars, he thought. All else being equal, Fred might have admitted an aesthetic preference for the "Dixie" flag over "Old Glory." But he was a loyal American and could never admit to such an outrageous opinion. It was a beautiful flag, though.

"It *is* beautiful," he murmured unconsciously.

"Fred, we can't stay all day," Bob whispered from the flag's outer edge.

Fred tore his eyes away from the flag. For an instant, it seemed another tear would form in the corner of his eye, but he managed to suppress it.

"You need to get back to your father. He'll be worried," Bob said, leading the way back down the stairway, which had seen its heaviest traffic vanish after the flag's display.

Fred stopped to take a final look at the captured Confederate flag. Josh Theuret and his cohorts were in the process of folding it for safekeeping. Fred found himself strangely saddened by the thought that the flag might never be flown, might never see the light of day, again.

*   *   *

Sherman entered the Bowman House, Jackson's finest hotel, not exactly in a rage, but in an elevated state of annoyance. He took a moment to get his bearings, removed his hat, slowly rotated his gaze clockwise, and found Grant and McPherson standing by the front window. He strode toward them, an abnormal quickness in his step. When they turned toward him, Sherman noticed both had drinks, probably whisky.

"General Sherman, congratulations on your glorious victory," McPherson said, raising his glass. Grant mimicked the motion, though his demeanor was, as usual, subdued.

Sherman was not diverted.

"I would offer congratulations as well, General, but the Rebels evacuated Jackson. That's not a victory; it's a gift."

"It's a gift I'll take any time," Grant said coolly.

Taking the hint to restrain his chronic bad temper, Sherman said, "Sir, there have been acts of pillage. Some of our troops have stolen rum from stores in town . . ."

"Bad rum, I hear," McPherson gibed, clearly under the influence. "The thieves will be duly punished without any assistance from the Army of the Tennessee."

"General, if we are ever to govern these people, we cannot be seen as criminals."

Grant sipped at his drink and said, "Sherman, we are already seen as criminals. We have invaded their lands and killed their soldiers. We are seizing their food, their drink, and their livestock. It is a condition of war that each side perceives the other as a murderous mob of plunderers. It cannot be helped."

Sherman's jaw tightened as he struggled to maintain his equanimity.

"You sent a courier, General," he stated, his eyebrows lifting as if he had seen a hawk fly over.

"Yes, I need to know your status."

Sherman took a moment to pour himself a drink, then shook his head and said, "There is not much to report. We took ten guns and suffered thirty-two casualties. The objective has been secured."

The "objective" was the southwest corner of Jackson, by which Sherman had entered the city. McPherson had come in from the west to join up with him and hopefully trap the Confederates between them. McClernand had not seen action in Jackson, having been ordered by Grant to take Bolton in the northwest to serve as an obstacle to the Confederate railroad traffic between Jackson and Vicksburg. Having lost over two hundred men, the defenders of Jackson were scrambling northward to regroup. The pincers formed by the joining of Sherman's and McPherson's Corps had served its tactical purpose of driving the Confederates from the field. It had not achieved its strategic objective of capturing the enemy and rendering him impotent. The forces of Johnston and Pemberton would survive to fight another day.

Despite his stoic demeanor, Grant was enjoying himself. He directed his colleagues to the front window and pointed to the building opposite the hotel.

"Do you know what that is?" he asked.

"The Mississippi State House," Sherman replied.

"Yes, the State House," Grant confirmed, grinning. "Jeff Davis's place. Do you remember what he said six months ago?"

"Something about throwing us back," McPherson suggested.

Grant's smile diffused to the corners of his mouth.

"He said, and I quote, 'that his fellow Mississippians would meet and hurl back these worse than *vandal* hordes.'"

The three men shared a good laugh, raised their glasses once more, and drank heartily.

"Vandal Hordes! That's pretty bad," Sherman said.

"It is," McPherson agreed. "About as bad as men can be. Evil, in fact."

"Let's face it, we are *bad, bad* men," Grant mocked.

The party atmosphere stayed alive for another hour but then began to wane. Grant wondered if he should slow down on the liquor but decided not to—for the moment. There was really no compelling reason not to imbibe alcohol. The Battle of Jackson was over if it could be called a battle. As was becoming his habit, the Confederate general Joseph Johnston had chosen not to risk his army against a superior Union army. It was a wise decision but was not a strategy that could be followed indefinitely. Yes, Grant concluded, he should definitely drink his fill and loosen the tension in his nerves and brain. It was the right moment. No one depended on his good judgment right now.

Grant had his lips pressed against the rim of his half-full glass when Charles Dana sauntered through the front door of the hotel.

"Charlie's here," Sherman warned, speaking over McPherson's shoulder.

But it was too late. Dana had noticed the glass, but, surprisingly, made no mention of it when he approached Grant. He smiled when he said, "We have another letter from Secretary Stanton."

Grant lowered his glass to waist level. Dana maintained the smile and said, "It has nothing to do with that, General. I think you'll find it good news."

Setting the glass on a nearby table, Grant waited while Dana extracted the letter from his breast pocket, then handed it over. Grant opened it and began reading.

Mr. Charles Dana
United States Army of the Tennessee
Vicksburg, Mississippi

Dear Mr. Dana,
Circumstances require that you direct General Ulysses S. Grant to lose no time in pushing his army to the Big Black and Jackson, threatening both and striking at either, as is most convenient. He will disregard his base and depend on the country for meat and bread.

General Grant has full and absolute authority to enforce his commands, to remove any person who, by ignorance, inaction, or any cause, interferes with or delays his operation. He has the full confidence of the Government, is expected to enforce his authority, and will be firmly and heartily supported, but he will be responsible for any failure to exert his powers. You may communicate this to him.

Very Sincerely Yours,
Edwin Stanton
Secretary of War

When he finished reading, Grant raised the dispatch to eye level and read it again.

"This sounds like I wrote it," he said.

"Some of it you did write."

Grant re-examined the opening paragraph.

"Oh, so I did. Well, it's a welcome change from his previous orders to stand ready for Nahaniel Banks."

McPherson offered Dana a drink. Dana accepted, with a tentative glance toward Grant.

"A successful strategy always trumps a *potentially* successful strategy," Dana said, taking his first swallow.

"*Here, here*," Sherman offered, raising his glass. "Here's to successful strategies. May they come early and often."

The toast was enthusiastically celebrated by the three generals and Dana. Even more enthusiastically received was the whisky.

Sherman was not finished. He turned to Grant and said, with a quizzical grin, "Do you appreciate what these orders mean, Grant?"

"Of course I do. It means Banks has to support us, not vice-versa. It means we don't need the approval of Old Brains to do what needs to be done, and . . ."

The others were frozen in attitudes of anticipation. Then Sherman spoke in a conspiratorial whisper.

". . . It means you can deal with insubordinate subordinates."

All of them chuckled, enjoying the implications of Stanton's order, but trying to be as discreet as possible in a room filled with revelers. It was understood that Sherman's reference was to Mc-Clernand.

McPherson offered another toast. After Grant had imbibed three drinks, Charles Dana cast a critical glance his way, but it was weakened by a good-natured chortle. Dana could hardly be critical of Grant's drinking when he was also intoxicated.

Rather than compete with Grant's whisky consumption—against which he had no chance of winning—the man from Stanton struck up a conversation with McPherson. Grant didn't mind. Many people found him wanting as a conversationalist. He was content to stand mute most of the time, exercising his oral talents only when, as Commander of the Army of the Tennessee, it was his duty to do so.

Ultimately, McPherson and Dana fell into a discussion of the relative merits of mules and draft horses as beasts of burden, which Grant and Sherman found thoroughly boring. They drifted to the hotel window and looked out. As the morning had become afternoon, the number and venality of looters had increased, their ranks swelled by escaped slaves, poor whites and Union soldiers. Anything was fair game—store goods, money, personal property. The only limitation was the size of the stolen item relative to the

thief's ability to carry it off. Some creative pilferers first stole horses and wagons, the better to carry off subsequent booty.

"Should we put an end to this?" Sherman asked, his expression somewhere between stern and sullen.

Grant looked askance at him before saying, "Our soldiers, yes.
It's bad for discipline."

"I'm sure most of the shopkeepers are good people. They don't
deserve this."

"We're not here to protect Rebels from their own kind, Sherman. We're here to put down a rebellion," Grant snapped.

The brisk remark was as emotional a statement as Sherman
had ever heard his friend make. Both were shocked by its intensity, Grant more than Sherman. But they shook it off and quickly
regained their equanimity.

"In fact, I'm giving you the task of destroying Jackson as a
railroad center and as a source of manufactured military goods.
You will remain in Jackson until the job is done."

Sherman breathed deeply and then let out a long, "Ye-e-e-s,"
punctuated by, ". . . of course. And when I'm finished?"

"Joe Johnston has pulled back. He's no longer a threat. We'll
be heading back to Vicksburg."

"What about Pemberton?"

Grant formed his lips into a grin. "You wouldn't want it to be
too easy, would you?"

The sarcasm was not lost on the red-haired general from Ohio.
For the most part, he shared Grant's contempt for the Rebel cause,
including as it did an indefinite extension of the institution of slavery. But he had made friends with southerners, even taught their
children as a schoolmaster in Louisiana. For the most part, he had
found them to be quite civilized and neighborly. Continuing the pol-
icy of subjecting black people to abject slaver was the one tenet of
inhumanity in their otherwise moderate philosophy. It was striking-
ly irrational, had been since before the American Revolution.
Thomas Jefferson had argued eloquently against slavery but had
never freed his slaves. George Washington willed his slaves to be
freed, but only after his death. Many southern aristocrats like
Robert E. Lee expressed a desire to abolish slavery but wanted to
do so on a timetable that would not destroy the economies of the
slave states. Why couldn't they understand that one more hour,
one more second of this evil institution was intolerable?

"Have you seen Fred?" Grant inquired.

"Not recently," Sherman answered. "The last time I saw him
was at breakfast. He was wearing your dress uniform and was
with that journalist . . ."

"Bob?"

"Yes."

"That was the last time I saw him too. I didn't see where they went. Did you?"

"No."

"I'm getting a little worried," Grant admitted, then pointed out the window. "I saw men in prison uniforms out there. And there's a building on fire a few blocks away. Is there a prison in Jackson?"

"Yes."

Sherman volunteered to comb the streets near the State House while Grant enlisted the aid of McPherson and Dana. He abandoned his whisky glass and was nearly out the door of the Bowman House when he ran into the two itinerants.

"Fred, where have you been?" Sherman barked, casting a critical eye at Bob.

"I almost had a Rebel flag, Sherman," Fred cried with an improbable mixture of happiness and misery on his face. "But another soldier got it instead."

Turning to Bob, Sherman said, "You should have brought him back sooner."

Bob's eyebrows lifted in surprise. "We were always surrounded by Union soldiers!"

As he stepped back through the hotel entrance, Sherman said, "Not everyone out there is a Union soldier. And I certainly wouldn't guarantee the good sense of every Union soldier."

Bob scowled but accepted the reprimand with, "Yes, sir. I'm sorry to cause any distress."

Sherman accepted the apology with a nod and a grunt, leading Fred into the hotel. Assuming his presence was no longer desired, Bob excused himself and scurried off in pursuit of greener journalistic pastures.

By the time they reached Grant, Dana had already departed on his assigned leg of the search, but McPherson was still at Grant's side. When he saw Fred's face, Grant rushed to the boy and knelt before him.

"Fred, where have you been?" Grant asked, gripping his son by the biceps. It was becoming the question of the moment.

"I almost got a Rebel flag, Dad!"

"Were you by yourself?"

"No, Bob was with me."

"Yes . . . Bob. Well, tell me what happened."

Fred frowned, then explained. "It was the flag on top of the building with the gold dome. A really big flag. But we got there too late. A soldier got to it before I did."

Grant put on his most authoritative expression.

"Fred, I saw that flag. I don't think you could have handled it anyway."

Fred reflected a moment, grimaced, then partially conceded the point. "Maybe. I'm pretty strong, though. Dad, it was such a pretty flag. It really was."

Grant was somewhat taken aback by his son's enthusiasm for an enemy flag, but he knew it was only an impressionable boy's reaction to a battle trophy. He was concerned that the boy did not appreciate what the flag stood for, what it meant, that he thought of it as a mere toy.

"Fred, I need to be serious for a moment," he said, gazing deeply into his son's eyes.

As a practicing adolescent, Fred was not looking forward to a lecture from his father. He started to frown, but realized it would not be a good strategy and transformed it into a bow and down-cast eyes.

Grant sighed and said, "In the eyes of many of our citizens, that flag is a symbol of the reprehensible institution of slavery. It is distressing to see that flag flying over so many state capitols."

"I didn't want to fly it. I just wanted to have it," his son protested.

"I know. I know. I'm not berating you. I can hardly criticize your for an activity my soldiers engage in. I just want you to un-derstand . . ."

The puzzled look on Fred's face suggested he was not compre-hending, so Grant paused, glanced briefly away, and carefully chose his words.

"The Rebels pledge allegiance to that flag, Fred, the same way we do to Old Glory. They are not all bad men. You should never think that."

"But you said it stood for slavery, didn't you? Slavery is bad, isn't it?"

Grant struggled to find words that would explain the tragic di-chotomy that was the Southern way of life. In truth, he had diffi-culty understanding it himself.

"Southerners are like all of us, Fred. They have their faults. It's just that theirs are really big ones—slavery and secession. But they have good points too. If they didn't, we wouldn't be fighting to bring them back into the Union."

Fred's face betrayed his bewilderment. He was not familiar with the concept of virtuous Rebels, so he stood blank-faced, fiddling with his father's sword while he thought. Finally, he spoke.

"What are their good points?" he inquired, obviously unconvinced that they had any.

Grant slowly exhaled. "Well, for one thing, most of the southern boys we come across aren't fighting for slavery. They don't have slaves, so why would they? What they are fighting for is to boot us out. They think we're invading their country."

"But it's our country too—"

Grant shook his head. "That's not how they see it. They think they have the right to secede from the United States and join the Confederacy, their new country."

The consternation in the boy's eyes was palpable. He was more confused than ever.

"But don't they?" he asked, gazing dolefully up at his father. "That's what freedom is, isn't it? Wouldn't we do the same thing if we didn't like them and wanted to get away?"

Grant shot a quick look at his colleagues, Sherman and McPherson, in search of a suitable answer to his son's query. But they were enjoying his quandary too much to be helpful.

"It's a complicated situation, Fred," Grant said, unsure of his ground. "I could say they gave up their right to freedom because they cast others into slavery, but that's too convoluted . . ."

"Con-vo-lu-ted?"

"Too complicated," Grant said, yielding to his son's limited vocabulary. All I can say is that, back in 1776, the men who founded our country made a deal. The deal was that all the states would come together to form the USA so the British could be defeated and sent packing."

"A deal," Fred said, still skeptical. "You mean like a bet?"

Grant was not a man to ignore an opportunity when he saw one.

"Yes, like a bet," he said. "Exactly. The new states were betting that, together, they could beat the British."

"And they did, right?"

"They did."

"Does that mean the Johnny Rebs will win our war too?"

Grant released his grip and stood, leaving his gaze on his son.

"No, it doesn't, not if I have anything to say about it. You have to realize, Fred, that the cause of freedom in 1776 was much more virtuous than the cause of slavery—"

"But you said most Johnny Rebs aren't fighting for slavery. They just want to give us the boot."

Hoisted on his own petard, Grant groaned inwardly and said, "Like I said, son, it's complicated. We'll talk more about it some other time."

As his father laid a hand on the boy's shoulder and directed him toward Sherman and McPherson, Fred started to protest. But he looked at his father, seemed to sense Grant's philosophical exhaustion and clamped his lips together.

The two generals had expunged the expressions of benign amusement on their faces when Grant confronted them.

"Would one of you find someone to feed Fred and put him to bed? I want to take a look around before I join him."

"Did you know your room is the same one Joe Johnston slept in last night?" Sherman asked.

"I did. Why?"

"Just thought you'd like to know," Sherman shrugged mischievously. "Tit for tat. It makes up for the time Beauregard slept in my tent at Shiloh."

McPherson volunteered to find someone to look after Fred, leaving Grant and Sherman by themselves. Anxious to get his tour of the city behind him, Grant looked for an aide to find him a horse, but then hesitated. He looked at Sherman.

"We'll discuss the matter, of course, but my inclination is to go after Pemberton and leave Johnston to his own devices for the moment. If we can get past Pemberton, we'll have Vicksburg."

"I agree, but what if Johnston attacks the rear?"

"I don't think he's prepared to attack. I should tell you, we intercepted a message from Johnston to Pemberton urging him to attack you now. I interpret this as meaning Johnston is not ready to attack us by himself."

"So, if we move fast enough, we can get Pemberton before Johnston has a chance to become involved. Is that your idea?"

"It is. All our reconnaissance says Johnston is retreating north of Jackson."

Sherman paced thoughtfully, considering the ramifications of leaving an enemy army in the Union rear while assaulting another enemy army. Under most circumstances, it would be considered an unwise tactic. It would leave the Army of the Tennessee sandwiched between two enemy armies. If both fought vigorously, it could present a serious problem. But he was convinced the twenty-five thousand of the Union salient were sufficient to deal with the possibility. He turned his attention back to Grant.

"Who would lead the attack?"

"McClernand," Grant replied. When he noticed the scowl on Sherman's face, he added, "It can't be helped. His Corps is the rear guard now. It will have to lead the attack when we turn around and face west. Last in, first out."

"Can he handle it?"

"I believe so. He has a whole corps."

Sherman nodded, then said, "Where?"

"Bolton Station. It's twenty miles west of Jackson and McClernand's corps is deployed just southeast of the town."

"What's the terrain like?"

Grant rubbed at the five o'clock shadow on his chin while he searched his memory.

"I'm not sure, but it is next to a piece of geography called Champion Hill. That should tell you something."

★ TWENTY-NINE ★

May 15, 1863, Edwards Station, Mississippi

The muscles in John Pemberton's brow tightened as he re-read the message from Joseph Johnston.

Sir,

> *I have lately arrived, and learn that General Sherman is between, with four divisions, at Clinton. It is important to re-establish communications, that you may be reinforced. If practicable, come up in his rear at once. To beat such a detachment would be of immense value. The troops here could co-operate. All the strength you can quickly assemble should be brought. Time is all-important.*

> *Your Humble Servant,*
> *General Joseph Johnston*
> *Dept. of the West, CSA*

The message was obsolete, of course. It had arrived several days earlier, and God only knew where Johnston was now. Had he successfully defended Jackson? Was he in retreat? Reluctantly, Pemberton had obeyed Johnston's orders and marched his army east, across the Big Black River, to where he was now—Edwards Station. This, in spite of President Jefferson Davis's warning not to get too far from Vicksburg. What was "too far," he wondered? Had he exceeded that limit? In a reply to Johnston he had said, *"I do not think you fully comprehend the position Vicksburg will be in, but I comply at once with your request."*

Pemberton had always been an obedient soldier, but he could not obey two masters. So here he was, at the outer edge of what could be considered "Vicksburg," fully complying with neither Davis's nor Johnston's orders.

Pemberton's reverie was interrupted by the sight and sound of a rider from the southeast. The young man was riding hard and had a look of incipient panic on his face. The other members of Pemberton's staff—Major Generals Carter Stevenson and William

Loring, and Brigadier General John Bowen turned toward the rider, who pulled up and strode directly for Pemberton.

"Sir, Private Ambrose Engle, sir," he said, saluting.

"From my division," said Loring.

Pemberton nodded his understanding and said, "What is it, Private?"

Private Engle paused for a much-needed breath and answered, "The Yankees. There are four or five divisions at Raymond. They appear to be preparing to advance on us.

Which would make a junction with Johnston at Clinton even less feasible than it already was, Pemberton concluded. Moving his army to Clinton would leave those four or five Union divisions in his rear and between him and Vicksburg. He could not accept such a risk.

"Whose corps is it?" he asked.

"General McClernand's, sir."

"That would make sense, General," Loring offered. "It was McPherson's and Sherman's corps that attacked Jackson. That would leave McClernand in the rearguard of the Union army. His corps would be the logical one to attack west if the Yankees were so inclined."

"They *are* so inclined," Pemberton insisted. "Grant wants Vicksburg, not Jackson.

There were no dissenting voices from that conclusion.

With a hundred competing thoughts going through his mind, Pemberton spun around to face west, fearful that the confusion in his face would shine like a lighthouse beacon. He had never been in such a situation before, and there was no one to help him through it. The members of his staff—Loring, Stevenson and, to a lesser extent, Bowen—were already wary of their northern commander. To do nothing was not an option. Turning back, he tried desperately to present a confident expression.

"We need a council of war," he said with a firmness he did not feel. Striding into his headquarters tent, he added a brisk "Now."

*   *   *

Adjusting the lamp flame for maximum illumination, Pemberton studied the faces of his generals. Of the three, Loring was the least physically imposing, with a pate as glossy as a billiard ball and the physique of a clerk. He had a rare ability to stir men with speech, however, and was Pemberton's most vocal critic. Loring was sitting in the darkest corner of the tent, his legs rigidly crossed, looking as if he might be happy to remain there forever.

Stevenson, one of a multitude of Virginia officers in the Confederate ranks, was a handsome Southern gentleman, whose thick sideburns framed his stern face like a woman's ringlets. With a straight back and crossed arms, he was stationed by the entrance with his eyes cast down, waiting for Pemberton to initiate the proceedings.

Of his three subordinates, Pemberton liked John Bowen the most. Unlike Stevenson, whose good looks verged on the effeminate, he exuded an unmistakably masculine aura with his well-trimmed beard and bold visage. Pemberton considered Bowen to be his most trusted officer, a trust that had been confirmed by his performance at Port Gibson in retarding the advance of Grant's army. Bowen was standing near the rear wall with his hands behind his back and his chin up. Like the others, he was impatient but held it in check.

"Well, gentlemen, we appear to have a predicament," Pemberton said, gazing down at the map spread out on the center table. "It seems we have General McClernand in our front. For this reason, I think the wisest course of action would be to consolidate our forces behind the Big Black River and let the enemy come to us—"

"Sir, I do not agree that relying on the enemy's bad judgment is a *wise* course of action," proclaimed Loring, who popped out of his chair and headed for Pemberton. Placing himself on his commander's left, he pointed to the crooked line representing the Big Black River.

"If we do nothing but wait, McClernand can close in on us from the southeast or Grant could come at us from Jackson."

Pemberton stiffened, then replied, "Are you suggesting we follow General Johnston's orders to join him at Clinton? If we do that, we expose our entire right flank to McClernand, and we will be in no position to defend Vicksburg."

Loring raised his open palms to resist Pemberton's stream of logic.

"Sir, sir, making a juncture with General Johnston is not the only option," he asserted. "Look here."

As Loring's right hand came down on the map, Stevenson and Bowen gathered around.

"Grant's supply line must come through Dillon," he said, pointing to a spot on the map five to ten miles southeast of their present location but west of where McClernand's forces had been detected. "If we can cut that supply line, the Yankees will either have to withdraw from Jackson or fight to re-establish their presence, at our leisure."

Grimacing at the idea of a leisurely battle, Pemberton said, "It would still take us too far from Vicksburg."

"Yes, a little farther," Loring snorted impatiently. "But it does not expose our flank, and we can always fall back across the Big Black and form a defensive line."

Pemberton took a deep but tentative breath and eyed the members of his staff, one at a time. He did not like taking his army any further from Vicksburg than it already was, but he could see he was outvoted. These were men of action, perhaps to a fault. They wanted to seize the initiative. Bowing his head to the inevitable, he said, "All right. I'll present this . . . plan to General Johnston."

*   *   *

When Johnston's reply came, it was terse and to the point.

Sir,

Our being compelled to leave Jackson makes your plan impracticable. The only mode by which we can unite is by your moving directly to Clinton, which will inform me that I may move to that point with about 6,000 troops. I have no means of estimating the enemy's force at Jackson. The principal officers here differ very widely, and I fear the enemy will fortify if time is left. Let me hear from you immediately.

> *Your Humble Servant,*
> *General Joseph Johnston*
> *Dept. of the West, CSA*

A deflated Pemberton rested his head in his hands and murmured, "So, he still wants us to join him."

A buzz of conversation radiated from the three staff officers. Unlike Pemberton, they were anything but despondent. Loring actually sounded cheerful. Stevenson was less sanguine but seemed to derive energy from his colleagues' enthusiasm. Bowen was more aloof, but his smile and indulgent laughter belied his composure. He gave Pemberton's shoulder a firm pat and said, "It will be all right, sir. The Yankees are digging in. They won't be active for several days. By that time, we'll have General Johnston's army and will be ready for them."

John Pemberton could think of nothing to say. Jefferson Davis, Joseph Johnston and his own staff were pushing him in contradictory directions, down paths he did not wish to tread. Arguably the safest course, at least for the moment, was to form a defensive perimeter within the borders of Vicksburg—Davis's preference. But this approach had one major flaw. It permitted the enemy to station himself at the outskirts of the city and impose a siege until the army, and the city's residents surrendered.

But that strategy was vastly superior to Johnston's plan to combine his and Pemberton's armies in Clinton in order to position themselves for an attack on the Federals in Jackson. For one thing, the plan presupposed that the Yankees would rest on their haunches until the Confederate juncture was complete. From what Pemberton had seen of Grant's military tactics, this did not seem to him a credible assumption.

The final alternative was Loring's suggestion to attack Grant's supply line at Dillon and starve him out of Jackson. Such a supply line had not yet been detected, but surely it had to be there. This plan was bold enough to satisfy his staff, yet safe enough that Jefferson Davis would—perhaps—accept it. If it succeeded, that is, which was by no means a given.

Pemberton's preference to form a defensive line on the west side of the Big Black was preferred by no one but him. However, as one of the few Yankee-born officers in the Confederate armed forces, he harbored a compelling desire to please.

Suddenly aware of the depths to which his meditations had sunk, he straightened his posture and cleared his throat.

"Gentlemen, we will depart for Clinton in the morning, God willing. But we will swing north of Bolton before proceeding there. I remain concerned about our right flank."

The faces of his generals revealed their contentment. They nodded with restrained but earnest enthusiasm. Loring, Stevenson, and Bowen were happy to give Pemberton his right flank in exchange for a bold initiative.

Still struggling with uncertainty, Pemberton averted his eyes from the expectant gazes of his staff and examined the map. He noted that Edwards Station, Bolton, and Brownsville formed a triangle with Brownsville at the northeast corner, Edwards Station at the southwest corner, and Bolton at the obtuse angle east of Edwards Station. Clinton, their new destination, was another nine miles east of Bolton on the Southern Railroad, with Jackson a comparable distance beyond that. Since they would be swinging north of Bolton, Pemberton studied the map of that region.

"What's this?" he asked, pointing to an oval shape with its major axis running southwest-northeast. "Will it get in the way of our march?"

Answering the call, Stevenson hurried over and said, "That's Champion Hill. It should not be a problem."

Pemberton cast a hasty glance at his subordinate, suspecting him of a degree of overconfidence.

"I think we would do well to set ourselves up on that hill so we can see what's coming. Do you agree?"

There were no dissenting voices.

Pemberton's feelings of anxiety were by no means assuaged, but he enjoyed a sense of security he had not felt since receiving Johnston's orders to march east. He and his army were going to have the high ground.

★ THIRTY ★

May 16, 1863, Headquarters of U.S. Grant

Grant was in his tent shaving—an infrequent event—when the messenger arrived.

"Sir, the Rebels are here, I mean, at Edwards Station," the young man stuttered. Realizing he had not saluted, he did so belatedly. Grant did not notice but continued hacking away at his beard.

"How many?" he asked.

"According to the crew—"

"Crew?"

The messenger did a hasty mental reorganization of his message and said, "The crew of the railroad train—"

"The Southern Railroad? We've captured one of their trains?" Grant asked, taking a wide swath at the brittle whiskers on his neck.

"Yes, sir. The crew of the train says there are about twenty-five thousand Rebels at Edwards Station."

Grant rolled the thought around in his mind. If it wasn't a trap, it was a golden opportunity to face Pemberton in the open field. He took his time finalizing the trim and turned back to the messenger.

"How did we capture this train?"

Confused, the messenger replied, "It was just there, in our midst, traveling east. We stopped it and boarded it. That's about all there is to tell."

While he toweled his face off, Grant exhibited a skeptical frown.

"Why would Pemberton send a train right through a Union army? He must know we're here. Hell, there's probably more candlepower in our campfires than there is in all the street-lamps of New York City. His scouts couldn't help seeing see us."

Uncertain whether the question was sincere or merely rhetorical, the young soldier meekly offered, "I don't know, sir."

Tossing the towel on his bunk, Grant allowed himself a shallow grin and placed a hand on the private's shoulder.

"I don't know either, son. Trouble is, I'm supposed to know these things, or at least be ready with a good guess. What do you think? Is General Pemberton setting us up for an attack or is he just not paying attention?"

Distressed by the possibility of making an incorrect assessment, the messenger uttered some semi-coherent remarks but managed to regain a semblance of equanimity.

"I think he's making a mistake, sir. We should go after him," he said with a hesitant bravado.

"We should indeed. That's what we'll do," Grant said as a ray of sunshine passed between the entrance flaps, giving the tent interior a more cheerful disposition. "Find me Generals McPherson and McClernand."

"And General Sherman, sir?"

"No, I'll send him a message letting him know what we're up to."

Sherman was busy burning Jackson, a task Grant considered to be strategically important. But he did not want to risk sounding like a warmonger. It could come back to haunt him.

*   *   *

Brigadier General Stephen D. Lee wondered what General John Bowen was thinking. Bowen was astride a gray gelding facing east from his position on the plateau of Champion Hill as Lee's brigade passed by on its way to deployment on the Jackson Road. Curious, Lee steered his horse toward Bowen. After an exchange of salutes, Lee barked, "Sir!"

Bowen casually diverted his gaze toward Lee and said, "Did you want something, General?"

With an expectant grin on his face, Lee replied, "I was wondering what you find so interesting."

Bowen gave a brief snort, pointed southeast and said, "At sunrise all those were campfires. Now they're just wisps of smoke."

"Yankees on the move?"

"Most likely."

"Does General Pemberton know?"

"He's been informed."

Which both men knew was not the same thing. Bowen was both concerned about and annoyed with his commanding officer. While he could understand Pemberton's confusion about whose orders he should follow and whose to set aside, he thought the displaced northerner would be better off making a firm decision and brooking no insubordination. He circled his horse around, studying the terrain. Despite his shortcomings, Pemberton had picked good ground. Bowen said so to Lee.

"Yep, I'll give him that. It is good ground," Lee acknowledged.

"We need something. There's not a whole lot of good ground between here and Vicksburg. There's just the Big Black."

Lee nodded languidly. Neither man wanted to think about the consequences of failure, let alone talk about it. Vicksburg must not fall to the enemy.

Redirecting the conversation, Bowen said, "Where are you going?"

"The Jackson, Road, sir. We're on the left of the line, and its flank needs to be covered. Not much happening at the Crossroads right now. I sent Colonel Pettus out to take a look. You know him?"

"Edmund Pettus, son of the Mississippi Governor?"

"That's him."

"Any word yet?"

"No, he should be back soon."

Bowen glanced at his watch. It was 8:58 AM. He was pleased to learn of Lee's initiative. Some officers would have stayed put, awaiting the inevitable. Lee was a good man.

"Is that where you think the Yankees' main body will come, the Jackson Road?"

Lee leaned forward in his saddle, pursed his lips and said, "There or the Raymond Road farther south, or something called the Middle Road in between. The Yankees have the advantage of numbers. They can go where they want. I just hope Grant comes by the Jackson Road. I'd like to get that bastard in my sights—"

"He's not a bad sort. I knew him in Mexico. He was a good horseman and a decent officer. Nobody took him for a leader, though. Your *cousin* Robert E. got those accolades."

"Grant must have changed."

"Must have."

"For better, or worse, depending on your point of view. Fierce sonofabitch on the battlefield."

"He is that. U.S. Grant—Unconditional Surrender Grant. That's what they call him."

"Up north, you mean," Lee said.

"Up north," Bowen agreed.

"I hope that's not how Pemberton sees him."

"He's a northerner," Bowen responded with an artful grin.

Stephen Lee made his exit with a crisp salute, saying, "Maybe we can talk later. I have to catch up with my brigade."

Bowen returned the salute and turned his horse south. Pemberton had deployed three divisions—Loring's, Bowen's and Carter Stevenson's—to shield the Confederate withdrawal and subsequent march to Clinton. Bowen's division was in the center, at the Crossroads where the Jackson Road met the Middle Road and turned sharply west. On the ride back he enjoyed the cool morning air and the grandeur of randomly spaced magnolia trees blooming in force. But even as he savored the lassitude of the morning, he knew it would not last. The day would turn hot and sticky before noon. It was springtime in Mississippi.

A mounted Confederate soldier was suddenly galloping at him out of the northeast. Had there been more than one man, Bowen might have thought he was in a panic, but, no, the rider was just trying to coax maximum speed from his steed. Bowen steered his horse to face the newcomer, who arrived flashing a hasty salute.

"Sir, General Lee wanted me to tell you Colonel Pettus has made contact with the enemy," he announced breathlessly.

"Where?"

"Jackson Road, the Champion House. Do you know where that is?"

Bowen visualized the local maps he'd studied, then said, "Yes, I think so. About a mile north of Champion Hill, isn't it?"

The courier nodded, struggling to control his horse. Bowen could see the horse was merely reacting to its rider's anxiety.

"Yes, sir," the cavalryman snapped.

"Where is General Lee?"

"Moving his brigade from the Crossroads to Champion Hill."

Bowen considered this and silently approved. He saluted the courier.

"Thank you, private. Now get back to your unit and give 'em hell."

The messenger smiled nervously, saluted again and headed back the way he had come.

In Bowen's mind, the news of the Yankee presence was not entirely unwelcome. They now knew where the Federals were, at least some of them. And it settled the issue of the link-up with Johnston. That was out of the question for the immediate future.

Bringing his horse to a comfortable trot toward the Crossroads, he mulled over his brief but incisive interaction with Stephen Lee. Had Lee not taken the initiative to seek out the enemy, it might have been hours before anyone knew they were coming. Then the Yankees would have the upper hand. Little things like that could turn the tide of battle.

How can we lose when we've got General *Lee* on our side? Bowen reflected whimsically.

* * *

Confederate couriers were not the only ones flying to and fro across the battlefields-to-be. Their itinerant Union counterparts were equally busy.

"Champion Hill, you say?" General John McClernand demanded to know. "The rebels are on Champion Hill?"

"Yes, sir," the courier said.

McClernand cast a questioning glance at General Alvin Hovey, whose division was attached to McClernand's corps and was leading the advance on the Jackson Road.

"Do we know who it is and how many?"

"No, sir. We're trying to find out. We do hold Champion House."

Hovey took a step forward to face the courier and said, "Are you with McGinnis's brigade?"

McGinnis's brigade was the lead element of Hovey's division.

"Yes."

"McGinnis made first contact?"

"Yes, sir."

"Good, good, fine job," Hovey murmured and stepped back to the spot he had originally occupied.

"Make sure General Grant is informed of this development," McClernand told the courier.

Grant was with McPherson's Seventeenth farther east on the Jackson Road, following Hovey's division. Normally an aggressive, sometimes reckless, commander, McClernand had been ordered by Grant not to engage the enemy until ordered to do so. Because of the occasional animosity between Grant and him, McClernand felt compelled to be on his best behavior. Glancing at Hovey again, he wondered if any of these feelings made their way onto his face. In fact, McClernand's face was so thoroughly covered with hair that only his eyes could betray any emotion.

"I'd better get forward a bit. Find out what's happening with McGinnis," Hovey said. "See if he needs anything."

"Good idea," McClernand agreed. "Go ahead. We'll be here."

Hovey gave a curt nod and mounted his horse. Along with an aide, he soon disappeared down the Jackson Road. Adhering to his newfound "good conduct" philosophy, McClernand did not even entertain thoughts of heroic deeds and political fame. Some other time, when Grant's orders were not so unambiguous. He found one of the cooks and had him prepare a steaming mug of hot coffee. With mug in hand, McClernand ordered his corps forward at a moderate pace westward on the Jackson Road.

Surely, *something* would happen soon. Then his corps, leading the charge on all three roads, would have an opportunity to distinguish itself.

As would John A. McClernand.

May 16, 1863, The Champion House

As they drove their horses westward, Ulysses S. Grant and James B. McPherson spotted the traffic jam ahead of them on the Jackson Road. Grant looked at McPherson, and once more wondered why his young colleague had decided to festoon himself in a full dress uniform. Grant was wearing a blue cotton blouse and fatigues, a working soldier's uniform.

"Wait here," he ordered gruffly. "I'm going to kick the collective asses of those wagon masters. We can't allow combat troops to be held up like this."

McPherson did as he was told, enjoying the unfolding melodrama. Grant urged his horse forward, stopped at the first wagon and uttered a string of expletives at the man in charge. Although he couldn't understand the details of the conversation—if a one-sided diatribe could be called a conversation—McPherson could tell by the wagon-master's bowed head and submissive posture that he was receiving a good tongue-lashing. Eventually, Grant let up on the man and proceeded to the next wagon in line, taking the sullen but co-operative wagon-master with him. Grant directed his captive to a station farther ahead while he delivered another scathing rebuke to the next man in line. In this way, Grant's verbal vituperation propagated down the line like a wave, instantly jolting successive teamsters into action. Within ten minutes, wagons were moving, and the road was clear.

When Grant returned, he took a moment to assure himself that troop movements were satisfactory, then turned to McPherson.

"Let's go," he announced, steering his horse around the parade of wagons and marching soldiers. Mounted on the well-groomed black stallion that complemented his uniform, McPherson quickly followed.

At the Champion House, a farmhouse with a surrounding porch, Alvin Hovey rushed out to meet the new arrivals.

"How's McGinnis doing. Where is he?" Grant inquired.

Hovey pointed to a bald spot, not quite a plateau, at the top of a hill to the west.

"That's Champion Hill. General McGinnis is up there with some Indiana cavalry."

"When will he be back?"

"Probably soon. He didn't take that many men with him."

"How many?"

Slightly embarrassed, Hovey replied, "Just two, a sergeant and another man."

"Who's the other man?"

"Another Indiana cavalryman, I suppose."

On any other occasion, Grant might have questioned the wisdom of sending only three men, one of them a brigade commander, to reconnoiter and enemy position. But his mind was spinning with other matters, not the least of which was the question of how well entrenched the enemy was in front of him. He would forgive Hovey if only McGinnis would return with the answer.

Hovey suggested breakfast and coffee to calm restless and taut nerves. Grant and McPherson accepted but refused to sit down, preferring to keep their eyes focused in the direction from which McGinnis would return, assuming he did. Eggs, bacon, and coffee were brought from the Champion House and hastily consumed.

"Sir, I think we should attack," Hovey suddenly blurted.

Grant smiled at his subordinate's proposal.

"Hovey, you always want to attack. Let's wait and hear what McGinnis has to say."

"Yes, sir, I understand, but—"

"The Seventeenth isn't up yet. You wouldn't want to run into the whole Reb army without McPherson's people, would you?"

"No, sir, but I—"

Belatedly realizing his arguments were long on emotion and short on reason, Hovey clamped his mouth shut and took a short stroll down the connecting road between the Champion House and the Jackson Road. Like McClernand, Hovey was a volunteer, but, unlike McClernand, he had no grandiose illusions about his place in the Army of the Tennessee.

Grant and McPherson maintained their positions, gazing west through field glasses in the hope of spotting McGinnis or a Confederate deployment. For twenty minutes, nothing but random skirmishing occurred between the two sides, creating an echo of sound and fury but signifying nothing. Then McPherson stiffened and pointed to a grove of trees two hundred yards west of the Champion House.

"Sir, I think there must be a company or two of Reb infantry in there."

Grant quickly swiveled his binoculars to the spot McPherson indicated.

"Where?"

McPherson made some fine adjustments to his pointing finger and said, "There."

What Grant saw were mostly trees, but trees that seemed to be swaying of their own accord. Then he saw a horse's rump pass by an opening in the foliage. Something was definitely in there, but he could not judge the size of the concealed force. Was it part of a larger deployment extending from the hilltop or was it just a scouting party?

"What do you want to do?" McPherson asked.

"Wait until your people come up. There's no rush."

Grant momentarily wondered if he might be suffering from over-caution, but dismissed the thought. There was no sense in attacking an enemy before you knew his strength. Given the elevation of the hill in front of him and the several stands of deciduous trees growing peacefully upon it, he would be willing to bet a brigade or two were hidden up there

"They're here," McPherson said, nodding to his right.

Grant shifted his gaze and saw John Logan with his division of McPherson's Seventeenth corps moving into position on Hovey's right flank. Logan had a massive mustache that enveloped his chin and neck, giving him the canine features of a terrier. Grant was glad to see them. Because of his trailing position at the close of hostilities in Jackson, McClernand now had the lead on all three roads: Jackson, Middle, and Raymond. It was a situation Grant did not like, but, short of moving McPherson's or Sherman's corps through McClernand's, there was not much he could do to prevent it. Even if he'd wanted to, he couldn't execute such a maneuver. It would be too difficult to pull off and would waste precious time. And McClernand, consummate politician that he was, would surely complain to the powers-that-be in Washington. Grant could not risk alienating Lincoln right now. There was too much at stake.

Logan spotted his two colleagues and steered his horse toward them. Greetings and salutations were hastily exchanged, and Grant looked at his watch. It was 10:15 AM.

When Logan was within listening distance, Grant announced, with his best stoic intonation, "It's time to go."

* * *

It was a magnificent, if frightening, sight, and Stephen Lee could not decide whether to stand in awe or run screaming from the field. From his vantage-point on Champion Hill, he watched the Union army form itself into battle array: skirmishers first, clearing the battleground of their opposite numbers in the Rebel ranks, then the infantry. Although he could not see Pettus and his scouting party, Lee assumed they would be retreating up the hill. If they did not, they would surely be killed or captured.

Handing his binoculars to an aide, Lee said, "What do you see, lieutenant? Can you tell whose corps that is?"

The aide, a mid-sized, light-haired Georgian, took the field glasses and studied a group of Union officers gathered just outside the Champion House.

"I can't tell. Too far away. I'd guess it was a division or two of McClernand's corps."

"Based on what you see or what you know about dispositions?"

The aide chuckled; he had been found out.

"Dispositions. McClernand was last in at Jackson, so he's got to be in the lead here. I have no idea what the man looks like."

Lee removed his gray slouch hat and used it to swat away a swarm of horse flies hovering around his steed's tail. The aide, still pressing the field glasses to his eyes, moved them to the right and froze.

"There's a young man with a neat beard, an older gentleman, and a short fellow smoking a cigar."

Lee confiscated the binoculars and held them to his eyes.

"The young one is McPherson, so it's not *all* McClernand's show. The cigar smoker . . ."

Lee lowered the binoculars and squinted as if to fine-tune his vision.

"The cigar smoker is Grant," he said.

"Really? Can I take another look?"

"Certainly," Lee said, then handed back the field glasses.

The flat bark of musket fire, faintly at first and then with more intensity, emanated from the left end of the line. Lee steadied his gaze in that direction and was rewarded with the sight of Pettus's skirmishers returning to the fold. They were being chased by Union skirmishers, who clearly held a numerical advantage of about two to one.

Turning to his aide, Lee screamed, "Tell the artillery to get their shells in the air and stop those people."

The aide, trying to control his skittish mare, gave the mandatory, "Yes, sir," and was off.

Lee dug his heels into his horse's sides and made a run for the left flank of the line. He wanted to learn what Pettus had found out and to find Colonel Alexander Reynolds. With the Union buildup on the Jackson Road, it was logical to assume Grant would deploy his forces to the right, to envelop the Confederates. If the Yankees were to make such an attempt, it was of the utmost importance that Lee's left flank link up with Reynolds's right flank. Otherwise, the Federals would pour through the gap like water through a sieve, and the battle would be over before it had barely begun.

The welcome sounds of booming six- and twelve-pounders resounded in Lee's ears. He smiled. His aide had indeed succeeded in lighting a fire under the gunners. He waited a second for the accompanying sounds of artillery shells exploding on the field of battle and was not disappointed. Pettus's pursuers would be driven back; he was sure of it.

★ THIRTY-ONE ★

May 16, 1863, The Battle of Champion Hill

A thin, not very athletic man with a naturally stern visage, Brigadier General George Francis McGinnis sometimes found it difficult to stir men into action. But it would be different this time. He had seen the enemy entrenchments on Champion Hill and knew what he had to do, what *they* would have to do. He was inspired.

"Sir, there are Reb soldiers over there," shouted one of the officers on McGinnis's left.

McGinnis's reconnoitering party was on its way back from Champion Hill to report its findings, and he was not expecting a confrontation. He glanced in the direction indicated by the officer and spotted a small group of Confederates in a clump of trees, trying to conceal themselves from view.

McGinnis weighed the pros and cons. He would have liked to attack the small company, but decided it was more urgent to report back to Hovey. The Rebels were probably on a mission similar to his. He would let them go for the moment.

"No, we'll go after Johnny Reb later, after General Hovey is informed of the situation. You ride ahead and let him know we're coming."

With a curt salute, the officer brought his horse to a gallop and disappeared down the eastbound Jackson Road. Two minutes later, McGinnis and the rest of his scouting party arrived at the Champion House to be greeted by Alvin Hovey and, somewhat unexpectedly, Ulysses S. Grant.

"McGinnis, what do you have for me?" Grant asked bluntly.

Dismounting, McGinnis said, "They're dug in, sir. That's a fine hill they're sitting on, and the Rebs are taking every advantage of it."

Unperturbed, Grant studied the faces of the scouting party, then brought his gaze back to McGinnis.

"How many are directly in front of us?" he inquired.

"Maybe a brigade."

"How many in those woods?" Grant asked, pointing to a forested area to the right of Champion Hill.

"I don't know. We couldn't get close enough to see."

Grant nodded and fell quiet, pacing forward and then back again, deep in thought.

"Sir, I'd like to repeat my proposal to attack, before the Rebs are ready for us," Hovey suddenly intoned.

Raising an open palm, Grant said, "Yes, yes, General. I know you're chomping at the bit to kill the enemy, and I can assure you —we will. But we can wait until General McPherson puts his corps in order, which, as you know, he's been doing for the last fifteen minutes."

Although Grant's matter of fact delivery was not intended to embarrass Hovey, it did.

"Yes, sir," was his only reply.

Grant resumed pacing, occasionally halting to study the terrain and the vegetation growing on it. Mississippi land seemed to have mantraps everywhere—vines, underbrush, gullies as deep and as treacherous as alpine slopes. Otherwise, there was little to see because neither side had as yet committed itself to serious action. The Rebels *were* lobbing artillery shells, most of which, in the absence of human targets, were doing little more than plowing the earth and making a deafening noise. How much quieter battlefields must have been before the invention of gunpowder, Grant mused.

He heard footsteps approaching and then heard McPherson say, "It's 10:30, sir."

Grant turned his head and said, "Does that mean you are ready to go?"

"Yes, sir."

Grant turned to view Logan's division of McPherson's corps forming a broad front. They looked imposing. He hoped the enemy would think so.

"All right, my orders are simple. Send a courier to recall Sherman," he said, pausing to focus his gaze on McPherson, "and attack."

*   *   *

Edmund Pettus listened to the whine of the twelve-pound shell overhead, trying to gauge where it would land, hopefully not on them. Instead, it exploded in midair. Instinctively, the two men raised their arms to shield against shrapnel fragments. None came close.

"Short fuse, too high," Stephen Lee muttered. "They'll find the range."

"They're coming," Pettus said stiffly, trying to mask his apprehension.

Pressing the field glasses to his eyes, Lee gazed between his horse's ears and said, "Yes, they are."

After he had returned from his reconnaissance of the Champion House, Pettus confirmed that the new arrivals were Logan's division of McPherson's Seventeenth Corps, who were deploying on the right of the Union line. He wasn't sure who was running the show in the Union center, but thought it might be Hovey of McClernand's Thirteenth Corps.

What Lee saw were lead elements of the two divisions making their way up Champion Hill. They were hindered by a profusion of vines and underbrush, but the advance was if a bit slow, orderly and determined.

One of Lee's aides, Lieutenant Joseph Laird, galloped in looking weary.

"Joe, what's the situation over there? Have we closed with Reynolds yet?" Lee shouted.

Laird pulled up on Lee's left side, opposite Pettus.

"He's not there, sir. General Pemberton ordered General Reynolds to escort the wagon train."

"Good God!" Lee groaned. "Who *is* over there?"

"I . . ." Laird stammered. "I'm not sure. General Stevenson . . . I think."

Carter Stevenson was Lee and Reynold's commanding officer, each of them commanding a brigade. Lee knew that the other two brigades, commanded by Seth Barton and Alfred Cumming, were on his right. That meant virtually no one was on his left. Pemberton's obvious desire to avoid a confrontation by retreating to a position closer to Vicksburg had left Lee vulnerable to envelopment. Lee would have to compensate.

"Lieutenant Laird, take these orders to the regimental commanders. Deploy all regiments farther to the left. Stretch them out. Who's on the left now?"

"The Twenty-Third Alabama, sir."

"Good. Send them at least another half mile out. Fill in with the other four regiments so there's not so much empty space in one place. Understand?"

"Yes, sir," Laird replied, reacting to Lee's sense of urgency by swatting his horse's rump a little too hard. The horse started to rear up, but Laird managed to regain control.

"One more thing, Lieutenant. Make sure Generals Cumming and Barton know what we're doing here."

"But, sir, they're on our right. I'll have to detour—"

"Then detour, Lieutenant. I can't leave Cumming and Barton in the same fix we're in, can I?"

Unaccustomed to formulating command decisions, an embarrassed Laird stammered, "Of course, sir. I'll . . . backtrack."

"And when you're done, come back and let me know what's happening on both our flanks. I don't want any gaps in the line."

Before Laird could utter another, "Yes, sir," Lee gave his horse a healthy swat and sent it and its rider speeding toward the Crossroads where the Jackson, Ratliff and Middle Roads met. Briefly thinking he had done all he could to improve his precarious circumstances, Lee suddenly realized he had not informed Pemberton. But Pemberton had ordered Reynolds to protect the wagon train and might not appreciate the threat. He thought about intercepting Laird and adding Pemberton's headquarters—the Robert's House—to his list of postings but decided to wait. He had more important matters to attend to and Carter Stevenson, whom Laird would surely locate, was in a better position to present the strategic picture to General Pemberton.

Lee felt, as well as heard, the massive explosions of Yankee shells as they found the range. As best he could, he sped along the line, alternately yelling, "Come on, boys, get those Yankees in your sights," and, "Left, you must move left. Our flank is in the air. Move left! Fill it in, boys! Fill it in!"

When he had moved halfway across the battlefront, Lee spotted some artillerymen moving their guns toward the peak of Champion Hill, which was topped by an ancient cotton field. He hurried over to them.

"Who are you boys?" he asked the four men struggling with four horses and heavy armament. "Where are you from?"

"We're what's left of the Botetourt Artillery," said the leader, a big man with sweat pouring from a naked skull into the abundant gray hair of his face and chin. "From Virginia."

"Virginians? What the hell are Virginians doing in *this* fight?"

"Can't rightly say, but we're definitely here," said the leader, flashing a tobacco-stained smile. "General Pemberton sent us."

Lee offered a grin of his own and asked, "What have you got there?"

The big man replied pointing to each of the two guns, "That one is a smoothbore six-pounder, and the big one is a twelve-pounder Napoleon."

"How soon can you get into this fight?"

"Soon as we find a good spot and get 'em turned around and aimed. Maybe half an hour."

"Fifteen minutes would be better."

The leader suppressed a snort of consternation, brandished his discolored smile again, and said, "I reckon it would. We'll give it a *shot*, so to speak."

"Thanks," Lee said, preparing to depart. For a minute, he watched the men laboring with their horses and cannon, wondering why most military activities had to be so unpleasant.

Suddenly, a shell screamed in. Lee leaped from his horse and dived to the ground, shoving his face into the dry grass and covering his head with his hands. Upon making landfall, the shell immediately exploded, the intensity of it threatening to pop his eardrums. When the noise had dissipated, he stood and took a good look around. A smoke-filled crater ten feet in diameter now occupied the void between Lee and the artillerymen. He turned his gaze toward them and saw four filthy figures rising lugubriously from the smoke-blanketed terrain.

"Are you boys all right?" he cried.

The big man finally reached a standing position, scanned his men, and brushed himself off.

"Looks like we survived, sir. Just sprayed us with a whole lot of sod and rocks."

He waved. Lee waved. Then Lee looked for his horse and found it standing beneath the branches of a big oak tree. Apparently, it had not suffered any physical injuries but was obviously unnerved. He approached it cautiously, whispering gentle nothings and gazing directly into its deep brown eyes until it let him grab its bridle.

"All right, boy. It's all right," he murmured soothingly, massaging its neck and snout. "None of us cares much for artillery. You're in good company . . . good boy . . . good boy."

After two minutes, the horse was steady enough for Lee to mount. He did, waved to the artillery crew, and directed his steed to the north. Still unnerved by the near fatal incident, he continued his monologue.

"Let's go, boy, gotta get there as fast as we can. Can't let those Yankees get through. Gotta clo-o-ose those gaps."

Eventually, realizing he was talking only to a horse, he clamped his mouth shut.

* * *

"Lee wants me to do what?" Brigadier General Alfred Cumming wanted to know. He was having a bad day.

Lieutenant Laird heaved a heavy sigh. He'd hoped his first stop on the battlefield tour Lee had sent him on would be brief. It didn't look like it would be.

"General Lee wants to make sure there are no gaps in the line. He has to move to the left, and he doesn't want the Third Brigade —your brigade—to become detached."

From his saddle, Laird gazed anxiously down at Cumming, wondering how to deal with the man. Since Cumming was a superior officer, he had little choice but to sit and listen.

"Tell General Lee I'm not sure I still have a brigade. Two regiments of my Georgians have already detached *themselves* to the Second Brigade. Tell him also that many more of the troops under my command have been detached to build the bridge over Baker's Creek and to defend the Crossroads. I can only stretch the men I have so far . . ."

Laird waited quietly, his head bowed, while Cumming recounted his troubles and complaints, starting with Pemberton's assignment of two companies to the Baker's Creek Bridge project and continuing with an appeal for sympathy. This was prompted by the fact that he'd had his present command for less than a week and did not yet know his officers, nor they him. Laird dutifully nodded his head, but, after three minutes of vituperation, had had enough.

"Sir, I have to go. Do you understand General Lee's concern?"

Annoyed by the interruption, but recognizing Lee's need to get on with his mission, Cumming grunted, "I believe so, Lieutenant, but—"

"And you will maintain contact with the Second Brigade?"

This irritated Cumming even more, but he kept his composure, smiled, and swallowed his pride.

"Of course, Lieutenant, we will do what we can. Did General Lee say anything about where he expects the Yankees to be coming from?"

"No, sir. I'm sorry, sir. I don't have that information."

"We will be forming a defensive line at the very top of Champion Hill," Cumming explained. "The Yankees could come at us from any direction. We've spotted them in the north and to the east. It will probably be one or both of those directions, I expect."

Cumming paused to suck in some oxygen, seeming to push his peevishness aside in favor of a more even disposition.

"Tell General Lee I will do my best—with what I have—to defend the hilltop. I will also do my best to hold the Crossroads. I'm not sure I can do both."

"And stay close," Laird added hesitantly.

Cumming smiled again. "And the Third Brigade will stay as close as it can to the Second Brigade."

This was not what Laird, and through him, Lee, wanted to hear, but it was as much as Cumming was willing to promise.

"Yes, sir," Laird said, barely pausing to salute before he was, once more, making his rounds.

* * *

Ten minutes later, Laird arrived at the Robert's House, west of the Crossroads on the Ratliff Road. Surprisingly, the only person in the front yard was a black servant, who was dumping table scraps into a hole surrounded by a clump of magnolia trees. The servant straightened as Laird approached.

"Can you tell me where General Pemberton is, my good man?" Laird inquired.

The black man, gray-haired and grizzly, chuckled at the salutation and pointed to the Robert's House

"He in the-ah," he replied with a wide grin.

Resisting the urge to salute every man he encountered, Laird hurried inside and found Pemberton enjoying an early lunch, accompanied by Carter Stevenson.

"Sir, I have a message from General Lee," he said, following the words with a lethargic wave of the hand that could have been a salute.

"Yes, Lieutenant, what is it?" Pemberton asked, his eyes rolling toward Laird.

"We are under attack, sir."

"Who is?" Stevenson inquired.

"We are, sir. General Lee, General Cumming. The Yankees are charging straight up Champion Hill at us."

Pemberton stood as if alarmed by the news. The reaction quickly passed, and he said, "Go on."

Laird hastily summarized the situation, focusing on Lee's inability to link up with Reynolds's brigade, and the reassignment of many of Cumming's men to other tasks.

"I'm glad I found you here, sir," Laird said to Stevenson. "General Lee is very much in need of reinforcing on his left flank. General Reynolds is not there."

Something in Laird's tone provoked Stevenson's ire. He growled, emptied his coffee cup, and glanced at Pemberton.

"Don't be impertinent, Lieutenant, we know where General Reynolds is."

Stevenson's level stare persisted for a half-minute, causing Pemberton to wriggle uncomfortably. Finally, he stopped and faced Laird.

"General Reynolds's brigade has been assigned to the Baker's Creek project. We must have that bridge to properly withdraw—"

"Withdraw?" Laird blurted, incredulous.

"Yes, Lieutenant, *withdraw*," Stevenson said tersely. His gaze shifted back to Pemberton, but his body language betrayed a predisposition toward Laird.

"We do not want to provoke a general engagement here," Pemberton interjected. "We were ordered by General Johnston to link up with him in Clinton. If possible, that is what I intend to do. If it is not possible, we will withdraw across the Big Black River. Either way, we will require that the Baker's Creek Bridge be in good repair."

"But, sir, there's already a battle in progress, and we have the high ground," Laird stammered. "All we have to do is defend it."

"Lieutenant, that will be all," Pemberton said with a raised hand. "You can rest assured matters are well in hand."

Laird could feel the frustration welling up in him. He glanced at Stevenson to see if he could garner any support on that front, but Stevenson averted his eyes.

"Sir, if you would just take a ride with me to Champion Hill, talk with General Lee . . ."

"Son, you are speaking beyond your rank, well beyond your rank," Pemberton said with forced politeness. Laying a hand on Laird's shoulder, he looked at Stevenson and said, "General Stevenson will discuss the matter with General Lee and ascertain what needs to be done. General Stevenson, would that be satisfactory?"

Carter Stevenson pursed his lips, then opened them to speak.

"It is. We will certainly need to understand General Lee's needs."

On that discordant note, Stevenson and Laird made their separate exits.

* * *

McGinnis was happy with the way things were going, but he was not ecstatic. The Rebels were retreating, however their withdrawal was more orderly than he would have preferred. He wanted to see men running for their lives; it was the only sure sign of victory. His attitude embodied no malice. It was strictly pragmatism.

Astride his piebald stallion, McGinnis was nearly jolted from his saddle by the nearby blast of an artillery shell. When the smoke cleared, he spotted the blood-soaked bodies of four soldiers lying on the ground, three of the four missing arms and two with truncated legs.

"Dear God . . ." he murmured, searching for, but failing to find a meaningful prayer. Canister shot had done the deed: a messy, violent assertion of death. He dismounted and checked the bodies for signs of life. There were none.

When another Rebel cannon fired off its payload, McGinnis tried to follow its trajectory with his ears. Its whine arrived directly overhead from a southwesterly direction. A subsequent blast seemed to emanate from a more westerly source and was less intense; probably meaning it was farther away.

So, he thought, *they have two batteries firing at us. Well, we can do better than that.*

McGinnis remounted his horse and continued in an east-to-west sweep of the battlefield. He could see his brigade fighting its way up the hill, adapting itself to the half-moon defensive line the Rebels had formed at the top. The Twenty-Ninth Wisconsin was attacking the northern front while the Eleventh Indiana moved in from the east. The Twenty-Fourth and Forty-Sixth Indiana filled in the space between. In some ways, the confrontation was beautiful. In most ways, it was horrifying.

But there was no time to admire or ponder the spectacle. Urging his horse forward again, McGinnis approached a staff officer of the Twenty-Ninth Wisconsin, who was leading his men through a thicket of vines and assorted Mississippi flora.

"Colonel, what is the situation here? It appears to be favorable for a final assault. Is that consistent with your judgment?"

The colonel hesitated, appreciating the fact he'd been asked for his opinion, but wary of committing himself too early.

"We're still three-hundred yards away, sir, and we haven't reached the crest of the hill yet."

"What's holding you up?"

"The Rebels, and these damnable swamp weeds," said the colonel, indicating the vines and underbrush at his feet.

McGinnis acknowledged the difficulty, saluted, and, without further embellishment, said, "I'll be back."

He resumed his easterly trek, then turned south, following the evolving line of battle. At each of the regiments in his brigade, he stopped to assess battle readiness and to review the battle plan with the regimental field commanders. That done, he hastened back to the Twenty-Ninth Wisconsin and found the staff officer to whom he had spoken earlier.

"Are you ready now?"

"We're closer by two hundred yards or so."

"That's close enough to get your head blown off."

The colonel joined McGinnis in a chuckle, though his heart was not in it. McGinnis dismounted and, approaching the officer, joined him in a semi-prone position on the ground, the better to avoid shrapnel and other airborne paraphernalia.

"Here's how we'll do it," McGinnis said calmly, gazing directly into the darting eyes of his colleague. "At this distance, the Rebs will only get off one volley before you'll be on them. After you've advanced ten paces or so, I'll make a downward chop with my sword, and the lines that have advanced will fall to the ground and cover themselves.

The plan was willingly, if not enthusiastically adopted. When they were within seventy yards of the Confederate defense, McGinnis swiped his sword downward with a definitive *swish*. As instructed, the members of the Twenty-Ninth Wisconsin fell to the ground, waited for the cascade of Rebel musketry and cannon to subside, then rushed the battlements. As the offense wrapped itself around the angle iron of the defense, McGinnis could see he had an opportunity to place enfilade fire on both segments of the line. Accordingly, he directed members of the Twenty-Ninth to turn toward the vertex of the, "L," from which they could fire on both the eastern and northern segments of the Rebel entrenchments. Cumming's Thirty-Fourth and Thirty-Ninth Georgia soon broke under the stress of musket balls making deadly contact with skulls, necks, and torsos, or simply simulating the terror of deadly bees swarming at them from what seemed like all directions. As they fled, some cried, some ran, some withdrew as they had been taught—slowly and, if possible, in tightly knit groups. None screamed. But the northern face of the Confederate line was no more.

Relentless, McGinnis wasted no time in giving the eastern side of the line an equal share of hellfire. He ordered the Forty-Sixth Indiana to enfilade the Thirty-Sixth Georgia, which they did with the help of the exotically festooned *Zouave* regiment. The Georgians defending the eastern arm of the Rebel line fell back when their commanding officer noted his precarious situation and ordered a retreat.

The sudden absence of a Rebel defense created an eerie hiatus. Gun smoke still hung in the air, the wounded could still be seen and heard writhing and moaning on the battlefield; occasional musket blasts still permeated the hazy atmosphere. It wasn't silence as much as it was the absence of cacophony. The sounds that remained were small and meek instead of large and boisterous, pleas for mercy rather than shouts of defiance.

Surveying the battlefront, McGinnis found the Twenty-Ninth's commander.

"Did we win?"

"I'd say so," the officer said. "At least for the time being."

"Think they'll come back?"

"Maybe, if they have enough boys left to make a show if it," he said, then, pointing to the left, added, "Look. The General looks like he's ready for a dress ball."

McGinnis and the officer curiously eyed the two men steering their horses along what had been the line. One was John Logan, commander of McPherson's Third Division; the other was McPherson himself. Logan's was a workingman's uniform—dirty, disheveled and wrinkled. McPherson was in full military dress; even his ebony black horse seemed to shine. Both were shouting words of encouragement at the Union troops. McGinnis knew from past experience that Logan's cheers would be little more than strings of expletives whereas McPherson's vocabulary contained only socially accepted epithets.

When they had finished pumping up their men, McPherson and Logan joined McGinnis and the Twenty-Ninth's commander.

"If you don't mind me askin', sirs, what exactly were you sayin' to those boys?" McGinnis asked.

Logan answered first. "I was just telling them that we've got to whip them here or go under the sod together. Give 'em hell. Give 'em *hell!*"

On the second "Give 'em hell" Logan propelled his fist forward for emphasis.

It was about what McGinnis had expected from Logan. He waited for McPherson's response but got none. Instead, it was Logan who, struggling to suppress a chuckle, replied, "General McPherson wants to give 'em . . ."

Without completing the statement, Logan glanced at McPherson, to gauge his commander's mood. Wearing a mild blush on his cheeks, McPherson's grin suggested he was in good spirits.

"Jesse," he said, finishing Logan's sentence.

The puzzled stares on the faces of McGinnis and his subordinate were absolutely vacant.

"Jesse?" McGinnis murmured cautiously, fearing he might insult McPherson with his ignorance.

"David's father," McPherson explained. "The David who killed Goliath. You remember him."

McGinnis and his staff officer exchanged glances. Neither was sure whether McPherson and Logan were serious or were pulling their legs.

It was at this moment that a messenger rode in announcing that the left flank of the Confederates was, "hanging in the air." McPherson and Logan briefly conferred, then rode off to the Champion House to plan how to take advantage of this fresh intelligence. McGinnis and the officer watched them as they made their way down the slope.

"Sir," the officer said, still baffled. "I surely have great respect for General McPherson, but 'give 'em Jesse' is just not a proper way of cursing."

McGinnis could not stifle a quick chortle. With a mischievous glint in his eye, he said, "You're right, Colonel. And I would certainly not expect you to follow the General's poor example. You may curse at will."

★ THIRTY-TWO ★

May 16, 1863, The Confederate Line Wavers

The vacuum Pemberton had created in the Confederate line by reassigning Reynolds's men to bridge building was rapidly filling with Yankees. For a while, Stephen Lee's Alabamans held fast, and could do so as long as the battle was dominated by musket fire. When the First Illinois brought its howitzers, the Rebels began to suffer heavy losses. Stephen Lee, who had been trying to fill his left wing with soldiers since discovering it hanging in the air, was on the verge of desperation. He turned to an aide.

"Give the order to charge those damned guns," he barked.

It wasn't long before he regretted his decision. The Twenty-Third Alabama led the charge but was halted by the Forty-Fifth Illinois and Twenty-Third Indiana after the Union artillerymen spotted the Rebels approaching. Rather than have his brigade cut to pieces, Lee reluctantly ordered a retreat. Before leaving the field, he sent a courier to Brigadier Seth Barton informing him of the Second Brigade's departure. It was a straightforward, "Must retreat. Good luck—S.D. Lee."

When he received the message, Barton and the First Brigade were just coming up. He looked to his left and saw the Union forces—John Stevenson's brigade of Logan's division—chasing Lee and his men into the forest between Champion Hill and the northbound branch of the Jackson Road. Barton sent three of his four Georgia regiments against Stevenson, with initial success. But the Union retreat was orderly and short-lived, and the Rebel offensive stalled.

It then got even worse for the Confederates. Stevenson's westerners started to roll up Barton's left flank, and he was forced to bring up the only reserve regiment he had into the fighting: the Forty-Second Georgia. It was not enough. To make matters worse, Brigadier General Mortimer Leggett of Logan's division accelerated the pace of the Union infiltration of the void Lee had left in his wake. Barton found his left flank being turned while his men were forced to endure enfilade fire on the right. The Union sharpshooters could hardly avoid hitting some unfortunate duck in the Confederate shooting gallery there were so many lined up. Not surprisingly, most of Barton's men panicked, fleeing through the trees to the Jackson road and to safety across Baker's Creek. Those that did not run accepted the inevitable by raising their hands in surrender.

The story was the same for the rest of the battlefield. Whether or not Stephen Lee's exposed left flank had caused the collapse was debatable. The Union forces were simply too numerous and too aggressive. The soldiers of Logan's division pursued the Rebels through the woods and onto the northbound Jackson Road like hounds after hares. John Stevenson's brigade overran the Mississippi Light Artillery after a hard trek across deep ravines and steep, thigh-burning hills. The Cherokee Georgia Artillery threw down their arms after making a token resistance by firing one shot from each of two Parrott rifles.

The prevailing philosophy among the rank and file of the Confederates was what it had always been and would always be for either side during a rout: *No sense getting killed for a cause already lost. Run or surrender, but avoid a bullet.* It was a perspective born of necessity.

It looked very much like a great Union victory, and the alleged victors were already celebrating, even though cannon fire could still be heard rumbling like lazy thunder across the rugged terrain. When he returned to the Champion House with his staff in the early afternoon, Grant observed that some rooms had acquired beds and medical facilities. He thought this a worthwhile development and said so to whoever he met—soldier or surgeon. But he worried that some of the medical staff might object if he lit up a cigar. They were always fussy about such things. He ordered an aide to find him a place to smoke where he could be confident of enjoying peace, quiet, a good cigar, and, most of all, freedom from petty harassment. The aide quickly found such a place near a back door and led Grant to it. The General thanked him, sat down in a comfortable chair, and lit up.

"Go find Logan and tell him he's making history today," Grant said with a smile of contentment. Soon he was surrounded by cigar smoke, a state of existence that could be improved only by the presence of a bottle of good whisky.

But that was out of the question until both sides tacitly agreed that the battle was over. He was confident it would be soon and fell asleep.

*   *   *

John Pemberton could see the aide was anxious to receive his orders, but Pemberton was not anxious to give any; the situation was starting to look desperate, and orders formulated during the heat of battle were frequently weighted as much by emotion as logic. However, he had no choice, so he folded his hands on the table before him, sucked in a deep breath, and glanced up.

"Tell General Bowen to move up and assist Carter Stevenson, and have Loring do the same, except for the men working on the bridge across Baker's Creek."

The aide saluted and turned to exit the Robert's House, Pemberton's *ad hoc* headquarters.

"Oh, and tell them I want them to crush the enemy," Pemberton added.

The aide made a half turn. Pemberton thought he detected a shake of the head before the soldier again snapped to attention and said with a controlled expression on his face, "Yes, sir."

This was clearly the appropriate action, Pemberton thought. Reinforce and, when possible, attack.

Saluting, the aide announced, "Sir, we already know General Loring can't move and that General Bowen has a heavy force of Yankees in front of him."

At least Bowen had given a reason for his immobility.

"Did Loring mention why he could not move?" Pemberton asked.

"Yes. I told you when I arrived, sir."

Drawing a blank, Pemberton made a querulous gesture with his hand and asked, "Did you? What was it then . . ."

"General Loring said he couldn't move because if he did, his right flank would be exposed to the enemy."

"Oh, yes, now I remember," Pemberton said, waving the hand in placation. "Yes, yes . . . well, you have my orders."

Befuddled by the command, the aide stammered, "Your orders, sir . . . ah, would you mind repeating them?"

"To move. Loring and Bowen are to support General Stevenson. Is that clear?"

The aide gave in. "Yes, sir. Of course, sir," he said, making a hasty exit and leaving John Pemberton alone.

In the privacy of the room and his solitary mind, Pemberton could not help ruminating on the burdens that had been his since coming to Vicksburg less than a year ago. He was to defend the city against the enemies of the Confederacy. *At all costs*, his master and mentor, Jeff Davis, would have added. Yet, if, as it was often said, Vicksburg was the Gibraltar of the Confederacy, why did she need so much defending, so many dead soldiers at her feet? He wondered how it could be done; if it could be done. If Vicksburg were to be defended, it would be best to do it at a place like

Champion Hill, on good ground of his choosing. But the Yankees had arrived in such overwhelming numbers!

Yankees! He was finally beginning to think of his former colleagues that way. Northerners, Philadelphians, westerners, all the myriad sub-groupings of citizens comprising the United States of America. What, then, was he? A Rebel? Of course he was. To his old friends and relatives in the North, he was worse than that. He was a traitor. *But I am not a traitor,* he wanted to cry out. *I am a defender of states rights.* The states should be governed by themselves and not by a gaggle of northern politicians trying to impose their special version of morality on the South. That's what the Declaration of Independence was all about, wasn't it?

He looked out one of the northeast windows to see how the battle was progressing, but it was too far away. The sounds of conflict reverberated from the direction of Champion Hill. It was maddening to be able to do nothing but wait for a definitive outcome. Never before having a field command, he had not understood how much of a toll waiting took on the nerves.

Proceeding to a kitchen cupboard, he looked in to see what was available to drink. He found coffee and a half bottle of Tennessee whisky. For a moment, he considered imbibing the whisky, but managed to get a grip on himself. What would his men think if they discovered he'd been drinking during the battle? But that would be the least of his concerns if he were to yield to the temptation. He might get drunk. Even if he didn't, it might affect his judgment.

Affect my judgment, he reflected sardonically. *Would that be a bad thing or a good thing? Maybe it would make me bold enough to decide whose orders to follow—Davis's or Johnston's.*

Suddenly, there was a jarring impact on the kitchen door, like a bag of flour or a body ramming into it. Pemberton rushed to the door and, bottle in hand, opened it. Seated on the ground in the doorway was a young soldier—smooth-skinned, auburn-haired and disheveled. He was just a boy, frightened, and cradling a musket across his body. When he saw Pemberton, he jumped to his feet, shifted the musket to his left hand and saluted.

"Sir," he murmured cautiously, as if ready to break into tears. "Sir, are you General Pemberton?"

"Yes, I am."

"Sir, sir," the boy repeated, "I need to go home. I'm . . . I'm all tied up in knots. I can't take it no more."

Then he did cry, but, after a brief outburst, stared relentlessly into Pemberton's eyes.

"General, sir, I don't want to die. Please let me go."

The boy started to shake. Stiffening, Pemberton grasped his shoulders and said, "Stand straight, son. Now, what's your name? And your unit?"

The boy struggled to regain his composure, trying several times to speak, but each time yielding to a flood of tears.

"Sit down, son," Pemberton said, leading him to a chair at the kitchen table.

When he had the boy settled, Pemberton discovered he still had the whisky bottle in his hand. He headed for the cupboard in the northeast corner of the room and grabbed one of the tin mugs there. As he returned to his disturbed guest, he poured a shot of whisky into the mug and handed it over. Then he took a chair across from the boy.

"I need to know your name, son, and your unit."

At first, the boy gazed in stupefaction at the mug, as if unsure of its contents. Then he swallowed it in one gulp and said, "Private Eli Jaffrey. Fifty-Sixth Georgia."

"Do you want another one?" Pemberton asked.

The boy nodded. Pemberton poured.

"Now, Private Jaffrey, let's just talk for a while. What do you want of me? I'll tell you truthfully—I have to send you back."

Jaffrey's face tightened, enough to squeeze tears onto his cheeks. He downed the whisky.

"Son, I must send you back. General Cumming would be very upset with me if I didn't. He's only got eight companies, and he has to hold Champion Hill. Do you understand what I'm telling you?"

The boy gave him a doleful look and said, "Yes. You want me to go back."

Pemberton waited for more, for Jaffrey to plead his case, but the boy only stared into the tin mug.

"The Fifty-Sixth is at the Crossroads. That's pretty far from the heavy action. Is it really that bad?"

"I saw my best friend get blown up by an artillery shell. He was there and then he wasn't, just a red mist and hunks of raw meat all over the place. I got some of his brains in my hair."

Jaffrey's demeanor was superficially calm, but Pemberton could see it was an illusion. The boy was simply drained of emotion.

"The Fifty-Sixth Georgia. Who is your commanding officer?"

"Colonel Pinson, sir."

"Pinson . . . Pinson. I don't think I know him. Is he a good man?"

"He's fine. Been with the regiment about a year."

"How about General Cumming? Do you have any thoughts about him?"

Jaffrey's voice took on a discordant timbre as he said, "Don't know him and he don't know us. He's only been the Fifty-Sixth's commander for a little while."

Then Pemberton remembered. Alfred Cumming had been given his new command only last week. A significant number of the troops under his command had never experienced combat. It was an unfortunate combination—a new commander leading raw recruits—and all too common in this war.

"Sir, could I ask a question," Jaffrey ventured.

"Of course."

"You have much battle savvy?"

"I fought against the Seminoles in Florida and was active in the Mexican War."

"They ain't Northerners."

Pemberton gazed into Jaffrey's deep-set green eyes, wondering what he was getting at and whether it might be wise to terminate the conversation.

"No, they're not, but they fought well."

"But they wasn't no kin of yours, was they? They was just good ol' boys that happened to be Indians and Mexicans. You didn't lose no sleep over shootin' 'em, did you?"

Now Pemberton understood. In his own way, Private Jaffrey was feeling the same pangs of disquietude as many members of his staff felt.

"I'm from Philadelphia, but my wife is from Virginia, and I have lived in the South for many years," Pemberton said peevishly. Rising, he added, "I think we'd best end our talk, Private. You need to get back to your regiment. Do you have a weapon?"

Jaffrey was quick to his feet.

"My musket, sir. I left it outside," he said, quickly reverting back to deferential status. Pemberton was saved further embarrassment by the arrival of two couriers, one from Cumming's brigade of Carter Stevenson's division, and the other from Cockrell's brigade under Bowen. The courier from Cumming was the first to speak.

"Sir, General Cumming requests reinforcements. He cannot hold the Crossroads unless—"

"But he must hold the Crossroads," Pemberton demanded. "I ordered troops to assist General Stevenson. They should have arrived by now . . ."

"Sir," the other courier interrupted. "May I say something?"

Consternation dominating his features, Pemberton ignored the impertinence and turned to the courier.

"Go ahead, private."

"Sir, Colonel Cockrell is here, sir."

Pemberton was at a loss for speech. He had seen no signs of Francis Cockrell and his Missouri contingent.

"Where?"

"Over there, sir," the courier said, pointing westward.

Pemberton rushed to a window that would allow him to view the Ratliff Road. He gazed out on the most wonderful sight he had seen in weeks: five divisions of Cockrell's Missourians accompanied by three batteries, all marching toward the Crossroads. If he had been a more devout Christian, he might have interpreted their arrival as manna from heaven.

Turning to Cockrell's courier, Pemberton said, "Tell the Colonel to report to me directly."

The courier obeyed and left. While he waited for Cockrell, he instructed Cumming's courier to remain but refrained from further discussion with Eli Jaffrey. When fifteen minutes had passed, Cockrell walked in.

"Colonel Cockrell," Pemberton said with clearly uplifted spirits. "If they are not already headed that way, would you direct your troops toward the Crossroads, please. General Cumming needs some help."

"Certainly, sir."

Pointing to Jaffrey, Pemberton said, "And please escort this young man back to his regiment."

"Which is?"

"The Fifty-Sixth Georgia, sir," Jaffrey snapped, trying to present a more courageous front than he had previously.

After Jaffrey retrieved his musket, he and Cockrell hastily departed, leaving Cumming's courier with Pemberton.

"Well, private, you may inform General Cumming that he will shortly have his reinforcements."

"Yes, sir," the courier said, turning to leave.

"Oh, tell me, how vigorous is the Yankee attack?"

"Very strong, sir. There have been . . . reversals."

He means it may turn into a rout, Pemberton brooded. It seemed to be a ubiquitous feature of this war. At one time or another, everyone retreated from a battlefield. There was only so much a man could be asked to do. Marching to a certain death was not one of them. The most a commander could expect of a soldier under his command was to try and kill the enemy before he killed you. If a man found himself alone on the battlefield, with a screaming enemy column closing on him, his ability to kill the enemy was no longer a credible option. Hastening rearward was the only sensible thing to do.

Pemberton asked, "How is the Fifty-Sixth doing?"

"They are holding their position, sir. But they are under heavy attack, like everyone else."

When Pemberton did not react, the courier turned and left. Pemberton stood silently, knowing he had done the right thing by sending Jaffrey back to his regiment, but fearing the worst.

★ THIRTY-THREE ★

May 16, 1863, Victory and Defeat at Champion Hill

Francis Cockrell was pleased to find the Fifty-Sixth Georgia holding its own. He looked back to see how far behind his courier and the Georgia private named Jaffrey were. He decided they were within spitting distance, and waited until they caught up. Then he pointed to the field north of Pemberton's headquarters occupied by the Fifty-Sixth.

"Lieutenant, deliver private Jaffrey to his regiment, then come back here."

"Yes, sir," chirped the courier, who waved for Jaffrey to follow.

Cockrell watched while Jaffrey was returned to his regiment and continued watching as the officer to whom he had been delivered gave him a severe tongue-lashing. Dejected and humbled, the private was then subjected to further humiliation by being dragged by his shirt collar back to his unit. It might have been amusing if desertion under fire had not been the offense. Cockrell resigned himself to letting Jaffrey off easy. Had the battle been lost, the young man might have been summarily shot in the act of flight. But the Confederacy could not afford to lose soldiers just because their courage sometimes faltered. Jaffrey would be given a chance to prove himself again, or die trying.

When the courier returned, Cockrell sent orders to the Fifth Missouri to join up with the left flank of the Fifty-Sixth. While the bugle was still sounding to initiate the deployment, the orderly ranks of the Georgians gave way to chaos. The Georgians tried to absorb the shock and then ran for their lives as an unbroken Union line advanced, mowing them down with murderous musket and artillery fire.

"What the . . ." Cockrell cried, silently cursing Jaffrey for claiming the Fifty-Sixth was standing firm. They clearly were not.

As he was attempting to organize his thoughts and assess the situation, he saw two Confederate horsemen approaching at a fast trot. When they were within recognition distance, he identified them as Robert Bevier and Owen Waddell, the first and second officers of the Fifth Missouri under Colonel James McCown.

"Colonel Bevier, I thought the Fifty-Sixth Georgia commanded the field. What happened?"

Bevier and Waddell halted their mounts next to Cockrell's, facing him.

"They did," Bevier began in a raspy voice. "But the Yankees decided to attack."

"Who are they?"

"The Yankees?"

"Yes."

Bevier paused to clear his throat. While he was dislodging phlegm, Waddell replied, "It looks like Slack's brigade, sir. You remember them?"

Cockrell did. Colonel James Slack's brigade had fought against Cockrell's at Port Gibson earlier in the campaign.

"I do," he said, adding, "Can't say I'm anxious to take them on again."

"It's a neighborhood brawl, sir, and you know how vicious those can be," Bevier said, his voice once more in working order.

The comment was a reference to the smattering of Missouri men among the other mid-westerners in Slack's brigade. Like Kentucky, Tennessee, Maryland and what was now West Virginia, Missouri had men fighting on both sides of the conflict.

Getting to the purpose of his and Waddell's visit, Bevier said, "We're having trouble linking up with the Fifty-Sixth since they appear to be . . . in some disarray at the moment. Colonel Mc-Cown wants to know if your orders have changed."

Before Bevier finished his sentence, a volley of Union musket fire filled the air with sound and smoke. The eyes of all three men swiveled toward the noise and saw the Fifth Missouri suddenly fall back, then try to reassert itself back into the fray. As it did, its left flank disengaged from the regiment next door—the Third Missouri."

"The order is to hold. It hasn't changed," Cockrell said with as much grit as his vocal chords could muster.

Union muskets quickly filled the separation with enfilade fire, killing Rebel soldiers at a rate that alarmed Cockrell and the two officers with him. Having confirmed the order to hold, he wondered if it could be done.

He was still wondering, as well as considering what words of inspiration he might deliver to his minions, when a company-size group of Rebels from the Fifth Missouri rushed by, screaming the Rebel yell, assorted epithets and a descant of, ". . . damn Yankee sons of bitches . . ." As they charged, the pack picked up various elements of the Fifth: first the color guard, then the lead infantry, then the stragglers and shell-shocked, and finally Cockrell himself.

Anxious to take advantage of the situation, Cockrell, Bevier, and Waddell followed the evolving action.

"The Yankees are coming from the right," Bevier observed.

Cockrell raised binoculars to his eyes to observe what was happening on the Fifth's right flank. Bevier was right: Slack's brigade was concentrated on that piece of battlefield territory. They might not be aware that he had two regiments that had not yet been brought up.

"You're right. Colonel Bevier, get back to the First and Sixth and tell them to move into position as rapidly as they can, then march toward that action over there. Major Waddell, you go back to the Fifth and inform Colonel McCown what we're up to. He'll need to tie his regiment to the First and Sixth pretty tightly."

"What about General Bowen, sir?" Waddell asked.

"When you're finished, find him and get his blessing."

Bevier spurred his horse and sped away, but Waddell remained, hesitant. Finally, he asked, "What if he doesn't give it, sir?"

Cockrell gave a rueful smile and said, "If he doesn't, tell him it was the best I could do under the circumstances. If he has other orders, bring them back to me. Otherwise, you can rejoin your regiment."

Waddell made a quick exit, leaving Cockrell to scrutinize what he could of the battle's development. He spotted a turkey buzzard hovering over the western slope of Champion Hill and could only assume there were many corpses lying beneath its perfidious gaze. Cursing the bird for its carnivorous instincts, he nevertheless wished he could borrow its wings and view the battlefield from above, where troop deployments—Union and Confederate—could easily be observed. Perhaps some day hot air balloons would be used extensively for such a purpose. For now, though, he and his fellow officers had to rely on ground level observations and couriers, an inefficient but necessary means of gathering intelligence.

As he watched, the six Missouri brigades formed into battle order and advanced. Martin Green's Arkansas and Missouri brigade moved into position alongside Cockrell's Missourians. He couldn't be sure, but Cockrell thought he detected a lull or at least a slowdown in the Union assault. He was trying to judge the significance of what he could see when a courier rode up.

"Sir, General Gates would like to see you."

"Gates? *Elijah* Gates?"

"Yes, sir."

Elijah Gates was the commander of the First Missouri's cavalry and an old friend.

"What does he want?"

The courier's face flushed with an *how-the-hell-should-I-know* expression, but he simply replied, "He didn't say, sir."

With the courier at his side, Cockrell cut across the irregular landscape to Green's brigade, where Gates' cavalry was providing the adhesion to bind the two brigades together, with Green on the right and Cockrell on the left.

"How are you, Colonel?" Cockrell asked, skulking up to Gates.

"Colonel, good to see you," Gates said cheerily.

"I'm glad to see you, too. We've been under some heavy fire."

"Come with me, Colonel," Gates beckoned. "I have something to show you."

The two men directed their horses to a position north of the Roberts House where there were few trees or hills to obscure sight lines. Gates pointed to the Yankee positions and said, "I think there's only one brigade out there: Slack's. We have two, yours and Green's."

Cockrell pulled the brim of his slouch hat down to keep the bright afternoon sunlight out of his eyes.

"Really? With all they've got, I'd expect the Yankees to send at least two brigades against us."

"They did, but the other one—I think it's McGinnis—is too far away to do Slack any good."

"So Slack is overextended?"

Gates smiled and hastily replied, "He is. *And* he has no artillery support. *And* his men are tired from climbing that damn hill and fighting all morning."

Cockrell liked what he was hearing.

"It sounds to me like we have a rare opportunity to outnumber the enemy and send him packing."

"That would be my hope, Colonel."

"Have you talked to General Bowen?"

Widening his grin, Gates said, "I think it would behoove you to discuss the matter with the good general. I'll stay here and keep pounding away with my guns."

Cockrell nodded his agreement and headed toward the front of what was rapidly transforming into a line of battle. The seam where Cockrell's brigade met Green's was not hard to find. The soldiers of both brigades were still scurrying to seal the breach between the two and make sure their brethren in the adjacent brigade did not inadvertently drift off. Cockrell ran into the First Missouri before he could find Bowen. The regiment's commander, Colonel Amos Riley, was busy overseeing a company of infantry preparing to advance.

"Colonel, what are you doing?" he asked abruptly.

"Sir," Riley said, offering a brisk salute. "General Bowen's orders, sir. "We're getting ready to attack."

"Just your regiment?"

"No, sir, some of General Green's people too."

Cockrell took a long look around, but could see no evidence of preparation except Riley's. He did see the five Missouri batteries rolling into position and aiming their guns at the remnants of Slack's brigade. It was not long before Riley gave the order to fire and twenty cannons boomed their deadly messages across the void separating the two armies. Like an echo, the thunder of each launch was followed by the report of an explosion in the Union ranks. Without artillery to support them, and being too far away to effectively return musket fire, the soldiers of Slack's brigade fell like ducks in a duck shoot.

Cockrell spotted John Bowen among the First Missouri infantry, seated on his horse and gazing intently at the enemy across the rugged terrain. Cockrell moved along his left side. Shortly thereafter, Martin Green rode in from the rear and placed himself on Bowen's right.

"Afternoon, gentlemen," Bowen said, his gaze unswerving.

"Sir."

"Sir."

A minute later, Bowen glanced quickly at each man and said, "Would you like to join me in leading the attack?"

"That would be unwise, sir," Green objected. "One or all of us could be killed."

"It would be unwise, General, but it would also be very effective," Bowen said, digging his heels into his steed's flanks. The horse reluctantly moved forward. Cockrell and Green followed. The Confederate response to the Union assault on Champion Hill was underway.

* * *

Zeke Jackson of the Fifty-Sixth Ohio was the first to notice what was happening. Zeke, a tall but bottom-heavy young man from Cincinnati, enjoyed predicting what the Rebels would do next. He was hopeful his observations would eventually reach the ears of Colonel James Slack, his commanding officer. Zeke wasn't sure he wanted to make the army a career, but he was sure that, whether he did or not, he would prefer to spend the rest of the war with a higher rank than private.

"Look, Jimmy, they're movin'," he said in the squeaky voice that belied his size.

"Who? Where?" burbled Jimmy Gallagher, Jackson's friend and colleague. Gallagher was as tall as Jackson but was thin to the point of emaciation. The skin of his face and neck covered his skull and spine like an old and brittle leather glove. When he spoke, it was with a nervous tick that seemed to set the whole head-neck assembly into resonance.

"Those boys?" he asked, a certain skepticism in his tone. "How do you know who they are?"

Zeke was not exactly sure who "they" were. The distance and the high afternoon sun made a visual examination difficult. So he said, "I don't know for sure, but we better keep an eye on 'em. They could be Rebs."

"I'll ask the Captain," Jimmy said.

Which he did by rising to his feet and cautiously making his way to the company captain. It wasn't far; an easy if unpleasant crawl over the dirt and rocks of a gradual rise in the terrain. When his friend returned, Zeke was still studying the oncoming troop movements. As they approached, the rail fence directly in front of him further obscured his view. Jimmy edged beside him, puffing from the exertion of squirming like a snake.

"Captain says they might be ours," he announced.

"Maybe, but I don't think so," Zeke said, packing himself into a small ditch and raising his musket.

"Zeke, what're you doin'? No need to . . ."

Before Jimmy could finish, a chorus of muskets let loose and he was struck in the neck by a musket ball."

"Ow! Damn!" he cried, touching the wound with a free hand. It came away bloodied. "Hey, I'm bleedin'," he groaned, mesmerized by the realization that he'd actually been wounded.

"Jimmy, for the love of God, get down!" Zeke enjoined.

The trance broken, Jimmy Gallagher promptly ducked his head and clawed at the earth in an effort to shield himself.

"Guess I was right," Zeke gibed.

"Guess you were," Jimmy replied.

"Let me take a look at that."

"All right."

Hurrying, Zeke propped himself on one elbow and gazed down at the wound on the back of his friend's neck. Then he touched the blood to determine its thickness.

"You're lucky, Jimmy. You only lost about a half-inch of skin. Bleedin' ain't too bad. I think I can stop it with a rag or somethin'."

"Is it big enough to get me outta here?"

"Prob'ly not. What's it feel like?"

"Like I got stung by the king of all bees."

"Bees don't have kings, just queens."

Jimmy grunted, conceding the point. Zeke explored his pockets, looking for something soft and porous to stop the bleeding. Finding nothing immediately suitable, he grabbed Gallagher's kepi and pressed the rear of it against the bloody furrow on Jimmy's neck.

"Hey, that's my hat."

"It's *your* neck, too."

Once it was clear Gallagher would not bleed to death, the two men got down to the serious business of battling the enemy. They heard the company captain shout, "Get up boys. Give 'em hell!" Zeke and Jimmy tried their best to obey.

There was no time to do anything but load and fire the Rebels were coming on so fast. But the Fifty-Sixth had a good defensive position and gave as good as it got, despite the Rebels' numerical advantage. They fought so well that the Confederates shifted to the Union right for better pickings. They found the Twenty-Fourth Iowa in relatively open, lightly wooded terrain with no natural defensive barriers. A murderous barrage of musket and artillery fire fell on the Iowans. They retreated, exposing the right flank of the Fifty-Sixth. With fire now directed at it from the north and the west, the Fifty-Sixth's defenses began to crumble.

"Goddammit, Zeke, we gotta get outta here," Jimmy cried, raising himself to a squat while he loaded his musket.

Zeke looked around to see what the other members of the regiment were doing. Some were already retreating. Others were positioning themselves for a retreat. Very few were staying put.

"I guess you're right," Zeke said, following his friend's actions.

As they fell back, Zeke and Jimmy saw men being picked off by sharpshooters from Cockrell's and Green's brigades. They ran just fast enough to keep out of some rifleman's crosshairs. Soon, they came across the captain, who joined them without a word, the enthusiasm of his earlier exhortations apparently degenerating into an instinctive concern for life and limb. In short order, the captain was leading the way.

"Runs pretty fast to the rear, don't he?" Zeke chuckled.

"Oh, don't be so hard on the Captain. He's a good man."

Zeke couldn't tell whether Jimmy was being sincere or sarcastic.

"Never seen him run *toward* the action that fast," he said.

"Would you?" Jimmy guffawed, gasping for breath.

Zeke didn't answer but craned his neck to see what was ahead. They crossed the Middle Road that came in from the south and effectively merged into the Jackson Road at the Crossroads. Some members of the Fifty-Sixth were abandoning their muskets to quicken their running speed. Zeke and Jimmy kept theirs, though there was no time to stop and reload.

"Where we goin', Zeke?"

"I don't know, followin' the crowd, I guess," Zeke admitted, then pointed forward. "Looks like we might be headed for them trees."

"Trees is good. Trees is good," Jimmy chanted as he gazed in the direction of Zeke's finger.

The two men ran like panicked deer for the copse of trees on the east side of the Crossroads, hoping to get some lumber between them and the advancing Rebels. While he was mid-stride in retreat, Zeke heard a loud but brief buzzing sound pass by his head. Simultaneously, his kepi flew off and landed on the exposed root of a sycamore.

"Holy . . ." he shouted, belatedly grabbing at his head, where the kepi no longer resided.

"You all right?" Jimmy inquired.

With his fingers, Zeke probed his head and hair, expecting blood. He found none.

"Looks that way," he said, scooping up the kepi from the fat root. Accelerating back to his previous pace, he glanced at the kepi and found a hole through its flat top. He stuck a finger in it and held it up. "Hey, Jimmy, they shot a hole in my hat. Look"

Jimmy watched as Zeke poked his finger into and out of the hole, grinning idiotically all the while.

Eventually, they noticed that their retreating colleagues ahead of them were slowing down. Catching up, Zeke and jimmy spied a line of Union soldiers facing them, some loading muskets, others holding them at the ready. The Captain stood in front of the line, shouting orders and overseeing preparations.

"I told you the Captain was a good man," Jimmy boasted.

"You're right again, Jimmy," Zeke said, trying for a subtly sardonic intonation. "You're always right."

The line Jimmy and Zeke had run into consisted mostly of members of the Fifty-Sixth Ohio and Twenty-Fourth Iowa. They could not very well continue retreating when their comrades in arms were standing fast, and they were not inclined to. Their arrival coincided with the formation of a second line of infantry behind the front line, whose members were now kneeling in position. They loaded then waited for an organized Rebel advance. At first, all they saw were skirmishers, men taking quick aim, firing from behind tree trunks then reloading using the tree trunks as shields. The bullets buzzed whimsically through the air, punctuated by staccato bursts of clipped sound as musket balls struck hard surfaces and ricocheted off others until their momentum was spent and they fell to the ground. It was like a high-velocity hailstorm, but deadlier. Zeke counted. A man in the front row fell about every ninth whizzing musket ball. If two or three of the men in front of him were shot, he would be exposed.

Then they arrived—*en masse.* Zeke and Jimmy could not believe their eyes. Rebel soldiers were coming at them from all directions except directly behind. The intensity of the maelstrom doubled.

Zeke tried to swallow his fear. He stared directly at the Captain, who seemed surprisingly calm. Zeke was certain the man was as scared as he was and could not help admiring his courage. The Captain glanced at the line, steadying it with the power of his eyes. Muskets were leveled and stabilized. A few stopped shaking altogether. Making a final visual appraisal of his target—the horde of Confederates was no more than fifty yards distant—he dropped his hand. The muskets of the front Union rank exploded in obedience.

As did the Captain's head. Grapeshot from Rebel artillery had not so much severed it as ground it into mincemeat. Oddly, the body took a second or two to fall, during which time shrapnel from another burst shredded the Captain's trousers, exposing his underwear.

Rebels also fell to the ground, but this did little to inspire the men of Slack's brigade. The enemy was advancing relentlessly toward them, a descant of Rebel yells rising above the cacophonous symphony of death.

"Let's go, Zeke," Jimmy said.

"Yeah . . . yeah."

Like the rest of their colleagues, Zeke Jackson and Jimmy Gallagher ran for their lives. It was the only sensible thing to do.

*　*　*

George McGinnis could not fathom what was happening. Had he not just given the Rebels a good thrashing and achieved a significant victory by pushing Pemberton's army off Champion Hill and sending it packing to the north? But now a swarm of Union soldiers was streaming past, hell bent for leather toward the Champion house and safety. There must be another Confederate division out there.

"Colonel, what Confederate forces do we know of out that way?" he said to his adjutant, waving a hand at the Crossroads.

The adjutant pulled out a map and opened it wide enough to study the area around the Crossroads. Holding the map so McGinnis could see, he said, "Could be Cumming again."

McGinnis shook his head and said, "His people were scattered every which way two hours ago. He won't recover that fast."

The adjutant reflected for a moment then offered, "Maybe it's more of Bowen's men. Do we know where they are?"

"Last time we had a report, they were down by the Raymond Road."

"Had they seen any action?"

"Not that I know of."

"They could have moved up the Ratliff Road to the Crossroads."

While that possibility was being contemplated, Cockrell's men elevated it to the status of certitude. McGinnis spotted Confederate infantry rushing in their direction with bayonets fixed and grim determination painted on their faces. For an instant, the only thought that passed through the mind of George McGinnis was how hideous were the faces of men when their anger took hold.

"Get the men in line," he shouted.

The adjutant obeyed. Without hesitation, McGinnis ordered one volley, then another. The Rebels struggled to clear a rail fence, making themselves vulnerable in the process. Some made it over; some did not. Of those who did, many fell dead or wounded before their feet could carry them forward. The battle was being won, McGinnis thought. The Rebel bodies were piling up at the fence, which, by this time, was giving way to the weight of the dying flesh adorning it.

A private from the Twenty-Fourth Indiana approached, fear consuming his pimpled, young face.

"Sir, we're runnin' out of ammunition," he announced breathlessly.

"We've got them on the run, son. Don't stop now," McGinnis exhorted. Then he added, "Anyone short of ammunition needs to scavenge whatever they can. Take the cartridge boxes from the dead and wounded. We need to keep the bullets flying. Tell everyone you see those are my orders."

The private gave a choked, "Yes, sir," and disappeared into the crowd of soldiers comprising McGinnis's brigade. It was not long before he realized the extent of the problem as one musket after another fell silent. He dispatched a courier for ammunition and reinforcements. He wondered how a shortage of ammunition could become a problem. Hadn't Hovey's staff planned for such a contingency?

Apparently not. It was one of those errors born of impromptu decision-making. They had taken Champion Hill, but, in the process, had overextended themselves, particularly their lines of supply. His friend and colleague, Jim Slack, was probably in an even more critical position. His brigade had advanced to the west side of the Crossroads, not waiting for McGinnis to catch up. McGinnis did not know for sure but suspected that the stream of fleeing Union soldiers were Slack's men. *God help them.*

He concluded that, in addition to men and ammunition, he needed artillery, and sent another courier to get it. What he got was a battery of two cannons from Osterhaus's division, led by a man he knew as Captain James Mitchell, mounted atop a white, if soiled, stallion. When the artillery pieces were in place and loaded with grape and canister shots, Mitchell ordered his men to fire. The grape and canister cut a wide swath through the Rebel ranks, finally knocking down the segment of rail fence that had survived the Rebel onslaught, and generating deeper piles of human flesh.

Under the heavy fire from the advancing Confederates, Green and Cockrell finally withdrew to lick their wounds and try again. After a twenty-minute respite, they were back and as energized as ever. McGinnis tried to rally his troops, but it was a near impossible task to encourage men to fight on without ammunition. Still, the battle raged on for an hour or more, hotly contested by both armies. Eventually, it became clear that the greater Confederate numbers could not help but prevail. The first to order a retreat was Captain James Mitchell, who was promptly shot from his horse and died before he reached the ground. In a belated and ill-timed afterthought, a lieutenant colonel from the Twenty-Fourth Indiana took up the colors and, waving them provocatively, scurried toward the line of gleaming bayonets rushing at him. He was greeted by blasts from at least six Rebel muskets and toppled to the ground, instantly lifeless.

Stupid, McGinnis thought, though he would never share the opinion with anyone. Lieutenant colonels were not supposed to act that way; gratuitous bravery was not on McGinnis's list of acceptable military behavior.

"How are we doing on ammunition?" he asked the adjutant.

"Not good."

McGinnis's stomach suddenly felt queasy. He had lost so many men taking Champion Hill, and now they would have to give it back.

"Withdraw," he barked at the adjutant.

Neither the adjutant nor the other members of the brigade needed to be told twice.

★ THIRTY-FOUR ★

May 16, 1863, Escape from Champion Hill

Cockrell's euphoria was real but tentative. His men were going to retake Champion Hill; he could sense it happening. But he also knew there were several Union divisions that had not yet been detected. Where were they? As he watched his own and Green's brigades secure the hilltop, his eyes beheld a welcome sight: Carter Stevenson's Georgians were coming up in his rear, and John Pemberton was at the head of the column. Cockrell spurred his horse over to the Vicksburg commander.

"I hear we have a victory," Pemberton said, offering a semblance of a grin.

"Maybe, but I'd like to know what's coming next."

Hesitating as though it pained him, Pemberton asked, "Have you seen General Loring or his division?"

"No, but I've been busy."

The two men shared a guffaw, Cockrell's more sincere than Pemberton's. Then Pemberton became serious.

"I need to find General Loring. I ordered him to attack earlier this morning, but I don't believe he did."

As Pemberton spoke, his head swiveled around so he could observe as much of the seized ground as possible. His head paused briefly as the Champion House came into view. Then it resumed its rotation. Cockrell wondered if he was searching for Loring.

"Maybe the general was caught up in some other action," Cockrell suggested, attempting to avoid the issue.

"Perhaps, but he will be needed to support General Bowen. As a member of General Bowen's staff, I am sure you are aware of that need, Colonel."

It was a mild rebuke, about as much emotion as Pemberton ever displayed. Though he did not think he deserved it, Cockrell accepted the criticism with a nod of acquiescence. Officers like Loring annoyed him. They disliked Pemberton for no better reason than his northern origins and made no bones about expressing that animosity. He had come from the enemy's world and was, therefore, to be held suspect in the purview of southern eyes. It might have been different if Pemberton behaved like a commander and "commanded" respect. But he was frequently indecisive, reluctant, and even timid. Cockrell felt sorry for him.

"I am, sir, quite aware," Cockrell said.

As if reading Cockrell's thoughts, Pemberton sighed and said, "You know, I've been very patient with General Loring. I've sent several couriers to him, asking him to deploy his men on General Bowen's right flank. He did nothing. In his absence, General Stevenson has done a creditable job of supporting General Bowen. I only wish . . ."

"Sir . . . I don't know why you're telling me this," Cockrell interjected.

"I must apologize for allowing my ruminations to run rampant, Colonel." Pemberton snapped, and then added, "Fatigue and frustration, I suppose. I did not mean to burden you with my troubles."

Cockrell tried to look busy. By this time, the ground had effectively been secured and a perimeter established. So, he sent a medical team to find the dead and wounded and bring them back. In the midst of this activity, a slow rider arrived. Despite the slouch hat that enveloped his head nearly to his ears, it was clear that Major Jacob Thompson, Inspector General of the Army, was bald. To compensate, he sported long black sideburns that extended down to his chin but no farther than his ear lobes. It was as if Thompson's head were a mountaintop and his ear lobes marked the line above which vegetation could not flourish.

"Good afternoon, sir," said Thompson with a salute that set his slouch hat into vibration.

"Good afternoon, Major," said Pemberton hesitantly. "But it could be better."

"You are speaking about my encounter with the good General?" Thompson queried.

"I am."

Before responding, Jacob Thompson looked askance and cleared his throat.

"He will not attack," he said.

"He will *not?*"

"Yes, he will *not*," Thompson echoed, embarrassed.

Pemberton took in a deep breath, then raised a dramatic arm and swept it back and forth as if painting the scene before him.

"Look at this, Major. General Grant's headquarters are down there in the Champion House. We have a golden opportunity to deliver him a crippling blow."

He gestured toward a regiment of Alabama troops coming up on Cockrell's left, then continued with what was, for him, a diatribe.

"We have men from Alabama, Georgia, Missouri here to drive the Yankee back to where he came from. The only troops missing are those from Mississippi, General Loring's men. The only absentees are those from the state in which we are offering battle to the enemy—Mississippi. Do I find irony in that?"

A silence descended while Pemberton re-established his composure and Thompson struggled to emerge from his melancholy.

"Sir, shall I find General Bowen?" Cockrell inquired.

His equanimity refreshed, Pemberton replied, "Yes, Colonel, it appears General Bowen's division will carry the greatest part of this attack on its shoulders."

"Should I return to General Loring and give it another try?" Thompson asked.

For an instant, it seemed as if Pemberton might be ready to boil over in anger.

"Tell him . . ." he began, the repressed rage in his face shining through like a new sunrise. However, he caught himself and added, ". . . Tell him I need him to put his division in the fight as soon as possible."

Thompson was happy to go. Cockrell went to find Bowen, though he could easily have sent a surrogate. When Cockrell returned with Bowen, they found Pemberton and Green surveying the slope leading down to the Champion House, discussing the plan of battle. Pemberton looked up as the two men approached.

"John, Francis, how soon can you form up?"

Bowen scratched his head and glanced at Cockrell and Green. "An hour."

"Good, good. We won't wait for General Loring. This will be your glory, General Bowen."

As he spoke, Pemberton smiled affably at Bowen, as if presenting him with a gift. Bowen did not respond, except to murmur, "Yes, sir. We'll get right to it."

Cockrell's brigade was the first to form up and the first to charge down Champion Hill after the scattered and disoriented remnants of McGinnis's brigade. They screamed the Missouri version of the Rebel yell as they ran, a sound not unlike the howling of hungry wolves. Cockrell wondered how the Yankees would react to the infernal noise.

* * *

"They sound like ten thousand wolves howling," said Jimmy Gallagher as he fled from Cockrell's charge.

Zeke Jackson thought that was an exaggeration, but did not debate the point. He, too, was in flight.

"Jimmy, we gotta stop runnin'."

"Why?" Jimmy huffed, mystified.

"Because, we gotta find some of our own boys and re-form."

"You ain't an officer."

"No, I ain't," Zeke retorted. "But I know we're gonna lose this fight if we keep on runnin'."

"We're gonna die if we don't," Jimmy shouted, ever the pragmatist.

Zeke reflected on both his and his companion's rationales, wondering which philosophy was appropriate for the present circumstances. On the one hand, he wanted to do his best to support the Union cause. On the other hand, he didn't want to die battling impossible odds. While his mind weighed the options, he kept his legs churning and his eyes peeled for signs of a Union defensive stance he and Jimmy might join. All he saw were blue coats hastening rearward or tumbling to the ground as Confederate musket balls and artillery shells cut them down. He made his decision.

"I guess it makes sense to keep on runnin'," he said to Jimmy.

"You're damn right it does," Jimmy retorted earnestly.

"But when we get to a place where our boys are makin' a stand, we gotta join 'em. Alright?"

Gallagher's response was instantaneous.

"I'll think about it," he called.

"You gotta do more than think about it, Jimmy. You gotta do it. We're soldiers. We gotta do our duty."

Despite shortness of breath and the distraction of concentrating his energies on speed maintenance and avoiding collisions with trees, Jimmy calmly expressed his opinion.

"I'll tell you what, Zeke. If I run into Ulysses S. Grant, I'll stop and ask him what he wants me to do about the pack of wolves chasing us. But until then, I'm gonna keep on movin'. Good enough?"

Jimmy smiled. "Good enough," he said and was content to match strides with his friend.

* * *

At the base of Champion Hill, General Marcellus Crocker and his subordinate, Colonel George Boomer of the Seventh Division of McPherson's Corps, were observing as much as they could of the action. Crocker was a handsome man with a neatly trimmed beard by Civil War standards but suffered from consumption. Boomer had no serious ailments, but his eyesight was bad, imposing on his face a persistently peevish expression.

The Seventh Division had trailed in behind Hovey's Twelfth and was not completely up to speed. Although the base of Champion Hill was becoming increasingly occupied by men moving swiftly in the wrong direction, Crocker and Boomer were unaware of the disaster that had befallen McGinnis and Slack. Crocker spotted a pair of riders galloping toward them from south of the Jackson Road. When they arrived, perspiring and anxious, Crocker saw that one of them was Colonel Clark Lagow of Grant's staff.

"General Crocker, you must move instantly to support General Hovey," Lagow said, loudly enough for nearby troops to hear.

"Instantly?" Crocker echoed, trying to suppress a cough.

Lagow responded, "Yes, General McGinnis's and Colonel Slack's brigades are under heavy attack."

"Why are we just hearing this? General Hovey could have asked for help directly."

"He did, but no one listened. General Hovey is not well known in the Seventeenth Corps."

Crocker grumbled. It was a common enough problem. You always jumped when an officer of your own unit gave an order, but tended to regard the authority of less familiar officers with greater skepticism. With the organization of the army corps and divisions into brigades and regiments recruited on a state-by-state basis, there were always strangers, even at the staff level.

"I must apologize for this . . . oversight," Crocker said with practiced humility. He thought about promising it wouldn't happen again but thought better of it.

"What does General Grant want us to do?" Boomer asked.

"George, don't worry about that," Crocker said stiffly. "Just bring your brigade up and, for God's sake, get them into the fight."

Boomer saluted and quickly departed to recall his brigade. When they were told what Grant had ordered, a sustained cheer erupted, matching the intensity of the Rebel "wolf pack" that was broadcasting from the crest of Champion Hill. The deployment of Boomer's Brigade, consisting of the Ninety-Third Illinois, the Tenth Iowa, the Fifth Iowa, and the Twenty-Sixth Missouri, was so rapid that they passed and hailed the retreating members of McGinnis's brigade as they charged up the hill.

Outside the Champion House, the figure of a short, bearded man in blue could be seen in solemn observation. It was Ulysses S. Grant.

* * *

Grant was worried but, as was his habit, calmly puffed on a cigar to soothe his nerves. He would have liked some Kentucky or Tennessee whisky but that would have been neither politic nor wise. He thought his decision to send Crocker's division into the fight was a good one, but he knew that anything could go wrong at any time. The charge of Boomer's brigade, for instance. As vigorous as it had been, it was uphill, and the Rebels were at the top, taunting Boomer's men with that damned howling. Grant could see the mass of gray uniforms up there and could not completely control the fear instilled in him by the shrill, incessant noise. He took another long look at the battlefield. There was actually more gray than that displayed by the wall of enemy soldiers. The musket fire from both sides had created a gray-brown fog that hung over the combatants like an ominous thundercloud. Only the men on the flanks were visible. The rest were immersed in the infernal grayness. The only things that could be seen at the interior were muzzle flashes that came and went faster than lightning bolts. Men were dying at an alarming rate.

"Will they make it?" a resonant baritone behind Grant inquired.

The voice was that of James McPherson, but Grant was startled nonetheless.

"If they don't, we'll have to fix it," Grant replied, exhaling a stream of cigar smoke.

McPherson nodded as if he completely understood what Grant meant.

"What happened?"

"Hovey's people got separated. Then Pemberton sent in a couple of Bowen's brigades. McGinnis and Slack had to fall back."

"What's your plan?"

"The plan is to whip the Rebels," Grant replied sardonically. "Just kick them off this hill and chase them back to Vicksburg."

Both men paused as the artillery duel heated up, hoping Confederate shells were not coming their way. Grant resumed his monologue.

"That's what a lot of people don't understand about this war. It is far better to go after the enemy than it is to lie back and formulate a grand strategy. Bobby Lee understands that. George McClellan does not. It's a hard lesson to learn because you're always haunted by your mistakes. You always wonder how things might have turned out if you'd taken more time to figure it all out."

"But McClellan's men love him," McPherson said, only half-serious. He and Grant had had this conversation before.

"By God, I would too, if I was a soldier in an army that never attacked the enemy."

Grant stopped abruptly, reluctant to expand his criticism of McClellan. He turned his attention back to the battlefield.

"I sent Hovey and Boomer in. They're good troops. If the enemy tries to stand up to them, he'll feel the consequences. And if we can make a showing—even a small one—I think he'll give way."

"Are you sending in anyone else?" McPherson queried.

Grant took a moment to reflect, then said, "Yes. As good as they are, Hovey and Boomer are fighting an uphill battle."

"Who do you have in mind?"

"Sam Holmes."

"Anyone else?"

Grant stood straight and wiped his brow. The hot, muggy weather was wearing him down. It was as effective a weapon as two infantry regiments.

"John Stevenson."

McPherson grinned quizzically and said, "All *my* people."

Grant smiled back and quipped, "Well, General, you haven't done much yet. Time you did."

The two men adjourned to the Champion House to discuss tactics and deployment. Stevenson's brigade had to be recalled from duty at the Bakers Creek crossing northwest of Champion Hill. Holmes had just marched in on the Jackson Road and was awaiting orders. He got them—Charge the hill and halt the enemy advance.

Which is what he did *post haste*, filtering through the remnants of Slack's brigade, most of them now at the base of the hill. Holmes's forces, consisting of the Seventeenth Iowa and Tenth Missouri, amounted to only about five hundred men, but arrived at a moment when Bowen and Hovey's forces appeared to be battling to a stalemate. The infusion of the Holmes five hundred buoyed the spirits of the Union men and discouraged Bowen's troops. It was a tug or war, and the Union side had gained another pair of arms. They weren't especially strong arms, but they tipped the balance to the Union side.

The Confederates of Bowen and Green had no choice but to withdraw. They did so, slowly but murderously, back up Champion Hill. A mounted regimental commander from the Tenth Missouri was shot three times and fell instantly dead, a monument to the stupidity of riding a horse into an infantry battle. In response to the stubborn Rebel resistance, the men in blue charged with bayonets, killing and maiming every gray-clad body in their path. Meanwhile, the mutual artillery bombardment continued unabated, massacring blue and gray alike. To a turkey buzzard circling overhead, it would have looked like a whirlwind, with eddies of furious activity continually breaking off the main vortex and dissipating into the aether.

At first, the chaos, being chaos, did not permit a straightforward sorting of victims and vanquished. On an individual basis, Yankee and Rebel soldiers were equal. The outcomes of man-to-man contests favored neither side; as many Federals as Confederates emerged victorious from these deadly bouts. But there were more Union men now. The Rebels were slowly being pushed back.

Then it got even worse. With the late afternoon sun shining brilliantly overhead, John Bowen received a message from Martin Green that a federal column was approaching on the Middle Road. Instinctively, he glanced south. From his position on Champion Hill, he did not have a good view of the Crossroads. But he knew that, if the federal column reached the Crossroads, he would not be able to withdraw from Champion Hill, and his troops would likely be massacred or captured *en masse.*

Bowen summoned the courier who had brought the news.

"Tell General Green to hightail it to the Baker's Creek Bridge. We can't hold here."

The courier acknowledged the order with a nod, but did not ride away, merely sat in his saddle with his head bowed in dejection.

"Son, you have to get going," Bowen urged with a gentle slap to the horse's rump. The animal stirred but stayed put.

"Sir, when are we goin' to stand firm?" the soldier demanded.

"Not here. There are too many of them coming from all directions."

"But there's not much between us and Vicksburg except the Big Black River."

"I know, I know."

"It's Vicksburg, General. We can't lose Vicksburg!"

But they could lose Vicksburg, Bowen knew. A month ago, he would have bet against it, but Grant had shown his cunning and taken advantage of his numerical superiority.

"We can't afford to lose an army, son, and that's what will happen if we don't get out of here," Bowen gently exhorted. "Now go, and tell General Green to skedaddle."

This time, he gave the horse's rump a sharp slap. Horse and rider headed for the Crossroads.

* * *

As he and the Thirteenth Corps approached the Crossroads, General John McClernand wondered why he had received no definite instructions from Grant. He could hear the sounds of battle beyond the copse of trees ahead on his right. Earlier in the day, he had sent a message to Grant asking if he should attack. The heat of battle would explain some of the delay in Grant's response, but surely not the entire interval from morning to late afternoon. So his approach on the Middle Road had been slow and cautious, almost lethargic, and still was. McClernand turned to look at the men of his corps and was pleased to see them marching in good order, stretching two abreast beyond his vision. He was proud of these men from Ohio, Indiana, Illinois and Iowa, he had, in fact, recruited many of them himself. They were from the same pool Grant had drawn from before being given command of the Army of the Tennessee. But Grant had not created his own corps, as McClernand had. McClernand sorely wanted that command. He deserved it.

"Lieutenant Brown, how far is it to the Crossroads?" he asked the aide riding beside him.

"A mile or two, sir."

"Any sign of enemy activity?"

"Yes, sir, at the Crossroads," the aide replied. "We should be running into Johnny Reb pretty soon."

McClernand winced. He did not approve of casual slang, including appellations like "Johnny Reb." Such language denigrated the nobility of the soldier, even if he was fighting for the Confederacy.

"Who is doing the scouting?"

"General Osterhaus, sir."

That made sense. Osterhaus's division was the one closest to the crossroads. In fact, he now recalled that he had ordered an advance, and that had probably put Osterhaus in a good position to reconnoiter the area.

God, he loved being the commander of an army It was so much more invigorating than running for office.

"Is General Osterhaus engaged? It sounds like there's a battle going on."

"I don't know, sir."

This response annoyed McClernand, but he managed to keep the irritation out of his voice.

"Has he made contact with the enemy?"

Lieutenant Brown was pleased to be able to report something and answered, "He says the Confederates have put up a roadblock guarded by several companies. The terrain is a problem."

"What kind of problem?"

"The General says it's a god-awful mess of sharp ravines and narrow hills."

McClernand rubbed his chin thoughtfully. No commander would blithely send his men into such a chamber of horrors. While he was weighing his options, another courier arrived. He recognized the man as one of Grant's aides. The courier saluted, dismounted, and strode directly to McClernand."

"Orders from General Grant, sir," the courier said, handing an envelope to him.

"It's about time," McClernand said, opening the envelope.

"General Grant's been busy, sir. The Rebels counterattacked and pushed us off the hill."

"The hill. I assume you mean Champion Hill?"

"Yes, sir."

Concerned that Grant might be ordering him into an immediate redeployment to save the day, McClernand read the message. When he had finished, he gazed over the top of the letter at the courier.

"General Grant wants me to attack if the opportunity presents itself."

It was a firm statement but was infused with questioning overtones.

"Yes, sir."

Re-folding the letter, McClernand lifted his chin and said, "That's not very clear. I was hoping for something more . . . definite."

Caught in McClernand's rueful stare, the courier started to say something, then thought better of it. Instead, he said, "Yes, sir. Should I inform the general of your status?"

"Of course. As you can see, my command is in good order. We have not yet encountered the enemy, but will, as the general orders, do so *if the opportunity arises.* General Osterhaus is, in fact, reconnoitering the road ahead and has discovered a roadblock protected by a sizable Rebel contingent."

"Yes, sir, I spotted it on the way here. About nine Rebel companies, I'd say, not much to be concerned about."

The unsolicited expression of opinion by a mere courier rankled McClernand's sense of propriety. He straightened and presented a sterner visage.

"I'll be the judge of that," he growled.

Rather than yield to the temptation of responding, the courier looked away. He kept his eyes averted for five seconds and then turned back to face McClernand, his expression unreadable.

"Sir, I'll be on my way now," he said with a snappy salute.

Before McClernand could organize his thoughts, Grant's man was already in motion. *Damn near insubordinate*, McClernand mused, wondering if he should report the man's behavior. But the thought passed, and he was back marching with his corps, trying to formulate a plan of attack that would highlight his corps' involvement. He wasn't sure which of his commanders should lead it. Osterhaus, maybe. He had the best opportunity.

"Lieutenant Brown, take a message to General Osterhaus. Have him take that roadblock."

"Now, sir?"

"Now," McClernand confirmed.

Brown disappeared with the same alacrity as Grant's courier had. McClernand then ordered a faster pace. If his corps were to be engaged, he didn't want to be late.

Despite his hesitation in attacking a Rebel emplacement situated on unfriendly terrain, General Peter Osterhaus did as his commander ordered and advanced, however hesitantly. Based on a sighting of a Confederate force marching north on the Ratliff Road, he believed his left flank to be threatened. When Osterhaus's Ninth division finally encountered the Confederates responsible for guarding the roadblock, the Union forces overwhelmed them with surprising ease. No one was more surprised than Osterhaus himself. He had wasted precious time and missed an opportunity to crush the enemy.

* * *

Much of the action now drifted from Champion Hill to the Crossroads and points south. With the Union Ninth and Fourteenth divisions approaching from the east, Pemberton's Headquarters—just south of the Middle Road—were now threatened. The Confederate divisions commanded by Stevenson and Bowen were giving way not only to McClernand but to McPherson in the north. Concerned about the developing situation and about his own presence so near the battle, John Pemberton wondered if it might be prudent to move his headquarters farther south. Then he received a terse message from Carter Stevenson, which simply said: "Fighting sixty to eighty thousand men. Cannot hold."

The message made up Pemberton's mind. He summoned an aide.

"Lieutenant, take a message to General Stevenson. Tell him General Loring will be coming to his assistance."

"When, sir? He'll surely ask when."

"As soon as I can find him."

The aide was uncomprehending.

"*You,* sir? Are you—"

"Yes, I am. Please get me a horse."

"But, sir, you're liable to be killed or captured if you go out there alone."

"If I don't go, I'll be killed or captured right here. Can't you hear the artillery? The enemy can't be far away. I need General Loring, and I need him now. I am the only officer I know who is not under direct assault . . . except, perhaps, General Loring."

Nervously, the aide, realizing he had few arguments at his disposal that could persuade his commander, gave the requisite salute and vanished to prepare a mount. When he returned with a saddled chestnut mare, he handed the reins over.

"Sir, if anyone asks where you are, what should I tell them?"

Thrusting a left foot into the port side stirrup, Pemberton said, "Tell them I'm looking for General Loring."

"But where will that be?"

"I don't know. If I did, I wouldn't be looking for him," Pemberton replied.

"But, sir . . ."

"Look, son, just tell anyone who asks to start looking out for me or General Loring. Find one of us and the other won't be far away. And if anyone does find the good general, he had better let me know."

The last statement was spoken with a finality that shook the soldier. Pemberton realized his anger was starting to mount and made a conscious effort to douse the flames. There was nothing to be gained by taking it out on an aide.

"I've got to go," he said as he swung his right leg over the saddle.

"Sir, could you at least tell me where you're going *first*?"

"The plantation road."

"That's the Ratliff plantation road?"

"It is," Pemberton replied, and spurred his horse into motion before the aide could ask any more questions.

★ THIRTY-FIVE ★

May 16, 1863, The Battle Shifts

Pemberton did not find Loring, but he did run into Abraham Buford, one of Loring's brigade commanders, on the plantation road. To satisfy Carter Stevenson, he sent most of the brigade to him. The remainder, consisting largely of the Twelfth Louisiana, was dispatched to the aid of Martin Green,

"Where is he?" asked Colonel Thomas Scott, the Twelfth's commander.

"General Green is that way," Pemberton answered, pointing toward Osterhaus's front line troops approaching from the Middle Road.

When he looked, Scott saw not only the advance of the Union line but fleeing Confederate soldiers, probably Green's men. It was at once a disturbing and a stirring sight.

"General, I've got to go."

"You do, indeed," Pemberton agreed.

The two men made their cursory salutations. Pemberton watched as Scott assembled his regiment in battle order and directed it at the freight train that was the Yankee onslaught. Assuming that Scott had the situation well in hand, Pemberton departed to resume his search for the evanescent Loring.

Scott was halfway to the inevitable clash when he realized he was confronting not a brigade, not two brigades, but what appeared to be an entire corps. His throat turned suddenly dry. He summoned an aide and gave his orders to his men in a husky whisper.

"Fix bayonets. Do not fire. I repeat, do not fire or yell out. I need to be heard, and I can't do that if you are all screaming at the top of your lungs."

The order caused a momentary spurt of consternation, but a blanket of uneasy silence soon descended on the Twelfth Louisiana.

"Good, good," Scott said, inching his horse forward. He was still whispering. "Now let's go get them."

The Confederate line advanced, as firmly and as steadily as its Union counterpart. It received Union fire, recovered from it, gave it in return, and continued its relentless march until it was close enough for bayonets. The killing and the accompanying cries of desperation seemed to rend the very atmosphere. One of Oster- haus's regiments—the Forty-Second Ohio—withdrew from the holocaust. The first brigade, under Brigadier General Theophilus Garrard, asked for reinforcements to halt the determined Rebels. Despite their numerical disadvantage, the Twelfth Louisiana was winning.

But it was not yet a victory. In spite of Osterhaus's instinctive caution and McClernand's lack of coordination, the Union re- gained its bearings and pushed back. It could not be called a bold thrust. Once again, Osterhaus yielded to the chronic Union temp- tation to overestimate enemy strength and halted his march re- peatedly. Elements of the second brigade failed to coordinate an attack and wound up splitting off in opposite directions. Eventual- ly, Confederate cannon that had been moved from Champion Hill and used to slow the Yankee juggernaut ran out of ammunition. Then the Yankees placed *their* cannon on Champion Hill, and it was the Rebels' turn to retreat. Bowen's division withdrew, leaving Buford's brigade and the Twelfth Louisiana to stem the Yankee tide, which they somehow managed to accomplish. Then, three things happened. First, the Union artillery focused its fire on them. Second, the soldiers in blue partially encircled the brigade.

And third, Buford ran into his commanding officer, Major Gen- eral William Loring.

"Sir," Buford barked skittishly, after a curt salute. "Did you know General Pemberton is looking for you?"

"I know," Loring replied indifferently.

"Shall I send a courier?"

"If you have to," said Loring in an abrasive tone of voice. He fixed intense, humorless eyes on Buford, who was keenly aware of his antipathy toward Pemberton.

"Sir, what should I tell him?"

"Tell him we're here," Loring said, scanning the scene as if gaz- ing upon it for the first time. "Where is *here*, by the way?"

"We're on the Ratliff Road, south of the Crossroads." Buford sullenly replied. He was not anxious to become involved in the game Loring was playing.

"Tell General Pemberton I shall be leading my division into battle."

"Sir, I don't know if that's a good idea."

Loring turned his face and his horse in Buford's direction.

"Not a good idea? What do you mean? It is always a good idea to plunge your foot into the enemy's ass!"

Flustered by Loring's coarseness, Buford struggled to put words together. "I just mean that we're in retreat, sir. We can't attack and retreat at the same time—"

Buford was in a quandary. Lloyd Tilghman's brigade was protecting the Raymond Road as a vital escape route, and Featherston was currently supporting Buford. Loring made the decision for him.

"I'll take Featherston's brigade," he said with a smile.

"Where will you take them?"

"To attack, of course, as I just told you."

Suspecting that Loring was attempting to outrun whatever orders Pemberton might be issuing, Buford asked, "But if General Pemberton needs you, where can he find you?"

"On Carter Stevenson's left flank. I understand he needs the support."

Pleased to see his commanding officer would be engaged in a fruitful activity, Buford said, "That would be fine, sir. I'll get General Featherston . . ."

"One thing, though," Loring said, turning his gaze and his horse in a tight circle before he shot a glance at Buford and asked, "Which way is it to the General's left flank? I'm a bit turned around."

* * *

"I wish to God I knew where we were!" an exasperated William Loring grumbled.

"It can't be far, sir," Buford replied. "I hear cannon and musket fire all around us."

"I hear it too, General Buford. But I also *see* grass and scrub brush all around us and not one enemy soldier . . . Where the hell are we?"

"Sir, I think it must be an old farm road. We must have accidentally turned onto it—"

"I know that, but how do we find General Stevenson?"

"We have his position. It sounds like we're headed toward a battle. If we just keep on going, we're bound to run into something, maybe the Ratliff Road, maybe the Jackson Road. Then we can get our bearings."

Loring turned his head to view the columns of Buford's brigade following behind. It was an awe-inspiring sight, but not exactly the kind of awe-inspiring sight a commanding officer wished to behold. The men looked tired, as they undoubtedly were, because of the need to repeatedly remove themselves from the road when it became too hazardous or overgrown to set a secure foot upon. He tried to figure out where they might have inadvertently been diverted to this country cow path, but could not. Suddenly, reality reared its ugly head in the form of a manure pile, into which his horse stepped, exploding the foul, wet offal in all directions, one of which was upward.

"Damn!" Loring screeched as the manure missiles splattered onto his lower pant legs. "Damn and double damn! I just had those washed."

Buford, whose pants had received a lesser dose of the putrid ploppings, secretly grinned at Loring's displeasure. With as much solemnity as he could muster, he said, "I'm not sure, but I think we're going northeast."

"Why do you say that?"

Buford pointed toward the sun, which was poised in the sky over their left shoulders.

"It's after three. That's about where the sun would be if that direction is west," Buford said, thrusting a finger toward a spot below the descending orange sun.

"Yes, yes, I see," Loring murmured, prodding his horse and then shouting, "Forward!"

Loring and Buford kept the members of the second brigade in motion for another mile and a half until they emerged onto a ridge that provided a good view of the surrounding countryside. What they saw was disconcerting. Rebel forces were in full retreat. It was four in the afternoon.

"My God, the whole army is on the run," he said almost wistfully.

Loring dismounted and rushed to the nearest fleeing Confederate soldier. Grabbing the man by his collar, he yelped, "Boy, you cannot do this. If you run now, all is lost! Don't you understand?"

The man ignored his plea, shook himself off, and resumed his flight. Loring tried the same tactic on another soldier, with the same result. He was up to number five when Buford strode cautiously toward him.

"Sir, they're not cowards. They just want to live."

Loring whirled around, barely contained rage in his expression. For a moment, it seemed he might try to browbeat Buford the way he had done with the other soldiers. But his body relaxed and the blood in his face retreated.

"I call no man a coward," he said, lowering his gaze. "Least of all the loyal soldiers of our beloved Confederacy . . ." he said, on the verge of weeping. "But we must win this fight. Don't you see? Don't you see . . ."

Buford did see, and he didn't. To him, today's defeat could become tomorrow's victory. It had happened before. It could happen again. But to lose Vicksburg would be a defeat on another level, a catastrophe. That possibility was the source of Loring's lamentations.

"We must attack soon, General Buford," Loring proclaimed. "If we don't, there will be no Confederate soldiers left on the field of battle."

"Perhaps another day?" Buford suggested lamely.

Loring only scowled, dismounted, and began gathering his staff to plan an attack. One of them supplied a map, which, in the absence of an elevated surface, had to be stretched out on the ground and secured with rocks. As a member of the staff, Buford joined in. The collective wisdom of the second brigade was kneeling on the ground or bent over the map when Pemberton's *aide-de-camp*, John Taylor, arrived. Taylor quickly made his way directly to Loring.

"Sir, orders from General Pemberton," he said crisply, but with a subtle overtone of irritation. "We are to retreat."

Buford wondered what was the source of Taylor's annoyance. He suspected it might have something to do with the long search for Loring.

"Are we, then?" Loring drawled, twisting the whiskers on his upper lip as he spoke.

"Yes, definitely. General Pemberton wants you to serve as a rear guard."

"Does he, now?"

Loring turned his back to Taylor and strolled ten paces eastward, deep in thought. To Buford, he appeared to be calmly watching the rout-in-progress. Then he turned and strode back.

"What exactly does General Pemberton have in mind for us?" he asked.

Seeing the map on the ground, Taylor moved toward it and pointed at a spot on the Jackson Road west of their current position.

"The Yankees have control of the bridge over Baker's Creek here, so we can't retreat by the Jackson Road," he explained, then moved his finger farther south and added, "So we'll have to use the Raymond Road Bridge."

"Are you sure the Jackson Road Bridge can't be captured? It was my intention to take it."

"Sir, let me repeat. We are in retreat. There are Yankees all over that bridge."

Loring was crestfallen and angry. He rubbed his chin and paced back and forth within a two-yard square of ground.

"Is the Raymond Road Bridge even big enough to handle the traffic?"

"There's a ford next to it."

"Do we have people there now?"

"Yes, Lloyd Tilghman. But he's outnumbered five-to-one."

Loring's disposition seemed to brighten. Tilghman, Buford knew, despised the northern-born Pemberton as much as he did. Like most Union and Confederate officers, Tilghman was a West Pointer, but was certainly not a mental giant, having graduated near the bottom of his class. However, in this war, good academic performance was not a guarantee of success. Robert E. Lee had done well in his studies, but so had George McClellan, whose battlefield performance for the Union could hardly be considered stellar. On the other end of the spectrum was Ulysses S. Grant. He hadn't been as far down the academic totem pole as Tilghman but had made an impression in only one course of study: horsemanship.

Loring smiled and said, "Lloyd Tilghman. Yes, he's a good man, good fighter. He'll hold until we get there."

"So you will serve as a rear guard?"

"Of course I will. It's my duty."

Loring's smile transformed into a smirk.

The Raymond Road, 5:00 PM

Despite the five to one advantage of the Union, Lloyd Tilghman did his best. His cannons—eight of them—were busily exchanging fire with the Chicago Mercantile Battery and the Seventeenth Ohio Battery. The exchange produced little more than sound and fury, signifying nothing much but a desire by both sides to maintain their distance from the enemy. At one-against-five, the Rebels had the more compelling incentive.

But General Stephen Burbridge of the Union Tenth Division eventually succumbed to impatience and sent a party of skirmishers to achieve what his cannons had not. Union sharpshooters advanced to an old building that had once been a slave quarters and settled in.

John Cowan and several of his subordinates from one of the Mississippi batteries approached Tilghman, jumping at the sound of every musket ball that buzzed by.

"Damn, it's dangerous out there," he crowed. "Bullets everywhere."

Tilghman snickered as Cowan dismounted.

"I think your boys better dismount too. Those Yankees are pretty close, and I can't tell if they are tryin' to shoot you or your gray horse."

"Can't we go after them? I'm not used to being shot at from this distance."

"I sent my son out with a few of our boys. That should take care of the problem," he said, then impulsively seized his rifle from its resting place next to a tree.

"Sir, I don't think you should expose yourself . . ." cautioned his adjutant, who was kneeling to lower his own profile.

"I'll be damned if I won't take a shot at those boys myself."

He quickly loaded, raised and aimed his musket, but was distracted by a Federal shell that exploded to his left. He grinned and said to Cowan and the adjutant, "By God, I do believe those boys are tryin' to spoil my new uniform!"

Before he could get his shot off, another shell arrived. This one sent a chunk of metal through his chest. Lloyd Tilghman, nearly cut in half, fell to the ground, unquestionably dead. The adjutant stood unbelieving at the sight of the bisected corpse, thinking that this is what happens to soldiers who are not among the brightest lights in the firmament. He did not share this opinion, but, instead, grabbed his slouch hat and flung it to the ground.

"Well, General," he cried, tears filling his eyes. Now you know them boys ain't tryin' to spoil your uniform. They're tryin' to kill you, and they just did."

* * *

With the death of their commander, the members of the Mississippi artillery did not know what to do. They kept up the cannonade, but it was obvious to all that Union firepower would ultimately triumph. It was into this mood of despair that William Loring and the second brigade entered.

"Where's General Tilghman?" he demanded of the adjutant, who was the only member of Tilghman's brigade to greet him.

"He's dead, sir."

The adjutant pointed to the lifeless flesh at the base of a red oak.

"Good God, Lieutenant, have someone put him back together. We can't leave him like that."

The adjutant strode off and found a private to perform the deed. When it was done, Loring approached Tilghman.

"Well, Lloyd, what were you playing at this time, taking potshots at the Yankees? If you'd had more common sense, you'd know they can shoot damn near as well as us. They're not all city boys. I guess you know that now."

Loring bowed his head and told the adjutant and Cowan to do likewise. Then he took his slouch hat, folded his hand over the brim, closed his eyes, and softly but firmly whispered the Lord's Prayer. When he was finished, he put the hat back on.

Turning to the adjutant, he said, "Who's in charge here, Lieutenant? You?"

"Uh . . . I'm not sure, sir. I mean, I suppose so."

"Well, soldier, in the absence of anyone else, I'm going to assume you are in charge. If it turns out you are not, I will thank you to hand over the reins to whoever is. But, for the moment, you are it. Do you understand?"

"Yes, sir."

"All right then. Get your artillery shells in the air and don't let the damn Yankees take your battery."

The adjutant hastily obeyed and was surprised by his ability to bark orders and have them obeyed. He seemed to have a natural talent for it and was busily supervising the bombardment and fantasizing about his future as an officer when Tilghman's son rode in with the squad of men he had led to harass the Union sharpshooters. The jaunty ebullience in his bearing vanished when he spotted the body. He did not ride directly to it but steered his horse toward the adjutant.

"Is that . . . my Pap?" he asked hesitantly, casting an uncertain glance toward the remains of Lloyd Tilghman."

The adjutant nodded, then bowed his head. He heard a horse being urged to a trot and looked up to see Tilghman's son riding away.

"Where's he going?"

One of the men who had just ridden in answered, "I think he's goin' to go kill more Yankees. If he can kill two or three, it will do him a world of good."

The adjutant glanced at the speaker to find him staring back with a wide, yellow grin on his face. He briefly reflected on the nature of a man who assuaged his grief by killing others. Then he returned to the business at hand: Killing Yankees by blowing them to bits.

*   *   *

William Loring successfully carried out his assigned task: a rear guard action to secure the Raymond Road and protect the retreat. After the Yankees seized the Crossroads, the stream of Confederate soldiers heading west became a torrent, but it was a controlled torrent. Pemberton left Bowen with instructions to hold the western bank of Baker's Creek until all units were across the bridge and Loring was ready to join the withdrawal. Then Pemberton and his staff turned their horses toward the setting sun. It was a quiet ride.

With the Union capture of the Crossroads came an abundance of booty: cannons, ammunition wagons, Confederate regimental colors, and muskets. Grant arrived in the late afternoon to meet with generals Hovey and Crocker, whose Twelfth and Seventh divisions were leading the charge. Grant was dressed like an ordinary private with no insignia to indicate his rank. As commander of the Thirteenth Corps, of which the Seventh and Twelfth divisions were a part, McClernand was also present.

Dismounting, Grant shook the hand of each commander and staff member. A nascent smile, barely perceptible, lifted the corners of his lips. Otherwise, his face was as deadpan as his attire was undistinguished. Silently, he stepped back.

"Gentlemen, we have them on the run. Would any of you like to engage in some stimulating pursuit?"

Nervous laughter floated up from the gathering.

"Sir, I don't like to be a contrarian, but most of our people are pretty well spent," said Marcellus Crocker.

"I appreciate that, General, but the good book of military tactics says that, after you give your enemy a good licking, you're supposed to chase him down. You should know that better than I. You got an 'A' in the course."

More laughter ensued. Crocker shrugged and said, "Whoever wrote that never had to hunt down a stampede of desperate men with guns."

"Even so, I don't want Mr. Stanton at the war office telling me I'm not doing my duty."

Grant paused to look around at the collective faces of his staff. Though their eyes were downcast, he knew that most agreed with him. It was just damn difficult to convince yourself to get up off your arse after a big battle.

He turned to McClernand.

"General, some of you men have seen action today but many haven't. I'd like you to organize the pursuit."

McClernand did not want the job, but could hardly refuse, given the chronically strained relations between him and Grant.

"Of course, sir," he said with as much enthusiasm as he could muster. "I'll give it to Eugene Carr."

McClernand executed the traditional salutations and regrouped with Carr and his Fourteenth Division. Carr recommended splitting his forces in two, one under Michael Lawler and the other under William Benton. In the action that followed, Lawler ran into Loring and his rear guard and, finding the Confederates ready, willing and able, could not launch an effective attack. Most of the Rebels escaped to the west side of Baker's Creek.

Benton had better luck than Lawler if being accompanied by one's commanding officer and his commanding officer can be called "good" luck. But there was a compelling logic to this abundance of superior officers. McClernand had received word that a strong Rebel force was approaching from the west, specifically from the direction of Edwards Station. John Stevenson's brigade of McPherson's Seventeenth Corps had already crossed Baker's Creek and was in a good position to confront the Rebels. McClernand told Stevenson to halt this force and turn it back. With the help of the Sixth Missouri Cavalry, Stevenson accomplished that objective, harassing the enemy until they were in full retreat.

This gave Benton the opportunity to attack Bowen's division, which had not yet replenished its supply of ammunition. Fortunately for Bowen, Loring's rear guard was still active and gave the division precious time to get safely across Baker's Creek.

Loring did not follow.

*   *   *

Atop his roan horse, one-armed William Loring considered the situations that faced him, his own and that of the division he commanded—Tilghman's brigade. He glanced one way along the Raymond Road, then the other, contemplating his options. For all he knew, the Yankees were just around the last bend in the road. For all he knew, all Confederate forces but his had already crossed the Baker's Creek Bridge.

"Sir, may I ask a question?"

The voice was John Cowan's, the officer in charge of the Mississippi battery providing the heavy firepower.

"Of course, Captain."

"I was wondering if we should be packing up," Cowan said, his gaze drifting eastward.

Loring heaved a deep sigh and said, "Soon, soon. Can you hold until sundown?"

Cowan's sigh was heavier than Loring's. Unconvincingly, he replied, "I think so."

"You think so," Loring echoed, without sarcasm. "Well, I think I'm going to save the division, and I want you to hold until sundown . . . even if it means being captured."

Cowan squirmed, obviously unhappy at the prospect of being captured, but replied, "Yes, sir. We'll try."

Loring fixed his gaze on Cowan, wondering how he might instill a bit more resolve into the artilleryman. Finally, he barked a curt, "Good," and directed his horse eastward to apprise himself with what was happening there. He spotted a patrol of Yankees, hid in a copse of trees, then re-emerged to pursue his reconnaissance. As the sun slowly descended in the west, he spotted a man on a horse riding toward him. Fearing that it might be a Yankee, he returned to the camouflage of the woods, but, when the rider was closer, realized he wore the Arkansas version of the Confederate uniform.

"Hal-lo, soldier," he cried out as the soldier passed.

Startled, the man prepared to make a hasty getaway.

"No, no, wait," Loring shouted, steering his horse toward the man from Arkansas.

I'm Major-General William Loring of the Confederacy. Who are you?"

"Lieutenant Meshak Spencer," the young man said smartly, executing an even smarter salute.

"Well, Lieutenant Spencer, where are you headed?"

Grinning with a set of moonlit teeth, Spencer said, "Why, to see you, sir."

The message was from a member of Bowen's staff, warning Loring to get moving and get himself across Baker's Creek because several Yankee divisions were converging on the Raymond Road and the bridge.

Handing the message back to the courier, Loring said, "Lieutenant Spencer, I thank your for doing your duty, but now I must be off."

The lieutenant was startled by the speed at which Loring accelerated past him, handling the reins with his only hand. For a moment, Spencer wondered whether he should follow, but he decided not to, having already delivered the message to its intended recipient. He turned his own horse west and spurred it into action. He wondered how, or if, with all the Yankees littering the countryside, he would make it across Baker's Creek. Again he considered following Loring. Finally, he decided to try a crossing somewhere north of the bridge. If he were challenged, he would simply surrender. It seemed a proper day for it.

* * *

"Captain, are you sure this is really a road?" Loring said as his horse sank knee deep into the mud.

"It's not what I said, sir. It's what the doctor said."

The doctor was a local physician who had volunteered information on alternate routes the Confederates might use to avoid the Federals.

Continuing, Cowan said, "He didn't call it a road. He called it a path."

Loring snorted derisively and said, "I don't think it's either one. I think it's a quicksand pit."

John Cowan allowed himself a brief snicker but pressed his lips closed when Loring did not join in.

"Where are we now?" Loring demanded.

"We're traveling parallel to Baker's Creek, about a mile east of it."

Cowan took a moment to check the status of his battery, thinking that, with all the cannon and equipment they had to move, they might be falling behind. In the dim twilight, he could not see them, so he asked for Loring's permission to send a man to locate them. Loring concurred, and a young soldier was dispatched to the rear of the column. He returned with a mixed report.

"Well?" Cowan queried.

The soldier braced his shoulders as if fearful of being chastised for what he was about to say.

"They're still with us, but it's slow going with the cannons. Don't think they can keep up."

"All right, all right, no sense crowing over it," Loring scolded. "Cowan, I know I've asked you the same question about every five minutes but where the hell are we? And don't tell me we are on a path parallel to Baker's Creek. I already know that."

"As I was just . . ." Cowan began with a sigh, then said, "I would guess we're about a mile from the crossing of the Raymond and Ratliff Roads."

"Any Yankees within shoutin' distance?"

"It's a crossroads, sir. There's probably Yankees all over it. They probably got the Coker house too. It's right at that crossroads."

"Maybe they'll be in the house celebratin' their victory," Loring suggested bitterly.

Loring and Cowan exchanged glances. Cowan said, "Not much chance of that, sir. Not tonight."

Loring nodded grimly. Cowan was right. The Yankees would secure their victory before allowing themselves the luxury of mirthful indulgences.

After appraising the situation, Cowan determined that twelve cannons and seven ammunition wagons should be abandoned.

Loring agreed, and the order was given. They would have to rely on stealth to make it past the Yankees at the Raymond/Ratliff intersection. Fortunately, night had fallen, and stealth amounted primarily to moving about as quietly as possible. The infantry, in small groups, made it across the Raymond Road without alarming any Yankee sentries. The horses and the caissons were another matter. Horses could not be persuaded to step lightly, and the caissons carrying the remaining cannons were chronic noisemakers, specializing in rattles, squeaks, and the occasional groan. Miraculously, the Confederates escaped across the Raymond Road without incident.

"Where are we now, Captain?" Loring asked, half in jest.

"On our way home!" an ebullient Cowan replied.

"I think the Yankees must be drunk. What do you think?"

"I agree. A sober sentry would have heard my heart beating."

Loring ordered a southwest course, the thought being to cross Baker's Creek well downstream of the bridge and join Pemberton at or near Edwards Station. However, a few miles into the journey a red glow began to expand into the western sky like a miscreant sunrise.

"What do you suppose that is, sir?" a bewildered Cowan inquired.

"Don't know," Loring said, his gaze fixed on the glow. "Could be Edwards burning."

Cowan could only stare at the distant conflagration in disbelief.

"Do you think . . ."

"Pemberton's been captured? I wouldn't be surprised."

"We'll think on it tonight."

Loring ordered a halt to the convoy for the night and, to the extent possible, silence. Men hastily bedded down, obeying the "silence" order almost instantly, except for a persistent chorus of snorers. These recalcitrants received further silencing from their cohorts, using blankets, jackets, hats and kerchiefs placed strategically over their snoring machinery.

The next morning, most of the division was up and around by daybreak. Loring, who had risen earlier than most, stood gazing toward the northwest, already feeling the heat of the sun on his neck. John Cowan, who had risen from a troubled slumber even before Loring, joined him.

"What are you thinking, General?" he asked.

"I'm thinking the same thing I did last night. That Pemberton has been captured."

"Are you sending out a patrol?"

Loring shifted his gaze to Cowan, presenting an expression that seemed more annoyed than concerned.

"We'll send a patrol out, but we need to make alternate plans."

Cowan's jaw felt as if it were frozen in place. Eventually, he managed to utter, "Alternate plans? What do you mean?"

"I mean, Captain, that if we can't flee west, we'll have to flee east," Loring chided.

It took Cowan a moment to comprehend. Then he said, "To join General Johnston in Jackson."

Loring gave a curt nod but said nothing.

"But that would be . . . I mean it would be against orders."

"Whose orders? Pemberton's? That man has sold us down the river, but I will be damned if I'll deliver!" Loring barked, spitting the words out like musket balls.

Cowan made no counter-argument. It was not his place to do so. Loring turned his division eastward, symbolically detaching it from Pemberton's command and joining Joe Johnston, a true son of the Confederacy. In the march to Jackson, Mississippi, he lost three thousand men, a few of them as victims of Yankee marksmanship, many as stragglers who simply could not maintain the lively pace.

* * *

The Confederate exodus to the west was, if anything, more frantic than Loring's escape to the east. There was as much confusion as fear: soldiers desperately inquiring about the status and location of their regiments, mule-drawn caissons without cannons scurrying this way and that, wounded men making their way through the chaos or falling by the wayside. Those with mounts frequently found them accelerating to an uncontrollable gallop, always in a westward direction, of course.

The Federal pursuit was vigorous if not entirely enthusiastic. No one wanted to die after a battle was over. At Baker's Creek, the chase gained momentum when Grant arrived, wearing his frumpish attire: a battered slouch hat, a blue cotton blouse, and a well-worn pair of cavalry trousers. The inevitable cigar was clenched between his teeth—his best friend and pacifier. Occasionally, he brought his horse to a halt, shook a hand or two, and murmured, "Well done." His comportment had few of the elements of a victory celebration. It was more like the attitude of a man who would rather be elsewhere but knew he had to take time to recognize the auspicious moment and the men who had given it to him.

The pursuit proceeded to Edwards Station, a small railroad town a mile or two northeast of a tight bend in the Big Black River. The Federals found the railroad station and several ammunition and supply cars in flames; the Confederate demolition teams had done their jobs. This took some of the wind out of Union sails and reminded the men of the Army of the Tennessee that they had had a long day and were hungry. But there was little food. A day spent killing and maiming the enemy was a foraging day wasted. This night, they would have to go to sleep without dinner.

★ THIRTY-SIX ★

May 16, 1863, The East Bank of the Big Black River

John Pemberton was as frustrated as he had ever been and ever expected to be. Besides having two masters—Davis and Johnston—who did not even try to coordinate their orders, he was keenly aware that the battle had not gone well. He was even more aware that, to some extent, the fault was his. His frustration was flavored by a persistent despair. This was his first field command, and he had been overcautious. It had been a mistake to leave nearly half his army in Vicksburg. Or had it? President Jefferson had ordered it. Even now, he was unsure who was the wiser—Davis or Johnston.

Riding parallel to the river, along the fortifications that had been hurriedly constructed, he said to Brigadier General John Vaughn of Tennessee, "Where in God's name is Loring? He should be here by now."

Vaughn slowed his horse to avoid a tree branch belonging to one of the trees cut down to fortify the defenses.

"Could be he waited too long. Maybe he got himself captured."

Reluctantly, Pemberton nodded. Loring's capture was a possibility; there was always the threat of capture when one military unit was assigned the task of covering the retreat of another. But he found it hard to believe. Loring was simply too much of a fighter. Although he disliked the man, he could not comprehend a Loring surrender. It couldn't happen.

While Pemberton was entranced in this doleful reverie, he heard Vaughn say, "It's General Bowen, sir."

Pemberton looked up to see John Bowen riding toward him alongside the breastworks. He smiled. Bowen was a good officer. Moreover, Bowen genuinely seemed to respect him.

"John, how are things going?" he asked as he shook Bowen's hand, waiting while Vaughn did the same.

Bowen was in charge of constructing the defenses.

"It'll keep the Yankees at bay for a while. We've got five thousand men and a mile of earthworks stretching north and south. Then there's the bayou to slow down any Yankee foolish enough to make a direct assault."

Bowen pointed to the stagnant, swampy and insect-infested moat beyond the fortifications. It certainly looked formidable, Pemberton thought. That and five thousand men from Vaughn's, Cockrell's, Baldwin's and Green's brigades. The twenty field pieces mounted behind the breastworks completed the illusion of a modern army preparing for a siege by a medieval enemy.

"Any sign of Yankees?" Pemberton asked.

"Here and there," Bowen replied stoically. "It won't be long."

"Any news from Loring?"

"No," Bowen said curtly, detaching his gaze from Pemberton. "And I don't know that I expect any."

It was a curious thing to say. Pemberton was about to ask Bowen what he meant when a scout came in astride a galloping horse. He was a youngster with too much auburn hair on his head and not enough on his cheeks and chin.

"Sir," he huffed, glancing first at Bowen then Pemberton, before saluting. "We spotted some Yankees a couple miles east of here."

Pemberton reflexively shifted his gaze to the east.

"We'll probably hear them before we see them," Vaughn commented.

The three officers concurred in that opinion. It was an hour before the first artillery shells arrived.

*   *   *

Ulysses Grant had wanted to inspect the forward units deploying around the Confederate stronghold at Big Black River. It was what every field officer was expected to do, at least by him. Officers owed it to their men to put them in positions of advantage, and that could not be done from a vantage point a mile to the rear of the battlefront.

Nevertheless, the inspection would have to wait. As soon as he'd brought his horse to a halt at an observation post near the Big Black, he heard a rider approaching. Grant dismounted anyway, and lifted a pair of binoculars to his eyes, sighting toward the Confederate defenses. He heard, rather than saw, the courier dismount, then approach on stealthy feet.

"Are you from General Halleck?" Grant asked without releasing his eyes from the field glasses.

"Yes, sir," the courier replied, a note of puzzlement in his voice. "How did you know?"

Grant lowered the binoculars to chin level.

"There's no reason to ride as hard as you did to tell me the Rebels are in retreat. Besides, you tread too softly. No one who has been in an all-day battle walks on his tippy-toes."

The courier, a lieutenant whose flat cheekbones, pasty white skin and light blond hair bespoke of a Midwest farming heritage, started to speak but thought better of it.

"Read it to me," Grant said, remounting the field glasses in front of his eyes.

"It's dated May 11. The General says he would like you to co-operate with General Banks."

"Nathaniel Banks, I assume?"

"I'm sure that's who he means, sir. He wants you and General Banks to cooperate in an attack against Port Hudson or Vicksburg."

"What do you think, lieutenant? Should General Banks and I drop what we're doing and start planning a joint venture that might or might not be practical?"

The stupefaction on the courier's face was classic.

"I . . . I don't know, sir."

Allowing himself a pinch of pique, Grant said, "Of course you don't. Neither does General Halleck. How could he know? His orders are six days out of date, and his assessment of our situation is probably twelve days out of date. See those Rebels down there?"

He pointed to the Confederate battlements and handed the binoculars to the young man. The courier squinted as he raised them to his eyes.

"We just booted them off a big hill back that way," he said, flipping a thumb in the direction of Champion Hill. "They're trying to get away, and we're trying to stop them. Does it look like I'm in any position to hold a hypothetical discussion with General Banks?"

"No, sir."

"Good, you understand. And I'm sure General Banks feels the same."

"What should I tell General Halleck?"

Grant sighed, struggling with the eternal question of how to deal with the politics of command.

"I'd rather just ignore him," Grant said. When he saw the look of horror on the courier's face, he backed off "But of course we can't do that. Just tell him . . ."

The courier waited quietly but anxiously.

"Tell him we have a rare opportunity to kick the enemy's be-hind all the way to Vicksburg, and it is my intention to do just that."

"Can I just tell him you have a rare opportunity to defeat the Confederates?"

"Certainly, certainly," Grant replied, trying to hide his amusement. Obviously, the courier was not going to send a message to Henry Halleck that involved kicking anyone's "behind," even if the recipients were Confederates.

Satisfied he had done his duty, the courier returned the field glasses and departed. Grant got back on his horse and resumed his inspection, using his binoculars to study every tree branch and every mound of dirt in the Confederate battlements, searching for weaknesses.

"Who's that?" he asked an aide.

The aide looked, saw nothing. Then Grant offered him the binoculars. After placing them properly against his eye cavities, the aide gazed in the same direction Grant had. He let out a choked chuckle and returned the field glasses.

"That's Iron Mike Lawler, he said. "Looks like he's advancing."

"Refresh my memory. Who is Iron Mike Lawler?"

"He's a good man," said a voice that did not belong to the aide. It was Lieutenant-Colonel James Wilson, one of the two members of Grant's staff—the other being John Rawlins—who had been charged by Charles Dana with monitoring Grant's drinking habits. "You've probably met him. Big man. Served in the Mexican War. He's got a brigade in Carr's division. What's he doing?"

Grant took the binoculars and looked for a big man. What he saw was a fat man wearing his sword belt like a shoulder strap. The reason was obvious. The sword belt would not have circumnavigated his immense girth. He wore no coat and was sweating profusely.

"He doesn't look like a soldier, but I think he's attacking."

"He would be. He's a good tactician. Probably found a weakness in the Rebel line."

Grant nodded, wondering what Lawler had found. He executed a wide visual sweep of the pending battlefield with his binoculars and said, "Well, I hope he found something. I'm not anxious to climb over that blasted pile of trees the Rebels have stacked in front of us."

* * *

"There's a break in the trees," Colonel William Kinsman told Iron Mike Lawler. "It's up at the north flank. Don't know why it's there. It just is. Flooding, maybe. Big empty space we can just walk right through. A bayonet charge would do it."

Lawler looked at him skeptically.

"Who are 'we,' the Twenty-Third Iowa?"

"Naturally," Kinsman said with a sly grin. The Twenty-Third was his regiment.

Lawler scratched under his right armpit where perspiration had accumulated in a fold of skin. The dam burst and a wave of sweat washed down his torso.

"I like your idea, but one regiment isn't enough. Get the other regimental commanders and I'll explain how we'll do it."

Lawler seated himself at a table while Kinsman summoned the commanders of the Twenty-First, Twenty-Second, and Twenty-Third Iowa, as well as the Eleventh Wisconsin. The Twenty-First and Twenty-Third Iowa took the lead while the other two regiments served as close support and reserve. The Twenty-Third Iowa was on the right of the Union line, which meant it would receive a heavier dose of Confederate fire than the other regiments.

It did. Kinsman was wounded and fell to the ground. After struggling to his feet, he tried a few tentative steps and then fell again, this time to his death. Command of the Twenty-Third fell to Lieutenant-Colonel Samuel Glasgow, who led his men across the Confederate earthworks to a vicious confrontation with the Rebel riflemen who had lain down the barrage that killed their commander. True to Iron Mike's philosophy, the charge proceeded with speed, agility, and firepower. Confederate bodies piled up in their rifle pits as the Iowans raked it with enfilade fire.

The men of Iowa had done their job, but the violence continued. Members of the Eleventh Wisconsin and Twenty-Second Iowa followed the victorious charge. After firing one volley, they thundered over the earthworks, creating chaos as they descended upon their avowed enemy. They, in turn, were followed by the Forty-Ninth and Sixty-Ninth Indiana regiments which, with help from the Twenty-Second Iowa, assaulted and rolled up the Confederate left flank. Rebel options were reduced to two: run or surrender. The choosing of one over the other was a matter of expediency. If you were distant from the nearest Yankee, you ran. If the Yankees were on top of you, guns blazing, the only nonlethal choice was surrender.

Iron Mike Lawler was weary from exertion, but euphoric from its consequences. Carefully dismounting from his horse, he walked toward the body of William Kinsman, the man who had conceived and executed the attack. He removed his sword belt from his shoulder and fell to one knee, praying for the soul of his fallen comrade. War, it seemed, was unfeeling and unfair. The bravest soldiers were always the ones to die first. Gently, he readjusted Kinsman's body from its undignified death pose to something resembling a man sleeping on his back. Sensing the need for something more, he muttered the Lord's Prayer, then used his sword as a cane to help him to his feet. He was preparing to mount his gray gelding when another contingent of troops marched through on its way to the battle. It was Brigadier General Mortimer Leggitt of Logan's Division. When Lawler signaled him to come over, Leggitt ordered his men to halt and complied.

"Might as well let your people rest," Lawler said. "The battle is over."

Leggitt cocked his head, listening.

"Sounds like it's still on," he said.

Lawler gave Leggitt an appraising look and said, "That's just cleanup."

"Did you get many of them?"

"Acres of 'em. Whole acres," he said in a tone free of emotion.

But Leggitt's troops were not emotionless. They gave a loud, sustained cheer of victory upon hearing the news.

Lawler took a final glance at Kinsman, hoping his friend was not yet so far removed from earthly concerns that he could not hear the collective sounds of human exaltation.

* * *

Major Samuel Lockett was appalled. From his vantage point atop the high ground on the west side of the Big Black River, he observed the Confederate retreat across the bridges he had designed and built. No, "retreat" was the wrong word. It was a rout. Then he saw the wave of Union blue pushing relentlessly at everything in front of it: men, horses, caissons, some of it plunging into the waters of the Big Black rather than be crushed by the horde crossing the bridge.

Lockett knew what he had to do. Repeatedly muttering, "Damn," "Sonofabitch," and an extensive repertoire of profane epithets, he climbed aboard a horse and galloped to the bridge. Once there, he rushed to the barrel of turpentine he had stashed next to one of the bridges and searched for someone to help him. He found a dazed soldier who seemed to be defying the general consensus by not hastening westward.

"Private, help me with this," he called.

The soldier appeared to hear, glanced this way and that, and finally pointed at himself.

"Me?"

"Yes, you. Come here."

The soldier obeyed and stood waiting for instructions.

"We're going to have to burn the bridges as soon as everyone gets across. I need you to help me dump this turpentine."

The soldier looked at the barrel, the bridge and what seemed like a battalion of men who had dived into the water, preferring to swim rather than deal with the dense bridge traffic.

"We'll wait until everyone is across *and* out of the water," Lockett assured the private. "For now, let's tip this barrel over and get the bridge ready for a fiery demise."

The two men tipped the barrel over and rolled it to locations specified by Lockett, giving each a heavy dose of turpentine. Then they waited until the swarm of Confederate soldiers crossed the river and could not be injured by flames. When only a few stragglers were left, he yelled some choice expletives and waved them on. Then he torched the turpentine and watched as it engulfed the wooden cross beams and railings. It was not long before the bridge was enveloped in orange flames and black smoke. Lockett saw his helper, mesmerized by the conflagration, looking on.

"I . . . never saw such a big fire before," the soldier murmured. "Never saw one start so fast before, either."

"Turpentine is a good fire starter. Look over there."

The private switched his gaze to where Lockett's finger was pointing. A demolition party was busily setting fire to the other bridge. The private moved away, as if fearful of catching fire himself.

"Let's get out of here," Lockett ordered.

The private did as he was told, and Lockett thanked him for his assistance. As the young man hastily departed westward, Lockett assumed he would likely join the throng of Rebels soldiers removing themselves from harm's way. He could not blame the man. He felt like running himself. But he hung back instead, enraptured by his handiwork and reveling in the destructive power of the fire as it seemed to swallow the two bridges whole. He had mixed feelings about what he had just done. Clearly, the Yankees would not be able to use the bridges; he had seen to that. But he had taken pride in those structures, and, like anyone with an impulse to create hated to see his work destroyed. But it was a fact of life in the military: a seemingly endless sequence of creation and destruction.

Taking a moment to salute the doomed bridges, he turned his horse west and, moving with enough deliberation that he could not be accused of cowardice, attempted to frame his experience in a fatalistic manner. He failed.

* * *

Sherman and the Fifteenth Corps had not been engaged during the battle and were still five to ten miles east of the Big Black River, near Bolton. He was riding with Colonel James Wilson of Grant's staff, whose pioneers would be of great assistance if it became necessary to build a bridge across the river. His corps was approaching the Big Black upstream of Lockett's burning bridges, a flanking maneuver. Sherman did not anticipate immediate action and was hoping to find some place to quench his thirst, the Mississippi summer day being typically hot and muggy.

"Are you as thirsty as I am?" he asked Wilson.

"Yes."

"Look over there," Sherman said, pointing to the farmhouse of what appeared to be a well-kept plantation.

Wilson looked, saw the farmhouse, and then spotted the two Union soldiers pumping water from a well in the front yard.

Exchanging nods of approval, Sherman and Wilson spurred their horses and sped toward the farmhouse. Sherman arrived first, dismounted, and signaled a hasty "at ease" when the men snapped brisk salutes.

"How's the water?" he asked.

"Cold," said the taller of the two, who seemed pleased, even amused, to find himself conversing with the famous general.

"May we have some?" Sherman asked, adjusting his chronic scowl to a forced but friendlier expression.

The men, of course, agreed, and the tall man, a sergeant, took a ladle and scooped deeply into the wooden bucket sitting next to the stone wall that surrounded the well. He handed it to his commander.

"To luck and God's grace," Sherman said, raised the ladle to his lips, and drank. Then he handed it to Wilson, who scooped his own portion and drank heartily.

With a fretful look in his eyes, Sergeant Tom Vollmer said, "Sir, you might want to look at this."

Sherman glanced in Vollmer's direction and saw a hand extended toward him. It was holding some sort of publication.

"What is it?" Sherman asked, reaching.

"It's a copy of the Constitution."

Why, in the name of God, is this man handing me a copy of the Constitution, Sherman wondered. *Does he think I'm doing something unconstitutional?*

Noticing his commander's consternation, the sergeant said, "We found it here . . . on the ground. Notice the title page."

Sherman took the document and looked at it. On the front page was the name "Jefferson Davis."

"Well, I'll be damned. Is this his place?"

"According to the local citizenry, he shipped his belongings here for safekeeping."

Sherman grinned devilishly.

"I'll bet he didn't expect William Tecumseh Sherman would wind up with it. If he was dead, he'd probably roll over in his grave."

Sherman handed back the publication, mounted his horse, and rejoined Wilson.

"You keep the book," he said, preparing to depart. "And if you ever run into old Jeff Davis, tell him William Tecumseh Sherman would like to have a constitutional debate with him some day. I'm only guessing, mind you, but I think there must be something he's doing that might be considered *un*-constitutional."

Wilson and the two enlisted men gave appreciative chuckles. Sherman got underway, waving to the sergeant and his companion.

"Come on, Wilson, we'll probably have to build a bridge today. We've got the only pontoons in town."

The Fifteenth Corps reached the Big Black by late morning and exchanged fire with a small complement of Rebels on the western side of the river. The Rebel force did not present much of a threat and surrendered within a couple of hours. Wilson's pioneers had a pontoon bridge laid by late afternoon, and members of the Thirteenth Illinois were crossing over by 8:00 PM.

Sherman's was not the only corps with orders from Grant to cross the river and chase down the Confederates. James McPherson had similar orders, but no pontoons. To help him, Grant ordered James Wilson to report to McPherson's corps, which would cross the river north of the recently ravished Confederate bridges. Without pontoons, all that could be done was to construct wooden cribs, fill them with cotton, and lay a plank road surface on top. It was touch and go, but the biggest challenge, the big Parrot rifles, made it over without sinking the bridge. Everyone, especially the pioneers, breathed a sigh of relief. It was early next morning before all the troops and heavy equipment were on the west side of the Big Black.

The Army of the Tennessee was on the move again, slowly but relentlessly.

* * *

General Joseph Johnston was confused and peeved but wasn't sure whom he should be peeved with. On May 16, he had received a message from the Vicksburg commander informing him of

Pemberton's intention to join him at Edwards Station. But he was almost at the destination, and there was no sign of Pemberton.

"Halt the column," he told an aide. "There's no point proceeding on until we know General Pemberton's situation."

The troops were happy to relax, chat and partake of food, drink, and masculine conversation. Johnston tied his horse to a stump and seated himself on the ground, resting his back against the gnarled trunk of an ancient sycamore. He was a thin man, balding but not completely bald, with a pointed chin and jaw line that gave him an emaciated appearance. His short beard also came to a point, clinging to the contours of his face and neck. He paused to take a long look at his troops, wondering what he should do and hesitant to believe Pemberton's message completely. For one thing, Pemberton had mentioned heavy skirmishing in his front. Another imponderable was Pemberton's relationship with Jefferson Davis. It had always annoyed him that Pemberton, even though under his command, received and usually obeyed independent orders from the President. That was no way to run an army. The field generals, like himself, should be making tactical decisions, not politicians in Richmond. Unlike many of his colleagues, Johnston did not personally dislike Pemberton, but the man could not seem to make an intelligent decision in the face of Davis's obsession with saving Vicksburg.

The aide returned and stood at attention facing him.

"At ease, lieutenant," Johnston said.

The aide adopted an at-ease posture, but still did not look comfortable.

"Lieutenant, why don't you go get yourself a cup of coffee, or . . . something?"

The aide saluted and said, "Yes, sir. May I bring you a cup?"

"No, lieutenant, I just want you to get one," Johnston replied testily. He instantly regretted the show of pique and added, "I would like some hardtack, though. Can you scare me up a few bites?"

The young man smiled and said he would, then scurried off to fulfill his mission. Johnston was thankfully left to his own thoughts. He weighed the pros and cons of continuing to wait for Pemberton or returning to Jackson. He imagined a confrontation with Davis over who should exercise control over the Army of Tennessee. In his fantasy, he won the debate, and that was how he knew it was a fantasy. Davis would always win such a contest. Not only was he better positioned to do so, but his finely honed forensic skills would make mincemeat of any arguments Johnston could come up with. It might be worth a try, though, after the war, in some print medium like a newspaper or book.

A mild commotion arose, and Johnston glanced up to see what it was all about. A courier was coming in. He got to his feet as the man dismounted, strode directly toward him, and said, "General Pemberton has been defeated, sir, at Baker's Creek."

The courier had forgotten to salute. Johnston decided not to make an issue of it but instead executed his own salute. Realizing his lapse, the courier did the same, with twice his usual vigor.

"Captured?" Johnston asked, dreading the answer.

"No, sir, he is returning to Vicksburg."

Of course he is, Pemberton mused.

"Let me read the message in your hand, son."

Embarrassed, the courier unfolded the message and handed it to Johnston.

Pemberton had indeed been defeated and was withdrawing to Vicksburg. What disturbed Johnston was a decision by the Vicksburg commander to abandon Haynes' Bluff instead of spending the men and materiel to defend it. Was he so blind he could not see that this would allow Grant unfettered access to the federal fleet on the Mississippi and all it could bring him?

"Lieutenant, you will stay here until I compose a message to General Pemberton," Johnston said, then summoned his aide and, with hands in the air, added, "Paper, pen, I need them."

Writing materials were promptly extracted from the aide's saddlebags and delivered to Johnston. Using the aide's back as a writing surface, Johnston penned his message in less than a minute. Without preamble, it read:

Sir,

If Haynes' Bluff is untenable, Vicksburg is of no value and cannot be held. If, therefore, you are invested in Vicksburg, you must ultimately surrender. Under such circumstances, instead of losing both troops and place, we must, if possible, save the troops. If it is not too late, evacuate Vicksburg and its dependencies, and march to the northeast.

Very Sincerely Yours,
Lieutenant-General Joseph E. Johnston,
Department of the West

"I'll ride to General Pemberton immediately," the aide said, taking the message from Johnston.

"Do that, and please impress upon him the importance of keeping Haynes' Bluff."

"I'll try, sir," the aide stammered, uneasy at being caught in a conflict between generals.

"Do you understand what's happening, Lieutenant?"

The aide thought for a moment, then answered, "Probably not entirely, sir, I know we lost *this* battle."

"In all likelihood, we will lose Vicksburg as well. There is just no way to save her."

"But there are good fortifications. I've seen them."

"That will hold the Yankees back for a little while, maybe a month. Then they'll simply starve us out. I assume you will be going back?"

"Yes, Vicksburg is my home," the young man said, his lips quivering.

Feeling sorry for him, Johnston said, "Do they still call her the Gibraltar of the Confederacy?"

The lieutenant smiled.

"Yes."

"She's a beauty, don't you think? The way the Mississippi sashays around De Soto Point. I've never seen anything quite that lovely."

"Yes . . . I know," the lieutenant said, clearly depressed.

Experiencing some dejection himself, Johnston dismissed Pemberton's courier and took a brief, thoughtful stroll. He successfully persuaded himself that Pemberton was not coming and that he should return to Jackson. He initiated preparations to that end and satisfied himself by overseeing the departure. When all was ready, he rode to the head of the column and ordered an eastward march back to his headquarters north of Jackson.

Half an hour into the march, his aide came alongside, bubbling with good cheer.

"Sir, did you hear about General Lee?" he asked.

"No."

"General Lee has whipped the Yankees at Chancellorsville."

"When did that happen?" Johnston asked, truly curious.

"Uh, I think about a week or so ago. They're calling it his masterpiece."

"And why is that?"

"Because he divided his army and defeated both Hooker and Sedgwick," the young man gushed. "Not many armies can do that."

Johnston's spirits were both buoyed and diminished.

"That's wonderful. I'll have to send my congratulations. Thank you for the good news."

What he would like to have done was complain to the War Department about the shortage of men and materiel in his own armed force. But he dared not risk tarnishing the image of Robert E. Lee, nor was he inclined to do so. Lee was fighting the more politically significant war, having to defend Richmond against a larger, if less inspired Union army. To date, no set piece battles had been fought in any of the northeastern states, but Johnston knew Lee was searching for such an opportunity. When it came, Lee would likely gobble up the available troops to take advantage of it.

Meanwhile, Joseph E. Johnston would make do with what he had, and become known as the general who, lacking the means to achieve a decisive victory, always managed to save his army for the next battle . . . and the next.

★ THIRTY-SEVEN ★

May 18, 1863, Richmond, Virginia

President Jefferson Davis and General Robert E. Lee sat across from each other at Davis's desk in the capitol building. Davis was reading an estimate of troop strength from the War Department.

Without lifting his eyes from the printed word, he said, "General, do you really need more men? You won at Chancellorsville without even inviting General Longstreet to participate. And you defeated two armies simultaneously. It seems to me your forces are quite adequate."

Lee meshed his fingers together as if in prayer. His gaze fell to the floor and then lifted to make a wide scan of the room and its other occupant. When he finally fixed his eyes on the President, there was sadness in them.

"Mr. President, Chancellorsville is an important victory for southern morale, but it has no strategic significance. What we need to do is take the war to the Union. An invasion of Pennsylvania, or Delaware, or even Maryland would show them we are a real threat to their tranquility."

"I think you have successfully disrupted their tranquility," Davis said with a wry grin.

"But they don't fear us. We are too far from the average northern citizen to make him tremble."

Davis rose from his chair and drifted toward a window through which luminous rays of sunlight were passing. He stopped just short of being bathed in the solar radiance.

"General Johnston and General Pemberton have requested additional troops and equipment. They are faced with the possible, no, the probable loss of Vicksburg if the government does not grant their requests. I think you can appreciate the strategic significance of a northern victory at Vicksburg. It would cut the Confederacy in two. We would not be able to effectively communicate with our loyal citizens in Texas, Arkansas, and Missouri, nor would we be able to conduct commerce on the Mississippi. The loss of Vicksburg would be a great loss indeed."

Annoyed, Lee got to his feet and strolled toward his president. He did not project a formidable presence but had powers of persuasion beyond those of the ordinary military officer. Supporting assets were a gentle face and a well-trimmed, grandfatherly gray beard. When he reached Davis, their eyes met again. His were moist.

"So it comes down to a choice between Virginia and the Mississippi River. I think you know where my loyalties must fall."

"It is not a matter to be decided by blind loyalties. You are a Virginian. You would naturally have her defense first and foremost in your mind. But—"

"And you are from Mississippi!" Lee retorted.

Davis sighed and retreated to a chair in the dimly lit recesses of the room. He looked old and defeated.

"As I've said, it is not a matter for loyalties. The Yankees have already seized my home. I have nothing to lose. If it were possible to lose Mississippi and keep Vicksburg, I would do it, but it is not!"

"Mr. President, I have heard you say that we've enjoyed considerable success at Vicksburg and that, at this time of year, the rivers will become too shallow to allow the Union fleet to pass."

Davis stared at Lee in disbelief.

"General Lee, I know you are not a political man, but you must understand that there is a difference between a public speech and reality—"

"I believe you also said the summer heat in Mississippi would discourage further Union campaigns in the Mississippi Valley."

Davis's naturally gaunt face took on the mien of a death mask as he listened to his most talented commander.

"General, I can assure you that General Grant is not a man to be taken lightly. For more than a year, he has been probing our defenses, attacking our outposts, and gathering his forces—land and naval—for a final confrontation at Vicksburg. He is a most stubborn and dedicated man."

Davis's words finally gave pause to Lee's deliberations. He clasped his hands behind his back and paced across the floor space illuminated by the streaming sunlight. Then he turned back to Davis.

"Tell me about Grant," he said.

Davis inhaled and released a breath, then said, "He was in the Mexican war."

"As was I," Lee said. "But I don't remember him."

"He had a good but unremarkable record in that war. His most exceptional characteristic is his horsemanship. He excelled in horsemanship at West Point, and I am told he showed great courage in one battle by riding past a contingent of Mexican soldiers while mounted on only one side of his horse, to put the horse's body between him and them."

"It sounds reckless," Lee responded, amused. "What would have happened if the Mexicans had simply shot the horse?"

Davis allowed himself a small grin.

"They didn't."

Lee smiled and nodded his head respectfully. He could appreciate good horsemanship. His father, General "Light Horse" Harry Lee, had been known for the same skill.

"Perhaps you met Grant at West Point," Davis suggested.

"No, he was behind me. I don't think our cadet years overlapped."

"His father got him his appointment to the Academy."

"Hardly an unusual circumstance. Did he want the appointment?"

The president of the Confederacy leaned forward in his chair, clasped his hands together and looked up at Lee.

"I don't think so, but he was a good son. He obeyed his father."

"Is it true he has a drinking problem?"

"He drinks, but I'm not sure it's a problem. It doesn't seem to affect his performance on the battlefield, not adversely anyway. Lincoln said he would like someone to find out what Grant drinks, so he can send a few cases to his other generals."

Lee laughed politely. It would never enter his mind to imbibe liquor during a military campaign.

"Mr. President, I have a plan to invade Pennsylvania that I would like to discuss with you," he announced. "I want to pose a credible threat to Washington and give Lincoln and his congress something to think about, to fear. I believe this could lead to a negotiated settlement of the war with terms favorable to us."

Jefferson Davis slumped further into his chair.

"And leave Vicksburg to its own devices?"

With a heavy sigh, Lee said, "An invasion of the north should give Grant pause as well. Even if it doesn't, it could result in a shift of Union forces from west to east. That would take some of the pressure off Vicksburg."

Davis remained unconvinced but allowed Lee his moment.

"General, I think you are a realist. Frightening Grant off is by no means a certain outcome. You may even need additional troops from the west to supplement your own invasion force. Can you show me, realistically, how such an invasion would proceed?"

Lee summoned an aide to deliver maps of Pennsylvania, Maryland, and Washington, D.C. When the aide arrived, he spread the maps across the table and stepped back, allowing Davis and Lee

the best angles for viewing. The maps showed south central Pennsylvania, Maryland, parts of northern Virginia, and what was now
the Union State of West Virginia.

"We'll cross the Potomac here," Lee said, pointing to a spot
north and west of Washington, "And work our way north."

"What's the objective?"

Lee wavered a bit, then said, "We would like to capture a major city, like Philadelphia, but the main objective would be to cut a
swathe through Union territory sufficient to alarm Washington."

"And force the government to settle the war on terms favorable
to us."

"Precisely."

With his index finger, Davis traced a path starting at the Potomac, sweeping north and east and finally south in an arc that
surrounded Washington.

"It looks like a good plan. What about your lines of supply?
Can you maintain them over that kind of distance?"

"I think so. But if we can't, we'll live off the land. This is farm
country, just like Virginia."

Lee shifted his pointing finger to an area south of the Pennsylvania State capitol, Harrisburg. The settlements all had names
ending in "town" or "burg," a sure sign of rural civilization.

"I should tell you that most of my cabinet favors your plan,"
Davis said. "With one exception."

"And who might that be?" Lee asked, a bit startled. His reputation was such that few citizens, politicians included, challenged
his military judgment.

"John Reagan," Davis answered. "In fact, he has an alternate
plan."

Lee could offer only a blank stare.

"My Postmaster General," Davis prompted.

With the blank stare still operational, Lee said, "Your Postmaster Gen-er-al."

"Yes, I know he's not a military man, but he is from Texas. It's
almost the same thing."

It wasn't, but Lee overlooked the *faux pas* and listened.

". . . He is, in fact, the only member of my cabinet who hails
from a state west of the Mississippi."

Politely maintaining his equanimity, Lee straightened his posture and stiffly intertwined the fingers of both hands behind his
back."

"And what is John Reagan's plan," he asked quietly.

Davis lifted one leg over the opposite knee and tried to appear
relaxed.

"He wants you to appear to be invading Pennsylvania by making lots of noise and bluster. Secretly, however, you will be sending Longstreet's corps against Grant, thereby relieving the pressure on Vicksburg."

As he paced in the brilliance of the sunbeams, Lee brought a thumb to his mouth and picked at a front tooth with a thumbnail. Reagan's plan did have merit that he appreciated. Under other circumstances, it might be an appropriate choice. But he could not turn his back on the strategy he had devised, which he firmly believed could end the war. Then he stopped pacing and looked directly at Davis.

"I think Mr. Reagan's ideas are sound. However, I think the fact of his Texas citizenship may be clouding his judgment," Lee argued, setting aside the possibility that his Virginia citizenship might be clouding his own judgment.

"So you still want to invade the North?

Robert E. Lee paused to reflect on the words "invade the North." His father, "Light-Horse Harry" Lee, had done just that following the War of Independence. But he had done it to quash a rebellion, not promote one. The Whisky Rebellion had pitted westerners in the Ohio Valley against the agents of the new federal law mandating a tax on corn whisky. The westerners objected because the new tax cut deeply into their profits, which were already minimal because of the need to transport the corn whisky over the mountains to eastern markets. Light-Horse Harry had crushed the rebellion, sending the whisky rebels down the Ohio River to Kentucky and beyond.

Lee could not escape the irony. Here he was, fomenting a revolution against the federal government when his father had done precisely the opposite. He was not distressed, only saddened by the poignancy of his extraordinary situation. He wondered what Light-Horse Harry would have thought.

"I do," Lee replied to Davis's question. He caressed the map with his fingertips and added, "I think it is the best thing. There should be very little resistance here. As we've noted, these are all rural settlements. That can only be favorable to our cause."

Both men perused the sector of Pennsylvania Lee's fingers were brushing against. Silently, they read the names of the communities: *Littlestown, Chambersburg, Taneytown, Gettysburg* . . .

May 18, 1863, Vicksburg, Mississippi

While he rode to meet Major Samuel Lockett for an inspection of the Vicksburg defenses, John Pemberton read the latest dispatch.

John Bowen was obviously angry with him and took no pains to temper his judgment. Although Bowen referred to them as "camp rumors," he recounted several challenges to Pemberton's loyalty that he'd heard, and another that had Pemberton handing Vicksburg over to Grant. This was of course, ridiculous and pernicious, and he was distressed that Bowen felt a need to repeat such trash. Bowen also wanted a council of war, and Pemberton was inclined to give it to him. Matters would have to be set straight.

He spotted Lockett riding out from the Fort Hill battery at the north end of the city. He folded Bowen's dispatch and stuffed it into his pants pocket. The two men saluted each other, and it was Lockett who spoke first.

"General," Lockett said curtly.

"Major," Pemberton said, trying on a smile.

"I think we're in pretty good shape, sir. All the batteries from Fort Hill to South Fort are manned and well stocked with artillery and ammunition. Our entrenchments follow the high ground and surround the city out to a distance of three miles down to South Fort. There are nine bastioned forts and stockades at one to two-mile intervals all the way. And, of course, Vicksburg occupies a position high above the Mississippi, so we have a natural defense against the Union ironclads and their big guns."

"Some of their big guns can still lob shells at us, or, more likely, the city."

"That's true, sir," Lockett admitted. "But there's not a lot we can do about that except—"

"Grin and bear it," Pemberton finished.

Suitably humbled, Lockett cleared his throat and said, "Yes, sir, except to grin and bear it . . . and give back as much as we get."

Easier said than done, Pemberton thought but did not say to Lockett. There would be no point in diminishing a good man's morale. Instead, he said, "I think our batteries can give the Union fleet a sound thrashing," putting as much confidence into the statement as he could muster.

"Yes, sir, but the critical defenses are those in the east. That's the direction the main Yankee thrust will come from."

Echoing the thought, Pemberton murmured, "I agree. The Yankees will be coming at us soon if they haven't started already."

Pemberton fell silent. The word "Yankee" still felt alien on his tongue and he wondered if Lockett had noticed his distaste for the sobriquet. While he was at it, he also wondered if Lockett was among those of his officers who disapproved of him because of his northern birth. But it was only a passing thought. The major was too good a soldier to indulge in officer corps melodrama. He knew his duty and would do it, regardless of how he felt about his commanding officer.

"So what do we need, Major? Surely, we could use something."

Lockett nodded affirmatively and said, "Artillery is not a problem. We have plenty of six-pounders and thirty-pound Parrotts to keep the Yankees from entering Vicksburg at their leisure. What we really need are shovels."

Surprised, Pemberton echoed, "Shovels!"

"Shovels," Lockett reaffirmed. "We have only a few hundred. If we can't get enough shovels, we won't be able to keep up with any damage the Yankees might inflict."

Pemberton sighed and said, "I suppose that applies equally to other tools and equipment that would be needed for the same purpose?"

"Yes, of course."

As a trained military man, Pemberton was keenly aware of Vicksburg's vulnerabilities. There were many ways in which war was distinctly unlike peace. One of them was that, not only were construction and repair projects more frequently necessary, but they had to be protected against premature destruction. This effectively doubled the manpower needed to accomplish any building task, as well as doubling the materiel and equipment required, in case some were blown up or otherwise destroyed by the enemy.

Pemberton followed Lockett on a guided tour of the Vicksburg fortifications, mentally noting the needs of each while Lockett recorded the same information in a journal. When he encountered the members of his staff, he told them to be ready for a council of war the next day at the Cowan House. Noon was the designated time. After two hours, Pemberton and Lockett found themselves nearly back where they'd started—a mile east of Fort Hill. They had just inspected the Stockade Redan, the smallest of the fortifications, when Pemberton heard a distant thunder.

"What's that?"

"Cannon, probably howitzers," Lockett said, turning his head in an attempt to identify the source of the noise. He pointed back along the path they had followed from Stockade Redan. "Over there."

Returning, Pemberton asked the officer in charge, "Is that Yankee cannon I hear?"

The officer quickly nodded and said, "Yes, sir, it's got us in its sights."

As if to punctuate the statement, a shell exploded fifty yards to the north. Fragments of dirt and debris rained down on the spectators.

"How far?" Pemberton asked, brushing himself off.

The officer donned his thinking expression, thought a while, then said, "Maybe a thousand yards."

Not far enough, Pemberton concluded.

"We need that council of war now," he told Lockett and the officer. "Send the message to my staff. There will be a council of war at my headquarters at 1:00 PM."

The Yankees were coming.

* * *

The war council was held on the front porch of the Cowan House, facing the Mississippi River. The day was brilliant and the sky a cheerful bird's egg blue, but the mood was anything but spirited. Some staff members stood, some sat, all seemed to be enveloped in a pervasive atmosphere of gloom. But dejection was not Pemberton's primary concern; that was hostility. At least half his staff considered him incompetent; a smaller fraction perceived him to be disloyal. Considering both allegations, he had come to the conclusion that he was certainly not disloyal, but there might be some truth to the charge of incompetence. He had not been decisive. A good part of this was because he had to answer to two masters, Davis and Johnston, whose orders were diametrically opposed. Nevertheless, he should have learned the game, played the politics, and then made a firm decision instead of simply falling back on Vicksburg. Bit it was too late for regrets.

Pemberton strode from one man to the next, trying to lighten the mood with a smile that, even to him, seemed artificial. Finally, he turned to face the assemblage.

"Gentlemen, there will be no evacuation and no surrender. We will hold Vicksburg."

A few, disparate cheers were uttered, but none contained a spark of enthusiasm.

"So we're just going to ignore General Johnston's orders?" asked Carter Stevenson from one corner of the porch. It was phrased matter-of-factly, a statement as much as a question.

"I would not put it that way. We are not ignoring General Johnston but obeying President Davis. We can't obey both, and President Davis is obviously the higher authority."

Another wave of commentary passed through the officer corps. Pemberton was relieved that its tonality appeared to be favorable.

"How long do you expect we can hold out, sir?" Martin Green inquired.

It was a fair question, but Pemberton had no pat answer.

"I don't know. Some of you, I know, would prefer to hold out to the bitter end," he replied with a glance at John Bowen. "But I don't think that's a practical point of view. I've already stated that there will be no evacuation and no surrender, but whether or not this is a viable strategy depends on how much assistance we can get from the government. I will write President Davis that it is my intention to maintain our forces in Vicksburg as long as possible, with the expectation that the government will do whatever it can to assist us."

"Sir, by the government, do you mean General Johnston? John Bowen inquired skeptically.

"I do. If—"

"Sir, General Johnston has only six thousand men-at-arms," Bowen said. "And his orders to you indicate a reluctance to attack the enemy."

"I appreciate that, General, but I think you will agree that we must try to succeed. Strategically, Vicksburg is the most important city in the Confederacy. If we lose her, we lose the ability to obstruct the enemy's freedom of navigation on the Mississippi. And we lose *our* freedom of navigation."

It was a sobering thought that every man was aware of at some level. The silence that permeated the atmosphere gave testimony to that awareness.

"We are in agreement then? We will hold out until General Johnston arrives," Pemberton summarized, putting the most favorable spin he could on their situation.

Most of the officers grunted in affirmation.

Seeking a little more than grudging acquiescence, Pemberton studied the face of each man—Bowen, Green, Stevenson, Lee, Cumming, Reynolds—each of them a division or brigade commander in his service. Then he noticed something.

"Where is General Loring?"

To Pemberton, it seemed his entire staff averted their eyes in unison. The exception was John Bowen.

"He's not here, sir," Bowen announced.

"Where is he?"

"He didn't make it across the Big Black River Bridge. If you'll remember, you appointed him rear guard."

"Didn't make it? What do you mean? Captured? Killed? What about his people?"

"Some of them are here. A few."

"What about Loring and the rest?"

Pemberton's insistent tone prompted Bowen to step forward so he could carry on a conversation without the staff overhearing. Inhaling deeply before he spoke, Bowen whispered, "The reports are that General Loring has joined General Johnston."

Pemberton took a moment to digest the news, glancing around to gauge the reactions of the others. But they were all engaged in real or contrived conversations about real or imaginary matters.

"That's good news, then. Isn't it, General?"

"It is, sir," Bowen replied with an awkward smile. "It is certainly better than being captured by the Yankees."

Pemberton tried to laugh, but the sound emanating from his throat was more like a squeal of pain. But he kept trying.

"I suppose that means we'll see him when he comes back with General Johnston to help us clear out the . . . uh . . . Yankees."

"I suppose it does, sir," Bowen said and then cautiously excused himself.

Pemberton felt as though he were being strangled, the words were so difficult to expel from his throat. He could not afford to show it, but he was mortified. He knew Loring had not joined Johnston out of necessity, but by choice. It was, in fact, an act of desertion! And he could do nothing about it.

* * *

"Where are the Rebel trenches? Can they be seen from here?" an impatient Ulysses S. Grant demanded.

Riding beside the Commander of the Army of the Tennessee, John Rawlins pointed in the direction of Vicksburg, along the track of the Southern Mississippi Railroad.

"The entrenchments are a couple of miles that way. The railroad tracks pass right through the center of the eight-mile arc, which surrounds the city all the way to the Mississippi River. The ditch itself is ten feet deep and eighteen feet wide. It's anchored by fortifications every mile or two."

Despite Rawlins's imprecations about getting too close, Grant and the lower ranking members of his staff followed the track until they recognized the outline of a redoubt.

"Sir, I think we should go back," Rawlins said nervously.

Grant grinned and said, "Don't worry, Colonel, I don't have a stash of whisky hidden out here."

"That's not it at all, sir. I'm concerned for your safety."

"I know, I know," Grant said with a dismissive wave of the hand. "I was just pulling your leg. We can go back now."

Which they did, with Grant occasionally craning his neck rearward in hopes of spotting something interesting.

"Do we have a good map of this area?"

"Yes, sir."

"With the Rebel defenses sketched in?"

"We're still working on that, but they are pretty much what we talked about."

"I don't suppose you have the map with you?" Grant asked Rawlins.

"No, sir."

Grant nodded and said, "All right. I'll go back now. I need to see how things look, and I can't do that without a map."

"Of course, sir," a relieved Rawlins replied.

Grant did not wait, quickly turning his horse and heading north. No one knew exactly where he was going, but his pace was not so brisk he couldn't be followed. Twenty minutes later, it was clear where he was headed: Sherman's corps. Rawlins's relief gave way to a new concern. Sherman was Grant's best friend and might have a ready supply of whisky on hand. Then Rawlins felt a wave of shame pass through him. How could he be so mistrustful?

* * *

Sherman did not remove the whisky from his breast pocket until he and Grant were alone on the heights above Vicksburg. Rawlins had been sent to retrieve a map of the city and its surroundings. They could see the masts of David Porter's warships on the Mississippi. The Rebel entrenchments at Chickasaw Bluffs were no more than two hundred yards distant.

"Here," he said, thrusting the bottle at his friend. "Don't drink too much. You have a battle to plan."

"When have I ever drunk too much?"

They had a good laugh over that bit of fantasy. Grant took two swigs, handed the bottle back, and, staring into the permanent scowl on Sherman's craggy, corrugated face, said, "That'll do. I just needed a taste to sharpen my wits."

Sherman looked as if he might comment on the remark, but restrained himself and happily put the bottle away. He turned back to his colleague.

"Grant, I'm going to give you a lecture," he began. Noting the look of dismay on Grant's face, he held up a hand and started again. "It has nothing to do with your imbibing skills. I simply wanted to say that I was wrong all along. If you'll recall, I spoke against moving downriver past the Vicksburg guns."

"Yes, you did," Grant said, trying to suppress a belch.

"And I advised you to wait for your supply trains, but you did not want to wait and said we could live off the land."

Grant gave a lazy nod of affirmation.

"Which we did, and here we are," Sherman continued. "Until now, I never thought this expedition would be a success. I never could see the end clearly until now. But this campaign has been successful even if we *never* take Vicksburg."

Grant hesitated, not knowing what to make of such a show of congeniality from Sherman.

"Sherman, I'm not sure what you're up to, but I have to say I don't agree with you."

"About what?"

"About taking Vicksburg. We have to take Vicksburg or the entire campaign will be pointless."

Sherman thought about that, bit off a hangnail and spat it on the ground.

"I didn't say we shouldn't take Vicksburg. I said the campaign is a success if we do or if we don't take her."

"Her?"

Sherman put on a crooked smile and waved an arm toward the city on the hill.

"Vicksburg. She's a woman, don't you think?"

"Not my kind of woman. Too . . . belligerent."

"That's because there is no romance in your soul, Grant, You're too businesslike."

"I thought you liked my businesslike approach to battle."

"I do, but I don't like your insensitivity to feminine characteristics."

Knowing he would never outwit his friend, Grant said, "All right. Vicksburg is a woman. But we still have to capture . . . her."

"Take her," Sherman corrected.

"What?"

"Take her. You don't capture a woman. You take her. It's the male imperative."

Grant looked at Sherman as if he were out of his mind and said, "You're crazy."

"Yes I am, and you're drunk. That's why we get along so well."

Grant pointed at Sherman's pocket and said, "I've barely had anything!"

"That's clearly why we are having this disagreement. You are definitely more agreeable when you've had a few."

Grant allowed himself a muffled snicker but decided it was time to get down to business.

"I want to attack Vicksburg at the earliest opportunity; the sooner, the better. We may have Pemberton cornered, but Johnston is still in our rear. I don't want to get caught between the two."

Sherman, who shared the same fear, said, "When?"

"Tomorrow morning."

It was vintage Ulysses S. Grant. Actions spoke louder than words. The discussion was suddenly interrupted by the crack of musket fire and the muffled lament of soil being furrowed by musket balls.

"Let's move back a bit," Grant suggested.

"Good idea," Sherman agreed. "Apparently, the Rebs don't know we've already won this battle."

The two generals steered their horses to a spot fifty yards back and halted.

"Are we going to have a council of war?" Sherman inquired.

"A meeting of the minds. Don't we always?" Grant replied.

"I suppose we do, but I couldn't swear to it."

Ignoring Sherman's gibe, Grant spurred his horse and called back to his lagging friend, "One thing I'll want you to do is to take Haynes' Bluff. We're going to need it to communicate with Admiral Porter and the Navy."

"That should not be a problem."

When they were in sight of the headquarters tent where Grant had instructed Rawlins to assemble his staff, Grant turned back to Sherman.

"Have you got that bottle stashed away?"

Sherman patted his breast pocket, grinned, and said, "That, too, is not a problem."

*   *   *

Rawlins had spread the map over several surfaces, around which the ranking staff members were gathered. Grant stood on the side opposite the tent entrance to take advantage of the light. He and the corps commanders had gone over the plan several times, and there was not much left to discuss. Nevertheless, he lifted his head and caught as many eyes as he could. "Let's go through it one more time. Sherman's Fifteenth Corps will attack from the north. He'll take Haynes' Bluff while he's at it and rendezvous with Porter's people. McPherson's Seventeenth Corps will come in from the northeast, directly south of Sherman, and seize the roads leading to Vicksburg from that direction. McClernand's Thirteenth Corps will fill in between the Seventeenth Corps and the railroad."

"What about south of the railroad?" Alvin Hovey asked.

Grant shook his head and said, "Too much empty space. We can't afford to spread ourselves too thin. Most of Vicksburg proper is north of the railroad. That's where we want to be concentrated."

He paused, glancing around for querulous expressions. Finding none, he said, "Tomorrow morning then. Bright and early."

May 19, 1863, Outside the Vicksburg Entrenchments

It was a beautiful day, but, in being so, was an ugly day for a battle. The men of Grant's Army of the Tennessee were in good spirits, not because they were looking forward to the inevitable conflict—no one in his right mind looked forward to that—but because of what they had accomplished. From Grand Gulf to Jackson and back to Vicksburg, they had licked Johnny Reb soundly. In their latest encounter, they had booted him off the last major obstacle—the hill called Champion—on the way to Vicksburg. If they looked forward to battle at all, it was to have it over and done with.

As they approached the Confederate line, their confidence diminished. Johnny Reb was dug in. There were forts on the left, redoubts on the right, and stockades scattered all along the trench line. Johnny himself could not be seen, and would not become visible until he stuck his head up, which he was not likely to do unless accompanied by a loaded and shouldered musket or rifle. Trench warfare—it was something new on the battlefield. It appeared that Grant's Special Order No. 134, that, "corps commanders will push forward carefully, and gain as close position as possible to the enemy's works until 2:00 AM" might not be feasible. If it was not, the rest of the special order—to, "fire artillery volleys as a signal for a general charge along the whole line"—was a pipe dream.

To make matters worse, Special Order No. 134 was not delivered to the corps commanders until 11:00 AM, making a comprehensive assessment of the battlefield and the enemy's relationship to it an impossibility. There was little preparation and much haste. When 2:00 PM arrived, many Union troops had to cross open fields, rugged terrain and man-made obstacles just to reach their assigned positions. Finally ready to advance, Sherman's men moved toward a Rebel emplacement called Stockade Redan and were mowed down, none getting closer than fifty yards from the objective. There were heroics on the Union side, but they were to no avail. Captain Charles Ewing carried the colors to the Stockade Redan. Ten men followed him and were immediately cut off from their units until darkness fell. Then they made their way back to the Union lines, the only casualty being Ewing's partially severed finger. A musket ball had taken the missing piece when he'd planted the colors. If there were any heroics on the Confederated side of the battle line, they were not as noticeable. They weren't needed.

The attack was halted in its tracks. Major Samuel Lockett had done a fine job on the Vicksburg defenses, and General U.S. Grant had not devised and executed a plan sufficient to cause their destruction. Far more blue-clad bodies than gray-clad bodies littered the battlefield. Union losses exceeded Confederate losses by a ratio of five-to-one. To boot, there was some shirking of duty on the part of Grant's staff. McClernand, and more surprisingly, McPherson, withdrew from the action prematurely, deciding that Sherman's corps, having seen little action during the Champion Hill campaign, should have the honor of taking it to the Rebels. He did, and his corps took three-fourths of all Union losses.

The citizens of Vicksburg were delighted, an attitude they expressed by cheering at every Union repulse. If Grant was discouraged, he did not show it. He knew that self-indulgent behavior was also self-defeating, and settled into the task of planning the next assault.

★ THIRTY-EIGHT ★

May 21, 1863, Aboard the Flagship *Black Hawk*.

From the deck of the flagship, *Black Hawk*, Admiral David Porter and General Ulysses S. Grant observed the burning of the *ad hoc* Confederate naval yard on the Yazoo River. With the capture of Haynes' Bluff by Sherman, the Union Navy now had complete freedom of movement on the Yazoo. Porter's Mississippi squadron had not, in fact, initiated the conflagration with bombardment; the rebels had done that, preferring the destruction of partially built ironclads to their certain capture by Porter. Confederate leaders were in agreement that the ironclads should be destroyed.

Cautiously, the *Black Hawk* approached the docking facility at Yazoo City. The heat was intense.

"What are we doing?" Grant asked.

"Docking. Just briefly. We have to put some landing parties ashore."

"Why?"

Porter grabbed the hand railings as the *Black Hawk* gently collided with the wooden superstructure of the dock. He waved his hand toward the unfinished vessels that were being eaten by flames.

"The Rebs have done a pretty good job of accomplishing it for us, but I want to make sure no gunboats ever steam out of this place."

Grant did not argue with this reasoning, but he might have. A gunboat was a gunboat, no matter who assembled it. It seemed to him that Porter could have made good use of a few more gunboats, particularly the giant vessel that had caught his attention. But all three hundred feet of it were being enveloped in a blazing inferno. Well, he reflected, Porter must know what he's doing. Grant would not risk disrupting the harmony of Army-Navy relations by questioning his colleague's judgment.

The fire utterly decimated the Confederate naval yard. Porter then turned to the Yazoo River and its tributaries for mopping up operations. The role of the U.S. Navy was not front and center, but its actions helped to simplify communications between Grant and Porter and maintain a tight noose around the city of Vicksburg.

Without the Navy's assistance, events might have taken a different course.

*   *   *

Alone in his headquarters tent, except for the friendly flask of whisky on the table before him, Grant considered his options. He knew he had a tendency to hurry matters along and tried to resist the impulse. Joe Johnston was still on his mind. Although Pemberton had shown little skill as a commander and appeared to be digging in for a long defensive campaign, Grant was keenly aware that an attack from the east by Johnston could inspire a more offensive Confederate strategy. For the Army of the Tennessee, it would be far better to fight Pemberton and Johnston separately than simultaneously.

He made his decision. Time was of the essence. Hastily, he took a final swig from the flask and shoved it into his breast pocket. Then he summoned his corps commanders: Sherman, McPherson, and McClernand. Within the hour, they arrived to find Grant standing behind his desk, scratching the heavy stubble on his neck.

"McClernand, how do you stand that long beard of yours? I can't let mine grow an inch without scratching the skin off my neck."

McClernand smiled, but the action was submerged in the tangled whiskers surrounding his lips.

"Mine is perfectly comfortable," he replied.

"Even in this heat?"

McClernand lifted his chin as if to display the massive growth attached to it.

"I would have to say the heat is not a bother to me."

Grant stood silently, wondering if McClernand was being truthful or was simply waxing superior. He set the thought aside and tried to do the same with his dislike of the man.

"Sirs, we failed yesterday. I failed yesterday."

"We knocked out a Parrott and destroyed a redan, and our artillery . . ." McClernand began.

"None of that constitutes victory. Victory is what happens when we take ground from the enemy and keep it. Show me where we've done that."

He waited. Sherman looked as though he might say something but declined.

"Exactly," Grant said, walking around the three generals. "We didn't lose, but we didn't win either. We just lost a lot of good men."

"General Grant," McClernand interrupted. "Those entrenchments are difficult to attack. In some places, we can throw enfilade
fire down on them, but most of the time we have to wait until their
heads pop out of the trenches, which they do as quickly as they
can and then duck back down again. It is very frustrating."

"I know, I know, so here's what we're going to do . . ."

For the rest of the day, Federal artillery bombarded Rebel fortifications. This was accomplished with two big, thirty-pound Parrott rifles and twelve lesser but effective cannons. This rain of
shells demolished the Third Louisiana Redan near the confluence
of McPherson's and McClernand's corps. The three-inch rifled
guns of the Second Texas Lunette, just north of the Southern
Railroad, were also rendered non-functional.

But the relentless bombardment of May 21 was just a prelude.
On May 22, Grant again summoned his corps commanders and
had them synchronize their timepieces with his, a first in the his-
tories of warfare and timepieces. The subsequent assaults by the
three corps happened with what might otherwise have been considered astonishing simultaneity. Other innovations abounded.
Because of the fields peppered with Rebel obstructions, infantry
attacked not on the usual broad front but in columns that could
easily weave in and out of the pathways between the stone and
steel Confederate welcome mats. To allow more rapid advance,
Sherman's men built artillery emplacements along the roads leading to Rebel positions. At great risk, McPherson's gunners moved
their artillery pieces to within three hundred yards of the Confederate earthworks to provide close fire support. McClernand conceived and created a twenty-two-gun battery, hoping to devastate
the enemy with massed firepower. Union sharpshooters meticulously studied the ground and found positions from which they
shot down at the enemy without much exposure to themselves.

Despite these bold and imaginative tactics, the May 22 attack
suffered the same fate as its May 21 predecessor. "Unconditional
Surrender" Grant was not, it turned out, invincible. Men who had
advanced far ahead of their colleagues crawled back; others carelessly risked their lives to retrieve battle flags they had just risked
their lives to plant a few hours earlier. Three thousand Union casualties told the story: Gallantry was no match for wisdom, and
this battle had been unwise from the outset. The enemy defenses
were simply too strong.

As Grant gazed over the scene of wanton destruction with
Sherman, a message arrived. He opened it, did a quick read, and
scowled.

"Who's it from?" Sherman asked, curious.

"McClernand."

"What's he want?"

Grant raised the message to a good viewing elevation.

"He says he's captured two forts and has the Stars and Stripes flying over them."

Energized by the news, Sherman said, "Is that possible? Do you believe him?"

Grant cast a skeptical glance at his friend.

"I think he believes it, but I don't."

Sherman paused to wipe perspiration from his brow just beneath the rim of his slouch hat and considered Grant's statement. Neither of them thought much of McClernand as a soldier, but Sherman was inclined to follow correct military procedure, which frowned upon feuds between officers, especially generals.

"What does he want us to do?" Sherman asked again.

"He wants us to support his breakthrough," Grant said with undisguised sarcasm.

"Then I think we have to accede to his request. He's a commanding officer in the field. His judgment should be credited."

Grant lifted his slouch hat from the table and slammed it on his head, eyes gleaming with anger, and focused on Sherman.

"All right. Let's get McPherson on board and get this 'breakthrough' under way."

*   *   *

By 2:00 PM, the three Union corps were ready for a second try at the Vicksburg defenses. Having stopped the Yankees once, the Confederates were using their experience to their advantage. As it had before, the union artillery barrage came first, but there was no shock value to it. The southerners were ready. The Union advance began confidently, with steady, measured steps. The Rebel fire was equally steady. At first, the Union soldiers fell sporadically, almost as if by coincidence. As they closed on the Rebel entrenchments, they became better targets and fell in inverse proportion to their distance from the Rebel guns. Charlie Johnson and Darren McGlover of Sherman's corps were among the attackers.

"How did those fellows get so far ahead of us?" Charlie asked.

Out of breath because of the quick pace of the advance, Darren gasped, "I don't know. They were supposed to stay even with us. Bad timing, I guess."

If Charlie and Darren had been aware of Grant's "synchronize timepieces" directive, they would have shared a good laugh.

"Who are they, anyway?" Charlie asked.

Darren pointed to the officer leading the charge on their right.

"That's General Ransom," McGlover said. "His brigade is part of McPherson's corps."

"Looks like they're gonna get hell," Charlie said.

The remark was prompted by a barrage of musket fire from the enemy trenches. Ransom survived it, but a third of the men in the first Union wave fell to the ground. As they watched, Charlie and Darren saw Ransom seize the colors of the Ninety-Fifth Illinois and shout at his men until they hesitantly followed him to the Confederate line.

"This is crazy," Charlie said. "We're gonna get killed, Darren."

"Prob'ly," Darren replied indifferently.

Surprised by his friend's tepid response, Charlie said, "Do you want to get killed?"

"Course not. There just ain't much we can do about it, one way or the other. Maybe the generals will call it off when they see it ain't workin'."

Charlie grunted a note of sarcasm in Darren's direction, which was followed by a grunt of acknowledgment from Darren.

When they were close enough to the Rebel entrenchments, the commanding officer of the Thirteenth Illinois' second brigade ordered the march to a halt. Charlie and Darren were happy to comply. Both men found a tree to hide behind and started shooting, taking care not to expose themselves to the blistering Rebel crossfire.

"Well, at least Colonel Manter ain't ordered us to fire by platoons," Charlie said. We'd get our heads blown off if he did."

"He ain't ordered us to do anything but halt. If that's on purpose, I surely do appreciate it. If it's just carelessness, let's keep it a secret a while longer."

Charlie endorsed the idea with another grunt. Suddenly, an especially intense barrage filled the air with whizzing musket balls, causing the two men to hug the ground as if it were their mothers' midriffs.

"Charlie, I think the first chance we get we should go back. You're right, this is crazy," McGlover said with a quiver in his voice.

Charlie lifted his head above ground level and gazed around. The assault had not only stalled but was beginning to look like a rout. Fearful of being spotted, few soldiers were hightailing it rearward, but many were surreptitiously drifting in that direction. Even with this backward trend, others were pressing forward. General Thomas Ransom, having planted his colors, was now standing on a stump, nervously preparing himself for a rousing speech. He obviously wanted to order his men forward but kept turning to face the Rebel entrenchments, as if trying to decide which way to go.

"Back, turn back," Charlie murmured.

"What's that?"

"Nothin'. I'm just tryin' to encourage the good general a little."

"To do what?"

"To save us all!" Charlie nearly shouted.

McGlover smiled and announced, "Amen to that."

Shortly thereafter, Thomas Ransom made up his mind and ordered a retreat. Having done so, he did not immediately climb down from his stump, but remained on it, shouting at his men and pointing to a ravine further back. Charlie could not hear the words clearly, but gathered from the heading Ransom's men took that he wanted them to make their way to the ravine and find cover. Charlie unconsciously nodded his approval.

"He's tellin' them to hide in that ravine," Darren observed.

"I know, but why's he look so upset?"

"They ain't stoppin' at the ravine, that's why."

Charlie looked again and saw several Ransom men emerge from the opposite side of the ravine and resume their sojourn to the rear. He turned his head and once more spotted Ransom, straight-laced and fuming on his stump while bullets whizzed past him from more than one direction. *Enfilade fire*, Charlie concluded. It was then that Charlie realized he hadn't fired a shot in a while. He tried to raise his musket to a firing position, but Darren halted the motion with his hand and mouthed the words, "Too late for that, Charlie."

Ransom's grand posturing lasted a few more minutes before an officer, keenly aware of his own vulnerability, crawled to Ransom and pulled his pant leg. The officer said something, Ransom replied with a growl, and the officer looked away and slithered back to his shelter.

"What just happened there?" Charlie wondered out loud.

"That boy just told the General to please get his head down, and the general refused and gave him hell for it."

"Why?"

Darren shrugged and offered, "He's a general . . . and he's unhappy."

It was as good an explanation as any, Charlie concluded, and probably accurate. He could not imagine what it was like to be an officer. You had to be able to think while musket balls were trying to penetrate your head and artillery shells were trying to blow you to smithereens. Worst of all, you had to give orders that you knew would likely get men, possibly yourself, killed. It was no wonder most officers were chronically cantankerous. Better to be a simple infantryman taking orders.

"Charlie, let's go. Everybody's leavin'."

Shaking off his reverie, Charlie was startled to find Union men scurrying to safety as rapidly as their legs would carry them. He looked for Ransom but discovered the general had vacated his stump.

"I guess we better," he said, struggling to keep pace with his companion.

With Confederate muskets and cannon booming away, a chorus of Rebel catcalls driving the Union retreat, and the screams of freshly wounded men all around him, Charlie was terrified. His legs would not churn as fast as his brain directed them to; his strides would not increase on command. What good were they if he could not outrun the horror enveloping him? Despite his body's disobedience, he kept trying, kept putting one foot in front of the other, until he collided with Darren.

"Whoa, Charlie, slow down. We're here."

Mouth agape with dangling strings of spittle, Charlie finally realized what McGlover was saying. He was safe! He had outrun death! Relieved, he bent over and grasped his knees with his hands. After taking time to catch a breath, he looked around. They had returned to the point from which the attack had jumped off. Soldiers, many of them with wounds, were sucking in desperate breaths, searching for companions, seeking medical assistance, or simply groaning in pain. Nearby cannoneers were still launching their ordnance, but with less urgent frequency than before. The pervasive mood was one of defeat.

"We lost the battle, didn't we?"

Darren cleared his throat and spat on the ground. When he looked up, his face was aglow with anger.

"'Course we lost the damn battle. Can't shoot the damn Johnny Rebs if you can't see 'em."

"Think they'll come after us?"

McGlover snorted derisively.

"Hell, no. Why would they? If I was them, I'd stay in my hole and take an occasional potshot. Why get uppity when the odds are already in your favor?"

Charlie thought about that but knew he was not expected to answer. Such matters were for officers, not him and Darren. Even if he had an opinion, it didn't matter.

It was an hour before the smoke finally settled, and the only sounds were the cries of the wounded remaining on the battlefield. Having escaped death one more time, Charlie and Darren tried to relax and enjoy a cup of coffee, but found it to be impossible in the presence of those unearthly strains.

"Someone should go and get those boys," Darren said in frustration.

"And who would that be?" Charlie asked.

Darren bowed his head. Like Charlie, he knew no one would volunteer for a humanitarian mission like retrieving the wounded without an acknowledged cease-fire by the opposing commanders. It was too early for that.

At the end of another hour, a corporal arrived with a message from Colonel Manter.

"Council of War," the messenger said. "Seven O'clock at the Colonel's headquarters."

* * *

All along the line, the Union advance wavered and, as individual soldiers decided they had had enough, came to a grinding halt. A command to withdraw was given and was enthusiastically obeyed.

But the Rebels were not finished. With only a field of dead or dying soldiers before them, they recaptured the Railroad Redoubt under the leadership of General Stephen D. Lee. Outnumbered by three-to-one, they suffered only one-sixth the number of Union casualties. At this rate, the South would easily win the battle of attrition if the armed conflict continued. For the Union forces, a new, less destructive tactic was needed.

* * *

Because they arrived at 7:05 PM, slightly late, Charlie and Darren had to stand in the outer ring of the gathering outside the tent of Colonel Francis Manter, the commanding officer of the first brigade of Sherman's first division. Manter was accompanied by his regimental commanders, including the commander of Charlie's regiment. Despite the heavy losses of the day's conflict, it was a crowded affair. Manter had six regiments under his command, five from Missouri, and the Thirteenth Illinois.

When it was concluded that all were present who could be present, a trumpet blasted assembly and the soldiers lazily regrouped into ranks and quieted down. A lull persisted for thirty seconds until the sounds of boots on packed earth were heard. Colonel Manter appeared outside his tent, fifty yards from Charlie and Darren.

"At ease," he said with bowed head. Then he looked up and added, "Boys, I don't have to tell you we've had a bad day . . ."

Murmurs of agreement, not all of them friendly, arose from the crowd. McGlover's was one of the least friendly.

Raising his hands in a calming gesture, Manter continued.

"Yes, we have definitely had a bad day, but it's the first in a long time. You all remember Champion Hill, don't you?"

They did and acknowledged their recollection with a sustained cheer. But Manter's face revealed disappointment and a persistent sadness.

Raising his hands again, this time to quell the noise, Manter said with a forced smile, "But things are looking up. First thing is, we're not going to be on the attack, at least not for a while. Second thing is, we have a new weapon."

Manter halted his discourse, apparently trying to establish an air of suspense. A murmur of puzzlement buzzed through the crowd.

"What do you think it is, Darren? Are we all gonna get repeatin' rifles?"

To those who got them, repeating rifles were a godsend, an innovation that allowed them to fire four or five times faster than they could with the old muzzle loaders.

"I don't know, Charlie. Let's just wait and see. He ain't gonna keep us in the dark too long."

Manter did not keep them in the dark much longer. He signaled to a pair of officers, who disappeared briefly into the tent and then returned with two objects, each covered by a burlap sack. When both sacks were in plain view, Manter abruptly uncovered the objects. The shiny metal of a brand new pick and shovel glinted in the setting sun.

"Boys, these are our new weapons. Everybody's going to get one or the other. You may have noticed that the Rebs have been shooting at us from protected positions in their earthworks. Well, we're going to take that advantage away from them. We're going to dig our own trenches clear up to theirs and give 'em hell . . ."

Charlie was not sure, but he thought Manter might be expecting a reprise of the cheer that had arisen at the mention of Champion Hill. If he did, he was disappointed. At first, the silence was complete. Then it burst into a whirlwind of conversational eddies.

"What do you think of that, Charlie? We're gonna be gophers, or maybe sewer rats," Darren said with undisguised sarcasm.

Charlie watched Colonel Manter and the two officers direct the men of the Thirteenth Illinois and the other regiments under his command into three tents to receive their picks and shovels. He was not reassured. It was not difficult to imagine the violence that would ensue when Union boys broke through into a Rebel trench. In the narrow confines of those ugly slits in the ground, the term "fighting in close quarters" would be a gross understatement.

* * *

That night, sitting alone in his tent, Ulysses S. Grant reflected on the day's events. The May 22 assault had begun as a setback, and should have been limited to that. But McClernand's request to support his, "breakthrough" had come and Grant had agreed to it, no matter how much he might blame the decision on Sherman's insistence. He was furious with McClernand's incompetence. What had John Rawlins said after the battle? "That bastard McClernand should be charged with a thousand lives." It was true. A day of reckoning with McClernand must come, and soon.

A feeling of profound melancholy suddenly engulfed him. He leaned forward and plunged his face into his hands. He could not deceive himself. The responsibility was his, and he would have to live with it. After ten minutes of silent grieving, he strolled outside and listened. That day's battlefield was beyond the copse of trees to the west, but he could still hear the moans and wayward cries for help from the dying, most, but not all of them Union men. Oddly, the sounds of death failed to stir him. The violence of the Rebel repulse had drained him, leaving only a shallow pool of emotion in his frayed and weary soul. He needed somehow to fill it up again, if not with passion, at least with thoughtful deliberation. He thought briefly of the whisky flask in his desk drawer on the other side of the room. He even turned toward it, as if about to fetch it from its lair, but rejected the thought. The battle was over. He had been beaten back. There was no need for whisky's soothing illogic. It was time to begin preparations for the next battle. That battle would not be as much a conflict of arms as it would be a sustained assault on the nerves and stomachs of Vicksburg's inhabitants, military and civilian.

Grant readied himself for a good night's sleep, though he knew he would not have one. There was too much to think about. Joe Johnston was still out there, and would have to be dealt with. He would need to consult with his staff and Admiral Porter about many things, among them the frequency and timing of artillery and naval bombardment, and how best to stop the flow of food and supplies to the city's residents. It was a daunting task, but he could not shy away from it. He was, if nothing else, a pragmatist.

One thing was certain. By this time tomorrow, Vicksburg, the Gibraltar of the Confederacy, would be under siege.

★ THIRTY-NINE ★

May 23, 1863, Outside the Vicksburg Defenses

The front line soldiers of Sherman's, McPherson's and McClernand's corps who had not received the new "weapons" got them on the morning of May 23. They were told that the trenches to be dug were to accomplish two things: keep the Rebels inside the Vicksburg entrenchments, and provide Union access to those entrenchments. To properly locate the Union trenches, which were to be roughly perpendicular to the Rebel trenches, Grant ordered all West Point engineers under his command to the task. Charlie Johnson and Darren McGlover were assigned to a digging detail between the Stockade Redan and the Graveyard Road in the northeast corner of the Rebel line surrounding Vicksburg. They took turns with two other members of the Thirteenth, Harry Harrison and Jacob Schively, alternately digging and, when provoked, returning fire. At the moment, Charlie and Darren were resting, but keeping an eye out for snipers.

"What do you think, Charlie? Did you ever think you'd be a sapper?" Darren asked, then spat a soggy wad of chewing tobacco into the trench they and their companions were digging.

Charlie took a swig of water from one of the two canteens they had brought to deal with the oppressive heat.

"I don't know what it means. How can I be a sapper if I don't know what it means?"

"It means you're a man digging a sap."

"It's just a trench. Why don't they just call it a trench?"

"Because it's a special kind of trench that only the attacking army digs to get at the army they're attackin'. And only those kinds of trenches, these saps, get one of those things."

Darren pointed at the sap roller, basically, a large, sapling-reinforced rolling basket filled with dirt and stones that was supposed to shield the sappers from enemy fire. Harrison and Schively were busily working in its shadow, making incremental but steady progress toward the enemy line.

"But what does it mean—sap?"

"It's a foreign word for that kind of trench," Harry Harrison interjected. Of the two current diggers, he was the eldest, with a crooked posture even when he was not wielding a pickax. With a pickax in hand, his frame was like an array of interconnected wires, bent at the elbows, knees, and hips, but otherwise straight. Harry signaled a need for water, and Charlie, crouching, made his way to where Harry and Jacob were digging.

"Here you are, Harry," Charlie said, handing the canteen to his co-worker.

"I think it's a French word," Harry continued.

"Why do you think so?"

Harry gulped some water and said, "It just sounds French to me, that's all."

Charlie considered that, wondering where Harry could have gotten a sense of the French language. Was he from one of the states bordering Quebec or some other French Canadian settlement? But that wouldn't be Illinois, would it?

Harry's face suddenly broke into a smile

"I'm just pullin' your leg, Charlie. One of the officers told me. You don't have to look so puzzled."

"I'm not puzzled, just curious," Charlie stuttered, embarrassed by his apparent gullibility.

Without warning, at least three musket blasts filled the atmosphere with sound. Musket balls struck the sap roller with dull thuds; others pinged off rocks in a random search for soft victims.

Charlie heard a, "Damn!" from Darren's direction, and, as soon as he was reasonably certain no more musket balls would be launched, cautiously made his way to his friend.

"You all right, Darren?" he asked.

"No, I'm hit," Darren replied in a conversational tone.

"Where?" Charlie asked.

"Here," Darren answered, rolling up his sleeve and exposing his right forearm. An angry but shallow red gash cut across the skin.

"That doesn't look too bad."

"It ain't too bad. I was hopin' for a bullet hole so I could get out of here. That's why I cursed. It ain't even a regular hole."

Charlie studied his compatriot's expression, thinking he might be joshing. Darren's features were utterly humorless.

"You don't want to get shot, Darren," Charlie stated officiously.

"I wouldn't mind it. Really, I wouldn't, as long as it ain't a bullet to the head or heart," Darren said, grinning.

Another round of musket blasts emanated from the Confederate side of the line. This time, it was Jacob who yelped.

"You hit, Jake?" Harry cried.

"In the leg," Jacob replied.

Leaving Harry to his earth-moving exertions, Charlie and Darren crawled to Jacob's aid. Propping himself against the sap roller beside Schively, Charlie looked up and asked, "Where is it, Jake?"

Schively rolled up his right pant-leg until a rough-hewn entrance wound could be seen on the fleshy part of the calf.

"Does it hurt bad?" Charlie inquired.

"Damn right it does."

"Did it come out the other side?"

"Hell, Charlie, I don't know," Schively said, wincing in pain. "Take a look and see."

Gently, Charlie rotated Jacob's calf until its left side was visible.

"No bullet hole this side. It's still in there," he announced.

"So I gotta get it out, right?" Schively said cheerily.

"Right!" Darren agreed with nearly as much enthusiasm. "Jake, you got my bullet, you lucky devil."

Charlie glanced at the wounded man and Darren, then at Harry, who deflected his gaze and resumed digging.

"All right, I guess that's the right thing to do," Charlie said, then added for Darren's benefit, "You planning on helping him?"

"I am. Jake, how well can you move that leg?"

"I can move it, but not too fast."

"You ain't gonna be runnin' no races, Jake. Not in these trenches."

"Keep your heads down. Don't do anything stupid," Charlie admonished.

Darren removed his kepi and stuffed it in his blouse, then dropped to his hands and knees to provide support for Schively.

"Don't worry, Charlie. The Rebs ain't gonna be as anxious to shoot at outgoin' Yankees as they are to shoot at incomin' Yankees. And if they do, you can shoot right back at them."

With a contented grin, Darren oriented himself for the trip out. Schively moved to Darren's left side in order for that leg to support most of his weight. Following this, he draped his left arm across McGlover's back and the three and a half-legged beast began its ungainly departure.

Charlie waited until they were out of sight and resumed his relaxed posture against the sap roller. The scraping and thumping of Harry's pick and shovel abruptly stopped, and Charlie looked over to find Harry readying himself to occupy the space next to him.

"I need a break," Harry proclaimed, sitting down and guzzling from a water bottle.

"Is it about my time?" Charlie asked.

"In about fifteen minutes you can have the honors."

"Why do you think the Rebs don't shoot at us more often? Even with this sap thing in front of us, we still aren't completely shielded. Look at what happened to Darren and Jake. Rebs might as well keep on shootin' until they get lucky."

Harry was thoughtful for a moment, then answered, "My guess is they are trying to conserve powder, or musket balls, or something else like that."

"Why would they be running out?"

"Think about it, Charlie. We've got them under a siege. Maybe they have plenty right now, but they have to know there won't be much coming in. They have to conserve anything they don't have lots of."

Charlie found himself nodding as Harry made his case. He had always respected Harry's opinions, even more so now.

"What do you think it could be?"

Harry shook his head, which pulled the taut, parched skin more tightly over his cheekbones.

"I have no idea," he whispered.

"I hope it's bullets. Be nice if they ran out of bullets."

This comment ended the casual conversation between Charlie and Harry. It was not that there was nothing left to say, but that neither man was comfortable lowering his guard. They were only yards away from the enemy trenches. Pretty soon, with further penetration into no-man's land, they would have to bring in a squad of riflemen for protection. With only Charlie and Harry present, the current situation could quickly become critical.

"Harry, I think we should get some more boys before we dig anymore. There's just you and me now," Charlie said meekly.

Harry imbibed his final swig of water and laid the half-empty bottle by the sap roller. Grunting copiously, he lifted his puppet-like body and continued digging. After one swing of the pick, he paused to gaze down at his colleague.

"They know there's only two of us now," he said, wiping sweat from his brow. "They'll send us a couple of boys."

"At least."

"At least," Harry confirmed with a grin.

Charlie allowed his lips to form into a smile, but it didn't last. He was definitely coming undone. His lips were twitching, his limbs were shaking, an inexplicable spasm had taken over his right cheek. It was an awful place to be, would be an awful place even without the threat of death.

I'm going to die, he thought balefully. Then, in a whisper, he mouthed the same words, "I'm going to die."

Sensing his friend's deteriorating state of mind, Harry offered another toothy grin and began, "N . . ."

The rest of the statement was abruptly cut off. Charlie saw the bullet hole appear in Harry's forehead and begin draining him of his lifeblood. A fraction of a second later, Harry fell to the ground, dead.

May 24, 1863, the Willis-Cowan House, Vicksburg

"Let me understand this," John Pemberton railed at John Bowen and the quartermaster he had brought with him. "What you are saying is that we have plenty of muskets, plenty of bullets, and plenty of cartridges, but not enough percussion caps to set them off. Is that right?"

The quartermaster, a short, middle-aged, hairless captain named Samuel Kroger screwed up his dried-prune lips and stammered, "Ye-Yes, sir. We have a million cartridges without caps."

Plunging his face into his hands, Pemberton said, "How in God's name did this happen?"

"I . . . don't know, sir."

To his two subordinates, Pemberton seemed to be crying, but he was not. He was greatly distressed, but panic, though perhaps justifiable, had not yet seized his spirit. Releasing his face from his hands, he looked pleadingly at Bowen.

"What can we do?" he asked. "Is there anything to be done?"

Bowen hesitated, made a groan of complaint, and said, "We could ask General Johnston to have his people smuggle some caps in."

"In their gray uniforms? No, that won't work. And if any of Johnston's men dress as ordinary citizens, they could be shot as spies."

"What about . . ." Kroger began hesitantly.

Bowen held out his hands and wriggled his fingers in a coaxing gesture.

"Come on, Captain, what is it?"

His voice breaking, Kroger blurted, "Why not regular citizens? They have more freedom to move about than we do."

Rising to his feet, Pemberton circled around Bowen and then made his way back to the captain.

"Who are you talking about? Housewives? Children? I don't think so."

"Why not, sir? If they're discovered, the Yankees won't shoot them. They're civilians. They might be put under house arrest for a while, but they probably won't even be detained. The last thing the Yankees need is more prisoners to take care of."

"I think it's a good idea, sir," Bowen piped in.

Startled by the remark, Pemberton turned to face his colleague.

"You do? You don't see any danger? We're supposed to be protecting civilians, not exposing them."

"We can't protect them without percussion caps," Bowen pointed out.

The logic of the argument overwhelmed whatever reservations were fermenting in Pemberton's head. He sat down, pondered, got up and paced, then sat down again.

"All right, we'll try it." He said hesitantly. "But the couriers will not include women and children . . ."

"They must include women and children," Bowen insisted. "Men are much more likely to be stopped and searched. We've already enlisted the aid of several volunteers."

Pemberton looked for the captain's reaction. He saw only a shrug.

Relenting, the Vicksburg commander banged his palms on the tabletop and said, "I suppose it's acceptable, at least for the time being. Captain Kroger, you can organize the mission and supervise the people who carry it out. Just keep me informed."

"Yes, sir, of course, sir," Kroger said with a snap in his voice and propelled himself to the door and out.

Pemberton sat still, letting his nerves settle. Then he fixed his gaze on Bowen and said, "Women and children, John, We're recruiting women and children to work for us."

"*God's work*. The defense of a fine city," Bowen replied.

"No, *God help us* would be more like it."

★ FORTY ★

May 28, 1863, Outside the Vicksburg Defenses

A quarter moon was poised overhead, its gentle light diffusing through a scrim of overcast. Bobby Thomas and his grandfather's ex-slave, Benjamin Boudreau Carter, clung tightly to the floating log they had selected for the journey past the Union naval patrol boats. The log was an old sycamore with a trunk nearly three feet in diameter and an abundance of branches for concealment. Ben had insisted on the branches, arguing that, aside from the concealment they provided, a "nek-kid" log floating past him would probably look strange to the eyes of any Yankee sailor scanning the Mississippi for interlopers.

"Mister Bobby, where are you?" Ben called out, adjusting the intensity of his voice downward to avoid tickling the eardrums of nearby Yankees.

"I'm over here," Bobby replied with less caution.

"Bobby, don't talk so loud. You'll get us caught," Ben admonished.

"All right . . . all right."

Ben heard a plop, and five seconds later Bobby's head broke the surface in front of him.

"Did y'all swim under that log? I tol' you not to do that. You goin' get caught in the branches."

"A . . . ah, I done it a million times."

"Not with me aroun', you ain't. Your grandpa gonna whip me good if I let anything happen to you."

"Like what?"

"Like drownd-in, that's what."

Bobby dismissed the idea with a groan of indifference and said, "I been swimmin' in the Mississippi long as I can remember. I ain't gonna get drownded."

"Well, you ain't me, and I ain't never learned to swim."

Bobby fell momentarily silent, acknowledging the truth of the statement. Ben had been a slave until his fortieth birthday, during which time he'd had few opportunities for aquatic entertainment. He looked into his black friend's liquid eyes to see if he could find the fear in them. He did, but, being thirteen years old, ignored any feelings of empathy the experience might have engendered.

"Ah, Ben, you're a scaredy cat!" he teased.

"I am for sure a scaredy *cat*, maybe even a scaredy *sheep* or a scaredy *cow*," Ben proclaimed, trying unsuccessfully to match Bobby's carefree mood. Then he returned to the comforts of peevishness.

"What you doin' on the other side of the log? You tryin' to get found by the Yankees?"

"I was checkin' the canteens," Bobby explained.

The ex-slave snorted in frustration.

"What you need to check for? Them caps ain't gonna come out them canteens. They all corked up."

Bobby raised a finger to his lips as they approached the lead gunboat, which was bedecked with so many bright lanterns it looked like a floating dance hall.

"I wasn't worried about the corks. I was worried about the cords tyin' the canteens to the log. I thought they might've come loose."

The eyes of both Southerners bulged as the sycamore drifted toward the gunboat. Unconsciously dipping his head down to avoid being illuminated by the ostentatious display, Ben asked, "Was they good?"

"Yeah."

Although Bobby probably could not see it, Ben gave a nod of semi-approval. He was still not ready to completely sanction Bobby's surreptitious underwater excursion. He was too fearful of the Mississippi's legendary undertow, a hydraulic phenomenon that often occurred near obstacles and sudden steps in the river bottom. Even under the best of conditions, the river was suffused with wavelets bouncing like square dancers on its surface.

As they passed the gunboat, a small, pudgy sailor strolled to the edge of the deck and began urinating into the river.

"Ow-wee, let's not get too close to that," Ben joked in a whisper.

"We got twenty yards on him. We're safe," Bobby chimed in.

After a lengthy release, the sailor buttoned himself up and re-turned to his post. By this time, Ben and Bobby were approaching the huge paddlewheel, which was turning slowly. It was not clear whether the engine was driving it or the boat was at anchor and the paddlewheel was rotating in response to the current.

Any tranquility the two sojourners might have felt at getting by the gunboat was shattered by the scream of an artillery shell from the Fort Hill battery. It landed thirty yards upstream of the lead gunboat and, upon exploding, doused it with a heavy shower, but did no real damage.

"Bobby, let's get outta here. Our own people are shootin' down on us."

"They ain't shootin' *at* us."

"I know they ain't, but it don't make no difference if we get blowed up anyway."

Bobby apparently concurred in this opinion because he swam to the front of the log, grabbed a branch, and, with his legs, propelled the ungainly transport downstream. The log missed the paddlewheel by a good fifteen feet. Then Bobby's head disappeared as he entered a hydraulic. Anticipating his own entrance into the same hydraulic, Ben tightened his grip on his support branch, closed his eyes, and prayed. He gasped at the drop, submerged, and resisted the temptation to suck in a quick breath. Then he popped above the waterline and rode the churning rapids downstream. That was the worst part, he thought, listening to the sounds of the turbulent water pounding on his eardrums.

"You all right?" he heard Bobby say.

It was then that Ben realized his eyelids were still closed. He opened them and saw Bobby treading water beside him. The boy had ridden out the hydraulic by himself, without the benefit of the sycamore as a life preserver. Ben was impressed but was not ashamed of his more cautious approach. After all, he did not know how to swim.

"You all right, Ben?" Bobby repeated.

Taking a breath, Ben sighed and answered, "I'm fine . . . I'm fine."

"Good. You stay here while I check the cargo, See if we lost any."

Without further warning, Bobby bent forward and surface dived under the tree again before Ben had a chance to complain. With as much haste as he could muster, Bobby worked himself around and under the log, checking the ties and fasteners. Not only did he inspect the canteens, but, much to Ben's chagrin, moved to the downstream end of the log to determine the status of the watertight boxes filled with percussion caps that had been stored in the hollowed-out trunk. The ex-slave was afraid they might encounter another hydraulic, one that would rise up with the swirling current and crash down on Bobby while he was vulnerable. But it didn't happen. Bobby's natural caution and agile athleticism in the turbulent water kept him from harm. When he had finished, Bobby swam back to Ben.

"They're all good," he said with a mischievous grin.

"That good . . . that good."

Other gunboats were looming ahead on the starboard side of the log, but none had as many lights as the lead gunboat, and the current was sweeping the two travelers closer to the Vicksburg shore. Here, a natural if small bay formed by two rock outcroppings slowed the current, allowing Ben and Bobby a brief respite.

Sensitive to the ex-slave's anxiety, Bobby said, "We're almost there, have to get by a few more boats and then we'll pull her into shore. See that on the other side?"

Ben swung his head in the direction Bobby was pointing across the river. He didn't see much except some big machines and what looked like the mouth of another stream.

"You mean them big machines?"

"Yeah, the machines and the opening in the shoreline. That's De Soto Point and that outlet is Grant's Canal. You know what Grant's Canal is?"

The glossy, black skin of Ben's face wrinkled in perplexity.

"I heard of it, but I don't know what it is."

Bobby chortled into the water, making a gurgling noise.

"Those big machines are earth-movers, steam-driven earth-movers," Bobby explained with obvious excitement in his voice. "General Grant got that canal dug nearly all the way across De Soto Point.

"Why he do that?"

"So he could bring his boats past Vicksburg without getting them shot out of the water by our boys."

"Mr. Grant must be a hard man. I wouldn't want to set me the task of diggin' up a whole river."

"It didn't work, though. The canal caved in before they could dig deep enough to let the boats with the deepest drafts pass through."

"What's a draft?"

"It's how far below the waterline a boat has to sink before it floats," Bobby said, giving the log a friendly pat. "This old boy has maybe two feet of draft. He's what you call *buoyant*."

Ben had no idea what buoyant meant and decided to refrain from asking another potentially stupid question. They drifted beyond the small bay, and the current picked up again, but never to a troublesome degree. Once the flotilla of Union patrol boats had been left behind, the sojourners searched for the red lantern that would signal where they were to land. It was another five minutes before a faint scarlet dot came into view.

"Theah it is!" Ben cried, pointing

"Good . . . good. Now we gotta get this thing to shore. Ben, do you know how to kick your legs in the water?"

"No, but I reckon I can give it a try," the black man replied.

Bobby said, "Don't kick like you run. Kick like a frog does."

"Huh?" Ben mumbled. "What you mean, kick like a frog?"

"Move both legs together, like scissors. It's easier than just kickin'," Bobby instructed. "If I could show you, I would, but my legs are underwater and it's dark."

Ben mulled over Bobby's proposal and tried to remember how a frog moved. He'd seen them jump, and wondered if that was what his young friend meant. Tightening his grip on his support branch, he tried to execute the machinations of a jumping frog. After several attempts, several of which rolled him onto his back, he felt the force of his thrusts pushing against the water."

"Hey, I think I done it," he exclaimed happily.

"Good. Now you have to move over here with me and do it."

"Why I gotta be on that side?"

Ben heard Bobby sigh in frustration, then regain his equanimity and calmly reply, "Because you're on the shore side of the log. If you kick from that side, you'll be pushing us farther out into the river . . ."

Before Bobby finished his explanation, the ex-slave had figured it out. Chiding himself for his ignorance, he said, "Right, right. But how I supposed to get over there? I can't duck under this log like you do. I drownd if I try that."

The two *ad hoc* sailors fell silent while considering what to do. Finally, Bobby spoke.

"Ben, tell you what. I'm gonna push this tree around until it's aimed at the shore instead of downstream. When I yell, you start kickin'. Can you do that?"

"I surely can," Ben replied with more confidence than he felt.

Though he could not see Bobby very well, Ben heard the boy's heavy breathing and the occasional splash of his feet breaking the surface of the water. Then he felt the log slowly swing around until the trunk was pointed at the shore. Bobby yelled "Go" and Ben began churning up the water with his legs. Within a minute, he was panting for breath but steadfastly continued the action.

"We almost theah, Mr. Bobby?" he gurgled.

"We're about fifty yards away. Be able to stand up pretty soon," Bobby said matter-of -factly.

Ben turned his attention to the red lantern, now closer and rushing toward them at a good pace. He quickly realized the movement was an illusion and that they were actually rushing toward the lantern instead of vice-versa. He kicked as hard as he could for another thirty seconds and then felt his feet touch the muddy riverbed.

"Hallelujah!" he murmured under his breath while he dug in his heels, bringing the big log to a halt. Together, Bobby and he pulled the trunk end onshore twenty yards downstream of the red lantern, which was now actually moving toward them.

"Bobby Thomas?" a chirping voice called.

"Mr. Ransford?" Bobby inquired hesitantly.

"Yes, yes, it's me. It's us," the voice replied.

Bobby was still for a moment, then whispered, "Who is 'us'?"

Ben could appreciate Bobby's concern. Harold Ransford, who owned a saddle shop in Vicksburg, was a slight but energetic man who had talked to Bobby's father and recruited Ben and Bobby for the "mission" of smuggling percussion caps to the Confederate forces defending Vicksburg. Ransford had wanted Bobby first and foremost, the logic being that the Yankees would not suspect a thirteen-year-old boy of being capable of conducting such a clandestine operation. But Bobby knew his way around the river, and his father was a dedicated Rebel. The fact that Bobby wanted to do it sealed the deal.

With Ben, it was different. He hadn't wanted to do it but felt a debt of gratitude to Mr. Thomas for setting him free. So here he was, soaking wet and about to be confronted by white men, all but one of whom he had yet to identify.

"Mr. Ransford, can you show me your face and tell me who else you got with you?" Bobby whispered cautiously.

"Sure thing," Ransford said, placing the lantern under his chin, the effect of which was to transform his face into a ghoulish mask of light and shadow.

Moving the light toward his two companions, Ransford said, "These two fellas are Jackson Toliver and Jesse Moonbeam."

Ransford positioned the lantern under each face, creating more ghostly illusions. Without a smile to soften the bleak contrasts, Moonbeam's expression seemed particularly frightening. Ben studied both men. He knew Toliver owned a small hardware store at the south end of town that Bobby's father occasionally used for nails and tools. He was not acquainted with Moonbeam, who still had not cracked a smile. Ben dare not say it, but he thought "Moonbeam" would be a good name for one of those tribes of white people who spent most of their time in the mountains making *hooch* and interbreeding with their own kind.

"Who you got with you?" Ransford's deep bass voice demanded to know.

He leveled the lantern below Ben's chin.

"This here is Benjamin Boudreau Carter," he announced.

"He's a Nigra!" Moonbeam protested.

"He's a good man, Jesse," Ransford chimed in. "He's also a free man and a loyal Mississippian."

Moonbeam was clearly unhappy to find himself working beside a black man. He stomped his feet and mumbled a few profanities while the others waited for the petulant squall to subside.

"Well, are we gonna get those caps or not?" Toliver said, his annoyance evident.

After a pause to gauge Moonbeam's inclinations, Bobby led the way to the log's cache of percussion caps. He hadn't noticed it before, but the three newcomers were wearing bandoliers across their upper torsos in which to stash the caps. Ben wished he had thought of that. Instead, he would probably be stuck carrying the watertight boxes or the canteens. Not wanting to present his back to Moonbeam, Ben hung back to allow the others to pass. All did but Jesse Moonbeam.

"Git movin', boy," Moonbeam insisted, halting abruptly until Ben stepped in front of him. With a blank but—Ben suspected— malevolent stare, Moonbeam watched and followed the black man's passage.

The percussion caps in the canteens were removed and stuffed into the bandoliers. As he'd expected, Ben got the job of transporting the six watertight boxes, each containing about fifty caps. Each of the four men carried approximately three hundred percussion caps, for a total of twelve hundred. It was a drop in the bucket, but additional smuggling operations would hopefully bring the number up to something equal to the million or so cartridges without caps that were lying useless in the ammunition depots. Because of his key role in the operation, Bobby did not carry any percussion caps himself but served as the keeper of the emptied canteens. They would be needed again.

Taking a final look at the hollowed out front of the log, Bobby said, "That's it. Let's go."

The next step was to get off the shore and into the bayou where Jackson Toliver had parked his wagon. Toliver led the way through the tall grass and undergrowth, diverting his path when he could to take advantage of the small patches of forestation peppering the landscape. Ransford was to his immediate rear, followed at some distance by the cluster formed by Moonbeam, Bobby, and Ben, with Moonbeam trudging lethargically ahead of the other two.

"Mr. Moonbeam, can you move a little faster?" Bobby urged. "The Yankees *do* patrol this place."

"You wouldn't want to leave your Nigra behind, now, would you?"

"Ben can keep up."

"I surely can," Ben agreed.

Moonbeam's eyes brightened as they focused on Ben. It was not a friendly gesture.

But Jesse Moonbeam did move a little faster, his chin riding high to show it was his idea and not Bobby's. At a half-mile into the trek, Ransford and Toliver branched off into a copse of cypress and oak trees. Moonbeam was not far behind, then, finally, Bobby and Ben. The darkness was nearly overwhelming.

"Ooo-wee, it's dark in here!" Ben opined, his eyes probing for crumbs of brightness.

Bobby laughed and said, "You'll get used to it. Just stand still and let your eyes figure it out."

Ben did as Bobby said. Sure enough, his vision came back, although he could make out only the outlines of the wagon and the three men standing behind its open gate. It was movement as much as vision that caught his attention. Ransford, Toliver, and Moonbeam were unloading their booty into a plank box at the rear of the wagon bed. The log had been put ashore about a mile upstream of the southernmost reach of the Confederate line. Consequently, they could load the wagon and transport the percussion caps to any place on the Vicksburg side of that line, that is, to any Rebel fortification that needed the valuable cargo. Ben was the last to deposit his boxes in the wagon. Bobby kept the canteens, then handed half of them to his companion.

"For the next time," Bobby said, handing Ben a big potato sack he'd retrieved from the wagon. "Put the canteens in this."

Ben obeyed, noting that Bobby had already placed his half of the canteens in another potato sack.

"If we get stopped by a Yankee patrol, it would look funny if we were carrying around a bunch of canteens," Bobby said.

"Gonna look funny us carryin' around filled-up potato sacks in the middle of the night."

Bobby giggled. "You're right, it would, but it does make carrying the canteens a sight easier, don't it?"

Ben acknowledged Bobby's good humor with a soft laugh.

"It does that. It does that."

By this time, the three other men had departed with Toliver at the reins of two workhorses pulling the wagon. They would ultimately take the cargo to meet a surrogate of General Pemberton, whose job it was to distribute the percussion caps to the units that needed them. There was nothing left for Ben and Bobby to do but return to their homes and await another request for their services.

As they strolled along a path that skirted the more swampy parts of the bayou, Ben's mood turned melancholy. He had never been enthusiastic about making the "trip," as Bobby called it. His limitations as a swimmer and the fact that it was his first time conspired to instill a mortal fear in him. The end of the journey had alleviated that fear, but he knew it had not disappeared. It would be there next time if there were a next time. And there was something else.

"You all right, Ben?" Bobby asked, sensing his companion's mood.

Ben sighed, was silent for ten paces, looked at the quarter moon depositing its frail beams on the Mississippi landscape, and said, "It's nothin . . . and everythin'."

"What's that mean?"

"It means my heart ain't in it," Ben admitted.

Bobby was more startled than annoyed.

"Why? Don't you want to help your country? Send the Yankees packin'?"

"I don't want to send nobody nowhere; I'm not sure what my country is. Can you 'preciate that?"

Bobby pursed his lips as if about to speak, then changed his mind, then changed it back again.

"The Confederate States of America. That's your country."

Ben nodded in silence.

"I don't know, Bobby, I surely don't know. I think it is when I'm with you and your Pap, but men like that Jesse Moonbeam would just a soon shoot me as say hello. He hates me, and I'll be blamed if I know why. The fact is, most of us *Nigras* is sons and daughters of people who was taken from some other land. Maybe that place is my country."

Ben could tell from the expression on Bobby's face that he was confused. He simply did not understand what it was like to be a black man in the South, slave or free.

Grasping at a passing thought, Bobby said, "But you don't even know what country your folks are from, or whether it's a country at all. It might be nothin' but a jungle."

It was a subtle insult, the implication that Ben's ancestors might have come from a place with no true identity, but he knew Bobby had not intended it as an insult and let it pass. Besides, maybe Bobby was right. Maybe the land of his forefathers did not have a proper name.

They kept walking for another mile before stopping to rest at a high spot along the river. The abundance of lamplight coming from the Yankee gunboats actually lent the night a festive quality. The ambience was enhanced by a relatively cool breeze that was passing by. Man and boy enjoyed the moment, reluctant to leave and rejoin the real world.

"My Pap will be disappointed," Bobby said.

"I know."

"So will the others. We thought you was one of us."

I ain't never been one of you, Ben thought, but said, "I 'preciate that, Mr. Bobby. I really do. I love Vicksburg, I really do. And I surely do like you and your Pap."

Bobby waited for more, but Ben silently glanced away.

"What *are* you gonna do, Ben?"

Ben shook his head, perusing his options. After the war, he could return to whatever was his native country, if he could figure out what that was, and whether or not the people in charge of that country would take him in. But he wasn't sure he wanted to live among people whose customs and language were alien to him. The second option was to stay where he was and put up with the multitude of Jesse Moonbeams who enjoyed nothing better than honing their skills at "Nigger-Knockin." The third choice was to move north, where, hopefully, there were fewer Jesse Moonbeams to contend with. But he wasn't sure there would be or whether he wanted to adapt to the faster-paced life of the North.

"I don't know what I'm gonna do, Bobby. Get me a wife for sure. After that, I'm not sure. It surely is a predicament. It surely is . . ."

*   *   *

The smuggling of percussion caps to the Vicksburg defenders became a community enterprise. With the exception of infants and the very young, every man, woman and child was assumed by the Yankees to be potentially culpable. Even with this widespread support, the shortage of percussion caps continued to be a problem. The Rebels compensated by minimizing their fire and pulling the trigger only when a "sure-thing" presented itself.

Not surprisingly, the Federals noticed the paucity of return fire from the enemy and attempted to take advantage of the situation by relentless bombardment of Confederate emplacements. In this effort, they shortly discovered a shortage of their own: a lack of siege guns. The Federal armies in the east had plenty of siege artillery, but, as of yet, no city to which they could lay siege. But

Grant's Army of the Tennessee had no siege guns. Yankee soldiers improvised by creating mortars from hollowed-out hardwood logs bound with steel-reinforcing bands. Using these "trench mortars" to lob six and twelve-pound shells was sometimes effective, always dangerous, and occasionally lethal to the men doing the shooting. But what they lacked in accuracy and safety, they made up for in sheer numbers. A multitude of *ad hoc* mortars were built with in excess of ten thousand rounds launched per bombardment. Together with the two hundred or more heavy artillery captured from the Vicksburg defenders, the trench mortars made a small but significant difference. Unfortunately for the citizens of Vicksburg, the shells struck the city and its inhabitants as often as they did the soldiers of Pemberton's army.

While demonstrating a limited effectiveness, the batteries of trench mortars could not get the job done. Searching for alternatives, Grant realized that Admiral David Porter had what he was looking for: big guns. When the General made the Admiral aware of his needs, Porter sent the gunboat *Cincinnati* to take out the Vicksburg batteries. The Vicksburg batteries fired back, and the *Cincinnati* was sunk, once again demonstrating that well-positioned, land-based artillery on high ground had the edge over floating gun platforms.

Unwilling to send another gunboat to its sure destruction, and equally unwilling to admit failure to Grant, David Porter compromised. He had thirteen naval guns dismantled and transferred to fixed ground positions. Scows were built to support an array of fifty to a hundred pound cannon and placed a mile from the city. Federal gunboats and their formidable firepower—mostly giant mortars—joined the fray, but at a distance, to avoid the *Cincinnati's* fate. Coupled with the considerable firepower Major Samuel Lockett had incorporated into the Vicksburg defenses, every night was a thunderstorm of bursting shells and flying debris, some of it human flesh.

★ FORTY-ONE ★

June 14, 1863, The Trenches

Sappers Charlie Johnson and Darren McGlover sat with their backs to the trench wall, a relatively safe position if any position in a "sap" trench could be considered safe. It was going on 8:00 PM and the sun was arranging its sunset halo for admiring onlookers.

"Darren, we should go back. It's gettin' dark."

"I'm all for that, Charlie," Darren replied, grabbing a pick and shovel.

Their latest companions, whom they knew only as "Schmidt" and "O'Neill," had left an hour earlier. Charlie and Darren had opted to stay the extra hour. They were close enough to the Rebel trenches to hear muffled conversations. There were still local conflicts going on, dominated by musket fire and hand-launched grenades consisting of round metal containers packed with powder and flight stabilized by a long tail. It was a typical evening in the Vicksburg trenches.

The sound Charlie heard as he arose from his squat was a simple "plop."

"Grenade!" Charlie yelled.

Both men dived face first into the muck of the trench floor and covered their heads with folded hands.

Nothing happened.

"What?" Darren said sharply, lifting his head to see where the missile had landed. Locating the oddly shaped object, he crawled toward it and held it up for Charlie to see.

"It's a bone, Charlie," Darren said, a mixture of relief and irritation flavoring his tone. "Some Johnny Reb's idea of a joke."

"It ain't a joke, Yank," said a voice from beyond the trench wall.

Charlie was the first to react. He grabbed his rifle and aimed it at the face peering down at them from atop the trench wall.

"No, wait, wait, I just want to ask you somethin'," said the Rebel soldier as he slowly raised his hands.

Charlie looked cautiously at the man to gauge his intentions. The soldier appeared to be about sixteen with sandy hair and acne. The sandy hair fell loosely to eye level.

"D'you boys know a boy named Tom Jones?"

Charlie and Darren gazed at each other, dumbstruck.

"I know maybe a hunderd Tom Joneses. Ain't exactly an un-usual name."

"I know, I know," the Rebel stammered. "But this here one is from Missouri, and he's my brother. He's a Yankee like you."

"What's your name?" Charlie asked.

"Jim Jones."

"So, Jim Jones, you want us to go find your brother from Missouri?"

"That's right," replied Jim Jones in all seriousness.

Darren and Charlie glanced at each other again, unsure how to respond. Yankee/Rebel fraternization during lulls in the mutu-al destruction was a common occurrence all along the line. But this was a cut above the norm.

"Well, maybe we could do somethin' for you, but we gotta make sure you ain't hostile. You got a gun?"

"Sure I got a gun, but I ain't gonna shoot it unless I get shot at."

"Well, why don't you just put that gun far behind you while Charlie or me tries to find your brother? This ain't a Missouri out-fit, you know."

Jim Jones's face momentarily clouded over in suspicion and fear, but he took hold of himself and pushed his apprehension to a remote place in his soul. In fact, he was exhibiting bravery, but none present recognized it as such. He backed up to his musket, gingerly held it up for the others to see, and laid it down twenty yards farther from the Yankee trench. Quickly and quietly he re-turned to the two sappers and slid into the trench.

"What do you want me to do?" he asked hopefully.

"Stay here with Charlie," Darren said. "I'll go and see if I can find your brother."

Darren hastened to the rear while Jim Jones brushed himself off and tried to look non-threatening to his new trench-mate Charlie, who was now holding his musket at the ready.

"I didn't get your name," Jones said, extending his hand.

Charlie shook it and replied, "Johnson. Charlie Johnson."

"We got a general named Johnson."

"I think you mean Johnston, not Johnson."

Embarrassed, Jones stammered, "Yeah, you're right. Joe Johnston, fightin' Joe Johnston. He's gonna . . ."

Charlie could imagine what the Rebel had been about to say. Something like, "General Joe Johnston. He's gonna kick your ass all the way to New Orleans." Or something similar. But the youngster managed to stop his overly energized mouth before in-advertently uttering something that might be offensive to the man holding the gun. He looked more sheepish now than before.

"We got our own ideas on ass-kickin'," Charlie said with a smile.

"I'm sure you do," Jones responded with obvious relief. "Hey, you got any generals named Johnson or Johnston in your army?"

"I maybe know one or two soldiers, but they ain't generals."

"Could be, though. You never know. We must have a dozen Lees in our officer corps. I'm sure you've heard of Robert E. Lee—"

"'Course I heard of Robert E. Lee."

"Yeah, yeah. Sure you have. We got another one right here, Stephen D. Lee. No relation to Robert E., though."

Charlie nodded and said, "I heard of him, I think."

"You have?" Jones said with a wide grin. "Well, I'll be a jack-ass's flea-bitten be-hind. I'll have to tell the General he's Yan-kee-famous. Myself, I gotta admit that once I get past Ulysses S. Grant and William Tecumseh Sherman, I got no familiarity with Yankee officers."

Charlie was inclined to say that Jones would shortly have a better acquaintance with Yankees after the Vicksburg garrison surrendered, but he suppressed the urge. It might be seen as bad manners.

With the demise of the officer corps topic, both men fell silent. Rather than concoct another subject of conversation, they relaxed with their backs against the Vicksburg side of the trench wall. Af-ter ten minutes, the more garrulous of the two—Jim Jones—spoke.

"This is a nice trench you got here," he said cheerily.

"A *nice* trench? It's just a trench."

"No, no, it's a nice trench. Wide. Deep, You boys are hard to find in a gun sight when your heads are down."

Charlie had had enough.

"It's a trench. That's all it is! And it ain't a friendly trench. It's here so's we can kill you better, which is the same reason you dig trenches, so's you can kill us better . . ."

The Rebel soldier was taken aback by the outburst and bowed his head as if he'd been scolded by a schoolmarm.

"Don't get hog-tied about it. I was just tryin' to be sociable."

"How can you be sociable with me when you're not even socia-ble with your brother?"

Shaken by the charge, Jim Jones said, "I am sociable with my brother."

"But you're a Rebel, and he's a Yankee. You might even wind up shooting each other some day. Ever think of that?"

"Yeah, 'course I have."

"Well?"

"Well, what?" Jones replied with a shrug.

"Well, aren't you afraid that might happen?"

"No . . . yeah. I keep my eyes peeled for him, though."

"But it could happen, couldn't it? Or he could accidentally shoot you?"

"Yeah, but it ain't likely. Most of the time his regiment ain't anywhere near mine," Jones said half-heartedly.

Feeling his irritation fading, Charlie asked, "Why did you and your brother choose different sides?"

"It's Missouri. We got both kinds."

Jones heaved a weary sigh and rested the back of his head against folded hands.

"I don't honestly know why. I guess you might say I was more attached to Missouri, and Tom was more attached to the U-S-of A."

"How can you be attached to a place that keeps men in slavery?"

Jim Jones leaned forward, extending his hands as if pleading for reason.

"It's easy. I'm from Missouri. I live there. We just don't like Yankees comin' down there and tellin' us what to do."

"Do you own slaves?"

"Me?" Jones chortled incredulously. "I got nothin' to do with slaves. Neither does my Pap and surely not my brother Tom. We're just dirt farmers."

"But . . ." Charlie started fitfully. He knew all the arguments for abolishing slavery but was not sure how to use them against someone who did not seem to care one way or the other. "But don't you think slavery is a bad thing?"

Jones's expressions went through a series of contortions that Charlie interpreted as a preparation for either total honesty or complete dissimulation.

"I suppose it is. I wouldn't want to be one, surely enough."

"You wouldn't want to be one? Is that all you have to say?"

"Well, uh, Mr. Charlie. It is for a fact all I have to say about slavery. Is there somethin' you want me to do?"

"Any decent person would resign from an army that holds black folks down."

"Well, I guess I just ain't decent enough," Jones said with an edge that hadn't been there before. He stared disdainfully into Charlie's eyes. "Tell you what, Charlie Johnson. If you get the

Yankee army out of Missouri, I will get *me* out of the army of the Confederacy, and I will do my best to get along with whatever Negroes cross my path."

Jones smiled and extended a hand, which Charlie refused to shake. The Rebel soldier wanted to see his brother and would probably sell his soul to the devil to achieve that end. The refusal had the effect of tightening the stress lines on Jones's face, but he tried to hide his annoyance by directing his gaze away from Charlie. For his part, Charlie kept his eye on the Rebel soldier and a tight grip on his gun. He was not about to trust any of the enemy, although this one did not appear to be interested in trouble making.

Darren McGlover and Tom Jones arrived five minutes later. Tom was an inch or two taller and maybe ten pounds heavier than Jim, but the family resemblance was obvious. Charlie rose to his feet as Tom approached and offered his hand. Charlie shook it and introduced himself.

"That's a damn sight more than I got out of him," said Jim Jones, who had also risen to his feet.

"That's because you're a damn seditious Rebel, Jim," Tom responded with a chuckle.

"I suppose I am. And you, brother, are a stiff-necked, self-righteous Yankee," the other Jones rejoined.

"And you, my deluded sibling, are . . ."

The banter continued for a minute or two while the brothers shook hands and embraced each other repeatedly. Darren pulled Charlie to one side.

"Let's let 'em enjoy the moment, Charlie. They ain't gonna see each other for a long time, maybe never."

Charlie nodded, understanding the sentiment. "How long?" he asked.

"Captain says fifteen minutes."

"That seems fair," Charlie said stiffly.

"You sound like you got your britches in a knot. What is it?"

Johnson hesitated, unsure whether he should mention his argument with the Rebel.

"We had a disagreement," he murmured.

"About what?"

"He's a slaver."

This caused a furrow to appear in McGlover's brow.

"That boy *owns* slaves?"

"No, he just . . . well, he doesn't . . . he isn't . . ."

"You mean he doesn't own any slaves, but he's fightin for the Confederate cause?"

"Yeah, that's about it, I guess."

"'Course he is, Charlie. He's a Rebel. But his brother Tom told me he's only doin' it to boot us out. Get the Yankees out of Dixie, or somethin' like that."

"Do you believe him?" Charlie asked with an earnestness that surprised his companion.

"I don't see why he should lie, do you?"

"No, I guess not."

Darren stood, rigid, staring at Charlie in dismay. Then he shook his head.

"Charlie, I don't know about you. What do you care about a bunch of darkies you never even met?"

It was a subject they'd discussed before, so Charlie steeled himself.

"It don't matter if I met them or not. They're still slaves, and they shouldn't be."

"Yeah, yeah, I understand," Darren said, trying to suppress a whine. It was clear he was not in the mood to discuss the matter further.

As hosts, Darren and Charlie kept to themselves while the brothers talked effusively of old times and new problems. Darren leaned with one arm against a trench wall, while Charlie curled up next to the sap roller. Evening had come and with it a diminution of military activity. *Thank God*, Charlie thought. He was tired of ducking his head every time he exposed it to hostile fire. Maybe he could actually get some sleep tonight.

Jim Jones glanced at his hosts and waved for them to come over. When they arrived, the two Illinois Yankees stared blankly at him and awaited an explanation. Jim Jones smiled and pulled a roll of bills from his pocket.

"Woo-ey!" Darren hooted. "Are those real? How much you got there?"

Tom Jones and Charlie joined in with audible expressions of awe.

"You mean are they Union or Confederate currency?"

"Yeah, which?" Darren wanted to know.

Jim Jones unfurled the bills and laid them flat on his hand.

"U.S. currency!" Charlie said with a start. Silently, he counted the stack of bills. His rough estimate of its value was two hundred dollars. "Where'd you get it?"

"Don't matter where it's from. It's for the folks back home."

The Rebel said this with such disarming frankness that all, Charlie excepted, believed him. Given the circumstances, Charlie did not challenge him.

"Here you go, Tom," Jim said, rolling the bills up and handing them to his brother.

Tom Jones accepted what, to all present, was a small fortune and hastily shoved it into his coat pocket. The brothers conversed heartily for another ten minutes, obviously trying to make up for months, perhaps years of silence. Then Darren reminded Tom of the terms of the visitation and led him back. McGlover was out and back in half an hour. He looked a little tense.

"Well, Charlie, Mr. Jones, it's been a good evening," he said.

"It has," Jones agreed, but with a wary eye on Charlie, to whom he again offered his hand. This time, Charlie relented and shook the proffered palm, albeit with little enthusiasm. Jones did not press the point but, as he turned to go, said, "See you boys sometime. Hope it's not in hell."

Though the Rebel's demeanor was unruffled, he disappeared with surprising alacrity. Noting Charlie's narrowed eyes and grim features, Darren said, "Well, that was different, don't you think? Maybe them and us ain't so different after all."

"You think he comes by them bills honestly?"

"I don't know, Charlie," Darren said with a sigh. "He could've."

"You don't think maybe he got 'em from a dead Union soldier?"

"Maybe he did, maybe he didn't. What difference does it make? Would it be better of one of our boys took the money? Either way, the dead man can't use it."

Charlie struggled to find a persuasive counter-argument, but all he could think of was that it was appropriate that U.S. currency remain in Union hands. But that did not begin to express the intense emotions he was feeling.

"Let's go back, Charlie," Darren said abruptly. "There's somethin' I need to tell you."

Having no idea what his friend might be talking about, Charlie nodded and followed in his footsteps. Darren proceeded cautiously, then spoke in a muffled voice.

"Charlie, you ever hear of an officer named Hickenlooper?"

"I know who he is—Captain Andrew Hickenlooper. He and his boys are tryin' to dig their way to that fort, the one the rebs call the Louisiana . . ."

"The Louisiana Redan."

"Yeah, the one along the Jackson Road, a mile or two south of us."

"That's it. Well, Hickenlooper and his boy made pretty good progress until they launched an attack. Then the Rebel artillery opened up and cut them to pieces."

"What are you getting at? What's this got to do with us?" Charlie said peevishly.

With unfolding hands, Darren pleaded for patience.

"It's somethin' important I heard back at camp. Just let me talk for a minute."

Charlie shrugged and obediently fell silent. Darren continued.

"Because they got all shot up in that attack, Hickenlooper decided to build a fort of his own across from the Rebel fort. They're gonna call it Battery Hickenlooper."

"And what's this battery supposed to accomplish?"

"It'll have cannons and sharpshooters. And . . ."

From the furtive look on his colleague's face, Charlie could see Darren had something more to say.

"*And* what? Are they gonna attack again?" Charlie inquired while he prepared to depart.

"*And* it will serve as a base for operations."

"Operations? What kind of operations?"

"Tunneling operations."

Charlie studied his friend's face. He saw both amusement and anxiety in it.

"Tunneling operations? What kind of tunneling operations? You can't shoot Rebs through a tunnel wall. All you can do is—"

Then Charlie understood. Darren was already nodding his head as the realization descended on Charlie's consciousness.

"They're gonna blow it up?"

"The whole god-damn Third Louisiana Redan!" Darren confirmed.

Charlie was stunned. He'd never heard of such a thing before. Was it actually possible to destroy an entire fortress from underneath?

"They're askin' for volunteers."

"I ain't volunteerin."

"C'mon, Charlie. We won't have to do any more than we already do every day. They're gettin' the boys with coal-mining experience to dig the tunnels. All we have to do is help them get close enough."

"What's close enough?"

"The ditch around the Rebel fort."

"That's pretty close."

As they started back to camp, Darren groaned at his partner's intransigence. He appealed to Charlie's patriotism, then to his sense of adventure, and finally to his pride. "It would be seen as a job well done," Darren reasoned. None of it worked. Charlie's final, "no," was enough to silence Darren for the rest of the hike back.

In the absence of Darren's pleading voice, Charlie's mind gave way to feverish contemplation. Whose idea was this, Grant's? Probably. In the course of the Vicksburg campaign, the general had already taken God knew how many extreme actions, from trying to re-rout the Mississippi River to sending gunboats into bayous barely deep enough to float a skiff. What kind of man would even imagine tunneling under an enemy fortress and blowing it to smithereens?

Charlie did not know the answer, but he was glad U.S. Grant was on his side.

June 15, 1863, The Northeast Corner of the Battle Line

Ulysses S. Grant could not see the Third Louisiana Redan from where he was standing, just northeast of the Graveyard Road in Sherman's sector. The Confederate fortress was a mile or two to the south in McPherson's sector. Too far to see, but it was on his mind. With him were John Rawlins, James Wilson, and General John Logan of McPherson's Seventeenth Corps.

Grant turned his head toward Logan and asked, "What's the status of Battery Hickenlooper?"

After he'd spoken the name, Grant could not help being mildly amused by it. How did anyone come by a name like "Hickenlooper?" It sounded like some mechanical contrivance for scaring the bejesus out of small children.

"We're coming along fine, sir. A hundred and fifty men are working on each shift. They should reach the Rebel outer trench in a week or two."

"Did you find enough coal miners to dig the tunnels?"

"They call them 'galleries,' sir."

"What?"

"Galleries, sir. That's what the coal miners—of which we found about three dozen—call them."

Grant gazed quizzically at Logan, puffed on the half-consumed cigar jutting from his mouth, and said, "All right. Galleries it is. What do these thirty-six men look like?"

"Big, strong, like you'd expect miners to be."

Grant mulled this over, slowly nodded his head, and said, "Let's sit down."

The staff seated themselves around the big table off to one side of the tent space.

"How are the sappers doing?" Grant asked Logan.

"Well, sir, they'll reach the outer ditch sometime today."

"I see," Grant said, circling the room with his eyes to gauge the reactions of his officers. Rawlins looked mildly surprised, but the others seemed unfazed by the news.

"You seem uncomfortable, Rawlins," Grant said. "Is anything amiss? Surely you were expecting this day to come. The sappers have been working day and night since early this month."

"Of course, sir, Rawlins said haltingly. "I'm more pleased than surprised. I didn't expect it to happen so soon."

Disinclined to pursue the matter further, Grant gave a nod and turned back to Logan.

"General Logan, do these coal miners of yours know what we expect them to do and what they're supposed to do it with?"

"They've been properly instructed, sir. And we've accumulated enough picks, shovels, and drills to do the job."

"Who's in charge?"

"Lieutenant Russell of the Seventh Missouri and Sergeant Morris of the Thirty-second Ohio."

"Do they have coal-mining experience?" Wilson asked.

"I'm not sure," Logan responded. "But I don't think so."

"Where would they get coal mining experience in the army?" Grant interjected. "They're officers. They don't work."

This generated a bubble of laughter, some of it genuine. Grant waved his cigar-laden hand in the general direction of Logan.

"Go on, General."

Logan quickly re-established his composure and cleared his throat.

"The gallery will be about five feet square, and will extend from the outer ditch perpendicular to the Rebel fort. We'll take it in about forty or fifty feet, then decide if and how we want to go farther."

"How long will that take?"

"Maybe a week."

"You can't do it in less?"

Logan started to shake his head but, under the resolute gaze of his commander, relented.

"Maybe less. The soil is easy to cut into."

"Is it strong enough that it won't cave in prematurely?"

"It's clay, red clay. It's pretty stiff, and we can add bracing if necessary."

"Very good," Grant said with as much enthusiasm as his subdued nature would allow. He leaned back in his chair and laid his feet on the table.

"Tell me more. How do you get the dirt out of the tunnel?"

Logan paused to lean back in his chair, but otherwise remained at attention.

"We'll have crews of six, some digging, some shoveling, and some removing grain sacks filled with the accumulated dirt. Each crew works steadily for an hour and is then relieved by the next crew."

Grant was pleased. Although he'd had his doubts—he always did—it appeared this might actually work. But the project had to be pursued vigorously to avoid Rebel countermeasures.

"Are the rebels still tossing grenades at us?"

"Grenades and artillery shells. They put fuses on the shells and roll them into our trenches. We think they might also try to reach the gallery with their own tunnels, and blow it up before ours is completed."

"We need to hurry then."

"We do."

Pausing to take a final puff on his cigar, Grant rose and brushed the accumulated ashes from his lap.

"How about June twenty-fifth? Will that be enough time?"

"I think so, sir."

"Will it be enough?" Grant said with a note of peevishness.

"Yes, sir. We'll be ready on the twenty-fifth."

Grant gazed querulously at the commander of McPherson's Third Division, wondering if he had pressed too hard. But Logan did not appear to be particularly stressed, and, to some extent, seemed relieved.

"Wonderful. Anyone have anything more to say?"

They did not.

"Good. We'll meet at Battery Hickenlooper on June twenty-fifth. The staff and I will draw up battle plans for the corps and division commanders. That's all, gentlemen."

June 25, 1863, Battery Hickenlooper

Much to his chagrin, Charlie Johnson had been drafted for duty digging the sap that would penetrate the Confederate outer ditch. He was accompanied by Darren McGlover, who had volunteered, and six other sappers.

"How far left to go, any idea?" Charlie asked of no one in particular. One of the men—whom Charlie knew only as Sampson—answered.

"Looks like we're almost there. Five feet, maybe."

The sap roller at the Confederate end of the trench suddenly burst into flame. Constructed of wicker and stuffed with cotton, it burned quickly and violently.

"Damnit, damnit, damnit, damnit!" Darren howled.

Charlie did not appreciate the profanity, but he did understand its cause. Without the sap roller, they would have no shield for the final five feet.

"Let's get on with it,' Charlie suggested. "Once we breach the wall, the sharpshooters can take care of any Reb who sticks his head through. And don't forget the six trench mortars we brought."

The sharpshooters were a select group of skilled riflemen led by Lieutenant Henry "Coonskin" Foster. The lieutenant and his men had built a tower near Battery Hickenlooper, from which they could fire down on any Confederates trying to shoot the sappers, without fear of being shot themselves.

Sampson helped Charlie and Darren put the fire out and remove the scorched remnants of the sap roller while the others continued digging. When the last piece of the sap roller was gone, Charlie and Darren retreated to where the trench mortars were stored. Darren grabbed two of the iron-banded, hollow log devices while Charlie struggled with a keg of powder. The two men then returned for the six-pound artillery shells that would be launched by the primitive cannons. As best they could, they set the mortars to lob the shells to a point ten feet beyond the Rebel side of the sap wall.

"Sampson, should we give those boys on the other side some hell?" Darren inquired.

Sampson, whose name belied his diminutive physique, replied, "Not yet. I'll let you know when we're about to punch through. Then you can hit 'em with whatever you want."

Darren nodded and waved to let his colleague know he understood. Charlie and he knelt before their loaded mortars, fire sticks in hand and aflame. The six sappers dug continuously for another ten minutes, then Sampson halted, turned, and mouthed the words, "We're ready," back at Darren and Charlie. Both cannoneers touched flame to fuse. Ignition was instantaneous. Quickly, the two men plugged their ears with their fingers and waited for the explosions. When it came, it was more like two stages of the same explosion, with Darren's mortar lagging Charlie's by a fraction of a second. While the launching of the two shells was nearly simultaneous, the arrival time was not. Charlie's shell hit the mark a good half-second before Darren's, and twenty feet farther west. Like a discordant descant above the chaos, screams of agony accompanied both blasts. As best they could, the six sappers punched through the wall and, like fugitives from hell, put as much distance as they could between the breach and themselves.

As Sampson passed by, Charlie yelled, "Make sure those miners know the wall has been breached. I don't want to get run over by Rebels."

Sampson sported a thumbs-up and said, "They already know. Here they come."

The last statement was accompanied by a finger pointing at the members of the Seventh Missouri and Twenty-Second Ohio, who had been waiting for the signal to move. They rushed forward with nearly as much dispatch as Sampson and the sappers were showing in the reverse direction. It was an odd sight because not every man held a musket, but every man did have a short-handled jack, a shovel, or a drill.

The two officers, Russell and Morris, halted when they reached Charlie and Darren, who were positioned on opposite sides of the sap.

"Private . . ." Russell began.

"Johnson," Charlie said, then directed a hand at Darren. "Charlie Johnson and Darren McGlover."

"Charlie, Darren, how long can you keep firing those things?" the lieutenant asked, indicating the mortars.

"Till they blow up, or we get blowed up, or we run outa shells," Darren answered in a manner, which, to Charlie, seemed gratuitously cheerful.

"We'd appreciate it if you could keep firing until we establish a gallery," Morris explained. "Once we're underground, they can't touch us."

Charlie noticed the sergeant was actually grinning as he spoke. *This man is as bad as Darren*, he thought.

"How long would that be?"

"Oh, maybe an hour."

An hour. An eternity.

"We'll probably have to get more shells," Charlie said, coughing. He glanced at Darren for concurrence.

Darren studied the stacks of mortar shells, then said, "I'll go get more. Charlie, you keep firin' away while I'm gone."

"Darren, I'd rather go—"

"I'll be back as quick as a whistle," Darren said, his gaiety undiminished. Before Charlie could object further, he was on his way.

Charlie felt, rather than saw the questioning stares of Russell and Morris. Reluctantly, he raised his head to view not only the two officers staring at him but the entire contingent of three dozen coal-miners. Charlie had never seen so many well-muscled men in one place before, many of them only half dressed in anticipation of a hot, sweaty experience.

"I'll cover you as best I can," he said, sucking a smile onto his face.

"Try not to hit us," Russell said good-naturedly, then, along with Morris, led his charges to the breach.

Charlie got off three mortar rounds before Darren, true to his word, returned with more shells. Both men quickly found the range and rained an armada of shells down on the Confederate defenders. At first, screams of pain competed with bursting shells for dominance, but these eventually fell silent. Charlie wondered if it was because the defenders were all dead or because they had retreated to safer ground. He hoped for the latter. Although he and Tom Jones had not gotten along particularly well, he found himself wishing the man good luck. For Charlie Johnson, such feelings were an epiphany he did not fully comprehend.

★ FORTY-TWO ★

June 25, 1863, Battery Hickenlooper

Grant had spent the morning doing what he could to take maximum advantage of the impending explosion. He had ordered an artillery bombardment to slow the flow of Rebel reinforcements, which would certainly be needed after the detonation. A hundred Union sharpshooters had been strategically placed to protect the assault force. That force would consist largely of Leggett's brigade of Logan's division—Illinois and Ohio boys with a smattering of loyal Missourians.

All of them were McPherson's troops. It was appropriate that he and Logan should join Grant for what might be the defining moment of the battle for Vicksburg—the obliteration of the Third Louisiana Redan and the invasion of the city.

From battery Hickenlooper, Grant gazed through binoculars at the members of the forlorn hope, who had positioned themselves as close as possible to the fortifications. At their head was Captain Andrew Hickenlooper.

Grant lowered the binoculars and turned to face McPherson.

"You tried to talk him out of it?" he asked curtly.

"We both tried to persuade him," McPherson replied, glancing at Logan. "But he was determined.

Logan said nothing, only nodded.

Grant shifted his attention back to the scene before him, where birds were unknowingly risking their lives by sweeping down into the field of fire between Battery Hickenlooper and the Third Louisiana Redan. A dozen of them lay dead or dying on the freshly dug soil bordering the trenches. The trenches were stuffed with men and materiel of Logan's brigade, who would follow the forlorn hope into the breach.

Finally, the Union guns fell silent. Sympathetically, illogical as it might seem, so did the Confederate guns, leaving the playful chatter of the birds as the only source of sound. Even that disappeared as the birds noticed the drop in noise level and, prey that they often were, suspected something threatening was afoot.

Like an earthquake from hell, the ground beneath the fortress lifted, taking Confederate troops, cannon and the Third Louisiana

Redan with it. The flash of the explosion followed only after the rising debris had dispersed enough to release its brilliant luminescence. The roar of the eruption was deep and persistent, like a stampede. The flash vanished as quickly as it had come, leaving a huge column of black smoke to hide the destruction it had wrought.

"My God, I never thought . . ." Grant moaned, awestruck by the spectacle of men being launched like artillery shells from the mouth of the gargantuan cannon that had once been the Redan.

McPherson and Logan were equally dumbfounded, nearly to the point of debilitation. Grant recovered from his reverie and raised his binoculars to watch the forlorn hope enter the breach.

"There they go," he said, a distant reverence filling his voice.

"God help them." was all Logan could say. McPherson had nothing to offer.

*   *   *

Like everyone else on or near the field of battle, Colonel Jasper Maltby was shocked by the magnitude of the blast. Unlike many, he was a member of Leggett's assault force and could not afford to remain a stunned onlooker. It was time for the attack to begin, but the way was blocked by debris.

"Get this rubble out of here. Now!" he screamed at the nearest soldier.

While a half dozen privates were performing this task, Maltby considered his tactics. Hopefully, the Rebels in the vicinity of his brigade were dead or dying. It would make things so much easier if he and his men did not have to dance between Confederate bullets.

When the debris had been cleared, Maltby arranged his men on both sides of the opening. Half of the ninety men under his command would provide covering fire while the other half rushed in.

"Go," he said.

The attacking half of the team charged through. Less than half of these had entered when the assault stalled, accompanied by a cacophony of musket fire and high-pitched screams. Twenty-one men returned. Maltby stopped one of them, a captain with a shoulder wound, named Austin Smith.

"What happened?"

Smith, a short but lanky man with a pockmarked face, took a deep breath and, in a trembling voice, replied, "The explosion made a big crater, but it left junk piles everywhere. There's a big one in the middle where the fort was. Some of the Rebs are hidin' behind it and takin' pot shots at us."

Smith paused for another breath and to subdue his frazzled nerves.

"There's also a trench that wasn't touched. It's behind the big junk pile and is protected by earthworks. Lots of Rebs comin' in that way."

"What about cover for us? Anything we can use?"

Smith shook his head.

"Just the junk piles but most are too small to shield a man. Except for what the Rebs are usin', it's wide open in there, just a big hole in the ground."

It was Maltby's worst nightmare. He briefly considered retreating but decided to try again with a slight adjustment to his original tactics.

"Captain, if any men are still in there, tell them to withdraw. We're going to try something else."

Smith was hesitant to re-enter the crater, but finally gave Maltby a compliant look and obeyed. He returned in ten minutes with four men. Maltby assembled them and the remainder of the assault team to present his revised strategy.

He was brief.

"We're changing tactics . . . a little," he shouted. "We'll still work in two teams, but we'll alternate—one team shoots while the other team reloads. Got it?"

Groans of disquietude could be heard throughout the assemblage, but no one offered a complaint. Maltby stood straight and spoke the Lord's Prayer aloud. Most of the brigade murmured the words, some synchronously, others lagging behind to delay the inevitable.

After the *amen*, Maltby took his musket and said, "Let's go."

He was not the first through but he *was* the fourth. For protection, he grabbed one of the makeshift shields Hickenlooper's pioneers had fashioned from logs. They proved to be cumbersome and, worse than that, deadly. Presented with partially concealed targets, the Rebels fired directly into the shields, creating high-velocity splinters scattering in all directions. It was almost as effective as grapeshot. Jasper Maltby fell, killed by a forest of wooden shrapnel.

* * *

Private Jasper Bennett looked down at the Union soldiers being slaughtered as they entered the crater through the breach. He felt somewhat exposed at the top of the debris mountain that was, for the Confederates, a protective parapet in the center of the crater. But he did not feel as exposed as the Yankees must feel as they did their best to rush in and seize whatever ground could be taken.

"Over to the right," he cried, doing his duty as a grenade spotter.

Two men, each pocketing four grenades and carrying an artillery shell between them, struggled up the Rebel side of the parapet. At the top, next to Bennett, they laid the shell down, peered over the edge, and launched their grenades at targets of opportunity. The result was three wounded Union soldiers, two of them clearly blinded by the grenades. Their shrill shrieks of pain and disillusion bounced off the crater walls and into Jasper's ears. He held a hand over each ear until the awful sound diminished.

"What are you gonna do with that?" he asked, pointing to the artillery shell.

"Roll it down the other side," said the younger and leaner of the two men. "Blow up some Yankees."

"Can't be very accurate."

"Doesn't have to be. It's a big bomb. All we have to do is get it within twenty yards of a Yankee, and it'll do the job," said the older man, a smug grin adorning his thin lips.

Bennett remained skeptical. Noticing his disbelief, the older man rolled the shell to the crest of the parapet, lit the fuse, and gave it a gentle shove over the top. It was not long before it was accelerating down the other side.

"Hold your ears," the younger man directed. "And duck your head."

His companion had already dropped to the ground and plugged his ears. The young man was close behind. Jasper took a little longer and, as he was lowering himself, spotted a Yankee climbing toward them on the opposite slope. He had a musket and a determined look on his face.

"There's a Yankee climbin' up at us," he whispered.

"I know," his youthful cohort said nonchalantly.

"But what if he makes it—"

Before he could finish, the artillery shell exploded, sending newly refined shards of debris everywhere, including the back of Jasper's neck."

"He ain't climbin' no more. He's flyin'" said the young Rebel with a demonic sneer.

Jasper took a moment to pop his ears, in hopes it would bring his hearing back to normal. It did not. Before rising to his feet again, he felt for the object that had landed on his neck. He knew what it was before he'd even had a chance to look at it—a human hand, a right hand.

Panic-stricken by the ghoulish specter, Bennett twisted his body to remove the foul thing from his line of sight. He started to rise but was quickly halted by another hand.

"Get down, you silly fool," said the older man.

Jasper turned his gaze toward his would-be savior and glimpsed a steely resolve in the brown eyes shining back at him.

"Sorry," he muttered, searching for something more to say. "By the way, I'm Jasper Bennett—"

"I know. My name is Seth, and this here is Andy," the elderly man proclaimed, deflecting his gaze to the youngster. Andy acknowledged the introduction with a nod.

"We should already know each others' names," Jasper lamented.

"We should, and now we do," Andy said, donning a less devilish grin than the one he'd reacted with moments earlier.

With a finger and an opposing thumb, Seth lifted the hand from Bennett's shoulder and tossed it to the Yankee side of the parapet. Still soft and pliable, it generated no discernible sound as it plummeted to the crater floor below. Even if it had, it would never be heard above the din of the incessant musket and artillery fire.

Jasper chanced a look down into the crater. He couldn't see a great deal, but what he did see filled him with foreboding. The crater was at least twenty-five feet in diameter and ten feet deep. It looked like . . . he didn't know what it looked like! The surface of the moon? An African desert?

"How could they do that?" he asked, dumbfounded.

"How could they do what?" Seth responded, already making his way down the slope for fresh weaponry. Andy was only a step behind.

"How could they make such a big explosion?"

"You know the answer to that. They dug tunnels under the Third Louisiana and filled 'em with explosives. Then they lit the fuse and 'Boom,' this is what they got."

"Yes, I know, but—"

"If you get enough explosives, you could blow up the world," Seth remarked with a wink as he descended the irregular slope of the parapet.

Surely not, Jasper thought. There weren't enough explosives to blow up the world. *Were there?*

He took a longer look at the destruction below and shook his head. Maybe there weren't enough explosives to blow up the world, but this was a good start. He hoped the end would come soon.

*   *   *

The carnage in the crater continued for a day and night. Finding themselves at a tactical disadvantage, the Federals compensated by throwing in more men. Observing this numerical disparity, the Confederates reacted by throwing in more of their men into the charnel house. The Yankees mimicked this move, and so it went. until, after much loss of life, the Union forces were able to reduce the casualty rate at their end of the killing field by constructing a casemate from the detritus in the crater—of which there was a plentiful supply. This *ad hoc* structure was strengthened by throwing dirt—of which there was also an abundance—onto it. The Yankees now had a protective barrier and withdrew to positions behind it.

But they held enough ground to force a stalemate. As the sun began its daily ascendance, the fighting and dying persisted. Grant finally conceded the futility of further offensive operations and called a halt. Something else had come to mind.

June 26, 1863, Battery Hickenlooper

Grant stared across the field of battle at the decimated structure that had once been the Third Louisiana Redan. It had been so thoroughly destroyed that it could no longer realistically be called a fortress. And yet the rebels had cleverly positioned themselves behind its skeleton to effectively forestall a Union victory. What was the minimum ratio of attackers to defenders needed for a successful assault? There-to-one? Four-to-one? He wasn't sure, but he knew it was too high.

Grant turned to John Rawlins, who, along with James McPherson, was at his side.

"Rawlins, find Hickenlooper and tell him I want him to do it again."

Rawlins and McPherson exchanged perplexed glances.

"Do what, sir?" Rawlins asked.

"Dig another tunnel. Blow up what's left of that . . . blasted thing,"

"The Redan? There's not much left to blow up."

Annoyed by Rawlins' recalcitrance, Grant glanced sharply at both men and said, "Look, I know it's not a particularly imaginative approach, but I think it's the most effective thing we can do short of another assault."

"Under the present conditions, another assault would be murderous."

"Exactly," Grant said. "And regardless of what the press frequently say about me, I only order men to fight if I think there's a chance to win. At the moment, there is not."

McPherson and Rawlins nodded, knowing the statement to be true. Grant's losses in men and materiel were high, but it was because he was willing to engage the enemy, not because he was reckless.

"How many saps do we have going?"

"Thirteen, sir."

"Are any of them closer to the Rebel line than the others?"

McPherson answered, "Not notably, general."

"Well, then, I suppose we'll have to take pot luck."

"When shall I tell Captain Hickenlooper to be finished?" McPherson inquired.

"Don't tell him; ask him. But let him know I would like to do it by July first."

"That's not much time," McPherson responded, suddenly realizing what Grant was trying to accomplish. "You want a victory by Independence Day, July Fourth."

"That would be . . ." Grant hesitated, unsure how to admit, even to himself, that political considerations could affect his judgment. "That would be my . . . wish."

As one of his closest friends, McPherson understood. After glancing at Rawlins for affirmation, McPherson said, "July first it is then. John, go and tell the good captain what he needs to know."

"Persuade him," Grant said, without a trace of humor.

The new mine—two thousand pounds of explosive—was detonated on July 1, 1863. It finished off the skeletal remainder of the Third Louisiana Redan. It nearly finished off a work party of eight slaves who had been conscripted to dig a countermine. But one, a gentleman named Abraham, was thrown a hundred fifty feet, most of it in Union airspace, and survived. His newfound federal friends promptly stationed him in a tent and charged ten cents a head to view the man who had literally flown to freedom.

July 1, 1863, the Battlefield

Depressed and weary, Generals Pemberton and Bowen inspected the repairs that had been made to the defenses on the Confederate side of the battlefield. The devastation was so extensive there was little of any substance that could be used to anchor a repair. It was like trying to reassemble a city after a tornado had struck.

"This is awful," Pemberton groaned, shaking his head as if he could no longer tolerate its weight. "This can't continue."

Bowen said nothing but knelt down to inspect what, at first glance, looked like a face hiding under a rock. It turned out to be the business end of a mop. He returned to an upright posture, wondering what a mop was doing on a battlefield.

"Do you want to call a council of war?" he asked.

Pemberton strolled on, seemingly mesmerized by the magnitude of the destruction. Glancing sheepishly at Bowen, he said, "They're going to do it again, aren't they?"

"They're still digging. I expect so."

Pemberton's head pitched back as if he'd received a mortal wound, but no cry of intolerable pain accompanied it, only a tortured simper of desperation.

"You know, the worst part of it is the wretched plight of ordinary citizens. Most of them can't fight, but they still suffer. Did you know they're living in caves?"

"Caves are much better protection against artillery bombardment than above ground structures."

"I hear they're eating rats."

"They're running out of mules, sir, like us," Bowen said, careful to avoid unintended sarcasm.

The two men took a dogleg around a boulder, whose rectangular facets identified it as having once been a creation of man.

"Sir, shall I set up a war council?"

"Yes, of course. Tomorrow," Pemberton said, his lips quivering. "What is tomorrow?"

"July second."

"Getting close to Independence Day."

They stared at each other, each feeling the surreal quality of the moment. As good citizens of the Republic, they had been taught to revere Independence Day. As Confederates, should they still hold it in high regard, as a symbol of secession from Mother England, or did it more certainly acknowledge the unbreakable bond with the Union?

"It's not our Independence Day," Bowen murmured.

Pemberton looked away as if embarrassed by the comment. For an instant, Bowen thought there might be some substance to the persistent rumor that, being a northerner by birth, Pemberton harbored secret sympathies with the Union. But he quickly dismissed the thought. There were officers who might better have handled Pemberton's responsibilities as the Commander of the Department of Mississippi, Tennessee, and Eastern Louisiana, but there were at least as many who would have done worse.

"Has there been any further word from Joe Johnston," Pemberton inquired.

"Not that I know of."

"I assume that means he's not coming?"

"That's been the thrust of all his communications lately. He doesn't like the odds. Too many Yankees between him and us."

"Too many Yankees . . ." Pemberton echoed. "That's what Grant did to us, you know. Split our armies. I'd have to admit he's a good commander. Do you know him?"

"We were friends before the war."

"Really?" Pemberton nodded, becoming thoughtful. "I met him during the Mexican War. We were in the same division. He was quiet, unpretentious. In fact, it's hard for me to visualize his face in my mind, he was so . . . insignificant. I do remember he was short. His face was . . . common. It gave nothing away, not even his identity. I would never have believed him capable of leading an army—"

Pemberton suddenly curbed his tongue. Bowen assumed he had done so rather than complete the sentence with: ". . . leading an army to victory." He appreciated his commander's tact.

"Let's get back. You can set up the war council while I review Johnston's correspondence. Maybe there's something . . ."

Pemberton let the sentence die a natural death. That was two incomplete statements in less than a minute. The man was starting to lose his composure.

July 2, 1863, Pemberton's Headquarters, Vicksburg

It was another hot day in the Mississippi summer. John Pemberton stood behind his chair in the parlor of the Willis-Cowan House and looked over his staff, who were seated around an oval-shaped oak table in the center of the room. The division and brigade commanders, except for Loring and his staff, were all present. Conversation was hesitant, sometimes stilted. All knew what the situation was, but were loath to talk about it for fear of acknowledging defeat. Some gazed back at Pemberton with despair in their eyes, others with disappointment, even contempt.

But, Pemberton thought, at least he could not be blamed for Joe Johnston's absence He pointed to the stack of dispatches on the table and said, "These are from General Johnston. I could read them aloud, but I think each of you should read them independently to see if I've missed something."

Abruptly, he sat down and adjusted his chair to fit his knees under the table. He shuffled the letter stack and handed it to the aide who would be taking notes. The aide handed it to General Carter Stevenson, who immediately began scanning the documents.

"Why don't we let the division commanders have the first look?" John Bowen suggested from his position on Pemberton's right. "So we can get the discussion underway."

All agreed, and Pemberton nodded. Maybe it wouldn't be too bad. Thank God for John Bowen.

The circulation of Johnston's dispatches created little excitement. It was obvious that, until Champion Hill, he had favored a link up with Pemberton, had even ordered the Vicksburg commander to do so, but was now unwilling to risk his army's defeat by a Union force with superior numbers. Johnston's decision was probably the better part of wisdom but, to Pemberton, it felt like a betrayal. It was a far cry from the attitude Johnston had expressed in a speech to the Mississippi legislature in 1862: "I promise you that I shall be watchful, energetic, and indefatigable in your defense."

Once the letters had been passed around and perused, Pemberton found he had little more to say. A few of the more vigorous brigade commanders proposed a breakout, but, once examined critically, it was easily demonstrated that a breakout would be impossible.

Bowen expressed the sensible logic.

"It should be obvious by now that Joe Johnston is not coming. Furthermore, the Yankees have dug trenches as deep and as wide as ours. To attack them would be suicide. They would have the same advantage that we, as the defenders, had. And we know they are laying more explosives."

He paused to look around the room. A chill silence greeted him. "I don't want any more men blown apart," he said somberly, forcing the words past his lips. "We can't win this fight. There is no way we can win this fight."

If anyone disagreed, he did not express himself.

Pemberton lifted himself from his chair, gathered in Johnston's dispatches, and tucked them under his arm.

"This council of war is adjourned. Tomorrow, we will offer our surrender on July 4, Independence Day." Some released sighs of relief and/or despair. Some stared at Pemberton with unabashed hatred. None registered an objection.

★ FORTY-THREE ★

July 3, 1863, the Jackson Road

Accompanied by Lieutenant-Colonel Louis Montgomery of Pemberton's staff and a bevy of officers, John Bowen led his entourage toward the Union line. The morning had been spent preparing the letter from Pemberton to Grant requesting a cease-fire to discuss the possibility of a Confederate surrender. General A.J. Smith strode out to meet the Rebels, halted next to Bowen's bay mare, and saluted. Bowen returned the salute.

"General Bowen, I'm Andrew Smith of General Grant's staff."

Dismounting, Bowen reached inside his breast coat pocket and removed an envelope. Handing it to Smith, he said, "This is a proposal from General Pemberton to General Grant—to stop the bloodshed."

Both men knew this was a euphemism for surrender, but were too steeped in military etiquette to let it show. Smith led Bowen and Montgomery to the headquarters tent, where Grant was waiting. When Bowen was within reaching range, the Union commander offered his hand.

"Hello, John, it's been a long time."

Bowen shook the proffered hand and replied, "Yes, it has, Sam."

"I've been busy."

"Me, too."

The Confederates followed Grant and Smith inside and sat at the table opposite their hosts, which included James McPherson. After a brief hiatus to permit all parties to meet each other and assimilate themselves to the situation, Grant leaned forward and flattened his hands on the tabletop. Smith handed the envelope to him and waited while his commander opened it, removed the sheet of paper inside, and raised it to a good viewing level. Grant gripped the letter with both hands and read, occasionally peering over its top edge. Finally, he laid it on the tabletop and shifted his gaze to Bowen.

"General Pemberton wants an armistice and negotiations," Grant summarized skeptically.

"Yes, with a commission to determine the terms of surrender."

Grant shook his head and said, "That won't do. The only terms I will accept are those of unconditional surrender."

The response was so abrupt and unemotional that Bowen wondered if he was joking. But he'd heard the nickname U. S. Grant had earned after his victories at Forts Henry and Donelson on the Cumberland River in Tennessee: <u>U</u>nconditional <u>S</u>urrender Grant. Bowen decided in favor of diplomacy.

"I think it would be best if I discussed this matter with General Pemberton."

Lighting a cigar and taking the first puff, Grant said, "That would be fine. I also think it would be appropriate to invite him to our next meeting so we can settle this promptly, don't you?"

Bowen and Montgomery concurred and agreed to meet later the same morning with Pemberton in tow. Grant watched as the Confederate entourage disappeared between the corridor of white flags that had been planted by both combatants and the citizens of Vicksburg. The message was clear: the rank and file wanted the fighting to be over.

"Sir, may I ask a question?" Smith murmured.

"Of course."

"Why did he call you Sam?"

"Because that's what I was called by my West Point class-mates. Bowen was one of them."

"Does the 'S' stand for Samuel?"

"No."

"What *does* it stand for?"

"Nothing."

Smith was puzzled and too curious to drop the subject. Grant noticed his dismay and explained.

"When I first entered West Point, someone in the administra-tion made a mistake. Somehow, my name was registered as Ulysses S. Grant."

Struggling to subdue his perplexity, Smith refrained from ask-ing the obvious question. Mercifully, Grant answered it anyway.

"Hiram is my other name, not Samuel," he said, mouthing he words as if his lips were soaked in lemon juice. "I am, in fact, Hi-ram Ulysses Grant."

Smith could only mutter, "*Hiram . . . Hiram?*"

After a pause to regain his equanimity, he said, "Sir, if you don't mind, I do have another question."

"About my name?"

"No. It's just that . . ."

"Come on, no need to be shy," Grant coaxed, turning his back so his cigar smoke would not envelop Smith's head.

"Well, how many men do you suppose they have? The Rebels I mean."

"My best sources say thirty thousand or thereabouts."

"What will we do with them? We can't feed and shelter them very long."

"Then we'll just ship them up north . . ."

Grant suddenly realized the critical flaw in his thinking. He whirled around to face Smith and barked, "Take a message to Admiral Porter. Ask him how many of his boats would be required to ship thirty-thousand prisoners to Memphis."

* * *

The dispatch from Porter was terse and to the point. The transport of thirty thousand prisoners to Memphis would leave him without a navy to secure the Vicksburg waterfront. Grant looked quizzically at McPherson, then A.J. Smith.

"What do you think? Should we parole the whole lot?"

"Sir, I don't think we have any choice. We need to maintain a naval presence," Smith argued.

"General Smith is right," McPherson said. "We can't keep Rebel gunboats off the Mississippi unless we chase them off with our own gunboats."

Although the problem had arrived late in his thinking, Grant agreed with the assessment. Nevertheless, he said, "We could be criticized. A free Rebel is a potentially dangerous one."

"Not as dangerous as the port of Vicksburg without federal gunboats," McPherson said earnestly.

Grant studied the well-groomed faces of his younger subordinates with fascination. Both were becoming fine officers, demonstrating not only an understanding of their own roles as army officers but an appreciation of the Navy's role in the taking of the Confederacy's Gibraltar. It was a rare combination. Even so, it was his decision to make.

"We'll parole all thirty thousand, but make them sign a non-combatant pledge."

"And if they won't sign?" Smith asked.

"Then we'll throw them in prison."

"And if all thirty-thousand won't sign?"

Grant looked helplessly at Smith, then at McPherson, who was enjoying the badinage. He threw up his hands.

"Then we have a problem. But I'm not going to worry about something that might not happen and probably won't. Let's go meet Pemberton."

Grant's small entourage proceeded to a pre-arranged location on the Jackson Road. The weather was not unpleasant, but a gathering of dark, foreboding clouds promised more interesting things to come. Grant hoped it was not a bad omen and, more rationally, that a deluge would not disrupt the proceedings and put everyone in a foul mood.

Their arrival was met by another mounted contingent, led by Pemberton and Bowen. The two groups dismounted, exchanged polite greetings, executed perfunctory handshakes, and waited for something to happen. Protocol demanded that the party that had called the truce speak first, but Pemberton appeared disinclined to follow that rule. Irritated, Grant was about to speak when John Bowen made the introductions.

The opposing commanders shook hands and Grant said, "I believe we were in the Mexican War together."

Pemberton gave an ambiguous nod and, ejecting the words like cherry pits, asked, "What are your terms, General?"

Grant hesitated, gazed into Pemberton's restless eyes, and said, "I believe my letter insisted on unconditional surrender."

Although the statement had been delivered calmly, Pemberton appeared to take offense. Above his dark, flowing beard, his face flushed pink.

"Well, if that is all you have to offer, this conference is at an end, and hostilities must at once be resumed," he said, nervously stroking the beard.

Except for Pemberton's animosity, the dominant emotion displayed by members of both delegations was incredulity. With the exchange of letters, it had been assumed that Pemberton's capitulation was assured. Yet, here he was, in defiance of Grant's clearly stated demands.

While he paced the neutral ground between the two armed camps, Grant pulled a cigar from his vest pocket and shoved it between his teeth. After a few tense moments, he finally halted and, with his back to the Union armies, approached Pemberton, withdrew the as of yet unlit cigar, and thrust his hands behind his back.

"Very, well, I am content to have it so," he said, his gaze lingering on the Confederate commander. Then he glanced at his orderly and barked, "Private, bring me my horse."

"Sir, I think . . ." Bowen interrupted. It was not obvious to whom he was speaking, and both commanders turned expectantly toward him. Glancing first at Pemberton then at Grant, he spoke hastily but with clarity.

"Sir, I think it would be appropriate for the staff officers to first have a thorough discussion of the . . . terms of surrender. Then we can continue the meeting with a clear objective in mind."

Bowen had not stated it explicitly, but all understood that his proposal assumed the temporary removal of the commanding generals from the negotiations. Fearing the action might be interpreted as indecision, neither commander withdrew completely. Instead, they adjourned to a small, nearby hill on which stood a nearly leafless oak tree. Though short on leaves, its branches remained, most of them peppered by shrapnel.

"I wonder whose army he fought for," Grant quipped, gazing at the tree.

"He's holding his ground, so he must be one of ours," Pemberton rejoined with a perfunctory smile.

Grant offered a cigar to Pemberton and struck a match to another for himself. Pemberton refused the offer and gripped one of the lower tree branches while he gazed wistfully in the direction of Vicksburg.

"You said earlier that we met in Mexico," he said.

Grant took a puff on his cigar and said, "I believe we were in the same division."

"I'm not sure I remember you."

"I didn't do anything particularly memorable. I was certainly no Robert E. Lee. He was the shining star of that war."

Pemberton paused to cast a quick glance at his opponent, wondering if the Union general was being sarcastic. Surely, the man must have a favorable opinion of himself. For more than a year, he had pursued the defenders of Vicksburg with a dogged determination. He wondered if any other commander, north or south, would have been as tenacious as Grant. Lee was a master of tactics and execution. Grant was like a hound, who, once he had an opponent by the throat, never let go. What Grant had said was true. He was no Robert E. Lee.

But he didn't have to be.

* * *

Bowen and McPherson led the negotiations with secretarial assistance from A.J. Smith. After several hours of ironing out the details and clarifying the fine points, the conference ended with an agreement that Grant would again present his terms, but with even more precision. The two delegations informed their commanders of the status of the negotiations and agreed to study the meeting notes until that evening, at which time negotiations would resume. The two mounted contingents then returned to their respective headquarters. When Grant arrived at his tent, a message was waiting for him. He opened it and scanned the contents. A shadow of concern swept across his face.

"What is it, Sir," McPherson inquired.

Grant handed the message to him and said, "Porter confirms that he can't ship thirty thousand prisoners north *and* garrison Vicksburg."

"We already know that."

"Yes, but now we have to tell the Rebels of their good fortune."

"Perhaps they already know."

Recalling Pemberton's odd behavior, Grant said, "Perhaps they do."

If Sherman had been there, Grant mused, he would have cursed and spit at the thought of releasing prisoners on the promise that they would go home and fight no more. But, in the end, he would have acquiesced for the same reason Grant would: the Army of the Tennessee could not do without Porter's navy. It was a fact of life that would have galled his redheaded curmudgeon of a friend, but, ultimately, a fact he would recognize as such.

Grant strolled away from his tent and leaned against the spoked wheel of a howitzer. Crossing his arms, he leveled his gaze at his staff officers.

"Well, gentlemen, it appears we will not be having unconditional surrender after all."

"We can still claim the terms were dictated by you," McPherson said.

Grant gave him a dubious look and said, "We might as well give General Pemberton his small victory. His petulance has earned it for him."

Glancing from one officer to the next, he allowed a slight grin to play on his face.

"But we should take as much advantage of the situation as we can. Smith, is thirty thousand prisoners the right number?"

"It is, sir."

"All right. Good. I want each of them to sign a written statement that he will not serve again during this war."

Murmurs of grudging agreement met his ears.

"I know. It's a lot to ask, but I want those signed statements by tomorrow. McPherson, you see to that."

McPherson groaned as if he might be in pain.

"Yes, sir. You want all non-combatant pledges signed and collected by July 4, 1863."

Grant nodded and said, "We'll supply horses, wagons and rations for all who sign. Make sure they understand this, and that they must skedaddle as soon as possible."

The revised surrender terms were presented to Pemberton that evening. The Vicksburg commander agreed to the terms on the condition that, to satisfy the demands of honor, the Confederates be allowed the time for a brief surrender ceremony. Grant replied that if he did not receive a favorable reply to his demands by nine o' clock the following morning, he would interpret it as a rejection and would act accordingly.

July 4, 1863, Vicksburg, Mississippi.

"They are not happy," James McPherson observed as Grant and his entourage rode past the Vicksburg citizens lining the street.

"Can't expect them to be happy," Grant said. "They suffered and lost. But they should be a little more contented now that the fighting is over. I'll be satisfied if all they do is scowl at us."

Grant watched a half-naked, little boy whittling a stick stare up at him with an unreadable expression that could have been fear, awe, enmity or all three. If it were enmity in the boy's face, it did not appear to have made it all the way to hatred, for which Grant was both grateful and amazed.

There was nothing to fear anymore. Early that morning, the ravaged Vicksburg fortifications had been adorned with white flags by Rebel soldiers as they made the short trek to surrender and stack their arms. There was no fight left in the defenders of Vicksburg, nor was there anything to fight with.

It was the same with the citizenry. The good men and women of Vicksburg were hungry and wearied by the incessant naval bombardment that had lasted more than a month. Many were homeless; some lived in caves.

At the Warren County courthouse, John Logan's regiment and Grant's staff officers came to attention. A Union soldier lowered the Confederate flag from the cupola and replaced it with the Stars and Stripes. Unexpectedly, white flags appeared in a number of windows along the street. Grant took no notice of these gestures and glared at any officer paying too much attention. There was no need to embarrass the citizens of the vanquished city.

They met Pemberton at a house on the Jackson Road, just inside the city limits. Fort Hill, with its massive artillery pieces, was off to the right, overlooking the nearly one hundred and eighty-degree bend in the Mississippi River that enveloped De Soto Point, which David Farragut had run past nearly a year ago. Though

Grant's visit would include an official debriefing of the Vicksburg officer corps, he hoped it would assume some of the character of a social event. He dismounted, his staff followed suit, and all climbed the steps to the porch where Pemberton and his officers gave the proper salutations.

"Sir," Grant said to one of Pemberton's aides. "I wonder if I might have a glass of water."

The aide clucked an, "of course," but did not depart for the kitchen. Instead, he made a casual gesture directing Grant toward it. In the kitchen, a black servant presented him with a glass of water. The servant was old, gray, and attentive. Grant thought he had never seen a smile last as long on anyone's face for as long as the black man's smile persisted.

The revised surrender terms were reviewed and accepted by an *out-of-sorts* Pemberton.

"The man doesn't know how good he is getting it," Grant whispered to McPherson.

"Maybe we should tell him," McPherson said, equally annoyed by Pemberton's sulking.

"No. It's much easier being a good winner than a good loser. Let him be."

The debriefing was short. Further in-depth interviews were left for administrative staff. Reluctantly but firmly, Pemberton affixed his signature to the surrender terms. So did Grant. Two of the administrative officers stayed behind while Grant and the rest of his staff made their way down to the riverfront to meet Admiral David Porter. The *Black Hawk* was there, along with most of the flotilla that had devastated the city with its long-range cannon. The smaller pieces were still active, but only in celebration.

Spotting Porter on deck. Grant tied his horse near the gangplank and dismounted. Porter, in his navy blues with double-starred epaulets and a freshly brushed briar patch of a beard, saluted.

"Afternoon, General. A fine day for a Fourth of July celebration, is it not?"

"It is."

"I wonder if historians will accuse us of planning it this way, finishing on Independence Day."

"They should. It was," Grant said, a shallow but unambiguous grin on his lips.

Porter ordered several midshipmen to find chairs for Grant and his staff. While they did, Porter retrieved several bottles of wine from a locker and ordered an aide to find glasses for all. The victory was toasted first, then Independence Day, then the army and navy and finally the soldiers and sailors who had done the job. Grant allowed himself to enjoy the luxury of a good wine coupled with what seemed like the most comfortable chair he had ever collapsed into. Porter pulled his chair next to Grant's, holding his glass and a full bottle high in the air.

"I don't know about you General, but I am enjoying this victory immensely," he announced boldly. Then he poured wine into his glass, sipped it, and stared straight at Grant.

"Sir, I would like to say that, if ever an army was entitled to the gratitude of a nation—"

"Hold that thought!" called a voice from the shore end of the gangplank. All eyes shifted in that direction. It was Sherman, waving what looked like a dispatch in front of him.

"This is from the War Department. As you may or may not know—we've all been a little busy lately—Bobby Lee has crossed into Pennsylvania. Looks like he's planning to attack Philadelphia or Washington and force an end to the war."

"Is Hooker still shadowing him?" McPherson asked.

"It's not Hooker anymore. Lincoln replaced him with Meade," Grant said.

"When did this happen?" Sherman said with his chronic scowl. He looked surprised, but not overwhelmed by the news.

"I don't recall. It was mentioned in one or two of the daily dispatches from Halleck."

"But—Old Snapping Turtle?" McPherson bemoaned.

It was enough to render the gathering of officers temporarily speechless. General George Gordon Meade was known more for his churlish disposition than his leadership qualities. He was competent, but competence had not been enough to keep McClellan, Pope, Burnside, and now Hooker on the job as commander of the Army of the Potomac. It was Lincoln's greatest problem with his eastern army: finding a military leader who could not only defeat Robert E. Lee but one who was bold enough to try and gritty enough to see it through.

"What's the situation in Pennsylvania?" a stunned John Rawlins inquired.

Grant briefly considered asking Rawlins if he wanted something stronger than wine, but concluded that Rawlins's sense of humor might not be up to the challenge. He stood and briefly studied each of his officers. Because of the fluid nature of what was happening back east and the dearth of information about it, he had not wanted to discuss the subject until there was something more definitive to say. But they were all here—the officers of the men who had taken Vicksburg—and he knew he had to share with them what little he did know.

"Lee is on a northeastern course from Maryland into Pennsylvania. He could be attempting to interpose his army between Meade's army and Washington."

"Where's Meade?" McPherson asked.

"He's following, but he has some catching up to do.

A rumble of commentary suddenly filled the air. All understood that if Lee defeated the Army of the Potomac, the capture of Washington and the government was the probable consequence. Such a victory for the Confederacy would render the capture of Vicksburg irrelevant.

"All right, so Meade is following Lee, but where is Lee? Has there been any contact?"

Grant searched his memory for the flurry of dispatches that had announced the presence of the Army of Northern Virginia on Union soil. There was a small town—what was its name? Then he had it.

"There was some skirmishing a few days ago at a small town called Gettysburg. There might be a battle going on by now. Or . . . there *might have been* a battle . . . already."

The wave of euphoria that had washed over every officer present just a few hours earlier suddenly vanished. Taking its place was a pervasive spiritual miasma, an empty feeling that the taking of Vicksburg might all have been for naught.

★ EPILOGUE ★

July 30, 1863, The Union Flagship, *Black Hawk*

The news from Pennsylvania was good. The Union had won the Battle of Gettysburg and sent Bobby Lee back to Virginia. *Hallelujah!* Grant could not keep the word from his thoughts.

He had come aboard Porter's flagship to relax and enjoy a reprieve from the seemingly endless administrative duties associated with disarming and paroling thirty thousand Confederate prisoners. He had expected to spend the afternoon with Porter, but the admiral was busy coordinating the activities of his fleet with those of Admiral David Farragut's fleet down-river. With the exception of Rawlins and Sherman, Grant's senior officers had all begged off with the perfectly legitimate excuse of being overwhelmed by paperwork. At present, only Rawlins was present.

Seated in a deck chair, Grant reached down for his bottle and raised it to his lips. The action immediately evoked a response from Rawlins, sitting in the adjacent chair.

"Sir, I think you should be more careful. If the press sees you drinking from a bottle of whisky, there will be hell to pay."

"Rawlins, the only time you get to cut me off is before an important battle," Grant grumbled.

"And who decides which battles are important?"

"I do."

"Don't worry, John, his judgment has been pretty good so far."

The voice was Sherman's abrasive rasp. He was coming toward them from the port side of the vessel, facing the Vicksburg waterfront. Grant and Rawlins were on the starboard side facing the rippling Mississippi and the downstream shore of De Soto Point.

Knowing he was outranked and outgunned, Rawlins looked like he might make a stand, but only uttered a brief sigh of frustration and turned his eyes skyward, as if seeking help from the almighty. After a moment of silence, he got to his feet and managed a half-smile.

"Sirs, at the risk of sounding insubordinate, I want you both to give me your word of honor that you will not overdo it and will stay away from members of the fourth estate while you imbibe."

Grant and Sherman glanced at each other. Sherman turned to face Rawlins.

"John, are you aware of President Lincoln's remarks concerning General Grant's drinking?"

"I am, Sir, but—"

"He said—to several members of Congress by the way—that if they would find the brand of whisky the General favors, he would gladly order some for distribution to his other generals."

Rawlins paused, then said, "I believe the gist of the president's comment was that, if the brand of whisky were identified, he would distribute it in hopes that it would create more fighting generals like General Grant."

Lowering himself into the chair Rawlins had vacated and raising a half-full mug of whisky that Grant had just poured for him, Sherman said, "I stand corrected, but you get my point."

"I do, but I would also point out that the president has never directly communicated such a sentiment to General Grant."

"Point taken," Sherman conceded. "But let's not argue. It's too nice a day, and we are all in need of restful meditation. Personally, I haven't felt this relieved since Nathan Bedford Forrest failed to kill me after Shiloh. Why don't you have a drink with us, John?"

Rawlins hesitated, looked at Sherman as if seriously considering the suggestion, and lazily shook his head.

"No, thank you. I'll get my restful meditation some other way."

That was all Rawlins had to say, leaving an uncomfortable void in the conversation. He filled it by excusing himself.

"Sir, if you have no objections, I'd like to go ashore and get some work done."

"Of course, if you feel you must."

"I do," Rawlins said and strode purposefully across the gangplank to his horse.

"Does he really have work to do?" Sherman whispered.

"There's always work to do. You know that," Grant replied. "But no, I don't think that's why he's leaving. I think he just gets tired of watching over me."

"Watching over you? It seems more like spying to me. For Dana and the War Department."

"It is, but I don't mind. Rawlins provides a useful service. He makes me aware of my limitations. He's been doing that ever since we both signed up in Illinois."

"I understand that," Sherman retorted irritably. "But why is he including me in his *don't overdo it* proclamations? I'm not a drunk. I'm just crazy."

Grant could not restrain a belly laugh, which he embellished by taking a large gulp of whisky. It filled his throat, stomach and outlook with satisfying warmth.

"How did you get that reputation, of being *crazy*, I mean?"

Sherman's demeanor shifted from sanguine to sullen. He took his time sipping his whisky, and when there was no more, refilling it. Then he looked at Grant, his chronic scowl mellowed by depression.

"It was that first battle at Bull Run. Losing it got me to thinking that maybe we wouldn't win the war. It preyed on my mind. When I was transferred to the Cumberland Department, it got worse. Lincoln promised me I would not be given a position with that kind of responsibility—"

"What? You didn't want a higher rank?"

"That's right. I didn't. I wanted to ease into the officer corps, not be in charge of a whole department. I didn't have the experience for that. But there I was, a new brigadier general in Louisville, Kentucky, overseeing thousands of men and making critical decisions."

"What difference does it make if it's one man or ten thousand? You're not a soldier if you're not responsible for someone, even if it's only yourself."

Oddly enough, this remark seemed to lift Sherman out of his funk. He got to his feet and started posturing and gesturing like a politician. There was even a grin on his grizzled face.

"That's the difference between you and me, Grant. It's the difference between you and every officer in the U.S. Army. You can handle the burden of command without letting it turn you into a blabbering nitwit—"

"Is that what you were, a blabbering nitwit?"

"I was. I surely was."

A hiatus ensued while both men reflected on the direction the conversation had taken. Then Sherman began patting himself down as if searching for a weapon.

"I have something here I want to show you, something I keep close to me at all times."

He finally found what he was searching for and pulled it from a coat pocket. It was a folded, dog-eared piece of paper. He unfolded it and held it up for viewing.

"This is a quote, from last year, of something you said during the Tennessee River campaign."

"God save me from my own remarks," Grant moaned.

"Listen, just listen, then we'll talk."

Sherman read, solemnly and succinctly, "The art of war is simple enough. Find out where your enemy is. Get at him as soon as you can. Strike him as hard as you can, and keep moving on."

Unfazed, Grant rested his arm on his thigh, moving his wrist and its attached hand in a circular motion. The whisky in the mug held by the hand formed into an inch deep, amber whirlpool. He cast an uncertain glance at Sherman.

"I said that?"

"You did."

"When?"

"1862."

"I must have been sober at the time."

"You were."

"Well, it sounds pretty good to me. What do you think?"

"It's perfect."

Grant shook his head. "It's *not* perfect. That's why it needs the, 'strike him as hard as you can,' part. So your enemy is in no position to profit from your mistakes."

Sherman sat his mug on the deck, refolded the paper, and returned it to its original hiding place.

"It's still perfect, or at least as perfect as it can be without benefit of omniscience."

"I am by no means omniscient."

"That's exactly my point," Sherman retorted, exposing his frustration-prone disposition. Without warning, Grant pulled two cigars from his breast pocket and offered one to his friend.

"Here, try this." He insisted.

Sherman bit off the end and shoved the cigar between his teeth. Grant did the same and then lighted both with a match flame.

"Think of it as a supplement to the whisky. Together, they'll drive the *crazies* away."

Sherman acknowledged the remark with a skeptical snort. After each man had inhaled and exhaled several puffs and created a localized fog of cigar smoke, Sherman said, "Grant, what do you think about Gettysburg?"

"What should I think? We won. *Old Snapping Turtle* Meade won. I'm happy for him."

"I mean, what do you think about their victory compared to ours? Have you thought about it?"

"A little. As I understand it, Lee attacked twice, once against entrenched Union positions at the top of a small hill, the second time against entrenched Union positions along a ridge. He failed both times."

"Little Round Top and Pickett's Charge."

"What?"

"The names of the battles: They're being called Little Round Top and Pickett's Charge."

"Oh. Strange how battles get named. *Pickett*. He's one of Longstreet's brigadiers, isn't he?"

"Yup."

"Did you know he was best man at my wedding? Longstreet, I mean."

Grant shot a quick look at Sherman, hoping his face would reveal what the ambiguous mumble had not. It didn't.

"James Longstreet is Julia's cousin and was my classmate at West Point." Grant added.

Sherman muttered, "Strange."

"Yes, it is . . . strange."

Rising to his feet, Sherman blew a smoke ring then faced his friend and said, "I'll tell you what else is strange, Grant, the fact that these two battles concluded on the same day, and that the day was July 4, Independence Day. Do you see the significance?"

Grant shrugged, "Divine Providence?"

"No, no, there's no need for Divine Providence. It's not a miracle. I'll tell you what it means. It means that historians will spend countless hours debating which of these two battles was most important to the salvation of the Union—Gettysburg or Vicksburg."

"And you are going to tell me which point of view is correct?"

"Yes, but only after I make my case. I do have pedagogic credentials . . ."

"Yes, I know. You were the headmaster—"

"Superintendent!"

". . . Superintendent of the Louisiana State Seminary of Learning and Military Academy. I've always thought that was a strange thing for a Union officer to have on his resume."

"Maybe, but I had the good sense to secede from Louisiana when Louisiana seceded from the Union."

"You did that."

"I did."

The alcohol was beginning to affect Grant's sensibilities. He was marginally aware of Sherman's pontifications but found his gaze drifting across the battered face of Vicksburg. It was a pretty city, beautiful in some ways, striking in its physical dominance of the Mississippi River. Crowning the city at its highest point was the Warren County Courthouse, an imposing structure of classic columns and porticos, itself crowned by a clock tower and, now, finally, an American flag. It was a stirring sight, strangely peaceful in the midst of such vast devastation.

"As I was saying," Sherman continued, trying to reinvigorate his audience. "If we might get back to my point, it is my opinion that both battles—Gettysburg and Vicksburg—are equally significant, but for different reasons."

Overcoming a yawn in progress, Grant covered his mouth and said, "How so?"

Sherman took a minute to organize his thoughts, then said, "Gettysburg is obviously the more important victory from the point of Union morale. Lee threatened Washington. That threat was removed, and Lee was sent back to Virginia with his tail between his legs."

Grant rose from his chair and meandered to the deck railing, leaning on it while he continued his survey of the Vicksburg landscape. Sherman followed, leaning one arm against the railing.

"So your point is that Gettysburg is the more significant battle—"

"No, no, Grant, you're not listening! You're daydreaming. Try to be more attentive."

Grant did his best to strike an *attentive* pose. "Can you be brief?"

"I'm not sure, but I'll give it a try," Sherman replied with a wry grin. "What I said was that Gettysburg is the more important battle politically and morally. Strategically, it has no significance—"

"Really? The capture of the national capital has no strategic significance?"

"Lee was not prepared to attack Washington. He would have had to contend with both Meade and an entrenched Washington garrison. He could never have won such a fight. There's too much geography in the way. He was simply playing to a northern audience. Lee knew that if he could register a victory on northern soil, the anti-war factions in the press and Congress would likely succeed in turning northern opinion against the war."

"He could have laid siege to Washington like we did here."

"It wouldn't have worked. Washington is a much larger city than Vicksburg. His supply lines would have been stretched too far, not to mention the number of troops he would have needed for a successful investment. If he could have attacked Washington successfully, he would have done it when he had McClellan on the run in Virginia."

The reasoning was sound. Grant had run the same thoughts through his mind and come to much the same conclusions. Still, the possibility of a Rebel army threatening Washington was not to be taken lightly. He offered Sherman a confirmatory nod.

But Sherman was not finished.

"By way of contrast, look at what the capture of Vicksburg does. First, it cuts the Confederacy in half . . ."

As he spoke, Sherman held up one finger, then the next.

"Secondly, and more importantly, in the long run, the southern states now have no way to get their cotton to market. International cotton exports are their only major industry. Losing it will ultimately lead the Confederacy to bankruptcy. You can't run a war without money. It will take a while, but it will happen."

"I know," Grant said, tapping his cigar against the railing to loosen the ashes. They fell to the deck like tiny shooting stars.

"I know you know. And I also know you are the only Union general who could have done it. Who else would have brought in dipper dredges to force the Mississippi River into a more accommodating path? Who else would have blown up a levee to create a new river from the Mississippi's inventory? What other *army* officer would have included the navy as part of his assault force? You *know* I thought you were crazy."

"You're a fine one to be judging my mental condition."

"As they say, 'It takes one to know one.'"

"Sherman, you're making a mountain out of a molehill. What you forget is that all but one of these *strategies*—if they can be called that—were unsuccessful."

"They were not unsuccessful. They exhausted the enemy and gave our men something to do until you figured out the *right* strategy."

"Or the next *failed* strategy—"

"Or the next *unworkable* strategy. It doesn't matter. It only matters that the last one be successful. And it was. And here we are . . . victorious! Hallelujah!"

Grant opened his mouth to speak but then closed it. Sherman turned and leaned his back against the railing, propping himself on his elbows. He took another puff on his cigar and released it on a vertical trajectory.

"I can see I'm embarrassing you," he said.

"You are."

"Good. Then I'll continue."

Sherman paused while they shared a good laugh. To shield himself from the Mississippi sun, he pulled the brim of his slouch hat over his brow and stared into Grant's face, which, unadorned by a framework of military garb, could have been that of an itinerant wayfarer.

"So, we've established that Gettysburg and Vicksburg have equal significance to the war effort, but that Gettysburg is a victory of *morale* whereas Vicksburg is a victory of *substance*. Do you agree?"

"I suppose so."

"That's good, but now I'd like to contrast your performance with George Meade's."

"It took him three days. It took us more than a year to take Vicksburg, from John Pemberton, not Bobby Lee."

"From Pemberton *and* Joe Johnston."

"We did not engage Johnston."

"Yes, we scared the bejesus out of him the first time we went to Jackson. Clever ploy if you ask me. But let's get back to Meade. All he had to do was find the high ground and wait for Lee to attack. That's what he did—with John Buford's help, of course—and the rest is history. If he hadn't done that, if he had let Lee take the high ground and lost the battle, Lincoln would surely have fired him. The Union victory at Gettysburg is more of a blemish on Lee's record than it is a tribute to the skills of Old Snapping Turtle."

Without further affirmation or denial of Sherman's arguments, Grant made his way back to the deck chair and put on the slouch hat he had left there. Then he secured the buttons on his coat.

"It's a nice day. I'd like to go for a ride," he said. "Would you like to come?"

"Certainly."

"Why don't you ask Porter and Rawlins if they'd like to tag along? I'll wait."

Sherman disappeared to the port side of the *Black Hawk*. Grant corked the whisky bottle and placed it under his chair for safe keeping. Within ten minutes, Sherman returned with Porter and Rawlins in tow, the latter effecting a hasty scan of the premises to discover the whisky bottle's location. A look of sublime relief suffused his features when he spotted it on the deck floor. It would have been a perfect moment to poke fun at his chief of staff, but Grant declined. It was not his style.

"Admiral, you're coming with us," Grant announced. "Do you ride?"

"I do, but, at the moment, I don't have a horse."

"We'll get you one," Grant said, casting a quick glance at his chief of staff. Rawlins scurried off to find the promised mount. Disembarking from the *Black Hawk*, the two generals and the admiral headed for the horses. Rawlins and the horse he had expropriated, a chestnut mare, were waiting. Porter was the first to mount. The rest followed, with Grant leading the procession on the Yazoo City Road. Sherman hurried to catch up with him.

"General!" Sherman called.

The shock of hearing Sherman address him as "General" disrupted Grant's normally detached disposition. It was their habit to address each other simply as "Grant" and "Sherman." Bringing his horse to a halt, Grant waited for his friend to come alongside and then urged his horse to a comfortable amble. Sherman matched the pace.

"Sir, I didn't finish my appraisal of your performance."

"You didn't? I thought you gave me pretty good marks," Grant said with a snigger.

"I did, but an appraisal is not really complete without a conclusion."

Grant cast a hesitant glance at Sherman but made no reply.

"General. To put it mildly, your leadership and mastery of the Vicksburg operation was astounding. Much of the time—most of the time—I didn't think you could possibly succeed, and said so. But you proved me wrong. *Vicksburg* is very much your victory. You are to be congratulated."

After a moment, a curt, "Thank you," escaped Grant's lips. Sherman said no more but allowed himself a blissful grin.

Because of the traffic on the Yazoo City Road, Grant slowed the four-man parade to a gentler pace. With the cessation of hostilities, some of the citizens of Vicksburg were departing the damaged city for nearby settlements that had not suffered the same degree of devastation. Yazoo City was one such destination and was probably where the majority of refugees were headed. There appeared to be no organization to the exodus, just a steady, unrelenting stream of people, some riding wagons stacked with belongings, some with their belongings packed on the backs of horses and mules, others laden with as much as their own backs could carry without breaking. As Grant's entourage passed by, nearly all took a pause to cast their eyes upon the four northerners responsible for their dismal plight. In those eyes, Grant could see anger, desperation, and sometimes nothing at all, but rarely did he find hatred. He had expected hate, had hardened himself to deal with it, and now found himself strangely ill at ease in its absence. A wave of melancholy swept over him.

"What do you think of these people?" he asked Sherman. "Do they hate us?"

"Of course they do, but they aren't soldiers. They have to let it go."

"What do you mean?"

"I mean hatred is an emotion that rapidly burns itself out. Unless you know how to replenish it, hatred either dies or is replaced by something that lasts, like resentment."

"Soldiers know how to regulate hatred?"

"Have you ever heard the rebel yell?"

"As often as you have."

"The rebel yell is their way of stoking the flames of their personal hatred. Do you think any man would ever charge across a naked battlefield unless he hated the people on the other side and wanted to see them dead?"

"I thought the purpose of the rebel yell was to scare the living daylights out of us."

"Well, there's that too," Sherman conceded with an amused grunt.

After the Fort Hill turnoff, the road became steeper, which was easily gauged by the heavier and more frequent wheezing of the horses. Some, but fewer, refugees continued to stream toward them, displaying the same gaunt faces and subdued hostility as those they had already encountered. Mindful of the unintended consequences of their actions, the four Union officers avoided conversation and, unless in response to the rare friendly gesture, did not exchange pleasantries with the itinerant citizens of Vicksburg.

At the Fort Hill battery, the four men dismounted, were greeted by the officer-in-charge, and were given a quick tour of the facility.

"This battery was a real nuisance," David Porter commented as he gazed westward at the panorama of the wandering Mississippi. "As you can see, Fort Hill has upward of thirty cannon to bombard our boats with. But we couldn't return the favor. Even our mortars couldn't reach this place."

"You have to give them credit," Rawlins said, his eyes scanning the big guns of Fort Hill. "They know how to defend a city."

"Did I mention that I met the man who designed and built the entire ring of fortifications around Vicksburg?" Sherman inquired. "From Fort Hill all the way to South Fort."

"If you did, I don't recall," Grant replied as he strolled westward.

Nor did the others.

"His name is Major Samuel Lockett. I met him in May after the truce was called."

"Only a major? He deserves a promotion," Grant opined.

"Well, I tried to hire him, but he refused. Something about loyalty to the cause. We had a spirited conversation, though."

"I'll bet you did."

Grant came to a halt before the ground fell away to the river. Before him, beneath a cloudless sky, was the shimmering Mississippi, flowing down from the north, then making a hard left and another hard right before continuing past Fort Hill and DeSoto

Point to resume its meandering journey south. His gaze swept to the left, where it found the outskirts of the city proper and, he thought, a jigsaw piece of the cupola atop the Warren County courthouse. Silently, he wished Julia could have been with him.

"This is a beautiful city. Pemberton should never have forced us to destroy it."

Laughing at his friend's clumsy sophistry, Sherman said, "I think John Pemberton might have seen things differently."

Acknowledging the rib, Grant replied, "You're right. He would have."

"But, in a way, they are to blame. Vicksburg was their 'Gibraltar of the Confederacy.' It was inevitable she would be attacked."

"*She*? You still see Vicksburg as a woman? I hardly think Vicksburg could be considered a woman after this battle."

"Ah, but that's where you're wrong, Grant. *She* was fighting for her children. A woman will always do that. It doesn't diminish her femininity."

Grant nodded, conceding the point. A grin crept across his face.

"All right, I yield. Again. She's a woman—"

"A lady."

"A lady then. What's the difference?"

"Ladies have titles."

"What do you have in mind, *Miss Vicksburg*?"

"Of course not," Sherman scoffed. "Something more elegant."

"And that would be . . ."

Sherman rested his chin on one hand and the arm to which it was attached on the other. His chronic scowl returned as the ruminations of his brain intensified. Grant briefly wondered if the 'crazy' Sherman were making a reappearance. But the scowl soon vanished, to be replaced by an uncharacteristically broad grin. Sherman bowed, stared soulfully at Grant, spread his arms and proclaimed, "General Ulysses Simpson Grant, may I present . . . *Lady Gibraltar!*"

*   *   *

★ POSTSCRIPTS ★

Johnston

The surrender of the Vicksburg garrison almost, but not quite, ended the conflict. Joseph Johnston and his army—reinforced by the portion of Loring's division that had escaped to Johnston's command after Champion Hill—was still a force to be reckoned with. As a response to Pemberton's pleas for a second front, Johnston moved his army as far west as the left bank of the Big Black River. There he waited, considering his options and anxiously listening for news of happenings in Vicksburg, which was unusually quiet. Finally, on July 5, he learned that the worst had happened: The Gibraltar of the Confederacy had fallen. Johnston turned and fled east to Jackson, where he set up a defensive front on July 7.

Sherman was assigned the task of chasing Johnston down, an occupation that would ultimately become something of a habit in the years following Vicksburg. After a hot, humid march under a blazing sun, Sherman's Fifteenth Corps arrived at Jackson on July 10. Despite a shortage of artillery shells—he had not anticipated another siege operation—the Union bombardment began the morning of July 12 and ended when the supply of shells was exhausted. Without the benefit of artillery, Sherman ordered his men to dig in. Johnston did the same, and for three days, trench warfare prevailed, with each side filling the air with swarms of deadly shot.

On July 14, a Union supply train containing the much-needed artillery rounds crossed the Big Black River on its way to Jackson. Johnston learned of its coming and ordered it to be captured or destroyed. Unfortunately for the Confederates, Sherman learned of the impending attack and sent a brigade to the Champion Hill battleground, where it would escort the train to Jackson. Rebel forces found the train, but also noted its heavily armed escort and decided pursuit would not be a wise course of action. The supply train reached Sherman the evening of July 16.

With the failed attempt to seize the supply train, Johnston once more retreated eastward. Under cover of darkness, his army of thirty thousand strong began its journey on July 16 and did not complete the evacuation of Jackson until the morning of July

17. With Johnston removed as an immediate threat, the federals were free to complete the tasks of confiscation and destruction they had begun in May. Railroads were rendered impassable, hotels, factories, warehouses, and anything that could conceivably aid the Confederate war effort were burned. By July 20, the disembowelment of Jackson commerce and industry was finished. Sherman returned to Vicksburg.

For his part, Joseph Johnston could claim he had saved his army from certain defeat, and would fight another day. During the remaining years of the Civil War, he would develop a reputation for saving his troops for the *next* battle. It would haunt him the rest of his life.

* * *

Banks

In the spring and summer of 1863, Vicksburg was not the only southern Mississippi town under attack by the Union. General Nathaniel Banks and the Army of the Gulf arrived in Alexandria, Louisiana with the intention of capturing Port Hudson, a settlement situated on the Mississippi River a hundred miles south of Vicksburg. Banks expected to link up with James McPherson's Seventeenth Corps. However, as a critical part of Grant's Army of the Tennessee, McPherson was busy dealing with Pemberton and Johnston, and could not assist Banks.

While Grant and the Army of the Tennessee, including McPherson's Corps, were crossing the Mississippi River, Banks fumed. He implored Grant to send his army south, or at least to loan him a division or two. Heavily engaged in his strategy of attacking Vicksburg from the east, Grant could not comply. Banks briefly considered sending his army north to join forces with Grant but abandoned the idea on the grounds that it would leave the Union garrison in New Orleans vulnerable to attack. However, he was still under orders from Halleck to join forces with Grant—somewhere. Unsure what to do, he journeyed to New Orleans, where he learned that Pemberton had shifted five thousand men from Port Hudson to Jackson in order to prevent Grant from seizing the Mississippi capital. To take advantage of Port Hudson's reduced garrison, Banks moved the Army of the Gulf across the Mississippi River at Simmesport, and then twelve miles south to Port Hudson. He reached his destination on May 22, about the same time Grant was making his major assault against the Vicksburg defenses. Two other Union divisions under Cuvier Grover and Godfrey Weitzel linked up with Banks to complete the encirclement of Port Hudson.

Confederate Major General Franklin Gardner—defending Port Hudson—knew he was in trouble. Assuming a Federal attack would come from the south, he had not reinforced the city's northern defenses. Despite his precarious situation, Gardner remained confident, issuing bold proclamations and promising to send any Federal soldier, "to hell before he gets to Port Hudson."

Although Banks's thirty thousand men at arms exceeded the troops available to Gardner by four-to-one, this was a deceptive statistic. For one thing, Banks's army had more than a few nine-month enlistees whose terms of services would soon expire. For another, the Confederates had installed fourteen heavy guns facing the Mississippi River and forty lighter guns protecting the landside of Port Hudson. Like Vicksburg, the terrain did not favor the attacker, especially against the riverside defenses. If an attack degenerated into an extended siege, Banks's men would have to fight in the intense heat of a Mississippi summer. Of course, so would Gardner's, but his men were better acclimated to southern weather. They were also on the defense, which did not require as much toil and sweat as would the physical and mental exertions of Union infantrymen rushing *pell-mell* across a battlefield.

Regardless of whether the balance sheet favored Union or Confederate, Banks was committed to the attack. The first assault was launched on May 27 and quickly fell apart. The organizational skill Banks had shown in maneuvering three disparate divisions into an encirclement of Port Hudson was not in evidence. The heavily wooded terrain, punctuated by cavernous ravines and steep, mountainous slopes, created a "perfect labyrinth." Troops from New York and New England came from the north, went in first, and were thrown back. The First and Third Louisiana Native Guards of the *Corps d'Afrique*, comprised of free blacks and former slaves, tried next. They gave a good account of themselves but were halted by the same geological obstacles as the New Englanders and New Yorkers.

A subsequent attack—this time from the east—fared no better. The Federals again were turned back in a pasture prophetically named Slaughter's Field.

Finally realizing that a general assault would not work, Banks temporarily brought the hostilities to a close. But he was not done. On June 13, he convened a council of war and devised a new strategy that would concentrate on two targets in the defensive line, one called the Priest's Cap and the other known as Fort Desperate. With little preparation, the attack began the morning of June 14. Conceived as a two-pronged assault—Paine from the east and Grover from the north—the prongs suffered from a lack of coordination, with Grover's entry into the fray falling more than an hour behind Paine's. The result was a disaster.

Despite his inability to penetrate the Port Hudson defenses, Banks was granted a Boone on July 7. On that day, Union general Price pulled into Port Hudson with a message from Grant. General John Pemberton and the Vicksburg garrison had surrendered. The Union troops under Banks rejoiced. The Confederate troops under Gardner who had fought valiantly were sobered by the news and wondered why their Vicksburg brethren had given up the fight. After discussing the matter with his staff, Gardner bowed to the inevitable and surrendered on July 9,

With the fall of both Vicksburg and Port Hudson, the Mississippi River was back in the Union and was now open to traffic all the way from Memphis to New Orleans. As importantly, the Confederacy was split in two. Though few Southerners completely understood the ramifications of the Union victory at Vicksburg, all would mourn her loss.

*   *   *

McClernand

Grant relieved John McClernand of his command on June 18, 1863, well before John Pemberton's surrender on July 4, 1863. For Grant, Sherman, McPherson and various other members of Grant's staff, it was a relief. As professional soldiers, they considered McClernand incompetent. For him, it was a bitter pill to swallow. He had recruited many of the men in the Thirteenth Corps and felt a deep humiliation at its loss.

The purported reason for the dismissal was McClernand's publication of *Congratulatory Order 72*, in which he praised the members of the Thirteenth for their, "constancy, valor, and success," but referred to the other soldiers of the Army of the Tennessee as, "followers," and to their actions as, "redemption from previous disappointments." *Congratulatory Order 72* was also critical of Grant and the other corps commanders—Sherman and McPherson. McClernand's most egregious action, however, was in releasing his *Congratulatory Order 72* to the *Memphis Evening Bulletin* and the *Missouri Democrat*. This enraged Sherman and angered the other members of Grant's staff.

While the embarrassment caused by McClernand's misdeeds was certainly a factor in his dismissal, it was not the only, or even the primary, reason. That was his performance on May 22, in which, during the assault on the Vicksburg fortifications, the political general claimed to have broken through and needed reinforcements. Since the assault had stalled everywhere else, Grant gave them to him. When he subsequently inspected the front where the "breakthrough" was supposedly taking place, Grant found no evidence to support McClernand's assertion. The reinforcements were withdrawn, and the fighting brought to a halt. There was no point in continuing the slaughter.

McClernand complained to his friend from Illinois—Lincoln—about his dismissal, but the President remained steadfast in his support of Grant. Lincoln eventually reinstated McClernand to command the Thirteenth Corps in February of 1864. By this time, however, the Thirteenth Corps was no longer a part of the Army of the Tennessee.

★ ACKNOWLEDGMENTS ★

I am indebted to the many authors whose writings provided source material for *Taking Lady Gibraltar*. These books include, but are not necessarily limited to:

1. Grant, Ulysses S, *The Autobiography of Ulysses S. Grant, Memoirs of the Civil War,* Red and Black Publishers, St. Petersburg, Florida, originally published as the *Personal Memoirs of Ulysses S. Grant, 1885.*
2. Flood, Charles B., *Grant and Sherman, the Friendship That Won the Civil War,* Farrar, Straus and Giroux, New York, 2005.
3. Foote, Shelby, *the Beleaguered City, the Vicksburg Campaign, December 1862-July 1863,* Random House, Inc., New York, 1991.
4. Arnold, James R., *Grant Wins the War, Decision at Vicksburg,* John Wiley and Sons, New York, 1997.
5. Shea, William L. and Winchell, Terrence J., *Vicksburg Is the Key, The Struggle for the Mississippi River,* University of Nebraska Press, Lincoln Nebraska, 2003.
6. Winchell, Terrence J., *Vicksburg: Fall of the Confederate Gibraltar,* Machinery Foundation Press, McCurry University, Abilene, Texas, 1999.
7. Bastian, David F., *Grant's Canal, The Union Attempt to Bypass Vicksburg,* Bard Street Press, Shippensburg, PA, 1995.
8. Neil lands, Robin H., *Grant, the Man Who Won the Civil War,* Cold Spring Press, Cold Spring Harbor, New York, 2004.
9. Marshall-Cornwall, General Sir James, *Grant as Military Commander,* Barnes and Noble Books, Inc. New York, 1995.

The staffs of the Jefferson Hills and Pleasant Hills Libraries were always helpful in pointing me in the right direction. I am especially grateful to the staff of the Jefferson Hills Library, whose unwavering help and support frequently went beyond any reasonable call to duty. Special thanks go to the U.S National Park Service at Vicksburg for its assistance, and to Mr. Ray Brancolini for his interest and support.

Last, but certainly not least, I want to thank Crystal Devine, Christin Aswad, Amber Rendon, and Sarah Somple of Sunbury Press, without whom nothing could have happened.

★ ABOUT THE AUTHOR ★

I am an incompletely retired, 75-year old father of three and grandfather of six, living in the South Hills of Pittsburgh with my wife, Jo.

My favorite fiction *genres* are historical fiction and mysteries, with Michael Shaara and Michael Connelly as favorite authors. *The Killer Angels* by Shaara is at the top of my favorite novel list, and also makes it as a favorite movie in *Gettysburg*, coming in at third place behind *To Kill a Mockingbird* and *The Big Country*. The latter may seem an unconventional choice, but the symbiosis of a compelling story line and Jerome Moross's vibrant musical score truly affected me, emotionally and intellectually.

Although I have not done any acting in thirty years, I do have some experience in little theater. I have been Nathan Detroit in *Guys and Dolls*, Daddy Warbucks in *Annie*, the Modern Major General in *Pirates of Penzance*, Edward Rutledge in *1776*, and assorted white liberals and bigots in *In White America*. These experiences have taught me valuable lessons in theatrical presentation, such as the importance of effective staging, the dynamics of dialogue, and how to compartmentalize dramatic moments.

I chose to write about Grant at Vicksburg because I like stories about real people who rise from adverse and/or humble beginnings to achieve greatness. Ulysses S. Grant was such a man.

59931181R00271

Made in the USA
Charleston, SC
15 August 2016